Xavier Wallace

SHAW INITIATION

JEFFREY + WALLACE

This novel has been deposited and catalogued with the National Library of Australia in accordance with the *Copyright ACT 1968*. Cataloguing-in-Publication information can be accessed via the National Library of Australia.

ISBN: 9781764141222

ISBN (eBook): 9781764141239

JEFFREY + WALLACE PUBLISHING

www.jwpublishing.com.au

XAVIER WALLACE

www.xavierwallace.com

Xavier Wallace

Xavier Wallace was born and raised in regional New South Wales, Australia. He attended public primary and high schools, before studying business at the University of Newcastle. He worked in Canberra for the Australian Government in both the public service and politics for over a decade. He has a Master of Politics and Public Policy from Deakin University. Xavier's interests include politics, government, national security, media and communications, philosophy, ancient history and mythology. He is an advocate for equality and human rights, including LGBTI+ rights. Live music, thriller novels and action movies occupy his time outside writing and work. He loves spending time with his family and friends, and his groodle, Atlas.

Xavier Wallace is the author of the Max Shaw spy thriller series.

Dedication

For my niece, Frankie, and Grandma, June.

Acknowledgements

I want to take a moment to acknowledge and thank my parents, family and friends for their ongoing support. I could not be the person I am today without your guidance, advice and love. Thank you for being there on the end of the phone line or always available to share a coffee or beer. You all mean the world to me.

To Matt, Tanya and Ryan, thank you for your thoughts on the novel and your help putting the finishing touches on it! Your encouragement and validation are truly appreciated, and I am so grateful for your friendship and love.

This novel is dedicated to my niece, Frankie. You're too young at the moment to read the novel, but let it be just a small example that you can do anything you put your mind to. Constantly question, challenge and explore. The world is yours and life is an adventure, so enjoy it!

Finally, the novel is also dedicated to my Grandma, June. From the hours after school doing homework at your dining room table to the many years since where we have shared our book collections, you have always been there to help and guide me. Your love and support have always been so welcomed and it is thanks to you that I have pursued my passion for reading and now for writing. Thank you for everything! P.S. I hope Pa would like the tribute.

The Max Shaw Spy Thriller Series

Shaw Vengeance

Shaw Initiation

Shaw Confrontation

Shaw Intervention

Shaw Reclamation

Shaw Salvation

SHAW INITIATION

By Xavier Wallace

Second Novel of the Max Shaw Spy Thriller Series.

Prelude

"'Vengeance is Mine, and retribution, in due time their foot will slip; For the day of their calamity is near, And the impending things are hastening upon them', Deuteronomy thirty-two, thirty-five," the archbishop said to his gathered flock inside a small old church on the outskirts of the city.

"'For the day of their calamity is near'. It is my flock, my brothers and sisters of faith, and their feet have slipped! And, ours is a vengeful God and He seeks retribution for their failures! 'I will also laugh at your calamity; I will mock when your dread comes', says the Lord, in Proverbs one, twenty-six. He will laugh at those who have turned their backs from His light and His way, and judge them accordingly."

"'O Lord our God, You answered them; You were a forgiving God to them, And yet an avenger of their evil deeds,' Psalms ninety-nine, eight. Our Lord is indeed a forgiving God, He in His never-ending, triumphant glory has seen fit to grant forgiveness to even the most wicked should they repent for their sins against Him and turn back to His glory and His light. But, should they fail to see the error of their ways, He will be an avenger, a punisher and on the day of their judgement, He will rain forth with the fury of His greatness and send the unbelievers, the sinners, the corrupted, the wicked, the un-repenting, straight to the gates of hell – their feet have slipped! They will suffer the bitter wrath of the underworld with its 'coals of fire; violent are its flames', as described in Songs eight, six. Their feet have slipped!"

"'And I saw the dead, the great and the small, standing before the throne, and books were opened; and another book was opened, which is the book of life; and the dead were judged from the things which were written in the books, according to their deeds', Revelation twenty, twelve through thirteen. He does not forget and when the book of your life is written, do you want to be embraced by the Lord and welcomed into His house or cast into the lake of fire and brimstone with the devil, the beast and false prophet where 'they will be tormented day and night forever and ever' as set out in Revelation twenty, ten?"

"My friends, today, like all those that have been and all those that will follow, is a day where we can choose to live in His glory and light, choose to accept that He is the way, to be righteous and go on to eternal life or to ignore Him and insult Him and choose to be condemned to eternal punishment in a fire that burns with brimstone. I know you are here today to reject false prophets and the words of the devil whispered in our ears or shouted by non-believers and sinners from the rooftops. I know that today you are here to repent and ask God for His forgiveness of your sins, for you know, as defined in Matthew ten, twenty-eight, you 'do not fear those who kill the body but are unable to kill the soul; but rather fear Him who is able to destroy both soul and body in hell'. You know that the Lord and only the Lord, can destroy the soul in the fires of damnation for their deeds. Their feet have slipped!"

"But today, my brothers and sisters, I ask, should not we, the righteous, stand-ready to assist our Lord in spreading His word, so that others too can turn from their wicked ways? Should not we, the righteous, reach out into the world and act by His command to show people the error of their ways? Should not we, the righteous, help send the wicked to judgement, so the Lord can read from their book of deeds and cast those He deems unworthy of entry into the golden streets of heaven into the brimstone lakes of hell? Their feet have slipped! For was it not Genesis nine, five through six, which states that 'whoever sheds man's blood, By man his blood shall be shed, For in the image of God He made man'? And, Deuteronomy twenty-one, twenty-one 'Then all the men of his city shall stone him to death; so you shall remove the evil from your midst'? And, Leviticus twenty-four, twenty 'fracture for fracture, eye for eye, tooth for tooth. Just as he injured the other person, the same must be inflicted on him?' A sentiment echoed by Deuteronomy nineteen, twenty-one 'You must show no pity: life for life, eye for eye, tooth for tooth, hand for hand, and foot for foot.'"

"The sinners of the world have committed offences against our Lord and against us, His righteous followers. Their feet have slipped! They have spread lies and falsehoods, they have ignored and disregarded His commandments, they have spat upon His church and His will. Their feet have slipped! Retribution must follow as our Lord says in Isaiah sixty-five, twelve through fifteen 'I will destine you for the sword, And all of you will bow down to the slaughter Because I called, but you did not answer; I spoke, but you did not hear. And you did evil in My sight And chose that in which I did not delight'. He has spoken and we must answer His call. It is time for us to rise up and enforce His will on earth to send some to judgment – for their feet have slipped, while giving others the opportunity to see their folly – for their feet have slipped, but they can return to the church, the light, the way and His embrace, so that they might live in eternal life by His side."

Chapter One

The noise was deafening as it echoed out of the harsh steel stadium and over the luscious green grounds of the university football fields. The rivalry between the two college rugby teams was fierce and their gathered supporters were cheering on their respective teams. Beer and cheap wine spilled from large red plastic cups whenever a player would make a break or a team would put more points on the scoreboard. The energy was electric, but explosive, more like a European soccer match than a local game of rugby, with the two teams at each other's throats readying for an all-in-brawl and their fans just as prepared to defend college spirit.

An older gentleman was standing down by the coach's box next to the field. He had taken up the position to get a good view, away from the crowd, and he had chosen to stand with the team wearing the red and white striped jerseys and socks. He wore a long navy-blue trench coat over a maroon fleece, caramel chinos and brown R.M. Williams boots, but even with all of those layers it was easy to tell he was fit with a solid build, clearly strong and athletic, like a former front-rower who had stayed in shape years after retiring from the game. A large pair of silver reflective aviator sunglasses hid his eyes and a neatly combed greying head of hair was cut short giving him a distinctive look.

The crowd behind him roared to life as a fit, young man in red and white stripes broke the line and took off at great speed towards the try line. He watched as the young man wove easily through the opposition pack and fended off two guys wearing solid blue with white V-neck jersey's. He was agile and nimble, solid but athletic. The red and white cheer squad behind the man in the navy jacket erupted as the young man crossed the line scoring the try. His team mates ran in and hugged and patted him on the back, while others jumped into his arms or up over the shoulders of their fellow team mates to get close to the try-scoring hero. They were ecstatic, they smiled and cheered and threw fist pumps, letting out their raw emotions.

The man watched the game until the whistle blew and the two teams began shaking hands. He watched the young try-scorer walk along the line noticing how he looked each of his opponents in the eye and congratulated them on a game well played, even though his red and white crusaders had won the match, he was humble, a true sportsman.

The teams filed off the field to their respective change rooms for songs, speeches and showers. The man in the navy trench waited for almost thirty minutes, watching the crowds milling around waiting for their teams to re-emerge for celebratory or commissary drinks. The college students were in for a big night and they were already well on their way, as the alcohol kept flowing.

The young try-scorer walked out of the sheds wearing a pair of dark skinny-legged jeans with a red and white college hoodie and a pair of red and blue Converse All-Stars. He had a pair of mirror-lensed Oakleys on and his beaten-up leather Lonsdale gym bag was slung over his shoulder. Only a metre from the door, he was embraced by a good-looking young man in a heavy dark green overcoat with a fur-lined hood and blue chinos, with a red and white college scarf hanging around his neck. He dropped his leather gym bag to the ground and hugged the young man, picking him up and embracing him tightly, before they kissed.

The man in the navy coat watched as he lowered him back to the ground and they spoke briefly, no doubt talking about the game and the young man's performance, until he spotted the man in the aviators staring at them. He said something to his partner and they both turned to look at the grey-haired gentleman. He nodded at them and continued to stare in their direction.

He squeezed his partner's hand then walked over to the man in the trench coat.

"Congratulations," the older man said. "You played well."

"Thank you," the young man said. "But, I'm sorry, do I know you?"

"No, you don't. My name is General Patrick Scott, but most people call me Hulk. I am the Head of Operations for the Australian Intelligence Service or AIS for short."

"General, as in Army General?"

"Yes, I was in the Australian Special Air Service Regiment for over thirty years before taking on my new role, setting up and running covert operations within Australia's top intelligence agency."

"It's nice to meet you, General, and thank you for your service. Forgive me though, is there some reason you were staring at Lachlan and me?"

"Yes, Mr Shaw. I'm here to offer you a job."

"A job? We only just met. How do you know you want to offer me a job?"

"Maxwell Kenneth Shaw, born 15 January 1985, at the Glen Innes Hospital to Matthew and Hannah Shaw local hotel proprietors. Attended Glen Innes Public and High Schools, before gaining entry into the Bachelor of International Relations and Bachelor of Psychology double degree at the University of Newcastle. In the four and a half years completed of your degrees, you have consistently topped your class achieving a high-distinction average across the board. You play rugby, tennis and golf, you surf and are in training to compete in your first powerlifting and body-building competition in three weeks' time, but your true sporting talent is in rowing and swimming. You went to Nationals for swimming at high school and had the potential to join the Olympic team had you decided to pursue that interest, and I believe you have a standing offer from the Institute of Sport in Canberra to join the Australian Rowing Team after you beat their best man head-to-head last year in a fundraising event for the team. You have been dating Mr Lachlan James Farrell for eighteen months. Mr Farrell is a country boy from Tamworth in North West New South Wales, born 20 March 1985 at the local base hospital. He too went to the local public schools before coming to Newcastle University to study medicine where, like you, he is excelling in his studies. You see Mr Shaw, I don't need to have met you, to know you."

"Okay," Max said taking a moment to absorb what he had just heard. "How did you find me? I mean, how did you know to come to ask me to join the AIS?"

"Now, that is a great question. Professor Long in the psychology department is a long-time friend of mine and he keeps an eye out for special and unique individuals for me. He put your name forward and I've spent the last six months observing you and doing all the background checks necessary for me to be here today."

"Right," Max said slightly shocked by the conversation. "So, what exactly are you asking me, General?"

"I want you to join the AIS. It will involve months of vigorous training, followed by years of on-the-job training honing of your skills."

"You want me to become a spy?"

"Yes, on completion of the course you would become a federal agent charged with protecting this country from terrorist attacks, gathering intelligence and conducting counter-intelligence operations, both here in Australia and around the world. Our agents are based in normal nine-to-five jobs, but work for us on the side, doing missions as necessary. The 'normal' job gives you cover to travel and gather intelligence covertly, while helping you hide the truth from suspects, friends and acquittances. Your employer will know your real job and will make arrangements for you to slip away when we need you."

"Why me, I mean, I'm just a normal guy?"

"Max, our country is at war and unlike the battles I fought in the Army, our enemies hide in plain sight, they attack from the shadows then disappear just as quickly into the crowd. We need agents capable of reading people and understanding their motives, someone able to get into the heads of these psychopaths and break them down, find out what makes them tick. We need people who can mimic their moves to find them, stop them and get out of there again unseen. Your lecturers tell me, you are the best student they have seen, in some cases, in their whole careers. Plus, you are fit and athletic, strong and agile, and highly-capable in a physical sense, which is important for field missions. So, no Mr Shaw, you are not just a normal guy, we need you."

"I'm going to have to think about it and discuss it with Lachlan."

"I'm sorry, but you can't do that, not yet anyway. In a few years, if you make it through training and become a full agent and you know Mr Farrell is the one, then you can tell him, but until then it has to remain a secret."

"I can't keep something this big from him. I love him, I can't lie to him."

"It is to protect him and you. It is for people, like Lachlan, that we need to turn up to work and ensure order and safety."

"Well, General, it seems I'm not the only one with a knack for human behaviour. Straight to the boyfriend needs protecting card. Clever."

"I tell you what, take a couple of days to think about it. Tell Lachlan I work for the Government and that I wanted to offer you a job in Canberra working for a Member of Parliament. One of your lecturers put us in touch given your international relations studies, which is close to the truth. Ask him if he would consider moving to Canberra when you finish your studies and tell him I will find him a great job in general practice or at one of the hospitals to help start his career."

"Alright, General, thank you, I will. How do I get in touch with you?"

"Here is my card. I look forward to hearing from you."

With that Hulk and Max shook hands, and Hulk walked off putting his hands into his trench coat pockets for the short stroll across the field to a waiting black Landcruiser. Max turned and walked back to Lachlan, who was pacing with an intrigued and questioning look on his face. Max took a moment to study the card as he walked. It had the Australian Government crest on one side and simply Patrick Scott and a mobile number on the other.

Chapter Two

The big black Landcruiser bounced along the small country road leaving a thick blanket of dust in its wake from the powdery red soil which covered the road surface. It swerved occasionally to avoid a bigger rock or dead kangaroo on the roadway. It had been well over an hour since they had left the bitumen leading to the nearest country town and there were no street signs showing the way. The driver was focused on the road and she was pushing the big car to its limits on the rough little road. Gum trees lined their route with their branches extending out creating a long narrow archway over the rocky dirt track. Max sat in the backseat hoping there were no cars coming towards them with each small crest of a hill the road seemed to narrow further and he was doubtful two cars would fit side-by-side on some sections, but they had not seen another car since hitting the rough grated road.

Max watched the countryside unfold outside his window, rugged, almost jungle-like bushland at times kept his view close, while other times it opened up onto vast paddocks with cattle or various crops. The car crested a little hill in the road and the sun shone through the windows as the tree line on both sides of the car stopped abruptly. The road ran through the vast open space, two hundred metres from the tree line they had just left until the next began, which had been cleared of all vegetation in perfectly straight lines. At the one hundred metre mark, a cattle grate and brand-new steel gate blocked their entrance. Max looked left, then right. A ten-foot high, razor-wire topped fence ran in both directions for as far as his eyes could see, framed on both sides by the two hundred metre-wide, cleared land. Every fifty metres a sign stamped with the Australian Government crest held a warning 'This is an Australian Government facility. Authorised personnel only. Trespassers will be subject to prosecution. Turn back now.' Max also noticed a bright red sign which hung beneath the other warning 'Live ammunition and ordinance used in this area. For your safety, do not enter.'

The driver wound down her window and the car filled with dust as their trailing cloud caught up with them. She reached out to a small panel and waved her hand in front of it. A small green light blinked and a faint beep sounded, before the big gate slid to the left, clearing their path. The driver crossed the cattle grate vibrating the car. When the rear tires hit the soft dirt of the roadway, she hit the accelerator, kicking up dust as the gate began to close behind them.

Twenty minutes later, the driver turned left into a driveway which was lined with smooth river stones leading down to a massive farm house. A small wrought iron sign hung next to the driveway entrance, 'The Wool Shed' it read. The big Landcruiser stopped in a carpark at the front of the house and Max climbed down dragging his soft cotton overnight bag and leather training bag with him.

"Welcome to the Wool Shed, Mr Shaw," Hulk said walking over shaking hands with Max.

"Thank you, umm, do I call you Sir or General or Patrick?" Max asked.

"Most people call me Hulk."

"Okay, fair enough. Hulk it is. So, does everyone get a nickname?"

"Most of you will end up with a nickname in here, some of them stick and become your official codenames or callsigns. Others we change because they just don't work or they've been used before. We use them in official reports, when we talk on the phone or via electronic messaging and when we are in the field, it's a way of protecting our identities."

"That makes sense."

"This is Kate Matthews," Hulk said introducing Max to his driver. "We call her 'Alpha'".

"Nice to meet you and thanks for the lift," Max said shaking Kate's hand.

"No fucking problem at all," Kate said. "Good to meet you too."

Kate was a tall masculine figure about the same height as Max, six feet three inches. She was rough and looked like she would have no worries at all in hand-to-hand combat. She had a short peroxide blonde crewcut with shaved sides and Max could see a tattoo, like flames or a tail on one side at the base of her neck, cut off by her tight black t-shirt which was tucked into her cream coloured cargo pants. She wore solid black combat boots which turned grey as she walked and dust kicked up over them.

"She has a particular style, you get used to it," Hulk said as Kate walked off. "Alpha's one of the finest soldiers I've ever worked with, tough as nails and takes no shit from anyone, including me, so watch yourself or she'll give you the physical explanation of how she came to get her codename."

"Alpha?" Max asked.

"Yes, as in Alpha of the group. She was the first woman to join the SAS and not only did she excel at everything we threw at her, she beat every one of her male colleagues. They started calling her Alpha, as in Alpha male, top of the list, most dominant."

"Oh right, can't imagine that's an easy road, taking on all those blokes on what I assume they consider their own turf."

"No, but she did it and now she works for me at AIS and here at the Wool Shed as a trainer. She's going to put you through some pain to see if you have what it takes."

"Okay, looking forward to that," Max said as the pair began to walk towards the large homestead on the property in the middle of outback New South Wales.

"We'll see about that."

"So, how does this all work?"

"There are fifty potential recruits here for training and assessment. Most of them won't make it, they'll leave the course, they won't have what it takes."

"And, you think I have what it takes?"

"That's what we are here to find out. Over the next few weeks, we will be testing your fitness, endurance and strength, we already know you are intelligent, but we will be testing your memory and recall under stress, and we will be teaching you survival, surveillance and interrogation techniques. I won't lie to you, Max, it will be the hardest thing you have done in your life."

"Did you personally recruit all of us?"

"No. Most come to me as recommendations from the military, intelligence and diplomatic corps. Others, like you, are first flagged by Professors at university and we start surveilling you to assess your suitability.

"You said 'we', that's AIS?"

"Yes. Here on site there are five instructors, including Kate and me. There is a doctor, a nurse and a psychologist. Together, we will be combining training and assessment, and gauging how you respond at each stage. We will also be testing your character against what we've learnt through our surveillance of you over the past few months."

"Right. It's a bit creepy knowing you've been watching me."

"We have an important mission, Mr Shaw, to protect Australia, her allies and her interests. We can only take the best of the best and we need to know before we approach you, you have nothing to hide and nothing that can be used against you by our enemies."

"Well, that seems reasonable, I guess," Max said climbing the steps up to the deck. "Wouldn't it be better to take people from the military, I mean, I don't have any military training?"

"We do take some from the defence force, but they don't always make the best spies. Sometimes we need to do things differently and after years of training, they can be hard to retrain. I'm learning it is sometimes better to start with a blank canvas, so to speak."

"So, you can train us right from the start?"

"Exactly, it means I don't have to kick out any bad habits. It also means people come with the ability to think freely, which means they are willing and able to see things overs can't and that's exactly what it takes in this game, an ability to think on your feet and adapt quickly to changing circumstances. The power of fast, effective decision making. Considered and informed, but decisive."

"Got it."

"As well as the instructors, there's a chef and three kitchen hands, and two maintenance workers and three cleaning staff based out here with us for the next few weeks."

The pair walked inside the massive old homestead. It was shaped like a large hollowed out square. A large veranda ringed the house, each room opening out onto it on one side. The rooms also opened onto a large hall which formed the centre of the old house.

"Apparently, this space used to house a long dining table for formal dinner parties for around sixty people," Hulk said as they walked into the grand hall in the centre of the house. "There was also a massive old grand piano at the other end when we bought the place. It looks a bit different now."

"I'll say," Max said as he looked around the enormous space which was now filled with mess hall style seating and tables at one end and fifty portable camping beds packed closely together at the other.

"Find yourself an empty bed and keep your shit tidy, we're all in this together and we don't have room for clutter. Your first training session starts in thirty minutes. Good luck and Godspeed."

"Okay, thanks Hulk."

Max walked over to a long row of camping beds as Hulk headed for one of the rooms around the edge of the hall. There were a couple of guys laying on their bunks napping or reading, and he could hear movement and chatter in other rooms around the main hall. He strolled the length of the second row of cots until he found one without any gear under it and sat his bags down and rifled through them for his joggers and a set of training gear which he gathered up before heading off to find a change room.

As he made his way around the parameter of the building, he looked inside the various rooms. There was a massive kitchen with pantries and a cool-room. There was a recreational area with a small library and television. A couple of potential recruits where watching the television and they looked him up and down as he walked past. Bedrooms with private ensuites and offices for the instructors and crew were all empty until he got to the last room. Inside a man was frantically typing away on his laptop, he looked up as Max walked past and stopped typing.

"Hello," Max said. "I'm Max, I just arrived and I'm just looking for the changerooms."

"Hi Max," Blake said. "Nice to meet you. I've heard a lot about you. Welcome to the Wool Shed."

"Oh thanks, nice to meet you too," Max said as he walked in and shook hands with Blake.

Blake stood and for the first time Max noticed how handsome he was. Blake was shorter than Max by a couple of inches, but he could tell he was fit and solid muscle. His sandy blond hair was cut neat and short, and he was clean-shaven with accentuated cheekbones. Max knew straight away he was a tough, masculine figure, but he had a softness and kindness in his eyes – his intense, piercing blue eyes.

"What did you say your name was?" Max asked.

"I, I'm Blake," Blake said nervously, before recovering. "Lieutenant Commander Blake Smyth. I work for Hulk, I'm his aide-de-camp."

"So, do you have a nickname too?"

"Do you mean a codename?"

"Yeah. Everyone around here seems to have one."

"Hermes."

"Like the Greek God?"

"Yes," Blake said blushing.

"Messenger of the Gods, right? Does that mean Hulk is God?"

"He said you were smart. Yes, that's exactly how I got the name."

"Doesn't hurt that you're young and fit either, I suppose?"

Blake just blushed again and put his head down.

"What's an aide-de-camp do?"

"I'm part personal assistant, part secretary, but Hulk hates the idea of someone fussing over him, so he gets me to filter briefs and messages, and generally keep him on track, more like a chief of staff."

"Oh wow, sounds like a hard job."

"It is, but I enjoy it. He is tough but fair, and I've got so much respect for a man with such an incredible career."

"I'd like to hear about it sometime."

"Yeah, I'd be happy to fill you in."

"Anyway, I better get going. It was nice to meet you, Hermes."

"And you, Max. Good luck and Godspeed."

"See you around," Max said as he pointed in the direction he thought he should walk to find the changerooms. "Sorry for interrupting."

"Anytime," Blake said as he nodded and pointed towards the changerooms.

A few doors down, Max found the changerooms. He nodded and said hello to a couple of his fellow potential recruits as he walked through. He found a spot and started to change. As he was doing up his shoelaces, one of the recruits made his way over.

"G'day mate," Flash said. "How's it going?"

"Hi, yeah good thanks," Max said. "I just got here and I'm looking forward to seeing what it's all about. How about you?"

"Yeah, tell me about it. I just got here this morning too. I'm not sure what to expect."

"I'm Max, by the way."

"I'm Jacob, but people call me Flash."

"You've got your nickname already?"

"Nah, I brought this one with me. Last name's Gordon, as in Flash Gordon."

"Oh right, fair enough. Well, good to meet you."

"Yeah you too mate," Flash said changing into his workout gear.

A whistle sounded and then a voice came over the internal speaker system telling them they had five minutes to get ready and be out front.

"Guess we better hustle," Flash said quickly doing up his laces.

They threw their gear on their bunks and headed outside.

Hulk, Kate and Blake were standing with two other instructors all in their workout gear on the grass outside the homestead. The recruits all stood around in front of them doing stretches to warm up.

"Let me take this opportunity to officially welcome you all to the Wool Shed," Hulk said. "There will be time to get to know each other and all of your instructors over the next few weeks, but for now you need to meet, Hermes."

Max watched as Blake raised one hand and gave a quick sharp wave to the recruits. He had changed into running gear and Max noticed his impressive physique under his tight grey t-shirt which was stamped with the Royal Australian Navy logo on the chest.

"Hermes is one of the quickest runners we have on staff over both short and long distances," Hulk said. "Try to keep up."

Hulk pulled out a pistol and fired it into the air. Blake spun on one heal and took off running down the long driveway. The recruits all started running after him, closely followed by Hulk and Kate, the large river stones crunching under the feet.

After a few kilometres, Max and Flash had worked their way to the front of the pack and had fallen into step with each other.

"Jesus, he's fast," Flash said pointing ahead to Blake.

"Hence the name, the quick and cunning emissary of the Gods," Max said. "Certainly God-like speed."

Six kilometres later, Max and Flash were the first to arrive behind Blake by the side of a lake. The two other instructors were already there waiting for them, they were sitting on a small pontoon in the centre of the lake.

"Get your breath lads," Blake said. "It's far from over."

"You don't even look out of breath," Max said between his own deep in hails.

Several minutes passed, Max and Flash were stretching as the last of the recruits, followed by Hulk and Kate arrived at the lake.

"Listen up," Blake said. "We're going to do a bit of a swim. You are to go out around the pontoon and back here to Hulk, then back out and around again, until he tells us it's our last lap. At which point we will swim out to the pontoon and tread water, until one of the instructors tells us to swim ashore. Got it?"

There were a few nods and some worried looks on the last of the recruits to arrive by the lake who were still trying to get their breaths back.

"Go!" Hulk yelled as he fired his pistol into air behind the group making more than a few jump on the spot.

Blake took off running into the water fully clothed, including his joggers, when he was deep enough, he dived in and started to swim. If the group thought he was fast on land, they were definitely shocked at his speed through the water. Max and Flash made it to the shore as Blake was running back in, he glanced at Max, but kept running then dived into the water and started swimming out again.

"Keep it up boys," Kate said as they ran around her and Hulk, and back for the water.

The last of the pack was halfway back to shore as they dived in for their second lap. On their fourth lap, they overtook some of the recruits and by the tenth they were a full lap in front of the last recruit. By lap fifteen, as they ran ashore, Max noticed several recruits had stopped and were laying in the dirt, while others were slowly walking back in the direction of the homestead.

"They quit!" Hulk yelled at Max and Flash. "You going to quit too?"

"No, sir," they both said as they ran around him and back into the water.

Five laps later and Hulk gave the instruction to swim out and tread water. Blake was already out there as they started into the water. When they arrived, Max felt the burning in his lungs. He felt heavy in the water as his shallow breaths meant he could not float properly which forced him to kick more to stay above the water. It was a vicious cycle. His face dipped below the murky water more than once and he spat it from his mouth as he resurfaced.

They had been threading water for around thirty minutes before one of the instructors on the pontoon looked at his watch then dismissed Blake, Max and Flash. As they made it to shore, Max wondered whether his legs could hold him, they felt like jelly. His muscles and lungs burned, he was exhausted.

"Well done, both of you," Hulk said. "Not many people can match Blake, but you certainly got close. Head back and grab some food and rest."

"Don't worry," Kate said. "You can just walk back, unless you want to run?"

"No, thank you ma'am," Flash said.

"Get out of here," Kate said.

The three walked back towards the farmhouse in silence for the first few kilometres, mostly out of exhaustion. The wind gently blew through the trees cooling their wet and already freezing clothes. Nearby birds squawked and whistled. Three kangaroos bounced across the road in the distance.

"So, how long have you worked for Hulk?" Max asked.

"I have been with AIS on secondment for four years, working directly for Hulk for the last three," Blake said.

"Do you miss the Navy?"

"I'm still in the Navy, but I get what you mean. Yeah I do sometimes, but that's why I like coming out here to help train the new recruits. It's great to feel part of a team, working together to achieve a result, but also to get away from the office and my computer."

"What did you do before this?"

"I started as a clearance driver, then moved into Navy Intelligence."

"That's how you met Hulk?"

"Yes, I was sent on a mission with an AIS team by one of my commanders. Originally, I thought it was just to help and do my bit, I later found out it was a trial. Hulk recruited me, and I came here and went through everything you will. You're in a for a big few weeks if you can make it."

"Can you tell us what comes next?"

"No, but you need to be ready physically, emotionally and mentally for what is coming. Most of your fellow recruits won't make it."

"Sounds ominous," Flash said.

"We can only take the best of the best. Trust me, when it is your life on the line, you only want the best people around you, you only want the best people on your team and you only want the best people protecting your back."

Chapter Three

Max's heartbeat thundered in his chest, his eyes suddenly open and he swung out of bed onto his feet before he knew what was happening. The sound was deafening as the airhorns sounded around the cots in the farmhouse. Once all the potential recruits were awake and on their feet the horns stopped.

"Good morning," Hulk said. "Put on your joggers now, you have thirty seconds to be outside."

Max and his fellow recruits all scrambled to put on their shoes then ran through the front door out into the brisk morning air. He was bouncing up and down trying to warm up, but the cold pre-dawn air felt even colder than normal, given he was only wearing his loose, thin black cotton sleeping pants and an old white t-shirt. The green lawn had a thin layer of dew and frost from the late-Autumn air. He looked around at his comrades who all had bed hair, they were trying to warm up and rub the sleep out of their eyes shuffling back and forth on the dewy lawn in their random assortment of pyjamas. Some wore boxer shorts and t-shirts, others wore flannelette pants and singlets. Max noticed one of the recruits, Travis he thought his name was, only had on a pair of underpants and his joggers, and he was standing in a daze. *Not a morning person*, Max thought to himself and smiled. Hulk and his trainers were all dressed in their workout gear standing on the deck of the farmhouse and the recruits all turned around to face them as Kate blew a whistle.

"We wake every morning at five for training," Hulk said. "Normally, we'll be doing PT, but today I thought we should test your orienteering and teamwork skills. We have broken you into ten teams of four. Each team will be given a map which holds the location of a secret item. You are to retrieve the item, together, and return here as a team, together. No man or woman gets left behind and let me tell you there are some obstacles along the way where you are going to need to work as a team to achieve your mission. Am I understood?"

"Yes, sir," all but one of the recruits yelled.

"Mr Travis, do you have something to say?" Hulk asked of the recruit standing in his old red underpants.

"No, sir," Travis said. "It's just bloody cold."

"Well, you were dumb enough to run out here in your underpants, that was a stupid choice. All of you take note, in this game we all have choices to make, some of which we need to make in a split second. Some you'll get right, others like Mr Travis, will be patently stupid and you will suffer for them."

The recruits all laughed at Travis who was shifting his tall, skinny frame uncomfortably from side-to-side, kicking the grass. His pasty white skin was turning a bit blue from the cold air.

"Over to you, Alpha," Hulk said to Kate.

"Alright shut up and listen," Kate said. "When I call your fucking name, come up with your team to collect a map from Hermes. As soon as you have the map, you can head out."

Kate read out the first few teams and Max watched as they spoke briefly looking at their maps pointing this way and that, before Max heard his own name.

"Shaw, Gordon, Williams, Travis," Kate said.

Max and Flash walked up together and met with Travis in his red undies, and one of only ten female recruits, Sally Williams. They all shook hands and headed up to collect their map from Blake, before heading to one side, out of the way, to discuss the plan.

"Alright," Max said opening the map. "Let's take a look."

"Here pass it to me," Travis said taking the map from Max and looking him up and down. "I've been in the Army for five years, I'm sure I can read a map better than some punk who just left high school."

"Maybe so, but I'm hardly sure I want to trust the judgement of a man standing in a pair of underwear it looks like he's been wearing since he was in high school. Did your mummy buy those for you?"

"You want to have a go?" Travis said as he grabbed Max by the shirt.

"Oi!" Blake yelled from the deck. "Not a good start lads, get your shit together or you can pack your bags and leave the program, what's it going to be?"

"We're all good here," Max said raising his hands quickly towards Blake. "Aren't we Travis?"

"Yeah," Travis said letting go of Max before whispering under his breath. "Typical, fucking fag, Navy wanker."

"Let's just get this over with, shall we?" Williams said.

"Agreed," Flash said.

They opened the map and saw a red dot marking the location of their item.

"It looks like it's a couple of kilometres past the lake we visited yesterday," Williams said.

"Nah, that's not the same lake surely," Travis said. "You've got it upside down."

"No, Sally is right," Flash said. "Look here is the farmhouse and the driveway, and here is the dirt road we ran along for the first couple of kays yesterday. Let's move."

"I think you're wrong, but whatever, I need to run for a bit to warm up."

"Well, off you go, lead the way," Max said.

Travis gave Max an unimpressed look before running down the driveway.

"What a massive dick," Williams said.

"Didn't look that big to me in those pathetic undies," Max said.

Flash, Williams and Max all laughed before folding up the map and running after Travis.

After a few kilometres, one of the instructors flew passed on a dirt bike kicking up dust over the four recruits as he sped off into the distance. When they arrived at the lake, they each took a moment to catch their breaths. Max's shirt and pants were clinging to him from the sweat and cool air made him feel cold. Travis must have been freezing. Max's white shirt was dirty from the dust the bike had flicked up. For the first time, he noticed both Flash and Williams were wearing flannelette pyjama pants. Flash's were blue and red striped, and he was wearing a blue singlet which had dark wet patches on the front and back from the run. Williams had green and purple spots on her white pyjama pants and a loose-fitting white shirt. She had brown shoulder length hair hanging loosely framing her face and a dark tan. She was only short, but solid and fit. She looked tough, but still feminine.

"Jesus, I thought it was bad yesterday," Williams said. "Try running that without a bra on, fuck, and these pants are hot to run in."

"Tell me about it," Flash said adjusting himself with a painful look on his face.

"Let's take a look at the map," Max said stifling a smile at his team mates. "We can go get this item, then get back to the house before Flash gets an injury."

"That would be painful," Williams said laughing.

"It already is," Flash said still adjusting himself, causing the three of them to laugh.

"What are you all laughing at?" Travis asked.

"Nothing," Max said looking at the map and smiling to himself. "It looks like a path on the other side of the lake leads down to where our item is, let's head around."

Max put the map away and the group walked around to the far side of the lake and down an overgrown path into the bush.

"Check this out," Travis said pointing down at the dirt. "Bike tracks, that fucker that rode passed us must be down here. Guess we are going the right way."

"I'll take that as an apology and move on," Williams said.

"Hmm, yeah, sorry. I'm not a morning person."

"All forgiven, right Max?"

"Yeah, sure, why not?" Max said. "Let's keep moving."

"Hey guys, I think we might only just be beginning this little challenge," Flash said from his position up the path on a little crest. "Come check this out."

Max and the others joined Flash to take in the scene before them. The overgrown bush had been cleared in a large rectangle and a huge obstacle course sat in its centre. Wooden beams and steel monkey bars hung above muddy pits and pools of cold, still water. Climbing walls, swing ropes, old tyres and barbed wire littered the course.

A whistle rang out from the far end of the course and the team sighted the instructor waving an orange flag, like the pin on a golf course. Once he was sure they had seen him, he placed it back in its holder and cupped his hands around his mouth.

"Come and get it," the instructor yelled before blowing his whistle again.

Max and the team wandered over to the first obstacle. A single wooden beam was suspended on a slight incline at waist height from a metal frame over a muddy pool of water. Two small platforms sat at each end of the beam for the recruits to use to climb up to the beam. Max jumped down to the first one and reached up for the beam, which was above his shoulder now he was on the platform, it rotated in his hands.

"Okay, so this rotates, just for an extra challenge to kick off," Max said. "Guess I'll head over first."

He hung from his hands on the beam and kicked his legs up around it and began dragging himself along. He made his way across gingerly, then dropped to the platform and turned back to watch Flash, then Williams copy his technique and join him on the opposite side.

"Fuck this," Travis said hanging from the beam by his arms not wanting to use his bare legs to slide across.

With each movement the beam rotated in his hands. He was only inching forward trying to counterbalance the beam, so he did not lose his grip. His feet were only a foot from the muddy water. Painfully slowly he crossed to the other side, he reached out with his feet for the platform and slipped slightly, but Max and Flash reached out and took an arm each and reeled him in.

"Thanks," Travis said.

"You're welcome," Max said turning around. "What's next?"

A series of horizontal wooden beams alternated at different heights along a rocky section of the course.

"Got to go over the tall ones and under the low ones," Travis said. "We did this a lot for PT in the army, we'll have to help each other at the far end, they get much higher."

"Okay then," Max said. "Let's do it, want to lead the way?"

"Yeah, let's go."

The first four beams were easy enough, over the first one which was just above waist height and under the second which was barely a foot off the ground. The third and fourth were both just higher than the first. As they all army-crawled under the fifth, they checked out the sixth and seventh which both sat around Max's shoulder height. Travis ran and jumped up onto the sixth beam and caught it pulling himself up and over, then repeated the action for the seventh. Max and Flash stood next to the beam and took a foot each as Williams ran and jumped for the beam, boosting her up. As she leapt to the ground on the other side, Max and Flash copied Travis's moves up and over. They repeated it on the seventh beam, Williams first, then Max and Flash. The team crawled under three beams before arriving at the final beam which was suspended seven feet high.

"Two of us should get boosted up to sit on the bar," Max said staring at the beam. "Once we are up there, the third person can be boosted up and over."

"What about the fourth?" Flash asked.

"They'll just have to reach and be pulled up, dead weight. I'll go up and then you, Flash. We'll help Travis and Williams over."

"Got it," Flash said. "Travis come help me boost Max up."

Max stepped into their hands, as they pushed up, he placed his palms down on the smooth wooden cylinder and pulled himself up before straddling the beam. Williams and Travis boosted Flash up and he sat facing Max just over a metre apart. Travis stood with his back to Max and Flash with his hands cupped in front. Williams ran at him then stepped up into his hands with her right foot and sprung up as he boosted her. Flash and Max caught her and helped her onto the beam before lowering her towards the ground on the far side.

"Alright, Travis," Max said. "Try to jump as high as you can, we'll try to catch you under the arms and lift you to the beam, then you'll need to help pull yourself up and over."

"Got it," Travis said. "If I can get to my waist, I'll be fine."

"Let's do it."

Travis took a few steps back then ran and leapt for the bar, Max and Flash reached down while holding the beam with their legs and one arm each. Max caught Travis under the right arm and Flash under the left, they pulled him up slowly until his hands could grab the beam and he started to help pull himself up. When he got to his waist, he said thanks to Max and Flash before rolling his top half over the bar and used his momentum to somersault over the beam and lowered himself to the ground. Max and Flash quickly followed.

Max led the team through the next two sections of the obstacle course. The first was simple enough, high-steeping through old tyres over fifty metres. The second was more daunting. A flat sheet of barbed wire sat about a foot above a muddy pit. Max army-crawled under it, trying not to get caught on the wire. At first the mud was only an inch or so deep, but it was freezing. He reached out and felt a deep hole in front of him. He crawled forward and his legs fell down into the cold watery hole. He breaststroked through the muddy water until he got to a section where the barbed wire took a ninety-degree turn straight down into the water in front of him. He looked ahead and saw about two metres of muddy water then the barbed wire rising out and forming a similar roof to that he had just crawled under. *Guess I'm going under it*, Max thought. He felt under the water ahead of him and sure enough the barbed wire sheet was running level with the surface of the water, but it was clear underneath it. He turned back and told the others what to expect then took a breath, closed his eyes and went under. Max felt up towards the surface to check for barbed wire, when his hand broke out into the air he came up and took a breath as he tried to wipe the dirty water and debris from his eyes and face, mist was visible with every exhale. He turned back to face his team who were all huddled watching for him to resurface. He had gone at least two metres passed the little barbed wire wall. The others followed hesitantly, Flash, Williams then Travis. Ten metres from the end, Max felt the ground rising again and he began army-crawling the final stretch out from under the wire. He ripped a three-inch cut in his shirt only a foot from the end. *Oh well, this shirt was fucked anyway*, he thought. He helped the others to their feet as they slid out from under the wire. Travis caught the same wire as Max's shirt, but without a shirt on to protect him, the wire traced a red cut down his back.

"Argh fuck!" Travis said.

"Oh shit mate, are you okay?" Max asked.

"Yeah, fucking wire got me."

"Turn around," Max said checking out the cut. "It's a couple of inches long, but doesn't look too deep. You'll definitely need a tetanus shot when we get back."

"Great. Fuck it. Okay, let's just keep going."

They ran down a small path to the next obstacle. A ladder ran up to a metal platform and a large structure which looked to be suspended over a clear blue swimming pool. One-by-one they climbed up to the platform and took in the sight of the next platform. A long length of monkey bars ran in a straight line before them, ending in a maze of ropes which looked to stretch about the same distance to the platform at the other end. Max looked down to a pool of water which ran the length of the obstacle and if it was anything like the muddy water they had swum through before, it was going to be cold.

"What's that about twelve metres down?" Max asked. "That won't be pleasant if we fall."

"Agree," Flash said. "Especially, given the temperature. It'll feel like smashing through glass. So, do you want to go first?"

"Well, one of us has to I suppose."

"I'll do it," Travis said. "See you on the other side."

With that he leapt from the platform and caught the third monkey bar with both hands and began to swing between them, each hand taking a new bar in front of him, then he stopped a few short of the ropes.

"Fuck, they get further apart before the ropes," Travis yelled back.

He put both hands on the bar and swung back and forth to get momentum then jumped forward taking the next bar. He repeated the move twice to the final bar. On the last bar, he again swung back and forth, building momentum before he released it and sprung forward for the ropes. He caught the second rope in, but slid down move than three metres.

"Fucking hell," he yelled. "I've ripped up my hand."

"You okay?" Williams yelled.

"What'd you think? Fuck!"

"Can you go on?"

"I'm going to try, but I hope you aren't one of those harassment in the workplace types."

"What? Why?"

But before he answered, Max, Flash and Williams watched as Travis hung from the rope with one hand and removed his red jocks and used his teeth to wrap them tightly around his damaged hand. The three laughed at the sight of their fellow recruit swinging naked between the ropes.

"Whatever it takes, I guess?" Max said.

"I think I'd rather fall into the water," Flash said.

"I wish he had," Williams said. "That's not an image that's going to leave me real fast."

They all laughed as Travis swung and landed on the platform at the far end, then Max stepped forward to take on the course. He clapped and rubbed his hands together to get rid of any remaining dirt and water from the previous obstacle. Satisfied they were as good as he could ask for, considering what they had been through, he reached out and took the first of the monkey bars. Like Travis, he swung one handed, left then right, between the first rows of bars until he got to the far end. He reached one further than Travis, but then swung with both hands between the last two. When he was ready, he swung from the metal bar towards the nearest rope. He caught it with both hands and quickly moved to catch it with his feet to wedge it between his joggers to stop from sliding down. He did slide, but less than a metre, the rubber soles of his shoes gripped the rope stopping him high on the rope. He used his weight to swing the rope side-to-side to slowly create some momentum. His forearms burned and his whole body was screaming at him to give up in exhaustion. His stomach growled looking for fuel after doing heavy exercise without breakfast, but he pushed on. He reached out for the next rope and got them moving in time before letting go of the first and swing onto the third. He repeated this sequence over and over, until he finally reached the far end and leapt for the platform. He landed on it, but slipped, falling to his knees, he rolled forward and away from the edge. When he got to his knees, he was eye level with Travis's naked groin.

"Oh fuck, Travis, put your pants back on," Max said.

"I can't I need them for my hand."

"No, we can't have that," Max said taking off his shirt. "Here, use this."

"You sure?"

"Definitely sure."

"Thanks Max," Travis said putting his underwear back on and ripping Max's shirt down the cut from the barbed wire into a couple of long strips which he then tied around his hand.

Williams had started her crossing and Max and Travis turned back to watch. Halfway through the monkey bars,

Williams had to use both hands to make the distance between them, given her much shorter reach. She was using a great deal of energy to leap between each rung. On the second last bar, she hung still for a few seconds to get her breath. From a cold start, she tried to move, but she needed to use her whole body to gather momentum and she was starting to fatigue. She swung back and forth determined to make it, she pushed herself hard then made the jump. Max watched as her hands hit the last bar, but she could not get a hold. She slipped from the bar and fell awkwardly towards the water. Luckily, she managed to get her legs under herself and they broke the water with a harsh slap, before she disappeared under the surface. Max, Flash and Travis held their breaths waiting for her to resurface. The seconds rolled by and Max considered diving in to find her, but then she came up and tapped herself on the head to show she was alright.

"You okay?" Max yelled down to her.

"Yeah," she said. "You were right, that stings."

"I bet. Can you swim up this end?"

"Yeah, I'll meet you at the bottom of the ladder when Flash comes across."

"Okay," Max said looking up to Flash. "You ready?"

Flash gave Max a slightly worried look before giving him a thumbs up. He started his way across, almost identically to Max, given their similar builds, but halfway through the ropes he was starting to fatigue and he was getting lower as he moved to each new rope.

"Come on, Flash," Max said. "You've got this."

"Not sure I do," Flash said making his way to the second last rope.

"Only a couple more to go, then you'll have to shimmy up the rope a bit and jump across. You can do it."

He swung to the second last rope and slid down, but caught himself just before his feet went off the end of the rope. Max watched as Flash tried to pull himself back up. It was slow, Flash's muscles must have been burning in this arms, but he managed to get a couple of metres back up the rope and started to swing it before moving to the last rope. He climbed the rope and began swinging it towards the platform, then he jumped. His right foot hit the edge of the platform and his left felt short, grazing his shin and hitting his knee. Max ran forward and grabbed his hand, but it was too late, Flash was falling too fast, and instead of helping him up, Max went over the edge with him. The pair fell fast and hard into the water below. Flash went in first breaking the water, arse-first. Max went in next to him arms outstretched like an Olympic diver. The water was freezing and took Max's breath away. He came up and took a deep breath, checking around him for Flash, who popped up beside him.

"Fuck mate, I'm so sorry," Flash said. "Are you okay?"

"You're heavier than you look," Max said smiling. "I'm fine though, are you?"

"Yeah, shit, Williams was right though, that stings."

"Tell me about it."

"You two alright down there?" Travis asked looking over the edge of the platform. "Hell of a splash."

"Yeah mate," Flash yelled up. "Come down and we'll head over and finish this off."

"You bet."

Max and Flash swam over to the side of the pool and pulled themselves out of the cold water.

"Were you a diver, Max?" Williams asked as she watched him pull his toned body from the pool, the water running down his chest and abs to his now very clingy black pyjama pants.

"No, but I'm a swimmer. Why's that?"

"A ten or twelve metre dive is no easy feat."

"I'm just lucky his fat arse broke the water first or it could've ended differently, that's for sure."

"Hey!" Flash said. "Well, actually, I guess that's fair, I did pull you in."

The three of them laughed as Travis joined them.

"What's funny this time?" Travis asked.

"We were laughing at Flash's fat-arse and these two falling in the water," Williams said. "Although now I think about it, we should all have a good laugh at how you swung naked like Tarzan to the end of the course."

"Least I'm dry, not like you, dumb fucks."

Flash and Max looked at each other, then without a word threw Travis into the pool.

"Oh, you arseholes," Travis said as he resurfaced. "It's fucking freezing. Help me out."

Max grabbed Travis's good hand and dragged him out of the water, while they all laughed.

"Alright, let's go finish this hey?" Max asked.

They all nodded and followed Max down the last little path. The instructor was standing next to the little orange flag shaking his head. He held up one finger, then pointed to the one last obstacle, a two-storey wooden climbing wall. At the bottom, six wooden beams made a set of steps up to a flat wall with a rope hanging centred from the top.

"Oh for fuck's sake," Travis said. "I quit."

"That's bullshit, Travis," Max said. "We're nearly there. We can do it."

"This fucking course is bullshit."

"Come on," Max said walking towards the wall. "One more, then we can go back and relax."

"Fine, off you go."

Max climbed up the beams to the rope, took it in his hand then used it to walk up the wall. Everything was burning and he was cold from the water and his wet pants, but he pushed on. At the top, he sat on the edge and encouraged the others to join him. Flash followed him up.

"Don't pull me over this time," Max said reaching down to take Flash's hand to help him up the last metre.

"Wouldn't dream of it," Flash said pulling himself up with Max's help.

Williams climbed up and over to join Flash on the other side.

"Okay, come on, Travis," Max said. "Last one, then we're out of here. Hulk said we have got to finish together. We can do it, we're so close."

Travis mumbled something under his breath, but started up the beams. At the rope, he grimaced in pain from his hand which was still wrapped in Max's ripped shirt.

"You've got this," Max said as Travis began to climb, the pain evident in his eyes.

"Fuck it, I'm losing my grip."

"Couple more steps mate and you're home."

Travis took a step trying to reach for the top of the wall. Max reached out and grabbed his hand and dragged him up the last metre, then they lowered themselves down to meet Flash and Williams.

"Thanks, Max," Travis said. "Not bad for a bloke just out of high school."

"Not bad for a bloke whose mum still buys their undies for them," Max said smiling and they all laughed. "Let's go get our item from the instructor."

"Well, that had to be one of the most interesting performances I've ever seen of recruits completing this obstacle course," the instructor said when they reached him. "I'm Doctor Ian Carter the AIS phycologist. Mr Shaw, Mr Gordon, Ms Williams and Mr Travis congratulations you passed the course, here is your item, take it back to General Scott, will you?"

"What is it?" Travis asked taking the box from Carter.

"It's your item. Take it to Hulk and he'll decide if he wants to share with you what's inside."

"This some mind-fuck doctor joke?"

"In your potential new line of work, you will often come into contact with items and files which you won't read or see. Your job, especially for the first months or even years, will be solely to find the items requested and deliver them. So, without opening the box, take it back to Hulk and he'll decide if he wants to share it with you."

"Thanks Doc," Max said taking the box from Travis. "We'll get it to him."

"Thank you, Mr Shaw, see you all back there."

The team walked back to the farmhouse, exhausted, tired and hungry. Halfway back, Doctor Carter rode passed on his dirt bike leaving them in a trail of dust. He was standing with Blake and Hulk on the deck when they got back. A few of the other teams were already back and sitting or lying on the grass awaiting instructions.

"Here you go, Hulk," Max said handing Hulk the box as he team stood beside him.

"How'd you go, Mr Shaw?" Hulk said. "Tired? Hungry?"

"Yes, sir, but we made it and we're stronger for it."

Hulk looked at Carter and raised an eyebrow. Carter nodded. Max looked at Hulk and Carter, then to Blake who was looking him up and down. Max self-consciously rubbed his right hand down his wet chest and abs. Blake locked eyes with him and his face flushed.

"None of the other teams, so far, have seen their items," Hulk said. "Do you want to know what's in the box?"

"Sir, our job was to deliver it," Max said looking back to Hulk. "I personally don't care what's in it. If you chose to share it or not, I'll be comfortable either way."

"That's the right answer, Mr Shaw. Here you go."

Max walked over and took the box back from Hulk.

"Open it," Hulk said as all the other recruits on the grass sat up to see what was in the box.

Max opened the box and found four envelops inside with his and his teammates' names on each one. He handed them out and they each opened their package. Max pulled out a photo, it was of himself and Lachlan, they were smiling like it was taken mid-laugh, the happiness radiated out of the picture. It was taken only a month ago, before a college ball, they were wearing new matching navy suits with white shirts. Lachlan wore a pink tie with blue spots and Max worn a blue tie with pink spots, and they are swapped their matching pocket squares which were just visible at the bottom of the picture. Max felt his heart race both in missing Lachlan and from the guilt of having lied to him about where he was. He had told him he was at a personal training camp before his competition, then he would be heading overseas with his family for a holiday, a trip on which he promised he would come out and tell his family he was gay, and most importantly, tell them he was in love with Lachlan, so they could start their life together properly. A tear welled in his eye as he looked up in exhaustion to Hulk and the others.

"There is a phone in there too, if you want to call him," Hulk said before looking to the others. "Same goes for all of you, but if you do, just be sure to tell them you'll see them soon, as I'll take it as a sign you've quit this program because you can't handle it."

Max took out the phone and looked at it, as the instructors and his fellow recruits all looked on. He stood still for a moment thinking about it, then looked at Blake who shifted uncomfortably, then to Doctor Carter who did not flinch just watched him inquisitively and finally to Hulk who smiled broadly as if mocking him. Max stared into Hulk's eyes, then without blinking or looking away, he flicked the phone onto the grass and walked up the stairs to the deck coming face-to-face with Hulk.

"Is that all, General?" Max asked.

"Yes, you are all dismissed for the rest of the morning," Hulk said after a few tease seconds. "Hit the showers."

"Thank you, sir," Max said walking towards the door, before turning briefly to point at Travis. "Oh and he needs a tetanus shot."

Chapter Four

Max woke at a quarter to five and quietly got dressed into his workout gear. The previous day was playing on his mind. After they had showered and eaten, the recruits had all assembled in the dining area of the homestead. On both sides, large projector screens had been set up for the first of a long series of daily briefings and lessons. The first two hours were spent discussing information gathering and communications theory. The second two hours were dedicated to a video presentation of weapons handling techniques and showcasing an array of weapons they would be trained to use. Following dinner, they spent another two hours discussing the psychology of a terrorist in a session led by Doctor Carter. Max had enjoyed the lesson, given his studies in psychology, but he kept thinking about Lachlan. He had definitely been distracted.

As he tied the laces on his second set of joggers, the others were drying outside, he reminded himself that Hulk was trying to get into his head, trying to break him and expose and exploit weakness. He would not fall for it again. He loved Lachlan more than life itself and wanted to be with him, but he knew what he was doing was for the greater-good, something beyond himself. He had to push on. He looked at the photo and smiled seeing Lachlan staring back at him. He breathed deeply then packed it away under his bed with his other belongings.

On cue, Hulk and the other instructors came into the room and blasted their airhorns. Flash, Max, Williams and a hand full of other recruits sprung up and ran outside ready to go, while others had forgotten the lessons of yesterday, most likely from exhaustion.

Outside the farmhouse, Max, Flash and Williams were stretching their tired and sore muscles preparing for whatever the morning had in store. Hulk, Blake and Kate walked out to address the recruits as Travis stumbled out wearing only a pair of joggers and blue undies.

"Mr Travis, what the fuck is wrong with you?" Hulk asked. "You must be a fucking moron."

Travis mumbled something under his breath.

"What was that?"

"Nothing."

"What did you say?"

"Nothing, sir."

"Good, you have sixty seconds to go back inside and put on a shirt and some shorts or you're done, go!"

Travis headed back inside as Hulk stared at his watch. The recruits and instructors waited, milling around on the grass. The door of the homestead flew open and Travis ran out pulling a shirt over his head.

"Fifty-six seconds," Hulk said. "You made it, but you just volunteered."

"For what?"

"I'm sorry?"

"For what, sir?"

"Today, we are going to be teaching you some basic hand-to-hand combat and you've volunteered to join me in the ring for the first demonstrations."

"Oh fuck."

"Indeed, get your arse over there now."

Travis started to walk over to the ring which was sitting in the front yard under the shade of a large gum tree. Earlier it had been covered in frost and dew, but one of the maintenance guys had roughly wiped it down. Travis climbed into the ring, closely followed by Hulk. The other instructors and potential recruits lined the grass surrounding the ring.

"Let's see what you've got, Mr Travis," Hulk said. "Try to take me down."

Hesitantly, Travis squared up, raised his hands and started to bounce around like a boxer. Hulk stood on the spot moving only occasionally to keep Travis in front of him. After a few seconds, Travis lunged, throwing a stabbing jab. Hulk moved effortlessly to dodge the incoming haymaker and open palm slapped Travis across the face.

"Did you just slap me?" Travis asked holding his face.

"There is something simple and delightful in a good hard slap across an opponent's face, it confuses them," Hulk said. "Look at his face. Shock, surprise, maybe a bit of pain, but mostly embarrassment. Come on Travis, here I am. Come get your payback."

Travis shook his head and yelled, then lunged for a second time. This time Hulk ducked under it and using Travis's momentum, pulled down on his arm and flipped him onto his back. Travis sat on the mat, his back to Hulk, trying to work out what had happened, then Hulk slapped him again from behind, on the same cheek. The recruits all laughed as Travis sat dumbfounded on the mat.

"If you get good enough at that move, you can dislocate the attacker's shoulder, putting you at a significantly stronger advantage," Hulk said. "Mr Travis, weren't you in the army before you got here?"

"Yes, sir," Travis said getting to his feet.

"Well, it's certainly gone to shit since I left by the look of it. Try again."

Travis and Hulk began bouncing side-to-side like boxers, with Hulk commentating and teaching as he moved.

"See his feet," Hulk said. "Constantly moving, that's good. Stay agile. Stay on your toes so you can move fast. But, where does your power come from? I'll give you a clue, it ain't your arms."

Hulk dropped down and threw two solid punches into Travis's stomach.

"Your power comes from your whole body, through your legs and torso, through the shoulder and out the arm. Stay on your toes to avoid punches, but plant them hard to throw your punches and generate the power, then back on your toes as quick as possible to avoid any incoming blows."

"Look at his hands, he's trying to bluff me, showing me a move with the right hand, but throwing a left. Your attack doesn't come from your hands, it comes from your shoulders. Always watch their shoulders."

Hulk blocked a series of punches.

"See. His shoulders are the giveaway. Left, left, right, boring. Textbook sure, but predictable. Here at AIS, we need to be ready for highly-trained opponents and we need to be better than them. I'm going to spend weeks training you all then we'll spend months honing your skills and perfectly your styles, so you can better even the best of the best."

Travis came in for another go at landing a punch on Hulk, but Hulk caught both his hands and stretched them out to the sides and threw a vicious headbutt down on the bridge of Travis's nose, busting it and spraying blood over his face.

"Boring always gets beat," Hulk said watching Travis fall to the mat. "Remember that, mix up your styles and remember there are no rules for our enemies, it's a street fight. You have a knife, cut them. You have a gun, shot them. You have a pool cue, use it. You have a handful of dirt, throw it in their face. Do what you need to, to win."

Two of the recruits dragged Travis out of the ring and took him to the medical rooms, on Hulk's instruction. Kate joined Hulk in the ring where the two demonstrated how to disarm an attacker with a gun and then a knife. Hulk said the same principles applied to other objects too. After an hour of lessons, the recruits broke into pairs and practiced what they had just learnt as Kate and Hulk wandered around nuancing their skills.

The lesson was followed by lunch then more theory lessons. They were shown a range of real threats terrorists had made against the country's leaders and institutions, which made what they were doing seem suddenly more real. There were hastily scrawled letters to the Prime Minister and ministers of the government. A video rolled showing terror training camps, a row of men dressed in black combat gear and head scarfs, wielding AK47s ran forward and dived into a small mound in a sandy desert, army crawled to the top and started firing. The footage cut to a van exploding outside an old concrete building, it tore open the whole side of the building, then a series of photos flashed onto the screen of Australian Government buildings, before cutting to a man in a balaclava and black bandana with white Arabic writing on the front.

Allah commands death to the unbelievers and those who have rejected His will. He also demands retribution on those who have wrong Him. The West has for too long rained down missiles and bullets on our people, and waged war on our lands in the name of democracy and freedom, when in reality you come to rape and pillage our countries for oil. Almighty Allah, has spoken to me, he commands the death of you, Governor-General, and you, Prime Minister, and all Australians for your blind support of the infidel American and Jewish dogs. It is time for you to pay for your crimes against Allah. Allah Akbar.

The instructors passed around photos of terrorist attacks which had succeeded in various countries. Car bombs, suicide bombers, lone wolf attacks, beheadings, stabbings and shootings. The photos showed the victims, as well as the sites, and the men and women who had carried out the attacks. They also received briefings on the terrorists' biographies, surprisingly a lot of them were just normal people, until something changed them. They were radicalised in local mosques and in most cases, it seemed like their local Imams twisting the word of their god was the source.

And, finally for the night, they were briefed on successful operations of AIS, CIA and MI6 where they had thwarted terror attacks. They ran through the intelligence gathered to carry out their missions. In a number of cases, individual agents had gathered the key pieces of intel needed to stop the attacks. They were also shown successful takedown operations where the terrorists were either arrested or killed, including the entry and clearance procedures. This was the role they would play if they were successful, they were all told. They were also shown files of successful counter intelligence operations where agents had planted false information or sabotaged equipment to derail attacks.

Max was starting to realise why he needed to succeed and why AIS's role was so necessary. There were people out there trying to hurt innocents and trying to destroy our way of life, and he could not sit by and let it happen.

Chapter Five

A man in priestly black robes walked along a cold dark street, the heels of his shoes clicking lightly on the footpath. With each step he kicked the robes forward and the ropes which hung from his waist bounced from side to side. His hands were crossed in front of him, each arm inserted into the sleeve of the opposite arm. His large gold cross, and purple, white and gold sash flapped in the cold winter breeze. His white collar was shining as he walked in and out of the street lights, but his face and head were hidden by a large loose black hood.

Two metres behind the archbishop was a tall, athletic man dressed completely in black. He was constantly scanning the street ahead, to the left and to the right, and occasionally, he would turn to look behind them. Satisfied, he would turn back and try to keep up with the archbishop. He was a rugged man with a sandy beard covering a web of purple and white scars which ran from his left ear down his jaw line and neck where it disappeared under his tight-fitting shirt. His cargo pants flapped in the wind as his heavy combat boots moved silently on the concrete path.

The two men came to a small alleyway and the man in the combat boots entered first. He walked past an overflowing commercial bin from a nearby restaurant which was already closed for the night. The alley stank of stale food and rotting waste, but it didn't seem to faze him. At the end of the alley, he knocked on a narrow dark blue wooden door, its paint flaking and chipped from years of neglect unveiling an old yellow paintjob beneath. A small window three quarters of the way up the door slid to the side revealing a cold and fierce set of eyes.

"What?" the man behind the door asked.

"Their feet have slipped," the man in the combat boots said.

The window in the door closed and the heavy locks slid to the side, and the door opened. The archbishop rushed through the door closely followed by the man in the combat boots.

"Hello, Haddad," the archbishop said to the man who had opened the door.

"Your Grace," Haddad said nodding slightly. "Please come this way."

"Thank you. Haddad, this is Daniel Curran the head of my security detail and one of my strongest supporters," the archbishop said as Haddad and the man in combat boots nodded to each other. "He will be your best point of contact for operations going forward."

"Understood, Archbishop Wright. Please, Imam Moghadam is in back room."

"Lead the way."

The three men walked through a maze of dark corridors and into a small dining room. An old wooden table sat in the middle of the room with eight metal framed chairs. A man with a black beard, dark skin and white robes sat at one of the chairs on the far side with his back to the wall.

"Good evening, Benjamin," Moghadam said. "Did you have any trouble finding the place?"

"Good evening, Abu," Archbishop Wright said. "No, it was no problem at all. Although the alley is quite unpleasant."

"Clearly it has been a while since you have been among the people, Your Grace. Welcome to the bottom of the world, do you see why change is needed or do you want to go back to your opulent mansion surrounded by servants and live out your days in ignorance?"

"That's not what I meant. I just meant it stinks out there. I am onboard."

"Good to hear. I was not sure whether you had the heart to go through with it."

"My cause is what matters and I am here to see our plan come to fruition."

"Their feet have slipped."

"Indeed."

"I understand your service went well? It was a powerful speech."

"It did, thank you."

"Did anyone discuss it with you?"

"Yes, several people were keen to discuss it at length, some were very supportive, others not so."

"The New Testament is still your greatest weakness when it comes to empowering your people for action. Forgiveness and absolution can only be truly given by God, not through confession. Reminding them of God's will, not Jesus Christ and His weaknesses, that is how you will motivate them."

"I agree which is why the speech was written as it was, but please let's not start arguing about who is right or wrong here, we have one purpose. My flock will come around, they just are not as used to this sort of thing as you people are."

"What is that supposed to mean?"

"You know what I mean."

"Perhaps you are right, we should move on before this ends badly. We have one purpose."

"Their feet have slipped."

"Yes, indeed they have."

"So, where are we up to?"

"Haddad will secure the devices in a few weeks. They are being built and will be transported to a safe location."

"Who did you get them from?"

"It is irrelevant, all you need to know is he is a believer in our cause and they will work as required. Where did you get to with the vials?"

"I have spoken to Katzenberg and Rothstein, they tell me things are on track. They will deliver the vials to your safehouse when you give me the location, so the devices can be loaded."

"Another surprise."

"What is?"

"The Jews."

"What about them?"

"I did not think they would go through with this either."

"They share our goals, Abu."

"We will see."

"They will deliver."

"What about locations? Have you got your list ready?"

"Yes, I want the first to be the warning at the Opera."

"Stop. Do not tell me where, I just wanted to make sure you had your targets."

"Yes, we do. Why don't you want to know? I want to know where you will be setting them off."

"No, we cannot share that information. If one of us fails or is captured, we cannot risk the other operations."

"What if we are near the locations?"

"Then we will die for our cause. Are you willing to die for what you believe, Benjamin?"

"Yes."

"Then it does not matter where and when they go off, just as long as they do."

"Yes, you are right."

"And, your team is ready?"

"Yes, Daniel here will be leading both of our attacks."

"And, he will succeed?"

"Daniel is a former SAS solider. If anyone can succeed, it is him."

"Well, it is good to have you on the team, Daniel. Do not fail."

"He won't."

"We should meet again, with the Jews, in a few weeks to ensure we are ready."

"I will find a time, you find a place."

"It will be done. Thank you, Benjamin. See you in a few weeks."

"Thank you, Abu. Yes, we will see you then."

55

Chapter Six

Max walked back to his bunk from the changing rooms wearing his training gear as other recruits started to wake and get ready. He put his toiletry bag back under his bed and headed outside where he found a row of brand new cars parked in the driveway. A Chevrolet sedan was at the head of the queue, it was black, like all of the cars, and covered in the same fine film of red dust from the drive out to the Wool Shed. Max walked over and looked through the tinted windows, checking out the interior.

"Fucking nice car, isn't it?" Kate asked. "You can open the door and check it out if you want."

"Yeah it is," Max said opening the door and sitting in the driver's seat.

"We each have a preferred vehicle, it's our go-to for missions if we are driving. It's your choice, basically, it's what you feel comfortable with driving both in general and when, well let's just say, you need to get out of there in a hurry."

"Is that what we'll be doing today?"

"Sure is."

"Okay, cool."

"You going to take the Chevy?"

"Yeah, I think so."

"Good choice. V8, supercharged, easy to handle, fast and able to blend into a crowd. All our cars are typical cars you would find on Australian roads, but the top of the line models with racing suspension, tyres and engines."

"What do you drive?"

"I normally drive a Landcruiser, like the one I brought you out here in. Sometimes you need raw power and mass, I like it. Big and safe. I drive Hulk around a fair bit too and it's easier and more comfortable to fit the bullet-proofing we need for him, as the head of the agency, inside it."

"Oh, okay. Fair enough. I would have thought it would be a bit slow."

"Not mine. It's got a supercharged V12 engine under the hood to get it moving."

"Oh nice."

"Yep."

"So, are we racing today?"

"Not exactly, we are going to learn defensive driving techniques and some methods of stopping a car you're chasing and getting out quickly."

"Sounds fun," Max said climbing out of the car as Blake and the recruits walked out onto the lawn.

"Let's go join the others."

"Good morning," Blake said addressing the recruits. "Today, we're going to do something a bit different. We won't be doing PT this morning, instead we will be spending the day relearning how to drive. I say 'relearning' because what we will learn today, includes a bunch of new techniques which will force you to forget some of the things you have learnt about driving, especially when it comes to the road rules and safety. Now, we aren't giving you a licence to break the road rules in your day-to-day lives, but if necessary in emergency situations, it will be necessary in your careers with AIS to bend or break some rules and well, I want to make sure you do it safely, while achieving your objective. Alpha, can you run them through the plan?"

"Yes, sir," Kate said. "Each of you will choose a vehicle. It is your personal preference and if you are comfortable with it, it will become your assigned vehicle. If you need a car for a mission, your chosen vehicle with all the latest kit, will be provided. Follow me."

Kate walked to the black Chevrolet sedan Max had been sitting in and opened the bonnet and boot. The recruits all checked out the shinning chrome engine under the hood, it was stamped with the General Motors badge. Kate set about pointing to various AIS additions to the car. Most of the technical bits went over Max's head, but ultimately, he figured most of it was put in to make it go faster, handle better and brake quicker, like a race car hidden in plain sight.

The recruits wandered down along the line of cars inspecting each as they went.

"Hey, you lot," Kate said. "Back here for a minute."

She walked to the boot of the Chevrolet which was still open and waited for the recruits to gather around.

"They come with everything you need to get by," Kate said reaching into the boot.

She removed a small fabric panel in the lining of the boot and entered a six-digit code. The floor of the boot rose on small hydraulic arms revealing an array of weapons and tools each sitting neatly in perfectly shaped cut-outs in a foam inlay. Max saw some familiar items, pistols, assault rifles, knifes, duct tape, rope, smoke grenades, pepper spray, cable ties and there was even a set of bolt cutters.

"Alright," Kate said pointing to Blake who had walked down to the cars. "Tell him which car you want to drive, then we can get started."

Once the recruits had given their preferences to Blake, they all jumped into the cars and drove down the driveway and out around the farmhouse, down another dirt road leading into the woods. A few minutes later, as the trees sped past the windows, they arrived at a massive square concrete arena. It looked like it ran for kilometres into the distance. They drove up onto the concrete and sped towards the middle where another Landcruiser was waiting, Hulk was sitting up on the bonnet, but he climbed down when the recruits filed out of the cars.

"Good morning," Hulk said. "What do you think of the cars?"

The recruits all murmured amongst themselves and spoke of their excitement to get behind the wheel.

"Good, good, good," Hulk said. "It's always a popular day, especially compared to the long runs or endless theory lessons, but before you get too carried away, it will of course be challenging. Not only will you learn from some of the best, you will also have to complete a series of tasks throughout the day. I hope you slept well. But first, let me introduce you to two very special guests."

Two V8 supercars came racing down the concrete arena towards the recruits. The cars were plastered with the logos of major and minor sponsors. They did two wide laps around the assembled group before stopping next to Hulk's Landcruiser. The two drivers got out and some of the recruits started muttering and smiling, their excitement clearly rising.

"For those of you who don't know, Max, I'm looking at you," Hulk said making Max smile. "This is Mark Thomas, five-time Bathurst 1000 winner, and Tammy Peters, the first woman to win Bathurst, just a few months ago. They are here to teach you how to handle a performance car. Show us what you can do, Tammy and Mark. Blake, set it up."

Max turned to watch Blake as the two drivers climbed back into their cars. Blake typed a series of commands into his tablet computer. As he hit the last button, a pole rose out of the ground next to Hulk with an orange light on the top and a set of four small speakers. It rose to fifteen feet and the light started to flash and an alarm sounded, before an announcement for people to stand clear. A ring of two feet high posts rose from the ground near the outer edge of the concrete, spaced every ten metres, each with a small red light at the top. Twenty metres inside, another ring formed with green lights, again they were spaced at ten metre intervals. Max watched as the two race cars entered the ring and sped around, anticlockwise, each taking a turn in the lead. Max listened to the recruits' excitement at the spectacle. The sound was incredible, they must have been pushing their engines hard to get their cars up around two hundred kilometres an hour and more.

"Prepare for the change," Blake said.

"Hey?" Max said.

"I was telling the drivers through their comms units to be ready, I'm about to change the track."

"Oh, okay," Max said turning back to watch the cars as Blake set about typing on his tablet.

All the lights on the ring turned blue and flashed three times before returning to red and green, then a series of new guide poles rose out of the ground creating a new track. The drivers veered left and followed the new course, keeping the red lights on the right and green on the left. Blake's new track had sharp turns and long straights, mixing up the driving conditions. Max noticed how the lights flashed in a pattern as the drivers were approaching corners, the faster the flash, the tighter the turn. The cars raced by, engines roaring as Max and the recruits whipped around to watch them pass. After two laps the lights flashed blue again three times and a majority of the poles lowered into the ground except for one lane leading the cars around then straight down towards the recruits. The two powerful cars stopped a few metres behind Hulk's Landcruiser and the engines stopped, leaving a silence hanging in the air which Max had become used to in the quiet Australian outback.

The recruits and instructors all clapped as the two drivers climbed from their cars and walked over to Hulk who thanked them for the work. Over the following hours each recruit took turns of being passenger then driver, under the instruction of the two race car drivers. Max took his lesson with Tammy who had spent the first few laps in the driver's seat explaining the car's handling, acceleration and braking procedures which aided the vehicle's response to maximise its speed, as they flew around the course. Max felt the car slowing into a corner before accelerating through, felt the acceleration pull him back into his seat along the straights and appreciated the smooth transition between gears as Tammy expertly handled the performance vehicle around the course.

"What sort of car do you drive?" Tammy asked Max as he climbed into the driver's seat.

"I'm not sure you want to know," Max said doing up his seat belt.

"Oh, that bad, hey?"

"Yeah, I'm still at uni. I've got an old Ford ute, it's a manual V6 with a sports kit in faded red with some scratched up chrome roll bars. You can take the boy out of the country, but not the country out of the boy, right?"

"I guess so. This is a slightly more powerful car than that, so we're going to take it real slow to start and then work up to some faster laps, agreed?"

"Sounds good," Max said pressing the ignition button and feeling the engine vibrate to life.

Max could feel the raw power as he lightly touched the accelerator moving the car down the lane. He completed the first two laps relatively slow compared to Tammy's, but certainly faster than he was used to driving. She gave helpful instructions as he went around braking earlier, accelerating later and picking lines and angles to take corners smoother to ease pressure on the tyres and to get the most out of a tank of fuel, as well as creating a more comfortable and stable ride. With each lap Max's confidence was growing and his reactions getting better, he was feeling more at one with the big car.

"Alright, Max," Tammy said. "Let's give it a bit this time. Go up to where you feel comfortable and get used to the higher speed."

"Okay, it's your car," Max said smiling.

"I'm sure Hulk will buy me a new one if you break it, but I'd prefer you didn't."

"Roger that."

"Let's go. Let's see what you can do, country boy."

Max hit the accelerator throwing himself and Tammy back into the seats. Out of the corner of his eye he saw Tammy adjust her seatbelt and he smiled. Max raced down the straight heading for his first corner, a not too sharp, veer to the left. He braked slightly and paddled down a gear, roaring the engine and squealing the tyres on the way through.

"Brake a little earlier," Tammy said. "Then change down gear to stop the engine from revving so hard, it'll make it a little slower, but not as violent."

"Got it," Max said keeping his eyes focused on the next turn.

As instructed, he slowed the big car feeling it pull back as he changed down a gear, then another, taking the right hand turn still at a considerable speed. He felt the car bounce and skid in the back, but maintained control.

"Feel that?" Tammy asked.

"Yeah," Max said.

"A bit quick. Slower into the turns and accelerate hard out."

On the next turn, Max overcompensated and slowed too much. He knew it without Tammy needing to tell him. Max completed the lap and Tammy encouraged him to go even faster on the straights which he did, knowing she would not push him beyond his limits. Each lap got faster and faster, but still nowhere near as fast as Tammy's laps. On most corners he managed the brake and gear changes as Tammy had explained, but on others they went through too quick, skidding the tyres and shaking the car. After several laps, Tammy told him to head back over to the recruits.

"Not bad for a virgin," Tammy said as they climbed out of the car. "You can still push faster down those straights, have confidence in the car, trust me, the brakes work. But, you should use more before heading into the corners."

"Yeah, okay," Max said. "Thanks so much for the lesson, I'll keep all of that in mind. That was a lot of fun."

"You're not the best I've seen out here, but you've got enough, I'm sure, to get you by. Keep practicing."

"Will do. Thank you."

"You alright, Tammy?" Hulk asked. "You look a little white."

"Yeah, I'm okay, Hulk. Max here is a bit too keen to ride the clutch and do some high speeds through the corners, but overall not bad. I think I'm a better driver than passenger."

"That you are," Hulk said walking over and shaking her hand and Mark's. "Thank you both for your time today, we really appreciate you coming out."

"Pleasure," Tammy said. "Good luck."

"Anytime," Mark said. "Yes, good luck and thank you all for your service."

The recruits all said thanks and shook hands with the pair before they left the arena.

"Alright," Hulk said. "So, now we've covered speed, it's time to discuss evasion and chase techniques. There will be times you need both. If you are pursuing a suspect, you need to know how to safely stop them, and alternatively, if you are being pursued, you need to know how to stop them from stopping you. We will be showing you how to successfully execute procedures, like the pit manoeuvre, to stop a car, but also how to disable it by taking out the tyres, the engine or, if necessary, the driver. We will work in a combination of teams depending on the technique and to show the various scenarios you may face. All clear?"

"Yes, sir," the recruits shouted in unison.

"Good. Set it up, Blake."

"Yes, sir," Blake said typing away on his tablet.

A row of three televisions rose from the ground in front of the recruits and the guide poles again raised into position this time in two large rectangles. Kate and Blake both walked over and climbed into their cars, Blake taking the wheel of the Chevy and Kate the Landcruiser. They raced off into the first rectangle before turning back to the wide-open concrete and parking. One of the televisions was showing live footage from the dash in Kate's Landcruiser, the other showed footage from Blake's, while the third was showing a zoomed in version of what Max could see from where he was standing, he figured there must have been a camera on the back of the televisions' frame.

"When you're ready," Hulk said into his comms unit and Blake took off closely followed by Kate. "Watch now as Kate performs the pit manoeuvre, see how she is coming up beside Blake, level with the rear wheels. She's going to nudge in and he'll lose control."

On command, Kate turned the big car into the Chevy and it spun around before coming to a stop. Kate had stopped her own car and was already out with a pistol raised aiming through the window at Blake.

"Perfect," Hulk said. "Reload."

Kate climbed back in and the two cars headed back down the road. Once in position Hulk gave them the order and they again took off down the concrete strip.

"Watch this time," Hulk said. "Kate will move into position to do it again, but this time, Blake is going to fight back."

Kate came level with the rear wheels of Blake's sedan, but as she moved to nudge him, he slammed on the brakes. Max watched for a few seconds, not really sure what had happened. Instead of stopping Blake, Kate was now the one who had spun out and stopped, and Blake had his gun raised running towards her window.

"Everyone see how that worked?" Hulk asked as a few of the recruits scratched their heads.

"I didn't," Max said.

"Let's check the replay," Hulk said pressing some buttons on the tablet Blake had been using earlier changing the vision on the televisions. "See here, she's in line with the tyres, he senses it, brakes, then smashes the accelerator down and turns into her. In the fractions of a second it took to brake, Kate had moved too far forward to perform the manoeuvre, but putting Blake in line with her rear tyres. When he hit the accelerator, he performed the manoeuvre on her, leaving her confused and unprepared, then he's out of the car, wielding his gun as if she's a terrorist now dead or under arrest."

"Okay, yeah, I see it now," Max said. "His reaction speed has to be precise."

"Yes, is does. Although, even if he missed the manoeuvre, he can try to evade as she shoots past or they collide and continue down the road side-by-side. Both options are okay, because he is still moving. That's the most important thing when evading, get the fuck out of there. Got it?"

"Yes, sir," the potential recruits all said in unison as Kate and Blake returned to the group.

"Okay, this time I need two volunteers. Let's see, Max and Flash, you're up. You'll be driving. In you get, Kate and Blake will explain as you drive over."

"Yes, sir," Max and Flash said.

Flash climbed into the big Landcruiser with Kate in the passenger seat, while Max got behind the wheel of the Chevy with Blake taking the passenger's seat.

"Okay, Max," Blake said. "We are going to drive straight along the strip like Kate and I did just before. They'll be chasing us. On the first run, Kate will move ahead and shoot at us with a paintball gun to show how to disable our vehicle. If she lands the shot, the vehicle will react. You just need to slow us to a stop. Got it?"

"It'll react?" Max asked.

"Yep. Be ready."

"Okay," Max said reaching the end of the course and turning around.

"Righto, ready?"

"Yep."

"Let's go."

Max accelerated the car, surprised to feel the same power as Tammy's race car he had driven earlier, but remembering Kate had told him AIS vehicles were basically race cars hidden in plain sight. Kate's Landcruiser with Flash at the wheel past them on the right. Max watched as Kate lowered the passenger side window of her car and stuck a gun out and aimed it in his direction. He felt himself grip the wheel harder and he flinched slightly as the gun fired. Max felt the car respond instantly, the steering wheel vibrating wildly, and the vehicle started swerving. Max braked and got the vehicle under control, slowing it to a gentle stop. As he looked up, he saw Kate standing only a metre away, aiming the gun at him through the window. Max climbed out to see what had happened. A large blue dot of paint was visible on the front driver's side tyre which had deflated.

"There's a sensor in the tyre and in the paintball bullet, a computer in the car flattens the tyre to make it feel like it's been shot for real," Kate said to Max and Flash. "It's an enhanced version of software in the car to change the pressure of the tyres to suit driving conditions, easily fixed."

Blake pushed a button on the entertainment system in the car's dashboard and the tyre reinflated.

"Good as new," Kate said. "Let's go again."

They got back in their respective cars and headed down to the end of the track. When Kate gave the order, Max accelerated, with Flash giving chase. Again, they moved ahead of Max and Blake, however this time, Flash moved the Landcruiser directly in front of Max. He watched as the back window lowered into the tailgate. Kate popped up from behind the tailgate using it for cover and support. She fired four rounds, two into the front grill of the Chevy and two into the bonnet, splashing blue paint across the metal surface. This time Max did not need to brake to slow down, the car did it itself with the addition of smoke and steam pouring from under the hood. The car stopped and as the steam cleared, Max saw Kate again training her gun on him.

On the third run, Kate shot the window beside Max.

"What the hell?" Max said as blue paint hit the window.

"You're dead," Blake said as the vehicle stopped and again, and Kate was out and beside Max within seconds.

"Is it our turn yet?"

"Sure is," Blake said smiling. "Back we go, but this time, whatever happens, don't stop unless I say so. Oh, and the course, it is going to change, so stay alert."

"Roger that," Max said turning the car around.

"Hit it," Blake said as Max floored the accelerator once they had made it back to the end of the course.

The Chevy sped down the concrete strip as Max noticed the lights flashing blue on the poles. In front of him a series of wooden walls made to look like streetscapes emerged from the concrete creating a maze like a downtown central business district. Blake pressed some buttons on the entertainment unit and a number of icons appeared on the windscreen as a heads-up display, including Max's current speed and distances to corners which it was mapping. It was also suggesting routes, although there were very limited options on a fake track. In the top righthand corner was a message display window.

"What is all this?" Max asked.

"Head's-up display," Blake said. "Didn't have that in the race car, did they?"

"No, they certainly didn't."

"You get used to it, it's really helpful on a getaway because headquarters help direct you out of the conflict and away to safety."

The heads-up display flashed warning of an upcoming corner with metres counting down rapidly. Max braked hard then shot right with Flash in pursuit. Blake undid his seatbelt, lowered his window and turned around to kneel on his seat. As Max drove through the maze of artificial streets aided by the HUD, Blake stuck his arm and head out the window and began firing at Flash and Kate. Two paintballs hit Max's rear window as two from Blake's pistol found the Landcruiser's windscreen dead centre. Flash accelerated alongside Max's window and he saw Kate smiling broadly with her gun trained on him. Max hit the brakes and turned to try the pit manoeuvre, however he missed it and Flash shot past. Two paintballs hit the windows next to Max, but he kept driving now giving chase. Blake climbed up and sat on the doorframe hanging most of his body out the window and fired into the tailgate of the big Landcruiser low and to the left, aiming for the tyres then he found his mark and with a splash of paint the big car slowed and began swerving wildly, before the brake lights came on. Max's HUD lit up with collision warnings. A red triangle with exclamation mark flashed on the windscreen. He slammed his feet down on the brakes, but it was not enough to stop the Chevy. They were going to hit. Max reached over and grabbed Blake by the belt and dragged him back inside, while he yanked hard on the steering wheel veering the car to the right moments before the two cars collided. The panels on the left-hand side of Max's car were dinted and scratched as it scraped the rear tailgate of Kate and Flash's Landcruiser, then smashed through a wooden cut out storefront.

"Sorry, fuck, are you okay?" Max asked as he stopped his car.

"It's fine, yes, I'm fine too, thank you," Blake said reaching for the door handle. "We'll talk about it in a minute. Get your gun it's in the door."

Blake climbed out of the car and immediately fired three shots into the window next to Flash then keeping the gun trained on Kate as Max arrived.

"The driver's dead or dying," Blake said. "Keep focused on the passenger. She's our target."

"Got it," Max said.

"All clear," Hulk said over the radios. *"Get back over here."*

Max and Blake, Kate and Flash headed over to Hulk and the recruits, some of them were smiling or sniggering as Max climbed out of the driver's seat.

"Well, Mr Shaw," Hulk said. "You and Blake successfully apprehended the suspect, but not before you nearly killed yourselves. You okay, Blake?"

"Yes, sir," Blake said. "He actually pulled me back into the car. I fired early. He saved me."

"Really?"

"Yes, sir."

"Well, that's something, I guess. Your first instinct went to helping your colleague rather than wildly evading. Well done. Although I will say, you need many, many more hours, days, months of driving before I get in a car with you."

"Yes, sir," Max said. "Thank you, sir."

As the group re-watched the chase on screen, a semi-trailer pulled up and four guys scrambled out of the big rig. They walked over to the Landcruiser and the Chevy, and set about cleaning off the paint and replacing the panels, and they refuelled the cars from the side of the truck which had rolled up like a large mobile pit stop. Once the cars were ready the recruits, including Max and Flash, took turns of driving or shooting in the car chases using varying courses.

Chapter Seven

Max sat in the comfortable leather chair in the corner under a tall lamp looking around the office. It was a converted bedroom in the old homestead. A bookcase took up most of one wall and it was lined with various books from military history and strategy, to psychology and medical texts. There were religious books from all over the world as well as texts debating the use of torture and the techniques which had allegedly been proven to work. It was a dark space lit only by the lamps. A large Persian rug gave the room a warm and relaxing feel, and a small fireplace kept it warm on the early winter's day. A small fragile looking coffee table sat next to him holding a coffee mug and two glasses of water. A second large leather chair was in the opposite corner where Doctor Carter was sitting with his legs crossed sipping his coffee.

"So, how are you finding the experience?" Carter asked.

"It is certainly eye opening," Max said.

"In what way?"

"In every way."

"Tell me why?"

"We're going to be here for a long time Doctor Carter if your questions are constantly going to be so basic, like 'why?'"

"What would you prefer I ask?"

"Ask what you want to know. Be direct."

"Okay, how are you feeling?"

"You can do better than that."

"Why don't you answer the question you think I should be asking?"

"I'm fine."

"Do you want to add to that?"

"You want to know if I am having issues with the training, if I have considered where this program could take me, if I can do it, if I can handle it."

"Well, have you considered it and can you handle it?"

"Yes."

"To both questions."

"Yes."

"Really?"

"I think everyone would struggle to comprehend what is in front of them after a training program like this."

"Fair point, but I did not ask about everyone, I asked about you. You said 'struggle', can you tell me why you used that word?"

"You know what I mean."

"Well, let's find out."

"I think until I have experienced it, it would be hard to tell you whether I can do it."

"So, you have some doubts."

"Yes."

"How does that make you feel?"

"Seriously?"

"Come on, Max. You know what I'm doing. You don't consistently top your classes in psychology without knowing what I am asking and, more importantly, why I'm asking it."

"You want to know if you should let me continue and if I am successful, you want to know if you can trust to put me in the field."

"You got it."

"I would never let the team down."

"Sportsmanship and teamwork are great qualities, Max. We need those."

"I can see that."

"I saw it when you saved Blake yesterday by pulling him back into the car."

"How do you mean?"

"You cared more about your teammate then you did about crashing the car and risking your own safety."

"I didn't want him to get hurt."

"Most people would have relied on their primitive instincts and swerved first, not thinking about their colleague, just hoping to save themselves."

"If I did that he would have been crushed."

"He knew the risks when he climbed out the window."

"It doesn't matter anyway, he is fine and that's all that matters."

"My point is, Max, it shows a higher order thinking, others before self."

"But?"

"But, how would you help the team and put them first, if you're not sure you can do the job?"

"It's not that I don't think I can do the job, it's that I'm still processing how I would deal with certain aspects of it."

"Like what?"

"Like taking a human life, like torturing someone for information, like losing a colleague even though he 'knew the risks', like lying to my partner, like forgiving myself and my team if we fail."

"You're scared to fail."

"Wouldn't you be, if the consequences of your failure were so high?"

"You don't think the consequence of my failure are high in this job?"

"That's not what I meant."

"Every time I sign off on a recruit going into the field, I know that I am signing off on them putting their lives, their teammates lives and the general public's lives in their hands and I can tell you that every time someone makes a mistake I question my decision."

"I misspoke and I apologise."

"Thank you and that's okay, Max, I knew what you meant."

"Even so, I'm sorry."

"Moving on, you mentioned torture and taking a human life, would it make it easier if they were a terrorist?"

"I'm not sure. I don't think so."

"Why?"

"Because while they are evil, they are human beings. Someone's son or daughter. Someone's brother or sister, father or mother."

"You care a lot about people, don't you?"

"Of course."

"And, that extends to terrorists?"

"You're putting words in my mouth, Doctor, and twisting them a touch, I didn't say that."

"I care for my family and friends, I even care for complete strangers, but it's not that I care about terrorists, I just struggle with the idea of inflicting pain or taking their lives."

"There's that word again. Struggle."

"Yeah."

"Let me ask you this, what do you think happens after we die?"

"Now, we're going deep, Doc."

"You wanted to go there."

"No, I thought you did."

"Well, here we are. So, what happens?"

"Honestly, I have no idea."

"What do you think happens?"

"Nothing."

"Nothing?"

"Yep. Nothing. We're here, then we're not."

"So, no heaven or hell?"

"No."

"How does that make you feel?"

"Like I want to live."

"You mentioned other people's lives earlier, but not your own. Are you scared of death?"

"No. I mean, I'd prefer not to, but I'm not scared of it."

"So, what drives you if it's not religion?"

"You don't need religion to be a good person or to live your life. Heaven and hell aren't the carrot and stick needed to guide me, I want to do what's right, because it is right, not because of some promise of an amazing or terrible eternity. I truly believe people need to live for now, enjoying our fleeting and relatively short lives in the history of the universe, not holding out hope for something better afterwards."

"Then why risk it all for this job?"

"Because someone has to."

"But why you?"

"Because I might have the skills to be able to do it and as I said I care about people and I want them to live their lives free from fear, free from terror."

"People like Lachlan?"

"There's the million-dollar question."

"Why do you say that?"

"You know why."

"Yeah, but why don't you tell me?"

"Because I love him and please don't ask 'how does that make me feel?'"

"Well, why don't you tell me how you can reconcile such a strong and true love, with all the things AIS might ask you to do?"

"That's why it's the million-dollar question, Doc."

"I know. Is there a million-dollar answer?"

"I think he would be supportive."

"Of you risking your life?"

"No, of me doing what I can to help people."

"You think that would be important to him?"

"Yes, he cares about people even more than I do, he'll be a doctor soon."

"You should very proud."

"I am. I know how hard he has worked. He will be an incredible doctor."

"What do you think he would say if he found out you tortured someone?"

"I don't know."

"Think he'd be upset?"

"He's going to be a healer, Doc."

"And, you'd be doing the opposite?"

"Yeah."

"So, you don't think he'll be supportive."

"About as much as I am."

"What if I told you it works?"

"Torture?"

"Yes."

"Does it or do they just tell you what you want to hear?"

"Sometimes they do, but we've got a lot of practice, we sort it out eventually."

"So, you believe it works?"

"Yes, but I have to say, like you, I was sceptical until I saw their resilience and determination. It's in their eyes, Max, a fire, a passion, a cause. They become less-human and more beast."

"Does that help?"

"What?"

"Seeing them as less-than-human?"

"You will see for yourself someday I'm sure, then we can talk about it again."

"And, what about getting tortured?"

"I'm sorry?"

"Do the terrorists torture the people they capture, our guys?"

"Yes, they have before."

"How do we get through that?"

"The best way is to be taught everything you are learning here to escape them in the first place."

"And, if I don't?"

"Then you need to find the reason to live and the reason you do this job, and make it your sole focus. It will help with the pain and help delay a breaking point."

"Everyone has a breaking point?"

"Yes, you know that, you've studied it."

"I studied the theory, I wanted to know if it's real."

"Yes, it is definitely real. Even people who have been through training and who have been tortured before, they break. They can delay it, but they break. It is the same with the terrorists. Their cause fuels them, makes them hard to break, but they do, eventually. And we need them to. They plan to drive cars into crowds, they want to set off bombs at concerts, they want to shoot or stab people who are just trying to get on with their lives, they want to fly planes into buildings. We can't let them, Max."

"You mention their cause, is it always religion?"

"Most of the time, although not always. Sometimes there are others pulling the strings behind the scenes or people doing it for money, some are just crazy lunatics who do it for no reason whatsoever."

"So, sometimes they just use zealots to get the job done?"

"Sometimes."

"Amazing isn't it?"

"What?"

"The power of religion. It has the potential to give people hope and comfort, and to be a force for good, but it also creates difference, ignorance and hate. Imagine the invincibility and sheer strength you would get thinking you are doing God's work. Why would you care if you died in the process? He's going to save you right? Seventy-two virgins await."

"Like anything, Max, in the wrong hands it can be dangerous."

"I've spent a long time thinking about it over the years, religion as a motivator."

"I know."

"How?"

"We've been watching you for a long time and you wrote a paper on it."

"You read it?"

"Yes. It was fascinating work, Max. In fact, your professor and I discussed it at length."

"And your conclusion?"

"We agreed with your position, religion can be a strong motivator for both good and evil."

"But?"

"But you wrote it with some emotive language."

"And you read something into that?"

"Yes."

"Dare I ask?"

"It seemed personal."

"You got that from the paper?"

"What happened?"

"Nothing."

"Don't shutdown on me, Max. You can tell me."

"I was fifteen and I was starting to become aware of my true self."

"It's a formative time in a young man's life."

"Yeah, but there was something different. I started to realise I wasn't like the other boys. You have to know how scared I was at the thought. I was at a country high school with so many rough and brutish types fed from a young age on stereotypes and what I have come to realise is a culture of toxic masculinity."

"What happened?"

"One night my friends and I were camping down by the river on one of their farms. While a few of us were swimming, one of the boys went through my bag and found my journal."

"What did it say?"

"I had written some things, you know, to get them out of my head. There was a boy at school, we were on the swim team together and I couldn't get him off my mind. He was sweet and friendly, and super fit."

"What was his name?"

"Tom."

"So, what did your journal say about Tom?"

"A few days before the camping trip we had a swim meet. The two of us were in the locker room talking, I noticed he was nervous, so I sat down beside him and put my hand on his back to comfort him and tell him he'd be great. I thought it was just pre-race nerves. He turned and faced me, then he kissed me. I didn't know what to do I stood up and backed away. I was so conflicted. He ran from the room feeling rejected and I felt bad for him, but I was scared someone might have seen, was scared of how it made me feel, but over the coming days I couldn't help it, I liked him."

"And that's what the journal said?"

"Yes."

"So, what happened?"

"The supposed friend on the camping trip showed our other friends and there was laughter and awful things said, not just about me, but about Tom. How they knew all along about both of us and how we were going to get AIDS, and how I was going to hell for my sins. Sins. Can you believe it? I kissed a boy and had feelings for him. How could that be a sin? If we were truly made in God's image then surely he wanted us to be gay, wanted us to kiss and wanted us to feel what we felt? I mean, why would he create us like that, if he didn't want us to be ourselves?"

"There is more isn't there?"

"Yes."

"What happened, Max?"

"They tied my hands and feet then put me on a raft we'd made weeks ago for a race downstream, and they floated it out onto the river and let the current take me as one of my supposed friends yelled out that this is what Jesus would have wanted and that he hoped I drowned so I could find out in person."

"My God, Max."

"Yeah, pretty fucked up right?"

"Anybody would be. So, what happened after that?"

"The river took me and I cried for what felt like hours, until I hit some rapids. The raft flipped and I went under. I thought I was going to die. I was hit by sadness and confusion, and I was struggling with rejection and heartache, then I embraced it. Maybe dying wasn't so bad in comparison to what would face me when I got home. But as I rolled around in the water the rope on my legs came loose, my survival instincts took over and I kicked up to the surface. Eventually I made my way to the side of the river, not easy with your arms tied. I used my teeth to untie my hands when I made it onto the bank, then I cried some more laying wet and muddy on the river stones. I was two towns down the river where a nice farmer found me and called my parents. Frightened of being rejected by them too, I wrote the whole thing off as a stupid game we had played on the camping trip. I went to school on the Monday after and pretended like nothing had happened. My friends were all shitting themselves with worry people would find out what they did to me, but I didn't tell anyone. I just removed myself from the group and found some new friends."

"And what about Tom?"

"We spoke a lot. He wanted to date, but I didn't even want to be gay let alone have a relationship. I was scared, petrified of people finding out. I told him what had happened and he was understandably horrified, but he was strong and starred anyone down who questioned him, even my old friends, he was fearless when they were around and they knew to leave him alone. I told him that we would always be friends, but I didn't want anything more. He understood."

"Do you still talk?"

"Occasionally. I reached out after I met Lachlan to tell him that I had found not only the one, but myself. He told me how happy he was for me and that he could hear the strength in my voice. I let him know what his friendship has meant to me over the years, that it was his strength that helped me and that we'd always stay in touch."

"And we're back to Lachlan."

"Yes, we are."

"So, why him and not Tom?"

"Why is the sky blue or the grass green, Doc? Because it is. Tom is a great friend and someone who influenced me and gave me strength, but it's not the same. Lachlan fills me with courage and makes me feel bulletproof, he makes me feel whole and makes me feel like I can do anything. He showed me that I didn't need to feel frightened, didn't need to doubt who I was and didn't need to hide. He loves me for who I am and I love him for everything that he is and will be, and we both know it beyond any doubt. He's my protector and I am his, he is my rock, my comforter, my lover and my soulmate. And, you know what, Doc, he is all that matters to me."

Chapter Eight

The following weeks rolled on in a familiar fashion, PT or combat training every morning at five, followed by a series of lessons or briefings slowly crafting them into intelligence agents. They all had frequent sessions with Doctor Carter in his study too. In their spare time, the recruits caught up on sleep or the latest television shows or read. Occasionally, they did get to text or call their loved ones. Max had called and text Lachlan a few times. He missed him so much, time apart was painful, but it was showing them how much they wanted to be together. Max lied about the holiday and assured Lachlan that the conversation with his parents would happen soon. They also said I love you to each other every time they ended the call. Max felt guilty but tried to channel it into training.

After only a few days at the Wool Shed, they had begun weapons training. Max had only ever fired an air rifle, other than a couple of nights shooting kangaroos on mates' farms when he was at high school. Flash was in the same boat. He and Max paired up for nearly every activity and they were becoming close friends. Max learned that Flash had been recruited thanks to university lecturers on Hulk's payroll, like Max had been. He was a gifted sportsman, like Max he participated in many sports, but it was hockey where he really excelled. He was selected for the Australian team and was training for the Olympics. Hulk had promised the coach Flash would return even fitter after a few weeks training. He was in his final year of study in law and global politics. Max and Flash were the only two recruits who had no weapons training, so Kate spent several days giving them intensive training, but they were quick studies and were soon capable of outshooting even the most experienced of their fellow recruits. Kate and Hulk often brought in friends of theirs' from across the government to help train or hone skills, including an expert sniper from the SAS. Max and Flash trained with him for days, followed by smaller weapons training with Kate, from pistols to MP5s and assault rifles. The pistol and MP5 in particular were becoming Max's favourites and he was getting very comfortable with each weapon.

One morning the remaining recruits, now only around twenty, headed for the shooting range in the bushland west of the homestead. Like the various obstacle courses, the shooting range was a massive cleared section cut from the dense scrub. It consisted of ten alleys which were covered by a mammoth steel structure and roof. To the right of the alleys was a hi-tech control room with a large bank of computers and a control panel which looked like a massive version of a sound mixer in a recording studio. There was an aeroplane hanger sized steel frame running the length of the alleys with electronically controlled glass and metal louvres which ran between each of the supports on the left and right flanks of the range. They were in the open position as was the retractable roof letting the sunlight and breeze through. Above the space reserved for the trainee to position themselves for their shot or throw, on every alley, was a flat screen television displaying a picture of the current target for that alley. The instructors and other recruits could assemble behind the shooter to watch their performance.

When the group of recruits arrived, Kate and Hulk were waiting standing in front of an electronic message board showing a list of their names running down the left hand column, across the other columns' headings were a list of weapons. Six of the ten alleys had a target consisting of a red dot in the centre, followed by a white ring, then a black ring, followed by another set of white and black rings on a rectangular white sheet of paper.

"Good morning," Hulk said. "Alpha here tells me you are ready for the competition. And, what's that you ask? Well, it's our annual competition to rank your weapons skills. Each of you will begin a series of tests to gauge your timing and accuracy with each weapon listed across the top of the board. You will be pleased to note, all your instructors faced off against each other to determine who was the best in each category. Your performance will be benchmarked against theirs'. For example, Colonel Jones who came in to train you on the sniper rifle, is the best on that rifle, so you'll be judged against his shots. Hermes is the best on a silenced pistol, Kate the MP5 and me for the assault rifle and throwing knives."

Hulk pulled out his hunting knife and threw it down the range at a row of close targets. It pierced the target on the far right, dead centre of the red dot, and the force almost knocked over the stand. The television above the alley beeped and a green dot pinpointed the exact entry point of the knife in the target and a list of green figures was displayed under the target to show its precise location. Hulk had hit the target at zero point one from the very centre.

"So, whose next?" Hulk asked as the recruits mulled about in disbelief at his impressive throw.

The first five recruits stepped up to their alleys to throw their knives for their respective targets. A buzzer above sounded and the recruits threw for their targets. Five green dots and beeps showed their results on the televisions and they each eagerly stepped back to look up as the other recruits began discussing and comparing. Three had hit the red dot but were at least an inch out from the centre. One hit the inner white ring, while the fifth candidate had hit the inner black ring.

The board next to Hulk and Kate updated to show their results and reordered itself putting the closest at the top. Hulk nodded through the glass to the control room and Blake pressed a series of buttons on the large control panel. A small metal rod holding the paper targets came out an inch then slid down into the ground along each alley on the range, knocking the knives to the ground, before a second rod, holding a fresh target rose to take its place.

The next two groups repeated the process before Max, Flash, Williams, Travis and a recruit named Kim stepped up for their turn. The buzzer sounded and they threw their knives. Kim's knife lodged in the inner white ring, while Travis's hit the point where the red dot connected to it. Williams hit the red dot about an inch and a half from centre, while Flash and Max had almost identical hits right in the centre of the red dot. They stepped back to see the precision stats. Flash was zero point three and Max zero point two from the centre. Hulk looked somewhere between impressed and pissed. Kate was smirking and Max could see Blake trying in vain to stifle a smile in the control room.

"Well done, all of you," Hulk said. "Next round, pistols. Alpha swap places with Hermes. You will each get three rounds, the closer the grouping on the target and the closer to the centre, the higher your score. Alpha reset the range please."

The six original knife targets, including the stands, completely sunk into the ground and were replaced by targets at twice the distance. They had the same red spot and white and black rings. Blake stepped forward and loaded his pistol. He put his left foot forward and he kept his shoulders square to the target and extended his right arm straight out in front placing the gun's sights in line with his right eye and his left bent at the elbow while his left hand cupped the right under the gun for extra support. He took a slow breath in then out and fired three shots. The recruits watched as the grouping was displayed on the screen, two shots had overlapped while the third was less than a centimetre away, they formed a small triangle right around the very centre of the red dot. Blake stepped back to see the display and the disappointment showed on his face, but he holstered the pistol and went back into the control room where Kate looked to be providing some encourage words.

The same three groups took their shots and while some were very good, none were even close to matching Blake. Some had good results on two of their shots, but the third went astray. Max and his group stepped up as the targets were replaced with fresh papers. They each loaded a fresh magazine into the pistols' chambers and took their positions. Max's stance was identical to Blake's, while Flash's mirrored it as a left hander. The buzzer sounded and the recruits fired off their three rounds at the targets, before standing back to watch the results on the display. The recruits standing behind the range were all chatting and pointing at the screens. Max and Flashs' screens were the focus of most of their attention.

"Pretty close," Max said. "I think you got me though."

"If I did it was only just," Flash said. "You have a perfect three entry points right next to the centre of the red."

"Yeah but I think two of yours are touching, like Hermes's shots."

The green text ran over the screen. Flash had beaten Max by only a millimetre and fell short of Blake's by the same measure. The recruits all clapped and said congratulations to Flash.

"Ahh, told you, you got me," Max said. "Well done, man."

"Likewise, not much in it at all," Flash said. "Good job. You been practicing?"

Max laughed and they shook hands.

"Alright," Hulk said. "The scores have been updated, it's time for you to take on Alpha here with the MP5, but this one will be different. It'll be a timed run, targets will pop up along the alley and you'll need to react quickly to take them out. Time and accuracy matters. Double tap each target, head and chest. Alpha will go first to show you how it's done."

Hulk nodded through the window of the control room to Blake. He pressed a number of buttons and then an alarm sounded with a warning telling everyone to stand clear of the range. A series of walls rose up from the ground on every second alley, turning ten open lanes into five closed walled alleys. As they were rising the roof also started to slide into position. Within minutes the whole range had been converted to an indoor stadium. Kate stepped forward and loaded her MP5 then stepped down into the middle lane. The buzzer sounded and she began to move away from the recruits down range. It was dark along the alley but every few metres a target popped up from the floor or fell from the roof. The targets were white rectangular sheets with the silhouette of a man from the waist up. There were two red dots marking the locations of the centre of the head and centre on the chest above the heart. Kate made her way down the range firing two shots into each target. At the halfway point, the recruits could no longer see her in the dark, other than the lights which lit up each time a target moved into position, so they watched on the screens above the lanes. Kate fired her final two shots and the clock stopped. The screen broke into small rectangles showing each of her targets and shots. She had hit each one in the red dots, double taps, head and chest. Some were perfectly centred, others not far from it. Kate's run was three minutes and thirty seconds, with a ninety-seven percent accuracy rating.

When Max's turn came around, he loaded his MP5 and stepped into his lane, he extended the stock and placed it against his shoulder and lined up the sights with his right eye. He took a couple of controlled breaths to lower his heartrate and ready himself. The alarm sounded and he started down the lane, he quickly heard shots coming from the other alleys, but knew the targets were completely random on each run, so none of the spectator recruits could memorise the layout from previous runs. A target dropped from the roof on his left and was lit by a small light. He swung quickly and fired two shots, head and chest, then kept moving. He took out a total of ten targets and he felt pretty confident as he walked back to the join the others.

"How'd you guys go?" Max asked as they returned.

"Yeah okay, I think," Williams said. "Couple went a bit wide but otherwise okay."

"I think I went okay," Flash said. "A bit slower than Alpha, I think, and you?"

"I feel pretty good actually, I like the MP5, feels comfortable."

"Here we go," Williams said pointing at the televisions. "Bit better than pretty good, Max. Ninety-eight percent accuracy in three minutes, twenty. You beat Kate."

"Well fuck me, Prince Charming, those lessons have paid off," Kate said. "Good job."

"Max, you're now leading the pack, with Flash in close second after his run," Hulk said. "Ninety-seven percent is outstanding, Flash, just need to work on that reaction speed."

The recruits all gathered to congratulate the two current leaders, except Travis who was staring up at his little screen. Eighty-five percent accuracy in four minutes. He was a long way off Max and Kates' scores, he was clearly disappointed and he gave Max an unimpressed look.

"Colonel Jones is now going to lead us off for the sniper round," Hulk said. "The longest confirmed kill sniper shot in the world is three thousand, five hundred and forty metres, which beat the previous official record holder at a distance of just over two and a half kilometres. Colonel Jones here helped trained a number of the men on the top twenty list and if we allowed the unofficial list to be published, you'd find his name in the top five snipers in the world. For this test, there will be two targets the first is at the end of the range, once you fire for the first target, a second target will pop up three quarters of the way down range and you will have ten seconds to hit that target before it lowers again. At this distance, if you are quick enough, your original bullet will likely still be in the air as you take the second shot. You will be using the HK417 with its extended barrel. The HK is fast becoming the choice of special ops teams the world over. At AIS, we use all three variants – the Assaulter, Recce and Sniper. The Assaulter is an option for each of you instead of the MP5 for close quarters if you successfully pass the course."

A row of lights illuminated the five alleys. The targets looked tiny in the distance. Max was not sure how far down it was, but guessed it was around one and a half kilometres. Colonel Jones got into position laying prone and completely still. Max watched as his breathing slowed, then a shot rang out, but Max continued watching Jones, he shifted very slightly and moved the rifle gently then he fired again. He cleared the rifle and stood, as the recruits checked the television screen. It was split in two, on the left was the first target and the right held an image of the second target. Both targets were of the human silhouettes, Jones's first shot had hit right in the centre of the red dot on the target's head and the second almost perfectly in the centre of the red dot on the chest of the closer target. Max remembered Jones had told him in training that the body was a better target in a rush because it is a bigger object to aim for than a head and does not move as much giving you a higher chance of hitting and killing the target. Jones had hit with ninety-nine and ninety-seven percent accuracy on the two targets, respectively.

As the potential recruits ran through their shots, Max was nervous to see some completely miss both targets, while another six only got one or the other. The handful of recruits who hit both targets had a wide range of results. Some had hit the silhouette, while other shots had hit the white rectangular sheet surrounding it – impressive shots at that distance, but they would have devastating consequences in the real world, not only missing the mark, but potentially hitting an innocent bystander.

Max laid motionless trying to control his breath and sight-in the far target. Even through the high-powered scope the target looked a long way away. With the walls still in place, the wind was minimal to non-existent making the shot slightly easier. A small red dot inside the scope lined up his target, then he fired, and quickly scanned for the second target moving the weapon slightly to readjust his position, then he fired. He opened his left eye in time to see the closer target lower back into the ground. He cleared the rifle, stood and wandered over to inspect the screens. Max had hit both targets in the red dot, like Jones, he took a headshot on the first and chest shot on the second. Flash was the only other recruit to hit both red dots, he had taken both as chest shots. Williams hit both targets, one in the neck and the second in the forehead, as it was lowering. Travis was staring in disbelief at Max's screen and he just shook his head and looked away as he saw Max watching him. Max looked back up to his own screen and saw both shots had a ninety-six percent accuracy, Flash had taken a ninety-four and ninety-three.

"I knew you'd come along way, Max," Jones said shaking Max's hand then Flash's. "But, I have to say I'm impressed and with you too, Flash."

"Yeah, well I'm not that easily impressed," Hulk said.

"Oh come on, Hulk, nineties after only a few weeks of training is outstanding and I'm a good teacher."

"Well, let's see, shall we?"

"Hmm, I'm sensing a bet coming on."

"One alley, same target, full range, you, Mr Shaw, Mr Gordon and I, one shot each."

"And the wager?"

"A hundred bucks each, winner takes all."

"Aren't these two uni students? I'm not sure they can afford that."

"Fine, I'll put in their shares, on one condition."

"And, what's that?"

"One of them has to get a higher score than me."

"Okay by me, what do you two think?"

"Yeah, I'm in," Max said.

"Love your confidence, kid," Jones said.

"Don't get too far ahead of yourself, Mr Shaw," Hulk said. "You'll most likely lose a hundred bucks."

"We'll see."

"That's the way," Jones said. "What about you, Flash?"

"Well, money's a bit tight," Flash said.

"Ah, come on," Jones said. "Maybe you'll walk away with four hundred bucks."

"Is this some little scheme the two of you dreamt up? I bet this happens every year?"

"One of the smart ones, Hulk," Jones said laughing.

"So, it would seem," Hulk said. "Well, now you know, you have a choice, you can man up and put your money on the table or you can whimp out, save your cash, but lose a shitload of respect."

"I know what you're doing, but I'm in anyway."

"Got him," Jones said. "What about you, Max?"

"You know I'm in," Max said.

"Two suckers," Hulk said smiling and turning to the control room. "Set it up, Blake, oh and let's make it a bit of a challenge."

As Jones was getting ready, the alley before him went dark and a series of fans started creating a cross wind and a sprinter system started, creating artificial rain. Max and Flash looked at each other and shook their heads. The other recruits all laughed and spoke in excitement.

"You're getting too predictable, General," Jones said as he fired his shot and five seconds later it hit the red dot.

"Nice shot, Colonel, I hope it's good enough," Hulk said.

The recruits all looked to the television, but the accuracy stats did not come onto the screen, Blake was making everyone wait. They could see how good a shot it was, it was sitting just a centimetre to the left of the very centre of the red dot on the forehead. Flash shot second and hit the red dot just to the left of Jones's.

"Shit," Flash said as the recruits all pointed and chatted amongst themselves.

"That is a great shot, Flash," Jones said. "Not a money winner in this game, but a seriously fantastic shot."

"Thanks."

"Just not good enough, Mr Gordon," Hulk said. "You can put your money on the table."

"Well, not just yet, Hulk," Jones said. "You and Max have still got to take your shots."

"Hmm, give me the rifle," Hulk said climbing down to take his shot.

He laid prone rested the rifle against his shoulder, sighted the target and fired. Max watched as the bullet slammed into the target, it hit the red spot, Max thought it was about the same distance as Jones's but to the right of the centre spot.

"I think we're tied there, General," Jones said. "One to go, let's do it, Max."

"Do you have the cash on you, Mr Shaw?" Hulk asked.

"No, I didn't bring my wallet, but I'm not going to need it," Max said as he smiled and walked past to take up his position.

"There is a difference between confidence and arrogance, I hope you hit the target," Hulk said.

"Confidence is good, use it," Jones said. "Don't listen to him."

Max took up position on the mat and aimed the rifle down range. His hands were shaking but he controlled his breathing and calmed his nerves. *Just hit the target and that'll be fine,* he thought to himself. *No, you've got this, you can do it.* Max sighted the target using the red dot in the scope, breathed out and squeezed the trigger. Max kept watching the target through the scope and five seconds later he blinked a couple of times to take in the picture. He was not sure he was seeing it correctly, so he jumped up and walked back. Jones was beaming with a smile ear-to-ear, while Hulk was staring at the screen with a cranky disposition. Some of the recruits were shocked, while others smiled and clapped, they did not need to wait for the scores. Max had shot the target right between Hulk and Jones' shots. The green stats displayed on the screen. Flash ninety-five percent accuracy, Hulk ninety-seven percent, Jones ninety-eight percent and Max ninety-nine percent accuracy. The recruits and instructors all clapped and cheered. Max smiled and shook hands with many of them, then he noticed Blake standing in the control room watching him, he smiled broadly then looked back down at the control panel when he saw Max smiling back at him.

"Well done, Max," Jones said. "Hell of a shot, mate. You're a quick study. If Hulk doesn't want you for AIS, you can come and work with me."

"Thanks, Colonel," Max said.

"Good job brother, great shot," Flash said hugging and patting Max on the back.

"Thanks Jacob."

"Well done, Max," Hulk said. "Not sure it was any more than a fluke, but it's still an impressive shot."

"Thanks, Hulk," Max said shaking his hand. "How about we spend the winnings on a few drinks for everyone?"

"It's your money, if that's what you want to do, I'm sure it can be arranged."

"You bet," Max said and the recruits all cheered again.

"Alright, well, I think we can call it a day," Hulk said. "We'll be noting down these scores and we'll have more to say about it over the coming days. Head back to the farmhouse and get cleaned up."

Chapter Nine

True to his word, Hulk had arranged drinks and a barbeque for the recruits and instructors following Max's win. The recruits all sat around sharing stories and talking late into the evening. A few hours later they had one-by-one pealed away to their beds for the night. Max and Flash had stayed up the latest talking about sports, politics, religion, life and love. Flash had spoken about his girlfriend, but sounded far from convinced she was the one. Max on the other hand had shared his love for Lachlan. He told Flash how they had met at university, the complex emotions he felt when he realised he was gay and could not simply choose not to be, and the torture of worrying what people would think.

"He was the life of the party, still is," Max said. "When he is in a room, people are drawn to him, I certainly was when I first met him. He commands attention without ever seeking it. I think it's a mix of intelligence, confidence and charisma, but it could just be those eyes or that smile."

Max closed his eyes and smiled thinking about Lachlan. Flash could not help but feel the love the couple shared emanating from Max.

"So, when did you know?" Flash asked. "That he was the one?"

"We were good friends, almost instantly," Max said. "But, that's all it was. For months we spent so much time together and we became really close. In hindsight, I think I had feelings for him the whole time, but I grew up in a small country town and being gay was just not accepted, almost unheard of, which of course is completely ridiculous. That's how it is though, so I had pushed those feeling aside and hid them deep. I even dated a couple of women along the way, but one night my world changed. In the midst of a crazy college party, we found each other and in that moment we both knew on some level how we felt. He kissed me, while we sat on the floor in my kitchen – so romantic, I know – that's when I knew he was the one. We spent the first of almost every night since together and while I had some hard emotions to get through and self-doubt, he filled me with courage, support and love like I've never felt, and I know I want to spend the rest of my life with him."

"Wow Max, that's amazing. I'm glad you found someone so special and that you've come to terms with your sexuality."

"Well, it's been a hard road, but I was born this way, I can't change it, but most importantly, I wouldn't even if I could. I'm me and people can love or hate it, but I'm not changing for anyone and I no longer give a shit what they think."

"Hear, hear," Flash said clinking his beer bottle to Max's. "I hope I find someone that special someday."

"I know you will, Jacob," Max said. "Pretty handsome, kind, intelligent, soon to be super-spy, you're a catch mate."

"Pretty handsome?" Flash said smiling and they both laughed. "So, does he know you're here?"

"No, he thinks I'm on holidays with my family and telling them about us," Max said taking a long drink from his bottle.

"They won't let you tell him?"

"No, not yet, could be years before I can tell him. I hate lying to him. It's killing me actually."

"So, why are you doing all this?"

"I felt like I had to. They say I might have the skills to help and if I do, well, why shouldn't I help? AIS and the military and intel agencies need the right people to keep our country safe, and if I'm who they need, why should I get to live free and safe, while someone else puts their neck on the line? I couldn't live with myself if I turned my back on that opportunity to help and do my bit, and hopefully protect those who can't protect themselves. People like Lachlan, who deserve the best life has to offer, I want to make sure no one takes that away from him."

"I completely understand. It's hard when they turn up and put it all on you, then to go through all this, it really hits home, how important the role they play is and how we can be a part of that. It's an honour just to be considered, but I'm nervous, I'm just hoping I can be the agent they need me to be. It's a lot of pressure."

"Yeah it is, but I think we are both doing well and they are as committed to getting us trained up and through the course. They've invested a lot in us and they want us to succeed, now and in the field."

"Yeah, you're probably right," Flash said yawning. "Anyway, I might hit the hay."

"Good idea. Thanks for the chat."

"Anytime brother. Goodnight."

By the time Max had cleaned his teeth and changed into his new white t-shirt and black cotton sleeping pants, Flash was out cold on his bunk on the far side of the room. Now with less recruits the cots were spaced further apart giving them some room to move. Max was asleep as soon as his head hit the pillow, but not long after he was woken as a strong hand slapped down over his mouth, he could feel and smell something acrid on his face. *Tape,* he thought and he struggled for a moment before passing out.

Max woke again and his heart raced trying to comprehend what was happening. He remembered the tape, then nothing until a sharp smell jolted him awake. He blinked in the darkness willing his eyes to focus. The cold night air brush against his face, hands and feet. He tried to move but couldn't, his wrists were tied and so were his ankles. He started to panic and trashed about in the metal chair trying to free himself. His wrists and ankles burned as they pulled against his restraints. As his eyes began to adjust to the darkness, he started to make out shapes. He was in a shed of some sort, but it was the shadowy figure standing in the darkness a few metres in front of him that made his blood run cold. The figure was dressed completely in black from head to toe, including a balaclava which was hiding his face. Max's heart was racing.

"You just think you are so fucking special don't you," the figure said in a deep voice. "You think you can just walk in here without any experience and be king shit, well let's see how tough you really are. I'm going to hurt you, then I'm going to leave you here in this cold shithole to die. They won't know what happened to you, but I will, you are being punished for being a smartarse and for shitting on people with far more experience than you and for being a dirty faggot."

Max was panicking and started to shake in fear. His mind raced. *Who is that? Why is he doing this to me? What have I done? I want to go home. I don't want to die. Is this part of the training or is he for real? He sounds serious.* Max again thrashed about in the chair trying to break free and defend himself, but it was no use, he was helpless. He tried to speak, but the tape held his mouth closed.

"What's that? Got something to say?" the figure said walking over and ripping off the tape. "I'm not surprised, you never shut up."

"Who are you?" Max asked. "Why are you doing this?"

"I just fucking told you why. You are a disgrace and you bring dishonour to people who have worn the uniform, but by far the worst thing, is your disgusting, unnatural way of life. I heard you speaking to Flash earlier about your boyfriend and I've seen you and that other fag in there sharing looks at each other. You sicken me and I'm going to punish you for your sins."

"For my sins, you're religious? How can you justify hurting or killing someone, weren't you taught to love your fellow man?"

"Yes, but I was also taught that homosexuality is a sin, punishable by death."

"And you think you are free to name yourself judge, jury and executioner in the name of your God?"

"He spoke to me. He told me do this."

"I think you should book some time with Doctor Carter, you're fucked in the head. God ain't talking to you, that's just your own fucked up thoughts swirling through your thick scull."

"And there you go again, always the smartarse even in the face of torture and death."

"That's not me being a smartarse, that's me telling you, you need to get help and quickly, you're a serious mental case."

"Is that really how you want to speak to someone who is going to hurt you?"

"You already told me I can expect pain and death, what have I got to lose from insulting you?"

"I'm going to make you suffer and I can make that pain last and make it hurt more than you could imagine."

"All because I'm gay and you're jealous, I'm presuming because I beat you on some of this course, and not because I'm not into you?"

"Fuck you," the figure said punching Max hard in the face.

"If you wanted to touch me, you didn't have to go to all these lengths," Max said smiling through the pain.

The figure punched him again and Max's head slumped to his chest, blood ran from his mouth and nose onto his white t-shirt.

"Not so smart now, are you?"

"So tough, punching a tied-up opponent, while hiding your face. Why don't you take that balaclava off and untie me so we can sort this out man-to-man, unless you're afraid of getting beaten by a fag."

"I ain't afraid of you," Travis said taking off his balaclava. "But, I'm going to take my time."

"Well, at least you've dressed for the occasion and I don't have the displeasure of seeing you in those filthy underpants again."

"Don't pretend like you didn't love it, fag, I saw you checking me out."

"Oh, I looked, but I wasn't impressed."

Travis punched Max in the stomach knocking the wind out of him and then again in the face. As Max sat trying to get his breath back and stay conscious, Travis walked over to the far side of the shed and found some items he was looking for. As he walked back, Max heard something dragging behind him, but could not tell what it was. Travis threw a towel over Max's face and Max tried to shake his head to remove it, but before he could the chair was kicked over and he fell backwards, hitting his head hard on the floor. His head spun and ached, but he stayed conscious, then Max heard a familiar sound. *Water,* he thought. *He was dragging a hose.* Max panicked again as the freezing water hit the towel on his face and sprayed wildly around his shoulders and chest, then he felt a rough hand clench around his neck. Travis was pinning him to the cold concrete by the neck and he was choking him. Between the hard grip on his neck and the wet towel, Max was struggling to breath and his heart and mind raced, then the water started again. Travis was holding the hose just above Max's mouth, water filled his mouth and nose, and he started to cough and choke as he gasped for air. *He's going to kill me,* he thought. *This is the end. I wish I never came here. I miss Lachlan and my family. I wish I told him how much I loved him and I wish I told my parents and family and the whole world how much he means to me.* He cried in fear and started to think about death, then the water stopped and the towel was whipped from his face. He coughed and spluttered expelling as much water as possible.

"Enjoy that, Max?" Travis asked. "See, this is what us real soldiers have learnt, to kill and torture. Makes you question shit doesn't it and eventually you might even feel like giving up, but then they win, don't they? If you give up? I think I'll win this round, you'll give up for sure, bloody fag can't handle it."

"I can't change who I am and I wouldn't even if I could," Max said raising his head to stare at Travis. "So, do your worst you narrow-minded piece of shit and live with the knowledge that I will die proud of who I am."

The lights came on in the shed and Max blinked, blinded by the light, dazed and confused.

"Good for you, Max," Travis said standing up and pulling Max's chair back up into the sitting position.

Max watched as Hulk, Carter and Kate walked into the large shed and stood before him.

"I'm glad to say your training is coming along nicely, Max," Hulk said. "When you first arrived I told you, this training program is designed to push you to your limits. You are going to want to quit, you are going to break and this was just the beginning. Travis here works for me, I told him to do this to you to find your breaking point. You confronted death and accepted it, without compromise or surrender. I will let you in on secret, there were fifty of you potential recruits out here at the start, after yesterday's weapons trials another five will be departing in the morning, leaving fifteen on the base training. I will be lucky if a handful of you make it through this stage. You've passed part one, but there is still more to come. If you want to go home to your boyfriend, Lachlan, and feel the warmth of his arms around you and live your life in peace and comfort or you want to run home to mummy at any stage, all you need to say is 'I'm happy for the terrorists to win'. You say that, you'll be dead to me, to this program and you'll be thrown out of here because you aren't the person we want working with us. Am I understood?"

Max nodded at Hulk.

"Am I understood?" Hulk asked.

"Yes, sir," Max said.

"So, what do you say? Do you want to go home?"

"No, sir."

"Why? I'm sure Lachlan is missing you dearly," Hulk said pulling a mobile phone out of his pocket. "Let's see. Here we are, 'Hi Maximus, just letting you know I'm thinking of you and I miss you so much, I can't wait til you come home. I miss your arms, your love and your smile. I can't wait to cuddle you and kiss you, and make love with you. I love you so much. Lachie.' Maximus, that's a cute pet name, oh and look he even put a little 'x' and 'o' at the end. That's sweet."

"I know what you are doing and it won't work, as messed up as your tactics are and as much as I miss and love Lachlan,

I know he would stand by my decision and respect it. I'm here to learn how to protect him and every innocent man, woman and child in the country. I will not fail."

"Good, then let's get started. Lieutenant Matthews, you know what to do."

"Yes, General," Kate said as she walked over and checked the tape on Max's legs and arms.

When she was sure he was secure she took out her hunting knife and cut away his clothes. Max squirmed and frowned at Kate.

"What? You want to go home already?" Kate asked.

Max shook his head.

"Then shut the fuck up," she said and punched him hard right on the nose breaking the skin on the bridge and putting him back into a daze.

Over the next few hours, Kate and her team put Max through various torture techniques from hosing him down with ice-cold water to sight and sound deprivation, and even more water-boarding. Exhausted, Max slumped in the chair. Kate walked over and gave him a sip of water.

"Are you okay?" Kate asked. "Want to go home yet?"

Max spat the water in her face and laughed.

"No, but I need to piss real bad," he said.

"You think your torturer's going to give a fuck if you need a piss?" Kate asked wiping the water and spit from her face before walking away.

Max was embarrassed but could not hold it any longer and pissed himself sitting naked on the freezing metal chair in the shed. The lights went out over his head and he suddenly felt very cold and alone as the winter wind whipped around him.

After what felt like hours, a man entered the shed. He was finding his way across the open space with a torch. He knelt at Max's side. Max was shivering, mist was coming from his mouth with every breath and his whole body was shaking. His lips, hands and feet were turning blue. The man placed his hand on the side of Max's freezing face. It felt warm, gentle, caring.

Max lent in against it savouring the feeling after hours of pain and suffering. Max looked up at the man as he took his hand away. He was more than handsome, he was beautiful. He had soft but masculine features. Short hair, clean-shaven and a caring look in his eyes.

"Hello, Max," Blake said. "Do you recognise me?"

Max nodded.

"What is my name?"

"Lieutenant Commander Blake Smyth, codename Hermes," Max said through chattering teeth.

"Max, have you had enough? Do you want this to end?"

"I want it to end whenever it is supposed to end."

"It's warm inside Max, do you want to come in?"

"Not unless this is the end of the training session."

"It can be, if you want it to be, you just need to tell me what Hulk told you to say and I can end it right now for you and we can go inside and get you warm."

"This is a trick, you are trying to get me to quit. Tell Hulk and the team to do their worst, I'm not going to quit."

"Good for you, Max," Blake said as he lent in and whispered in his ear. "Find a reason to fight, find a purpose, find something to keep you grounded. Why are you doing this? What is your motivation? Find it Max and I won't lie, you will still feel the pain, but it will become more tolerable, more manageable and you will be able to delay any breaking point beyond what is thought to be humanly possible. Good luck."

Blake squeezed Max's hand and held it for a few seconds, then patted it twice before walking back out of the shed guided by his little flashlight.

Max thought about what Blake had said. There was only one thing powerful enough for him to endure anything they could throw at him, Lachlan. Lachlan was his world. He knew he loved him from the moment they had met and knew they were going to spend the rest of their lives together. Lachlan was the one. He meant what he had said to Hulk, he was joining AIS to keep Lachlan, and innocent people like him, safe. He wanted to protect people, especially Lachlan, from pain and from suffering. He wanted to stop terrorists and he wanted to end those who sort only death and destruction. Lachlan was the key to his motivation and his determination. He thought about Lachlan and felt warmer. In that moment, he knew he would make it through their training program.

As the dawning sun started to rise, Max woke in pain. He felt like he had been set on fire. He started to scream and cry. His eyes focused on Travis who was spraying him with the garden hose. The water was bitterly cold, but after a night in almost freezing conditions, it felt like he was being hit with acid or fire. He closed his eyes and tried to focus through the pain, then he stopped screaming and embraced it. *Lachlan,* he thought to himself. He smiled broadly then opened his eyes and locked them on Travis. Determined, resolute, unbreakable. Travis shut off the hose and walked out of the shed.

Hulk and Kate walked in, followed at some distance by Blake.

"So, how are you feeling, kid?" Hulk asked. "Ready to give up?"

Max nodded his head back summonsing Hulk to come closer. He whispered something faintly.

"What did you say?" Hulk asked. "Speak up."

"Closer," Max said in a barely audible voice.

Hulk lent in closer, Max threw his head back then violently forward with frightening speed. His forehead smashed down breaking Hulk's nose, sending him scurrying backwards, cursing.

"FUCK NO, SIR!" Max yelled. "BRING IT ON!"

Blake smiled and put his hand to his mouth to stifle a laugh. Kate smiled, she was impressed, not too many people could get the drop on Hulk, but this kid had. They were so much alike, both had problems with authority, both had pure raw power and motivation, and both hated to lose.

"Get him out of that fucking chair," Hulk snapped at Kate. "Two minutes, then I want you in the ring. Got it?"

"I'm ready now," Max said. "Cut this tape, let's do it."

Hulk rolled his shoulders and neck, and spat out blood which had poured from his nose into his mouth. Kate and Blake cut the tape on Max's wrists and ankles. He stood on shaky legs and quickly ran through his mental checklist starting at the head. His whole body felt tight and stiff and sore. *Don't do this,* he thought to himself. His body was giving him confused readings after the torture he had endured, but he wanted and needed to let out his anger and frustration. He walked outside, still completely naked, and climbed into the boxing ring. It was dewy and slightly icy underfoot. Hulk walked out and climbed into the ring as the remaining trainees, including Flash, came out of the house to see what was going on. It must have been quiet the sight. The recruits looking down from the deck to their naked fellow trainee who looked to be burning with rage and their hard-arsed instructor, who had put them through hell over a period of weeks, with what looked like a broken nose.

"Let's see it if that body can match the mouth," Hulk said as he squared up.

Max moved into position and raised his fists. Ready. Kate and Blake had walked over to the ring. Max sprung forward with surprising speed given the pain he must have been feeling from the cold. He threw a left jab and two quick hard right crosses which Hulk blocked easily. Hulk reached out with his left fist and shoved Max backwards.

"What have I taught you?" Hulk asked. "What happened to not being predictable? I could stand here and block that shit all day. You haven't got it, just quit."

"Never," Max said leaping forward off his left foot, drawing back his right hand in mid-air and throwing a vicious right cross which connected with the side of Hulk's face. As Max landed, he slightly crouched to the left and drove up transferring all of his power through his body, starting from his left ankle, up through his leg and torso as it moved back slightly as his left shoulder and arm recoiled then flung them forward with astonishing speed. His left hand rocketed with explosive force and smashed into Hulk's torso just below the ribs on the righthand side. The force of the two blows had knocked the wind out of Hulk and he was hunched over trying to get his breath back. Max capitalised and jumped forward bringing his right knee up and slammed it into Hulk's face. He groaned and fell to the mat as blood poured from his broken nose. Max looked to Blake and Kate who were both standing next to the ring in shock. They had never seen any recruit best Hulk in the ring. Max looked down at Hulk.

"Definitely, not predictable, but you still have more to learn," Hulk said smiling through bloodied teeth.

Hulk swept his leg around hard into the back of Max's ankles and he slipped on the dewy mat. He fell hard smacking the back of his head on the hard surface. In a daze, he felt Hulk scrambling and tried to move away, but Hulk had hold of his legs and dragged him in. Hulk climbed on top of Max and unleashed a flurry of punches. Max tried in vain to block them, but missed more then he blocked. He was getting pummelled and the last thing he saw as he passed out was the worried look on Blake's face.

Chapter Ten

"Your Grace," the waiter said. "Your table is ready, if you would like to follow me."

"Yes, thank you," Wright said following the waiter.

"There will be four of you?"

"Yes, please send the others through when they arrive," Wright said taking a seat.

He looked around the expansive restaurant which sat overlooking Sydney Harbour. Curran was sitting at a nearby table keeping watch on everyone in the room, but neither acknowledged the other's presence. Sunlight was flickering on the water's surface outside the window, it was truly a spectacular view. Tiny sail boats on full tilt sped past as the cream and green ferries pushed back and headed for the other side of the harbour. Occasionally, a jet boat would race between them with screaming tourists enjoying a thrill ride. A little seaplane was revving along trying to find room to take off and monstrously tall cruise ship was docked at the Quay. Trains, buses and cars raced their way across the Sydney Harbour Bridge which looked almost close enough to touch.

"Hello, Benjamin," Katzenberg said. "It is a beautiful day out there."

"Hello, David," Wright said standing to shake hands. "Yes, indeed the Lord has blessed as with such splendour."

"David, you remember Uri Rothstein," Katzenberg said pointing to Uri. "Uri, this is the Most Reverend Benjamin Wright, Archbishop of Sydney."

"A pleasure," Wright said shaking hands with Uri.

"Your Grace, it is good to meet you too," Uri said.

"Please, join me."

"Thank you," the two new man said taking their seats.

"Are we waiting for anyone else?" Katzenberg asked.

"Yes, I've asked Phillip Hogan to join us."

"Hogan, Stevens and Hill?" Uri asked. "That Phillip Hogan?"

"Yes, Phillip is a close friend and one of my closest followers."

"I did not know that," Uri said. "He is one of my biggest clients."

"Yes, I know. That's partly why I wanted him here."

"I don't follow."

"He told me about your project."

"Which project?"

"The second one."

Katzenberg and Uri exchanged worried looks.

"Let's not play games with each other," Wright said. "We always intended this to be two-fold. The Arabs don't get it. They just want everyone dead, including themselves in a lot of cases. We do not want this to spread too far. It needs to be controlled. I knew eventually the three of us and Phillip would need to discuss how we limit the impact."

"Yes, well, of course we were going to share it with you."

"I am sure you were."

"We don't have any desire to share it beyond this table though."

"You don't want to include Moghadam?"

"No," Katzenberg said. "This is a great opportunity for us to rid ourselves of them. Is that okay with you?"

"Yes. My thoughts exactly. Where are we up to with the vials?"

"They are still a little while off, but we have tested the original product," Uri said. "It works. Twenty-four hours start to finish maximum. One of the tests was only sixteen hours."

"Is it painful?"

"Yes and gruesome."

"Charming."

"We wanted it to seem nasty and awful to inflict more chaos and concern. It is something people will definitely believe the

Arabs capable of, it's almost torture before death. They are into that sort of thing. More retribution and punishment than just getting the job done."

"And the second project, how is it progressing?"

"Hogan is still working on it. I am sure he will be able to fill us in when he arrives, but it is looking optimistic. We handed over the formula for project one, so he can clearly see the active ingredients. I do not believe it will take him long engineer it."

"And mass production?"

"Hopefully, ready before the deadline."

"Good to hear. This is exactly what we need, people always turn back to their faith in times of need."

"With the world like it is, more religion can only be a good thing, Your Grace. Whether they believe as you do in the Bible and the Old and New Testaments, or whether they believe as we do in the Tanakh, Torah, Nevi'im and Ketuvim, only good can come from it. They need to return to us, they need to turn away from their wicked ways, and this is what will help them see the light."

"Their feet have slipped."

"Yes, my friend. Their feet have slipped. Some will still go on to face judgement and damnation, but those willing to embrace God and His way, they will be spared. Lord, may it be so."

"Amen," Wright said taking up his wine glass in cheers to his companions.

Chapter Eleven

"Max," he thought he heard someone say as his tried to open his eyes.

"Max, are you okay?" Blake asked.

"Blake?" Max asked unable to open his eyes properly after the beating he had received from Hulk.

"Yes, Max, it's Blake. Are you okay?"

"I feel like I've had the shit kicked out of me, but otherwise I'm just peachy."

"Well, I don't want to alarm you," Blake smiled. "But, you did just have your arse handed to you. Naked. In front of the others."

"I thought I had him."

"You got further than anyone I've ever seen," Blake said resting a cold pack on Max's face.

"Is he pissed?"

"A bit, but secretly I think he's impressed too."

Max laughed.

"I thought I'd do what he would do in that situation."

"That you did, but you're going to be in for an even harder time now."

"Great," Max said cringing. "It's already been a massive few weeks, there's what, less than ten of us left? Surely, we must be nearly through."

"I'm afraid the five o'clock starts continue, you're not done yet."

Flash walked into the room.

"Oh, I'm sorry to interrupt," Flash said as Blake pulled his hand back quickly and dropped the ice-pack. "Sorry, didn't mean to frighten you."

"No, it's fine," Blake said standing and shifting uncomfortably. "I was just checking in on Max."

"I can come back," Flash said.

"No, please come in," Blake said. "I better get back out to the training ground. I'll check back in later."

"Thanks for coming by," Max said.

Blake nodded and smiled then left the room.

"That's interesting," Flash said.

"What is?" Max asked.

"The way he looks at you, you must see it?"

"I can't see much right at this moment in time."

"Oh, yeah," Flash said getting a closer look at Max's face. "What were you thinking?"

"That psycho tortured me, he was trying to break me and I wanted to show him I wouldn't break, so I headbutted him. I think I broke his nose, then he challenged me to a fight. I thought I had him, Flash."

"So did I, especially when he hit the mat. Where'd you learn to fight like that?"

"Lachlan and I train twice a week at a local martial arts school. He took it up when he was a kid for self-defence because he was getting harassed at school. I asked him about it before we started dating and he encouraged me to come along and I thought why not, you know, I thought it would be good for extra fitness on top of my training regime and the various sports I was playing. But mostly, I did it to spend time with him."

"Well, I think you caught him off guard."

"Yeah, but it was worth it. I will get his respect soon enough. But right now I don't care, I just can't wait to get home to see Lachlan, it feels like we have been out here for ages. Oh God, I hope my face has healed by then," Max said gently touching his face, grimacing from the pain.

"I'm sure it will be fine. Just keep icing it. I imagine my turn in the shed is coming soon, hopefully I won't come out of it like you did."

Max sat up and reached over to grab Flash's arm.

"Believe in yourself and know it will end, it's going to suck mate, but you can get through it," Max said.

"Thanks, Max," Flash said.

Over the next few days, Max's wounds began to heal and he continued his training and assessment. He was one of only eight, from the original fifty, potential recruits still in the program. Flash had made it through the torture training stage and was still suffering some of the effects, mental, not physical. He and Max continued working together to complete their training and support each other. In endurance training, they kept in step with each other. On obstacle courses, they helped each other over and under barbed wire, through mud pits and rope courses, up and along wooden walls and logs, and they were in sync jogging through the high stepping tyre course. In individual exercises, they shouted encouragement and advice to each other. They became a team and even closer friends.

"Today," Hulk said. "We are going to run another drill on aggressive hostage retrieval. You will break up into two sets of three and one set of two. Flash, Max, you're the group of two, Hermes will join you as your third. Alpha, over to you."

"Thank you, sir," Kate said. "Over the last few weeks, you have studied and trained on entry procedures and hostage negotiations, well today, we're going in hard. Sometimes words just don't cut it. In your teams of three, you will take it in turns of clearing the house. Inside there are ten cardboard cut-out hostages and they are being held by an unknown number of terrorists, played by our instructors. They are armed, as you will be, with paintball guns. If you get hit, you're dead and out of the session, your team will be left to fend for themselves without you. Remember your training. Shoot to kill, but do not injure or kill the hostages. Everyone clear?"

"Yes, ma'am," the group of potential recruits shouted.

"Good, you three are up first," Kate said pointing to Max's team.

As they gathered their weapons, Hulk made his way over.

"Watch your backs in there," Hulk said walking past and lowering his face mask. "Death will be lurking around every corner."

Max, Flash and Blake put on their gear and got into position near the door. Kate fired her gun into the air and the team moved in. Max took the lead and snuck through the door moving right. Flash moved in second and went left. Blake was last and went straight. They moved quietly but quickly into the main hall where the bunks and mess were located. Various new obstacles had been arranged throughout. Max signalled to follow him right. Room by room they swept, following the same pattern, Max right, Flash left and Blake centre, first, second, third, repeat. In the fourth room, one of the instructors, dressed as a terrorist, leapt out from behind an open cupboard. Max was the first through the door and a paintball slapped into the wall beside him. Flash entered and put a paintball into the instructor's chest and Blake put a paintball square in the centre of his fellow instructor's face mask.

As they entered their six room, the large commercial scale kitchen, Max heard a paintball gun fire multiple times and turned back to see Blake standing in the doorway, lowering his gun, he had been shot in the back five times by one of the instructors. He shrugged his shoulders, he was now out and walked back towards the front of the house. While Max and Flash were distracted, Hulk popped up from behind the centre island and unloaded multiple shots. Max dived to the floor as two paintballs hit Flash in the chest.

"You're out, Flash," Hulk yelled. "Just me and the little prince here to have fun in the kitchen. He'll be with you shortly."

"Shit," Flash said shaking his head and leaving the room.

"Righto, little prince," Hulk said kneeling behind the island. "Let's get this over with."

"Why little prince?" Max asked as he franticly looked around the room stalling for time.

"Well, we were discussing it earlier, Alpha thinks you're Prince Charming. Actually, she was giving shit to one of our instructors at the time, so I think it was mostly about teasing him using you, not coming up with your codename. However, I also used it on your file for the last couple of years of surveillance we did on you, given your studies in psychology and politics, as in Machiavelli's 'The Prince'."

"It's a good book, not sure I'm a master of the dark arts, but give me time and we'll see."

"Yes, we will, but I think it's a fitting codename."

Max did not have time to consider his new codename, because while Hulk was talking, he had reached out and silently grabbed a pan from the rack opposite. He hurled it down the length of the kitchen and it clattered around loudly as it bounced between the stainless-steel bench and the wall, and eventually onto the floor at the end of the room. Hulk sprung up and began firing in the direction of the sound, as Max snuck around behind him.

"Not quite as good as I had hoped, Prince," Hulk said as he rounded the bench expecting to see Max on the ground.

"No, I know I've still got a lot to learn," Max said as he fired two shots, one above the spine at the centre of his back and the other into the back of Hulk's head.

"Oh, fucking hell," Hulk said. "Well, off you go, you've got terrorists to kill and hostages to save."

Max left the kitchen scanning as he moved. He went past Blake's room and headed for the changerooms. He entered and crept along the wall to the right. He moved through the locker room towards the showers and he snuck a look around the door into the shower room. The cardboard hostages were all in the middle of the room, but there was no sign of any of the instructors. Max walked in, but he did not notice the fishing line running between the doorframes. A catastrophic bang rang out and the hostages, shower room and Max himself was covered from top to bottom with bright pink fluorescent paint. Max was stunned and stepped back in shock.

"The hostages are dead and so are you," Hulk said walking in behind him.

Max removed his tactical glasses leaving a perfect paint free stripe across his face, he looked down at his hands and gear, and for the first time, since Travis had waterboarded him, he realised this was not a game. Death was a real option and it could come quickly.

"Don't worry, kid," Hulk said. "It's not a mistake you'll make again."

"No, it's not," Max said walking from the room.

A few hours later, Max was sitting alone on the veranda. He and Flash had had dinner in the hall inside and sat mostly in silence, thinking about their respective performances in the day's course. Over the weeks they had been at the Wool Shed they had been tested and retested, and trained and pushed to their limits. They had learnt new skills, built their fitness and athleticism to new levels, and the two of them had become very close, but over the last few days they were forced to consider more. Forced to confront death and the fact that they could die or others could if they failed or got even the smallest thing wrong. It was a sobering thought.

"Hey Max," Blake said walking out onto the veranda. "Want some company?"

"Yeah sure, Blake," Max said. "I'm just getting some air."

"I brought out some wine, would you like a glass?" Blake said offering Max an empty glass which he then filled.

"Yeah, thanks Blake," Max said taking a sip as Blake filled his own glass.

"Hell of a day."

"Yeah, tell me about it."

"The traps are built in to test you all and force you to realise the reality of the work you'll be doing if you are successful. It's dangerous and not everyone comes home at the end of the day."

Max took a sip of wine.

"And, you have to be ready for that, Max. We can't save everyone and we can't stop every incident from happening, and sadly there are times we can't save our team or ourselves either."

"I get it, Blake, I've been giving it a lot of thought since I was covered from head to toe in a figurative death a few hours ago. It couldn't be clearer. I know the risks, but tell me, who will stop them if we don't? Why should I just sit back and let others take all the risks to protect me? Why should my life be any more valuable than anyone else's? We all want the perfect life and we all hope these terrorists will just disappear, but the reality is, they aren't going anywhere and someone needs to be ready to stop them."

"You're right, Max. That's why we are here. There are people out there who want to destroy our way of life, people who chose hate and terror over love, freedom and democracy. We didn't ask for the fight, but we're in it and we need people who are willing to risk it all to stop them. Is that you?"

"I think so," Max said looking at Blake. "I want to do my bit and I want to protect those who can't protect themselves. If I have the ability and the skills to do it, I'm in."

"Good to hear," Blake said taking a sip of his wine. "Can I ask you something?"

"Sure."

"The other day, when you were in the shed, what got you through it? I saw the change in your eyes."

"Well, I just remembered what you said to me, about finding a reason to fight."

"And, what was it?"

"It was Lachlan, my boyfriend. I would do anything for him and to protect him. It's for him and people like him that I'm here. I just want him to be happy and safe, and I want to make sure he can have all that and more. And, I'll stop anyone that tries to take that away."

"He must be a special guy."

"He is the very best person I know. I love him and I want to spend the rest of my life with him. I've known it since the moment I met him."

"Oh wow," Blake said smiling to hide his own emotions. "How long have you been together?"

"Three years, but that's like what ten, in gay years?" Max laughed.

"Yeah, that sounds about right," Blake laughed. "How'd you meet?"

"We met at uni, he and I were constantly together and we worked really closely organising events and lectures and things at our college. I always enjoyed spending time with him and there was always something in the back of my mind pulling me towards him, but at the time I didn't know what it was. I had never really confronted the fact I might be gay, I had always dismissed it, mostly out of fear. I grew up in the country, Blake, and it was just so frowned upon. I was so frightened of being rejected by my family and friends. But, then one night, Lachie and I found each other, sitting drunk on the floor in my kitchen, and we got close. I was so nervous, but then he took my hand and we kissed. My world changed forever in that moment and we've been together ever since."

They sat in silence for a few minutes and drank their wine.

"How about you?" Max asked. "Are you married or seeing anyone?"

"No," Blake said. "The last person I was with couldn't handle the time apart when I was on deployment, they got so jealous and always questioned where I was and who I was with, they constantly accused me of cheating. Turns out, they were the one cheating. Anyway, I found out, I left and haven't looked back."

"Sorry to hear that mate. Sounds rough."

"Thanks, Max."

"Can I ask why you use the neutral pronoun?"

"I'm sorry?"

"You don't have to tell me, but I was wondering why you used the word they, instead of he or she."

"A few years in the masculine environment of the military will do it to you. I understand what you are saying, Max, about growing up in the country and being afraid of people finding out, I'm gay too. I just don't really tell anyone or talk about it. My parents weren't cool with it, they threw me out of home at fifteen. I got the train to Sydney and slept in Hyde Park for a few weeks before I met a lovely guy, he was six or seven years older than me. He worked for a youth centre, he was so kind. He gave me food and water, and I lived at the centre for almost two years while I finished school. The recruiting guys came to one of the careers days at school and I knew I couldn't afford uni, so it seemed like a good option. I signed up and they put me through uni, paid for my degree and gave me a home and a different kind of family."

"I'm sorry to hear about your parents. Do you talk to them at all?"

"No. I haven't spoken to them since that day."

"That must be tough, I'm sorry."

"Don't be. It's their fault, but I forgave them a long time ago."

"You're a bigger person than most, being able to forgive. How about your friend from the centre, do you still keep in touch?"

"Yeah, every year I try to get back a few times to help out. I donate money every fortnight to help payback by helping others who need to use the centre."

"That's nice."

"It's seriously the least I could do."

"So, what's the military really like with it? Homophobic?"

"Yes, on the surface, but there are a lot of men and women who disagree with that part of the culture and are trying to change it. And, there are more of us in the ranks than people would think."

"What about Hulk and the crew at AIS?"

"They are incredibly supportive. The best thing is they honestly don't care, as long as you can do the job, that's all that matters. You'll see, soon enough, we are a pretty close unit.

We have to be considering what we go through and how much time we spend together."

"Fair enough, I look forward to that, if I get through this. It must keep you really busy?"

"Yeah, especially when we have a training and recruitment intake like this one. It's pretty intense, just another reason I haven't found Mr Right."

"Well, they don't know what they are missing. You're fit, intelligent, caring and, I hope you don't mind me saying, really good looking. I'm sure you'll find someone who will treat you with the respect and love you deserve. Tell Hulk he needs to give you more time off."

"Thanks, Max," Blake said blushing. "Not sure he'll do that. I hope you're right, it's very kind of you to say. I'd love to find a love like you have with Lachlan."

"You will," Max said. "Speaking of, I should call Lachie soon. Thanks for the wine."

"Anytime," Blake said as the two stood and parted ways.

Chapter Twelve

Max left the shower room, which had been scrubbed clean of the pink paint overnight and changed into his training gear. He joined the seven remaining potential recruits and the instructors outside on the short walk to the weapons training range. After weeks of training, Max had excelled at weapons handling and it was becoming second nature. Pistols, rifles and knives were becoming almost like an extension of his own body. He moved them fluidly and with precision. He had shown the competition was no fluke by continuing to perform at the top of the class.

"Good morning," Hulk said as the recruits walked in. "This training program has been designed to both test and teach you. It is based on a combination of training programs used by the CIA, MI6 and their predecessor organisations. Churchill set up the Special Operations Executive to disrupt the Nazi's during World War Two from behind enemy lines. They were responsible for changing the course of the war by sabotaging supply lines, assassinating senior SS operatives and leaders, and providing intelligence to SOE command about Nazi troop movements, while disseminating false information to throw the enemy off course. AIS agents, like their SOE cousins, have to survive during covert operations right under the nose of their enemies. Using secret identities, you must hide in plain sight and become experts at sabotage, burglary, avoiding detection, survival, assassination, communications as well as what Churchill described as 'ungentlemanly warfare'. Over the next two days, you will hike in teams of three to a designated location on the map you will be provided. At the location, your mission will be to observe and assassinate the target, while avoiding or taking down the security they may have. On site, you will need to gather any relevant intelligence pointing to the criminal organisation's next moves. You'll need to call it in and await further instructions. I have brought in a number of AIS agents to act in the roles of the target and security, plus there will be guards along the route. They will be hostile. Avoid them, take them out or try to talk your way past them. Depending on where they're located, they will either arrest you or kill you if they don't believe your story or simply for seeing you. Again, you will be using paintballs, but if you're hit, you're dead. Alpha will join Max and Flash, but otherwise the teams are as they were yesterday. Collect your tablet, pistols and MP5s from the tables at the side, and feel free to take whatever other supplies you think you might need. Move out when you're ready."

Max, Flash and Kate moved to their table and checked out the tablet. There were two files on the tablet, a photo of their target and a map with a single blue dot hovering above a farmhouse several kilometres away. They put on their combat gear, holstered their guns and collected paint maker rounds for their weapons, and hung their hunting knives from their belts. They took a backpack with binoculars, rope and tape, and also decided to grab some ration packs and water, flashlights and a first aid kit. On their way out, Max also took a small steel briefcase from the rack.

"We should make our way here to this structure," Max said pointing at the tablet. "Looks like a shed of some sort. We can hide our gear there then trek up and do a recce of the target location, then make a plan of attack from there. Agreed?"

"Yes mate," Flash said. "Good idea. It's a fair way, so we'll probably need a break then anyway. Given the time, it'll probably be late afternoon by the time we reach the target location."

"Yep, we should get moving," Kate said. "I'm following your lead, Prince."

"Prince?" Flash said.

"Yeah, we think it works. Don't you?"

"Like Prince Charming? Not sure about that."

"Depends who you ask around here I guess," Kate said nodding at Blake who was walking out of the range with Hulk.

"Oh I see, yeah okay, I guess that works."

"What are you talking about?" Max asked.

"For a spy in the making it's a worry you can't see it," Kate said.

"See what?"

"Nothing, don't worry about it. Hulk also said something about Machiavelli too, so maybe that's more fitting."

"Yeah, I'd say so," Flash said smiling at Max. "Let's move out."

After two hours of solid walking through dense scrub, the team stopped to surveil the little shed they had spotted on the map. There was a guard wandering the perimeter, he stopped occasionally to check his surrounds, satisfied he kept walking. The shed was made of rusted iron and large old wooden supports held up the roof. It was surrounded by tall gumtrees which hung over the structure and deep red dusty soil ringed the shed. It was getting dark as storm clouds rolled in, but occasionally a beam of sunlight would shine through.

"I can only see one guy," Max said. "Looks like he's got a pretty consistent pattern. What do you think, take him out or capture him?"

"Capture him?" Flash asked.

"Yeah, let's try to take him alive and question him about the target location."

"What do you think, Alpha?"

"I'm not able to tell you what or how to do anything on this mission, I'm just to do as directed, so I don't give your team an advantage over the others. Sorry."

"Oh, okay," Max said. "I think we should capture him. Agreed?"

"Yeah, how do you want to do it?"

"I'll go down this way," Max said pointing out the direction on the tablet. "I'll wrap around to the right of the shed, the trees and bushes should give me pretty good cover, then I'll make a quick dash across and wait for him to stop near the corner. Once he does, I'll sneak up and knock him out. When he's out, you two come down and we'll clear the shed together. Flash you take up position here in this tree line. If it looks like he's getting the better of me, take him out. Alpha, you can wait in the tree line, between Flash and I, again be ready to back me up, and keep an eye out for any other guards. If you see any, take them down, that goes for you too, Flash."

"Ack," Flash said.

"Roger that," Kate said.

"Great, let's move."

Max moved quickly and as silently as possible in the dry bushland. When the guard was on the far side, he increased his pace between trees, timing his burst runs between cover. As the guard rounded the corner and stopped to check the tree line, Max quickly checked Flash and Kates' positions. They were making their way down towards the front of the shed at a steady pace. As Max got closer to the edge of the tree line, there was a crack of thunder and it started to rain. The guard made his pass and stopped by the corner, looking up at the heavens. It was so dry, the rain would be welcomed by the farmers around the area. Max quietly snuck out of cover and got behind the guard, then he wrapped his arms around his head and neck, putting him into a sleeper hold. The guard fought back stamping on Max's foot and trying to grab his groin. Max jumped up on the guard's back and wrapped his legs tightly around him and squeezed his knees together digging into his ribs and again helping cut off his oxygen supply. The guard was massive and he flung Max around trying to dislodge him, but Max held firm. As the guard started to slow, he reached for a Maglite hanging from his waist and flung it at the shed wall. The heavy metal flashlight hit with a loud bang and Max watched in fear, waiting for whoever was inside to come through the door. The guard passed out as the door flew open. Max rolled to the side, using the guard as a shield, as a row of paint makers hit the guard along the back, then Max heard four shots from the tree line. Flash and Kate had both seen what was coming and stepped out and shot the second guard from the shed, two shots each, both head and chest. He fell to the ground and laid still. Max was impressed by the agents' commitment to this training session, they fell without complaint and without moving. Max was on his feet and moving quickly, Flash joined him on the left and Kate behind as he went through the shed door and headed right. Flash was in second and went left, and Kate came in last and moved straight ahead. Max heard two shots and turned to see Kate taking down a third agent. Double-tap, head and chest, the guard fell to the floor.

"Clear," Max said.

"Clear," Flash said.

"All clear, here too," Kate said.

"Hmm, well, looks like we have a change of plans," Max said.

"Yeah. The guard you knocked out took three in the back, plus these two are dead, so we'll have to head straight up and surveil the target. We won't be getting an information from them."

"No. Let's drag them in here and take a moment to regroup before we head out."

Max and Flash went outside and picked up the big guy, while Kate dragged the guy from the doorway inside. Max was still impressed at how the agents stayed in character. Flash took a swig of water then passed it to Kate who took a good couple of sips before passing it to Max. He sipped at the canteen, deep in thought.

"Let's check their pockets," Max said. "Maybe they have something we can use. Empty their pockets onto this table."

They took one guard each and emptied their vests and pockets. They collected extra rounds for their weapons and put all the other supplies on the table. Max found a tablet on the guard Kate had taken down from the back of the shed.

"Here we go," Max said sitting it on the table. "Flash, you got our tablet?"

"Yeah mate, here you go."

Max sat the tablets side-by-side and retrieved a small cord from the backpack. He connected the two then unlocked his team's using his thumbprint. He closed the map and opened an AIS app he had been shown in training a few days ago. The app opened and he typed in a series of commands, telling the tablet to hack the device it was connected to. After a few minutes, he pressed the copy files button on his tablet and they downloaded from the guards' tablet to his team's. Once complete, he passed the tablet to Flash while he packed away the guards' tablet and the cord into his own backpack, as a spare.

"What have we got?" Max asked.

"Well, it's got our three headshots and a short file on each of us, so they know we are coming, who we are and what we look like," Flash said. "So, there'll be no bluffing them. There is a document with a number on it."

"Just a number? What is it?"

"Zero, four, zero, six, one, one, two, zero."

"Too short for a mobile number."

"Not sure what it's for but I assume it's important if it's on here."

"Good point. What else you got?"

"Here we go, an email saying food will be delivered at nineteen-thirty hours here and twenty-thirty hours at the target location."

"Fuck, if they come here, they'll find these guys missing and set off the alarm, but if we take out the food guys, the target will know when their food doesn't turn up."

"Why don't we take out the food guys and go in their place?"

"Yeah, but there will be a contingency, they'll know we could have found the information, so they could be ready for that. We need to break up. One or two of us needs to go ahead and check out the scene. And one or two of us need to stay for the delivery guys and to take their vehicle."

"We have the element of surprise here at this location, they might not be ready for one of us to be here to take them down. One person here can take down two people, there won't be more than two, surely."

"That's true and the other two can do surveillance and look for a way past the guards to the target."

"Maybe the delivery will serve as a distraction and we'll be able to find a window while they're pre-occupied?"

"Or we can make it a distraction?"

"What do you mean?"

"Well, let's say they know we could be rolling up in the van, let's make them think we are, but while they're all targeting the van, we'll actually be on the other side going in for our man."

"Yeah okay, great thinking, but how?"

"You and I will go ahead and surveil the house. We'll look for an entrance away from the delivery road and observe the guards and their routines. Alpha will wait here in the tree line outside and take down the deliver guys and steal their vehicle. On approach to the house, Kate, you'll need to find a way to crash it or make it a distraction in some way to draw their attention, but I need you to flee into the bushes nearby and open fire on any guards who come your way, but I want you to find cover and disappear. I want us all to finish this together. So, crash it and move away fast. Got it?"

"Fuck yeah, I can do that," Kate said smiling. "Sounds more fucking fun than I thought it'd be. Let's do it."

"Here take this," Max said passing Kate the tablet. "We'll use the guards' one in my backpack. What's the number on the back?"

"Seven, eight, one, one."

"Got it. Let's move out, Flash. See you up there, Alpha."

"Good luck and Godspeed, boys. Go fucking get it."

Max and Flash gathered their supplies and took some of the guards' extra rounds, then headed for the target location.

Chapter Thirteen

Max and Flash bunkered into the small hill overlooking the target location. They covered themselves in mud and leaves for camouflage in the cold, dark and wet scrub about two hundred metres from the big old farmhouse. It was still raining and it was hard to see through the trees. Max held the binoculars to his eyes to take in the scene. The farmhouse was not quite as big as the Wool Shed, but it was still a large old country house. It had a similar wooden deck running around the perimeter of the property and a small shed on the left where the delivery road ended. The house was raised up a couple of metres and a big set of stairs led up to the front door. Max presumed it was the same or similar at the rear of the property. The open space under the house was hidden by thin wooden lattice. Each room looked to open onto the deck with small French doors and some had large bay windows. Max checked his watch, nineteen hundred hours, Kate would be preparing to take down the delivery guys.

"Let's split up and meet around the back," Max said. "You go left and take the tablet, check out the road and let Alpha know if there are an issues and guards waiting. I'll head right and try to get closer to the house to see if I can spot our target. I'll meet you fifty metres into the scrub at the rear."

"Ack, good luck mate."

"You too, see you soon."

Max and Flash went their separate ways keeping low and quiet, stopping behind cover occasionally as they made their way around the house. Flash took a wide arch around to the left, as Max cut in and moved closer to the house. Max was only twenty metres from the house and could see inside through some of the big windows. He counted four guards in the front room, they were sitting around chatting drinking coffee. Several others were dotted about in rooms down the right side of the building and there were two guards walking in opposite directions around the deck. Every two minutes they would pass each other on the left then the right side of the house. Max watched as one of the perimeter guards looked into the room second from the back of the house and nodded, then Max saw him, their target, sitting working at a table in the second room from the back. He waited for the other guard to pass and watched as he too looked in and nodded at the target. Max crept away from the house and took a wide arc around the rear of the house to find Flash. As he did, he kept an eye on the house and the guards. He sat in the overgrown bush and waited. He was right, there was a big set of stairs leading up to the deck at the rear of the house, almost perfectly centred. He heard a noise to his right and raised his gun, but saw Flash smiling back at him.

"Don't shoot," he whispered.

"How'd you go?"

"Good. I messaged Kate, the shed is empty. She's en route. I also gave her the location of a small hiding spot just down the road. She should be able to bunker in there."

"Okay, good. I found our man, second room from the back now on our left as we approach the house. The two guards are a problem. They pass every two minutes on the left and right of the house and nod at him when they pass. It gives us thirty seconds to get up and through the door before one of them comes around the corner."

"Okay, shit, not much time."

"No, especially if that door is locked."

"Yeah, true," Flash said borrowing the binoculars to look at the door. "Old school lock, should be easy to pick."

"You are far better at that than me, so how about this, you head straight for the door and pick it if it's locked. I'll head left and stand ready to take out the guard. If I have to I'll take his place and walk around and take out the other guard too?"

"Okay, but the goal is to get in without them seeing us?"

"Yes. We'll need to move quickly, left. You'll be in first, so clear the first room and I'll head for our target. There are at least eight guys inside."

"Yeah I saw four, plus the two on the deck."

"Okay, so let's put the number at around ten inside, plus the two outside and the target."

"Got it."

"Okay, when the guard walks past we move."

"Ack, let's do it."

They started moving forward to the edge of the tree line, careful to stay in cover. When the guard walked passed the backdoor and towards the corner, they moved quickly and silently across the backyard. The mud and puddles splashed under their feet, but they made it across without the guard turning back. They took the stairs three at a time and Flash went straight for the door, silenced pistol in one hand and lock-picking wire in the other. Max stood three metres to his left and aimed for the nearest corner waiting for the second guard to swing around.

"Got it," Flash said shoving the wire back in his pocket and taking his gun in his left hand.

Max backed away towards the door and followed Flash through. It clicked shut moments before the guard turned to walk that stretch of the deck. They waited, holding their breaths, but heard his footsteps continue on. Max pointed for the room on the left and Flash moved silently, as Max moved past him, he heard the short, sharp hiss of Flash's silenced pistol. He had taken down a guard in the backroom. Max ran into the target's room, dived and slid on his right arm which was holding his silenced pistol. He slid past the target and curled in under the window, keeping the target in his sights, but low and close enough under the window that the guard could not see him.

"Don't move," Max said. "Nod to your mate as he walks past or I'll put a bullet between your eyes."

Max watched as the target nodded to the guard through the window.

"What is your organisation's next move?" Max asked.

"I'm not telling you shit," the target said.

Max shot him in the knee cap, the target swore, even a paintball at close range would hurt.

"Oh fuck," he said clutching his knee.

"Flash, quick," Max said as Flash ran into the room and took up a mirrored position to Max aiming his gun at the target. "Nod to your friend when he passes again."

The target nodded out the window and Max jumped up and punched the target in the mouth.

"Oh, for fuck sake," the target said. "Here fuck, it's all on this tablet."

Flash took the tablet and copied the files.

"Ready, Prince, files are downloaded," Flash said. "And, I got a message from Alpha. She's one minute out."

"Roger," Max said aiming at the target and firing two rounds into his chest.

The agent played his part and slumped in the chair as Max opened the window. The guard looked in to nod as he past, but stopped in his tracks when he saw the target slumped in the chair with the paintball marks on his vest. Max jumped up from under the window and fired two shots into the guard and he fell to the ground.

"Let's move," Flash said opening the door and checking the hallway.

They moved for the backdoor as an almighty crash echoed through the house. Max and Flash had moved through the door as the sound from outside startled the guards into action. Flash and Max ran across the back deck and down the side deck. The perimeter guard was stopped looking back towards the shed. Flash put two paintballs into his back and he jumped, then fell to the ground. They hurled themselves over the rail then bolted deep into the bush, before heading left to loop around for Kate. Max watched as the guards started firing in the direction of the vehicle. Kate had smashed it right through the little shed, demolishing it. They kept moving, running fast in the darkness, then Flash veered right and Max followed taking them further from the house.

"Alpha," Flash whispered as they came to a stop two hundred metres from the house. "Alpha."

"I'm here, lads," Kate said. "How'd you go?"

"We got the files, we should move," Max said.

"You two crazy fuckers pulled it off, I can't believe it. Well done."

"Thanks, we should move though before we check them out. I don't want us to be seen."

"Agreed," Flash said. "The first shed is burnt now, so maybe we just need to go bush for a while?"

"Yep, let's move," Max said leading his team deeper into the dense bushland.

They ran through the slippery mud and thick overgrown bushland for around half an hour, until they were satisfied they were far enough away to avoid detection. They sat down and shared some water.

"So, how'd you get away from the delivery van?" Max asked.

"When Flash messaged me and told me the shed was empty, I decided to make it the target. I stopped at the end of the delivery road and got out and let it run down the road. I tied the steering wheel to keep it on track, but I was free and clear well before they knew what was happening. I just hid in the spot Flash told me to. Fucking easy as."

"That's awesome," Max said. "Great thinking."

"All Flash's idea."

"Love it. Well done mate."

"We make quite the team, the three of us," Flash said.

"Sure do, don't know whether the others will make it through their tests," Kate said. "I don't think I've ever seen a team get this far. Normally, they fuck it up."

"I guess we haven't finished yet though, have we?" Max asked. "We should look at the files."

Flash took out the tablet and started scanning through the files.

"It looks like they've got plans to blow up a defence base and they are storing their equipment nearby," Flash said. "We better call it in."

"Yeah, get the files to Hermes and ask what's next?" Max said as Flash started typing on the tablet.

"Done," Flash said. "Now, I guess we just wait."

The team ate some cold rations while sitting in the rain waiting for instructions. Max knew that part of the training was to teach patience and survival in any conditions, so he sat quietly with the others just waiting and preparing for what was to come.

"Here we go," Flash said holding up the tablet. "Instructions are to move in and sabotage their equipment. Intelligence says that they know their leader has been taken out, so they've moved forward their plans and expect to roll out in the early hours of the morning. So, we need to move now and take out the equipment before they can use it."

"Alright, let's move," Max said.

"Yep, let's go fuck these terrorists up," Kate said handing Max the steel briefcase he had taken from the range. "Oh and here, you can carry this, I'm sick of carrying it. You left it at the shed."

"Excellent," Max said. "Thanks for that."

Near the location, Max had crawled forward painfully slowly keeping his profile low and the noise down, even though it was still pouring rain and he was covered in leaves and mud, the rare streak of lightning lit up the sky and everything under it, including Max. He had kept to the cover as best he could to minimise the chances of being seen and was now laying prone in an inch of mud less than twenty metres from the nearest guard. There were four in total guarding the perimeter of the storage shed. He inched closer and closer, then lightning lit up the sky and he laid still and lowered his head to hide his face. He waited a full minute before daring to move again. When he was sure he had not been detected he inched closer then rose to kneel on one knee. He slighted the closest guard with his silenced pistol and waited, then it happened a rolling clap of thunder and lightning forked across the sky above. Max fired two shots into the vest of the closest guard and rushed forward to catch him, he quickly dragged him back into the bushes and hid him under some leaves, before taking his place standing sentry on the corner of the shed. He mimicked the way the guard had been standing, moving slightly on the spot shifting his feet and looking out into the bush for threats.

He took the chance to look at the guard to his left. He was facing away from Max, kicking the mud and looked to be getting restless standing in the rain. The guard on his right was also looking away, staring intently at the tree line. Max made his move and stepped back towards the door of the shed and opened it slightly, and quickly ducked his head in for a look. Satisfied it was clear, he reached in and rested his tablet next to the door, with the camera facing in towards the equipment, then stepped forward back into his sentry position leaving the door opened a few inches. He stepped on the spot, just as the guard on the right glanced in his direction. Max pretended to scan the tree line and the guard turned away again.

Max waited for ten minutes before he heard some movement in the bushes to his left, he turned to check if the guard had heard it. He had not moved or looked, so Max nodded in the direction of the sound and it started again, a slow, low hum and some rustling of the undergrowth and muddy puddles. Max watched the guards and scanned for the object making the sound, then it appeared and gently nudged forward. When Max was certain the guards were not looking, he nodded towards the little drone and it sped out of the bush, past him and through the door of the storage shed. The drone was inside for two minutes then slowly came back out behind Max and he held up one finger behind his back to tell it to wait. The restless guard was looking in his direction.

"I'm just gonna take a piss," the guard yelled towards Max and he gave him a thumbs up.

Max turned and gave the guard on his right the all-clear signal, and when he turned around he gave the drone the go signal and it sped back into the bushes across from Max. After relieving himself, the guard to his left moved back into position and continued to stare off into the distance.

It was almost twenty minutes later when Max heard the signal he was waiting for, an explosion rang out in the woods to his right, maybe fifty metres past the guard to his right. He watched as the two guards he could see raised their weapons and headed in search of the cause of the sound. Max grabbed his tablet and ran as fast and as hard as he could into the bush in the opposite direction. His legs burned as he powered up and over a little rise and zig-zagged through the jungle-like bush land. Low branches slapped his face and body as he ran, and muddy water splashed up his legs. He ran for several minutes veering slightly left before correcting and heading right. As he swerved right, he heard the second explosion, this time he knew it was contained in the shed. The sound echoed throughout the scrub and he smiled to himself and kept running. He thought about the little remote-controlled drone, as planned, it had entered the shed with two fake C4 bombs attached to it, like the pink paint bomb Max had set off in the shower room, and he imagined the inside of the storage shed was now similarly covered, so was part of the bushland to the right of the shed, where the guards were headed. The little all-terrain drone had been in the steel briefcase Max picked up at the range and Kate returned to him after taking out the target. Flash had used the second tablet to drive it down, plant the bomb in the safest place using the tablet Max had set up, and then it had sped out and around in the bushes to find a distraction point.

Max pulled out his tablet and checked his position. Five hundred metres straight ahead he found Kate and Flash, laying waiting for him in the mud.

"Call it in, Flash," Max said. "Mission complete."

"You got it, Prince," Flash said. "Well done."

"Couldn't have done it without you both, thank you. We do make a good team."

"Well fucking done, boys," Kate said. "I've seen troops with years of experience who couldn't pull of the crazy-shit you did tonight. Seriously, well done. Now, tell Hermes to come get us the fuck out of here, I'm freezing my tits off."

Flash sent the message and the three shook hands and congratulated each other. The tablet beeped and Flash smiled.

"What's it say?" Max asked.

"It's from Hermes, he says congratulations," Flash said. "Hulk and Carter are reviewing our performance and a car is en route to pick us up."

"Thank fuck for that," Kate said. "I'm sick of this mud and rain."

"I thought you'd be used to it?" Max said smiling. "Tough Army chick like you."

"I've had more than my fucking fair share of this shit. It's your turn now."

"He said one more thing too," Flash said.

"What's that?"

"Winners' choice, there's fresh hot coffee in the pot or cold beers in the fridge."

Chapter Fourteen

"Congratulations on your performance, Max," Carter said sitting in his dark study. "I'm not sure I've seen any team get through the assassination and sabotage stage, like your team did. I haven't seen you since then, I just wanted to say, well done."

"Thanks, Doc," Max said. "So, what's on for today?"

"I've seen you twice a week for the last few weeks and I understand why you have made this commitment, you're patriotic, but it's more than that, you have a sense of duty, like you owe it to the country to do your bit. It's certainly honourable, but I want to come back to a couple of topics, in particular, I want to know how you feel about, death and love."

"Okay, but we've discussed them at length. I'm not sure what more we can discuss, but I do appreciate you being more direct."

"You know what I want to know."

"You want to know if I can take someone's life?"

"Yes."

"I'm pretty black and white there, Doc, if someone has broken the rules or intends to, then they need to be dealt with. If I know they are going to hurt or kill someone, I will do what it takes to stop them."

"Even if that means taking their life?"

"Yes, they don't deserve it anyway."

"Why do you say that?"

"If they think they can take a life for their cause then they are wrong and must be stopped. There is no cause worth taking a life for."

"What about your cause? You have admitted this morning you're willing to kill for it."

"That's different."

"How?"

"They seek to hurt and kill innocent people in the name of religion or money or power, I would seek only to do it save lives or to right wrongs."

"Right wrongs?"

"Yeah, if they succeed and hurt or kill civilians, if it comes to it, I'll kill them to balance the ledger."

"An eye for an eye?"

"No, more like a life for an eye."

"So, it's not actually balance you're looking for?"

"No, I think we need to scare them and their friends, and make some examples of them. If they hurt us, we will find and kill them. If they succeed, we will come back at them twice as hard."

"Does the tit-for-tat not just escalate tensions?"

"In Roman times, a Roman citizen could walk to the edges of the empire free from harassment and harm, simply for being a citizen of Rome. That's the sort of fear we need to project. Do not come at us or we will find you, hunt you down and put you in the ground. We need to move beyond stopping terrorist attacks to permanently deterring them from even being considered. Our citizens shouldn't live in fear, nor should any man, woman or child who seeks freedom, choice, democracy and liberty, but those who seek to terrorise, harm and murder, they should be the ones living in fear."

"I'm sure Hulk is going to love that answer, you are sounding more like him every day."

"I'm sorry?"

"Nothing. What about love?"

"It is the single most important thing in the world."

"Worth fighting for and dying for?"

"Yes."

"And, what about Lachlan?"

"What about him?"

"How do you think the two of you will go being separated often for you to train and complete missions?"

"It would be easier if I didn't have to lie to him. I hate lying to him."

"It's for your and his protection, and for the protection of the AIS and this program. You'll be able to tell him soon enough, if he is the one that is."

"He is. I am going to spend my life with him."

"How do you think he'll take it? Finding out you lied to him for years?"

"It will upset him, but he knows how much I love him and if he understands the reasons, I'm sure he will be okay."

"How would he cope if you got injured or didn't come home at all?"

"As anyone in that situation would, Doc. That's a stupid question."

"Maybe. But it's also a real possibility."

"I understand that, I got covered in a very real reminder of that not that long ago, when I set off the trap in the shower room. And, when that psychopath, Travis, waterboarded me."

"Yes, how did you feel?"

"Seriously, Doc?"

"Yes, seriously, how did you feel?"

"Awful."

"Why?"

"Because of Lachlan."

"Because he'd miss you?"

"No, because I'm not sure if he knows just how much I love him and because I haven't come out and told my parents and family and friends, that he is the most incredible person I have ever met, that we are in love and that he is my life, my soulmate, the one."

"So, why haven't you told them?"

"I wasn't sure how they would take it and I wanted to be sure he was the one first."

"Fear of rejection?"

"Yeah, but I don't care about that anymore. I've got him and he is all I need. Anything more than that is just a bonus."

"Fair enough, Max."

"He thinks I'm telling them on this trip. He thinks I'm overseas with my family. I'd like to duck home and have that conversation before I go back to see him."

"I'm sure we can arrange that, Max."

"Thank you."

"And how will your parents know to cover for you if he asks them about the trip?"

"Hulk said he would take care of that for me."

"Okay, that's good. Well, no more questions from me, unless there is anything else you'd like to discuss?"

"Not today, thanks, Doc."

"You should know, by the way, you've found your balance."

"In what way?"

"Lachlan and your love for him and for the people around you, plus your desire to help and protect them, that will balance out anything you need to do for AIS, including torture and killing. You're in a good place."

"That's good to hear. I certainly feel better about it all."

"Good, I can see that, but it's nice to hear it too."

"Okay, thanks, Doc, see you later."

"No, sorry, Max. We aren't done quite yet. We've finished the discussion session, but I need you to complete these tests. We have a series of behavioural, psychometric and recall tests for you to do. These just help me get a more complete picture of you and your profile."

"No worries."

"You will have sixty minutes to complete the first two tests, then I will come back in for the third. Good luck."

Carter put two test papers in front of Max then left the room. Max checked the time on the wall then started the tests. The first was a series of questions asking him to choose between scenarios and pick the best or most appropriate answer from a list. He completed it in twenty-four minutes, so started the second. It was sixty psychometric questions where he had to choose the next shape in a sequence. He completed it with a few minutes to spare, so sat in silence waiting for Carter to come back into the room.

"How'd you go?" Carter asked wandering in.

"Yeah pretty good, I think. Finished both."

"Alright, that's great. The last test is about recall. You will read a passage of information, then I will ask you questions about it, following which you will read two more datasets and I will then ask you questions about all three sources. Got it?"

"Yeah, ready when you are."

Carter gave Max the first passage which he read then they ran through a question and answer session, before Max took the second and third datasets to read. They were much more complex, facts and figures, complex equations and several profiles of individuals. Max read it all and nodded for Carter to begin, but before he could the door of the room burst open and a man in a balaclava ran into the room and fired several shots from an MP5 wildly into the air. Without thinking Max jumped from his chair and in one smooth motion, dropped to a knee and hurled the chair over his head towards the gunman. It smashed into the gunman and he fell to the floor and scrambled for the door. Max gave chase, but Carter grabbed his arm.

"Take a seat, Max," Carter said.

"Who the fuck was that? Was that part of the test?"

"What was he wearing?"

"A balaclava, navy polo shirt and caramel chinos, maybe brown boots."

"Anything else?"

"A watch on his left wrist, small face, brown band."

"And the gun, what was it and how many shots did he fire?"

"MP5, I think it five shots."

"The second data set you saw had a dollar amount and a CEO profile, what was the figure and who was the CEO?"

"One point seven billion dollar annual revenue. Mr James Parkinson."

"In the third data set, there was a formula, can you remember it?"

"I can write it down, I don't know what all the symbols are."

"That's fair enough, here you go," Carter said handing Max a piece of paper and pen which he scrawled the formula on. "Perfect. AIS agents need to not only react, but to think under pressure and recall is one of those vital skills we need you to have. You need to be able to get in, absorb the information and get out, sometimes under fire or a lot of stress, and you will need to adapt and overcome to achieve your mission and bring back the intelligence you have found."

"Wow, okay, so I just chucked a chair at one of the instructors?"

"Yep."

"It was Blake, wasn't it?"

"How do you know that?"

"His build and, now I think about it, the watch. I'm sure I've seen him wear something similar."

"Not similar, one and the same. The test's over, Max, you better go find him and say sorry."

"Sorry? I thought he was trying to kill me and you for that matter."

"Well, thanks for having my back. I will see you again soon."

"Anytime. Thanks, Doc."

Chapter Fifteen

"Today, we are going to run another real-world hostage scenario," Kate said standing in front of what looked like a brand new four storey building built in a valley down from the rifle range. "You will abseil down to the third floor and make entry. Inside there will be a number of cardboard terrorists and hostages. Your task is to take out the terrorists without hurting any of the civilians. There are also traps, Prince, so you more than anyone need to watch out for them."

The four other remaining recruits laughed and looked at Max, he just smiled back at her.

"We are using live rounds," Kate said. "Weapon safety is paramount. Remember your surrounds and if you hear an alarm sound, you are to immediately put your weapon to safe. Understood?"

"Yes, ma'am," they all shouted in unison.

"Flash, you're up first," Kate said. "Oh and this will be a timed run, you have five minutes to clear the third and fourth floors, and make your way back to the roof with this chest."

Kate held up a small wooden box.

"Get the package, clear the floors and get back to the roof," Kate said. "Five minutes. All of you get to the roof now."

A few minutes later, Flash geared up and abseiled down smashing the window on the third floor. Max heard the gunfire ringing out in the building below as Flash made his way through the course. He burst through the door on the roof with the chest in hand. He ran over and passed Kate the little box.

"Four minutes, thirty seconds," Kate said pausing the stopwatch. "Not bad. Well done."

The recruits, Max included, patted Flash on the back and congratulated him as Kate took the chest back down into the building, placing it in its hiding spot. She then headed down to the first floor and entered an observation room. Hulk, Blake and Carter were re-watching Flash's performance on a row of televisions.

"He's got pretty good form," Kate said watching the little screen.

"He does things by the book, a bit heavy on the rounds expended, but overall very good," Blake said.

"It's a pass from me, we need to work on his reaction speed, but he's in as far as I'm concerned," Hulk said looking around the group and they all nodded their agreement.

Blake pulled Flash's file and wrote 'cleared for field training' in the relevant box and co-signed and dated it with Hulk.

"Alpha, send in the next one," Hulk said to Kate as she turned and left the room.

Kate made her way back up to the roof stopping on the third floor. Workers had replaced the glass panel and cleared the broken glass from Flash's entry, and had left the floor. Good to go again.

On the roof, Williams geared up and started her run by abseiling off the roof. Again, gunfire rang out below. Max and the others milled about staring at the door waiting for her to re-join them. Eventually, she burst through the door and placed the small chest on the ground in front of Kate.

"Five minutes, fifty-six seconds," Kate said. "Sorry, but that's a fail."

Williams hung her head as the others rallied around to console her. Kate went back inside and replaced the box, and headed to the observation room.

"She's been generally very good across the board," Blake said.

"Yes, she has talent, but I'm not sure she's good enough," Hulk said. "What do you think, Doc?"

"Look here," Carter said pointing to a monitor. "Slight hesitation before firing, but generally pretty good. I think we can improve the performance."

"So, you think on everything you've seen to date she should pass?" Blake asked.

"Yes, I do, Commander."

"General?"

"Let's pass her, but keep a close eye on her," Hulk said. "If that reaction speed doesn't change within weeks, she's out."

"Yes, sir," Blake said as he wrote a note on Williams's personnel file and co-signed and dated it with Hulk.

"Let's go again, Kate," Hulk said.

"Yes, sir," Kate said leaving the room and heading back to the roof.

She sent the third potential recruit over the side of the building and started the clock. The new window pane smashed and several shots rang out, then a wailing siren sounded. Kate waited for full minute before entering the building. On level three, she found the recruit standing next to the wooden cut-out of a female hostage hugging her daughter. The two-dimensional woman had a perfect hole right through the centre of her forehead.

"Get back to the roof," Kate said to the potential recruit before heading downstairs to the observation room.

"Fuck me, one extreme to the other," Hulk said. "One recruit hesitates before shooting and this guy is too quick to shoot, and kills a fucking woman in front of her daughter. God, could you imagine the shit-storm that would rain down? He's done. Frankly, he was lucky to even get to this stage, but no more."

Blake and the others just nodded, before he again wrote a note and signed and dated the file with Hulk.

"Alright, Prince Charming's turn," Hulk said. "Let's see if we've taught him anything."

Kate headed back to the roof and told Max to get ready. He walked over and clipped the abseiling line to his vest before checking his MP5 and flicking off the safety. He stood staring over the edge collecting his thoughts and mentally preparing. After a few seconds, Kate fired her pistol and without thought

Max leapt from the building letting the line whip in the wind behind him as he fell. Max had spun around to face the building as he jumped from the roof, as the line caught at the top, Max came level with the third-floor window and put three bullets into it as he swung forward and through the cracked window. Glass shards scattered across the floor as Max fired four bullets, two for each terrorist cut-out, head and chest, in the first room. He retrieved his hunting knife from his belt and cut the line he had abseiled in on. A terrorist cut-out holding a frightened hostage, popped out of the wall at the end of the room. Max threw his hunting knife with astonishing force, it flew through the air end-over-end until it pierced the terrorist's throat. It hit so hard, it almost broke the head off the wooden figure. He swept quickly and quietly. In the second room, he found two more targets and fired rounds into both, as he was leaving the room a sound behind him made him turn. A cut-out of a woman, holding her daughter, both with terrified gazes on their faces sprung from the wall. Max paused and held his fire, before moving towards the third room. Inside the third room, a group of hostages were surrounded by three armed terrorists. The one on the left was pointing his gun at the hostages, the one on the right's gun was pointing at the floor and the one in the centre's gun was pointing at the door. Max fired two shots into the face of the terrorist on the left, followed by two, head and chest, on the centre guy, and two for the guy on the right.

Max turned and left the room, ejecting his empty magazine onto the carpet and replaced it with a full one while walking. He clicked it into place and chambered a round as he headed up the stairs. At the top, he put two bullets into a terrorist guarding the door. He kicked the door open and took out two more terrorist cut-outs. He cleared a room on the left before heading for a second room. As he went to enter, he noticed the tripwire running across the doorframe. He cut the wire with a set of plyers from his vest and snuck a quick look around the door. Four terrorists were standing guard by the chest. Max threw a flashbang grenade into the room and a second after it exploded, he entered and put two bullets into each target. He collected the chest and made his way out into the stair well and up onto the roof and placed the chest in front of Kate.

"Three minutes, fifteen seconds," Kate said smiling and patting him on the shoulder as she walked passed him and back downstairs.

In the observation room, Hulk and the team were reviewing Max's performance on the little monitors.

"Look at this," Blake said pausing the video as Max's feet smashed the glass. "He didn't abseil down, he jumped backwards to swing in. It would certainly bring with it the element of surprise."

"Then," Blake said letting the tape play before pausing it again. "He cut's the line, unlike the others who wasted time unclipping it. Our terrorist at the end of the room appears and instead of dicking around changing to the gun, he throws his hunting knife and nearly destroys the wooden figure with the force of it, that would kill any man and he knows it, look how he is already moving while the knife is still in the air."

Blake played the video showing the knife leaving Max's hand and he pointed to the screen as Max began to move before the knife smashed through the terrorist's neck. The team watched as Max went room by room taking down the terrorists.

"He is on autopilot, Hulk," Carter said. "He is moving and acting like he has been doing this for years. He doesn't hesitate at all, but still maintains control and successfully avoids harming the hostages. See how he took out the guy with his gun pointing at the hostages first, risking his own life to save theirs', then he took out the next riskiest the guy pointing a gun at him. He is showing logical thought under pressure with a priority on preserving life. And, here we go upstairs, he caught the tire-wire which isn't a surprise following the bathroom incident, but that's not all, he snuck a look around the door and used a flashbang. None of the others did that, he knew in a real-world scenario four on one would be too difficult a feat, so he disorientated them before taking them out. Each cut-out, like the others, were textbook takedowns, two shots each, double-tap, head and chest. You did well finding this one, Hulk."

"I found him at Newcastle University," Hulk said. "I got a tip-off from a friend of mine who's a psychology professor and it was backed up by one of his colleagues in international relations. I put him under close surveillance for months and turns out, not only did he have the brain, but he is a natural athlete. He swims, cycles, plays rugby, tennis, he has a standing offer from the Australian Rowing Team to join them, he hits the gym five to six times a week doing some amateur body-building, and, as I found out the hard way, he's getting pretty good at martial arts which he took up for self-defence with his boyfriend, Lachlan."

"I spoke to him after that," Carter said. "He told me, he thought that's what you would do in the same situation. I tend to agree, you would be very likely to headbutt your captives and challenge them to hand-to-hand combat, even though you were naked and frozen solid. It's no wonder he made it this far, you've found a younger version of yourself."

"Hmm, he's too sensitive though," Hulk said. "Certainly, more bloody sensitive than I am."

"I don't think that's a bad thing, Hulk," Carter said. "He is a complex young guy and yes he is sweet and very caring, but we could use a bit more of that around here. I think it gives him balance, in fact, I think it will keep him more grounded than others. And, judging by his performance just now and from his test results, and the hours I've had him under observation, it doesn't look like anything will hold him back in anyway."

"But, what's motivating him? How do I know he won't turnaround and quit when it gets too hard? When it becomes real."

"Love," Blake said shyly.

"What?" Hulk asked.

"You asked what's motivating him, it's love, mostly for Lachlan, but he knows the world isn't perfect," Blake said. "He knows he is lucky and he wants to protect what he has, and wants to protect those who can't protect themselves. He knows there are terrible people in the world and he wants to stop them. He told me that if he has the skills and ability to do the work we require, then it wouldn't be fair to sit back and let others do the job and take all the risk. He wants to do his part and he knows somewhere deep inside that he can do it."

"I agree," Carter said. "It's a definite yes from me."

"Me too," Blake said.

"Yeah and me too, boss," Kate said from behind them as Hulk looked over his shoulder at her. "He's a machine. I've never seen anyone do this course so quickly and over the past few weeks he's been out there on endurance and obstacle courses keeping pace with Blake which is not fucking easy, that's for sure. I can't keep up with you, Blake. Max is a natural leader, I've experienced that first-hand during the survival and sabotage course, he drove those results. And, well, he nearly beat your dumb arse after hours of torture in the shed and you're one of the toughest sons-of-bitches I've ever met. He's got it. With all-due-respect, sir."

"Alright," Hulk said turning back to face Blake. "Well, what are you waiting for?"

Blake wrote 'cleared for field training' in the relevant box on Max's personnel file and signed and dated it before passing it to Hulk.

"Next," Hulk said as Kate left to go back to the roof to put the remaining potential recruit through the course.

Chapter Sixteen

Max, Flash and Williams all passed the course and were cleared for field training. Hulk had told them to take some time off and said he would be in touch in a few days to continue their training. Max took the opportunity to head home to see his family. Hulk accompanied him on the first day to discuss Max's important new role working for the government, leaving out the fact he was a spy. He told them about an opportunity which had come up for Max to work for a local Member of Parliament and he asked them to cover for Max for political reasons. They bought it and Hulk headed off.

Max wasted no time in coming out to his parents and telling them all about Lachlan. While he could tell they were both surprised and maybe even a little bit sad, he knew they understood. His mum said how excited she was to meet Lachlan.

After a couple of days at home, he got the train back to Newcastle and Lachlan met him at the station. He ran over, Max dropped his bags and took him in his arms. They hugged and kissed on the platform like no one was watching. Max was swept up in the emotions of their reunion thinking about everything he had been through from the endless training to the torture and everyday it was Lachlan who got him through it.

"I want you to know, I love you," Max said still holding Lachlan. "More than anything in the world. I missed you so much."

"I missed you too, Max, and I love you too. Don't ever go away that long without me again. Come on, you've got to tell me everything."

"Okay babe," Max said lowering Lachlan back to the ground before picking up his bags and holding Lachlan's hand to walk to the car.

They drove back to the college, made love and fell asleep in each other's arms.

At five the next morning, Max woke out of habit, grabbed one of his training bags and snuck out of their bedroom. He went to the gym and did a light weights session, before swimming eighty laps of the pool. When he got back to the room, Lachlan was up doing some reading.

"Good morning mister," Max said dropping his bag and starting to undress. "How'd you sleep?"

"Soundly, in the arms of the man of my dreams," Lachlan said staring lovingly at Max. "And, might I say, he is damn fine too. Woah boy, how much gym time did you have on holidays? You're even sexier than I remember and those arms feel bigger."

"Yeah I did a bit, but you're the sexy one," Max said wrapping a towel around his waist before crawling onto the bed to kiss Lachlan. "Want to join me in the shower, then we can go grab some breakfast and a good coffee?"

"Stupid question," Lachlan said smiling and kissing Max then grabbing a towel as they stumbled out the door towards the shower.

They made love in the shower, changed and head down to the beach for coffee and breakfast.

"So, do you remember that old guy who was at the football a couple of months ago?" Max asked.

"The one who came over after the game?" Lachlan asked.

"Yeah."

"Yes, I remember him. Why?"

"He offered me a job. Working for a Member of Parliament. He's a Shadow Minister."

"Okay. That's great, Max. Congratulations. A job offer before we've even finished uni is amazing. How did he find you?"

"One of my lecturers called him. Apparently, my marks and some of my essays stood out, and so they put my name forward and this guy wants me to come try it out."

"That's so great, Max. Yes, your grades are amazing, I'm not surprised they want you. Although, did you say Shadow Minister?"

"Yes."

"You would want to work for those conservative arseholes?"

"Not really, but it's more about his portfolio. He's Shadow Defence Minister and I think that would be really interesting, and if they win, he'll be Defence Minister. Imagine the opportunities and doors that would open. Plus, there will be opportunity to travel and get involved in policy making, and maybe even some media type work."

"That's true. It's a fantastic opportunity, I'm so proud of you," Lachlan said turning and hugging Max. "I love you."

"I love you too, but that's not all. We'd need to move to Canberra."

"Oh right, okay. I've only been there once on a year six excursion."

"I've never been there, I've heard mixed things. All I know is it's cold."

"Not if we're there together," Lachlan said smirking.

"Naughty," Max said smiling and tickling Lachlan. "I told them, I would think about it and discuss it with you before I agreed to it."

"Are you crazy? This is an incredible opportunity, Max, you can't turn it down."

"I will, if you don't want to move to Canberra or don't think I should do it."

"You would do that for me?"

"Yes, Lachie. You are the only thing that matters to me, not where we live or my career, I don't need or want anything in life, other than you by my side."

"You are so sweet, God, I love you so much," Lachlan said as a tear welled in his eye. "I would do anything for you and I will follow you wherever you go. I only care about spending my life with you too."

They kissed and hugged on the café bench, until they were interrupted by their coffees arriving.

"I'm so happy, Lachie."

"Me too, Max."

"Oh and there's one more thing, he's found you a job too."

"What?"

"To help push us over the edge, he found you a job too at the local private hospital."

"God, they must really want you."

"And, the hospital really wants you. They've contacted your lecturers and well, I'm not the only one with outstanding grades. They're ready to make you an offer."

"Seriously?"

"Yes, Lachie. I know you want an amazing career too and this will give you the best possible start, on top of your incredible intellect and amazing grades."

"Well, what are we waiting for?"

Max smiled broadly and kissed Lachlan passionately.

Chapter Seventeen

"For non-believers, the reckoning is near," Moghadam said to his assembled followers in the dark and muggy mosque. "And Allah awaits, to question the good and bad, the virtuous and the evil, the faithful and the non-believers to weigh up the sum of their life and choose their fate. Will they join Him in paradise or suffer a fate worse than death being flogged and stabbed with irons and cast into the flames of the underworld? Rest assure the infidels will be punished! Their feet have slipped!"

"Allah alone can determine what comes next and He is waiting for us all to join Him. The western world has been corrupted by false gods and idols, and by atheists spreading their lies. Their feet have slipped. The west has opened its arms to promiscuity, homosexuality, vulgar behaviour, blasphemy, free thinking, radical feminism, democracy and the ability to question, and atheism, while continuing to spread mistruths about Islam and waging war against our people under false pretences. Their feet have slipped!"

"They claim their God and values supreme without thought given to alternative viewpoints. They claim their system of government to be the best without thought given to the disgraceful people who they choose to represent them. They claim women and gays to be equal without thought given to sins they have committed against the word of Allah. Their feet have slipped. Well my brothers, it is time for their reckoning. Time for them to meet the one true God, Allah. Will you join me in rising up against these people who betray Allah? Will you join the fight to spread His word across this nation and throughout the world? Will you help me send the non-believers and infidels to their reckoning? Their feet have slipped! Inshallah, we will be successful and put an end to their wretched ways. Allah Akbar."

Moghadam walked off the stage to cheers and applause from his followers.

"Congratulations, Imam Moghadam," Haddad said. "The word of Allah flows through you to recruit new followers to our cause."

"Thank you, Haddad," Moghadam said. "Are the devices ready?"

"Yes, I will pick them up and move them to the facility. Have you heard from the Archbishop about the vials?"

"No. The Jews must be dragging their feet. We may have to provide them with some incentive."

"What would you like me to do?"

"Wait until I have spoken to Wright, I will call you if we need to give them a push."

"Understood. We should discuss," Haddad said but was interrupted by shouting from the main hall.

"Get out of here, Haddad," Moghadam said. "I will handle this, but if you do not hear from me, take over and see this through."

"Allah be with you."

"And with you."

Haddad ran to a storeroom at the rear of the building and fled through an escape hatch, as Moghadam walked back into the main hall. Twelve combat uniformed police officers dressed in black with balaclavas, reflective lensed goggles, helmets and tactical vests had surrounded Moghadam's followers who were all on their knees with their hands behind their heads.

"What is going on here?" Moghadam said. "This is a place of worship. You cannot do this!"

"Imam Abu Artan Moghadam?" one of the officers asked.

"Yes."

"Put your hands on your head. You are coming with us."

"What are you talking about? I am a man of faith. You would arrest a religious leader."

"Well, arrest might be a bit generous," the officer said walking over and clubbing Moghadam across the face with the butt of his MP5 and knocking him to the floor.

"You will pay for this insult," Moghadam said as one of the officers placed a hood over his head and cuffed him.

"Shut the fuck up, you terrorist piece of shit," the officer said dragging him to his feet and escorting him to the car.

"You cannot do this," Moghadam protested as he was shoved into the rear of the car.

"Imam Moghadam, you are now in the custody of the Australian Intelligence Service and we need to have a little chat," Hulk said removing his hood as Kate put the car into drive and took off down the road.

Chapter Eighteen

A few days had passed since Max and Lachlan had discussed moving to Canberra. They had spent time organising themselves and planned a trip in the coming days to visit Canberra, meet their new bosses and start looking for a house. Max got a call from Hulk who told him to get to the Newcastle Airport. He told Lachlan he needed to go to Canberra for a few days to do some training and left for the airport, where he found one of the AIS helicopters waiting for him. They flew for a couple of hours before landing on the front lawn of the Wool Shed in Western New South Wales.

He dropped his bag inside the door of the big homestead and headed for the shed, where he had spent that long night being interrogated, to find Hulk and Kate standing in front of a man tied to the same chair he had sat in. At first, he thought it might have been another round of recruits, but when he got closer, he saw the scars and cuts, and saw the blood dripping from his mouth and nose.

"Codenames only, Prince, okay?" Hulk asked.

"Yes, sir," Max said.

"This is Imam Abu Artan Moghadam," Hulk said. "Known to his cell as Little Bear which is what Artan means apparently. He is responsible for planning a series of terrorist attacks, including one in Adelaide which we stopped. We picked him up after a little hate speech he gave to his followers and now we want to know where the rest of his cell is located and where and when the next attacks are planned to take place."

"Okay," Max said. "Why am I here, sir?"

"Well, you successfully completed the course and have moved into the on the job training phase," Hulk said. "This means you get to ride shotgun with some of our more qualified agents until you are ready and you start today. Watch, observe and learn."

"Yes, sir."

Kate walked over and waved smelling salts under Moghadam's nose waking him up.

"Mr Moghadam, you are in the custody of the Australian Intelligence Service," Hulk said. "You are no longer in Adelaide, I will not tell you were you are, but I can assure you, you are a long way from anything or anyone. No one will hear you scream and if you escape, which you won't, but if you do, it's hundreds of kilometres to the nearest town. We will find you before you reach it and you will be right back here. Am I understood?"

"I am not worried," Moghadam said. "Allah protects me and it's Imam, not Mister."

"Hope he turns up soon, for your sake," Hulk said as he walked over and drove his knife through Moghadam's forearm.

Moghadam screamed in pain and thrashed about in his chair as blood started dripping to the floor.

"Jesus Christ," Max said. "What the fuck are you doing?"

"I'm doing whatever it takes," Hulk said. "You need to be willing to as well."

Hulk grabbed the knife handle and twisted it in Moghadam's arm making him scream out again in pain.

"Where are the rest of your terrorist mates?" Hulk asked.

"They will die before they surrender and I will die before I give them up," Moghadam said.

Hulk ripped the knife out and stabbed it down into Moghadam's thigh. It pierced the skin and buried two inches deep into his leg.

"Fucking hell, Hulk," Max said as he paced back and forth trying to expel some of his nervous energy.

"I told them you were too fucking soft for this," Hulk said. "If I'm right, you can leave now."

Max stopped pacing and ran his hands through his hair, but he stayed in the shed.

"So, where are your friends?" Hulk asked.

"Please don't let him do this to me?" Moghadam said looking to Max. "Please."

"Tell him what he needs to know," Max said looking up at Moghadam. "And, the pain will stop."

"That's more like it, kid," Hulk said smiling and turning back to face Moghadam.

Hulk grabbed the knife and twisted it slowly in Moghadam's leg.

"You will tell me what I want to know," Hulk said still twisting the knife. "It is only a matter of time and pain, but you will tell me."

Over several hours, Hulk continued to torture Moghadam using various techniques while Max and Kate watched on until it was time for a break. Hulk and Kate left the shed and Max paced trying to collect his thoughts. *God, I'm not sure I can do this,* he thought to himself. *It is so brutal, so barbaric, do we really need to sink to their level to win?*

"Help me, please," Moghadam said interrupting his thoughts. "He is killing me while you watch on."

Max looked around the room and then to Moghadam, and for a moment questioned whether Moghadam had been reading his body language and if his thoughts had betrayed him.

"Did you do what he says you did?" Max asked.

"I was never going to go through with it. I was told I would be killed if I did not help."

"Why should I believe you?"

"Because I'm telling the truth. Please, can I have some water?"

Max walked over and grabbed the hose, turning it on and letting the water run on the ground next to Moghadam.

"You're thirsty hey?" Max asked. "Well, why don't you tell me why you just lied to me and then I'll give you some water."

"I did not lie."

"Oh yes, you did. I have been watching you for hours, Mr Moghadam, and what you don't know about me is that I study psychology and human behaviour, it is apparently one of the reasons they hired me. You were lying, so why don't you tell me where your comrades are and then I'll give you some water."

Max took a sip from the hose then wiped his mouth on his sleeve, as Moghadam moved his tongue over his dry lips in thirst, it had been more than a day since he had water.

"There are four of my men still in Adelaide and one in Sydney," Moghadam said.

"What are their names?" Max asked.

"Asfour, Awad, Qureshi and Toma are in Adelaide, and Haddad is in Sydney."

Max gave Moghadam a sip of water from the hose it was barely a few drops before he took it away.

"Please, I need some more water."

"You can have some more when you tell me exactly where they are."

"There is a safehouse not far from the Adelaide Airport, two kilometres north of the airport and three blocks east," Moghadam said. "And, there is another in Western Sydney near Parramatta Train Station, three blocks west. Now, please, can I have some water?"

Max gave Moghadam several mouthfuls of water from the hose then turned it off.

"I've told you everything I know, please don't let the other man back in here," Moghadam said.

"He doesn't work for me," Max said. "Quite the opposite, it'll be up to him what happens next."

Carter walked into the shed and called Max over.

"What are you doing?" Carter asked. "Hulk won't like you in here talking to the prisoner without him, let alone giving him water. For all we know, water deprivation could be part of the torture."

"That's better than the knife, that was barbaric," Max said.

"We do what we need to do, Prince, to keep people safe."

"But, don't we let them win when we lower ourselves to their level and when we become as savage as them?"

"It most cases, it is the only thing they understand. You saw what happened, he gave you names and locations. I have been doing this for a long time. It's not pleasant, but it works."

"Don't you have a duty, as a doctor, to look after people? Lachlan and I discussed it, the Hippocratic Oath."

"I believe I am adhering to the Oath, Max, or at least its modern-day version known as the Declaration of Geneva from the World Health Organisation. It particular, I would draw your attention to two lines – 'I solemnly pledge to consecrate my life to the service of humanity' and 'I will maintain the utmost respect for human life'. What we do helps to protect humanity and life, Max. The many over the few."

Max looked down at the ground and nodded his head slightly, as he shuffled on his feet.

"I'm sorry," Max said. "I hope I didn't offend you?"

"It's quite alright, Max," Carter said. "What you have witnessed here today is traumatic and you are right to question it. As a loving human being, especially one who is in love with a doctor-in-training, I would be more worried if you didn't question it, but I can assure you, it is necessary to get the information we need to save others from suffering, from injury and from death. Remember you said you wanted them to fear us, this is part of how we do it."

"I guess, I just wasn't expecting it to escalate so quickly and violently."

"What the fuck is going on in here?" Hulk said marching into the shed with Kate close behind.

"I was collecting my thoughts then I was going to follow you, but he spoke to me," Max said. "He asked me for some water."

"And you fucking gave it to him?" Hulk said his face beginning to turn red with anger.

"Yes," Max said.

"I told you he was too weak for this," Hulk said turning to face Carter.

"He didn't quite tell you the full story, Hulk," Carter said.

"There's more? Well, this better be good or you're done," Hulk said turning back to face Max.

"He gave me the names and locations of his cell."

Hulk looked at Carter.

"He showed a willingness to give Moghadam water, but only if he got the names first," Carter said. "And, he gave them up."

"Hmm, well, okay then, you better hope they are the real deal," Hulk said. "Hermes, call in it in."

"Already done, General," Blake said over the intercom.

Blake had been sitting in an observation room with Carter watching Max since the moment Hulk and Kate had left the shed.

"The chopper is ready out front when you are," Blake said.

"Well, don't just stand there holding your dick," Hulk said looking at Max. "Go gear up, time to put your skills to the test in the real world."

Chapter Nineteen

Max sat in the rear of the Landcruiser trying to control his thoughts and nerves. He was on his first real mission after all the training and he was anxious to say the least. Kate was driving and Hulk was in the passenger seat on his forth call since they hit the motorway. The AIS helicopter had taken them from the Wool Shed and had flown to Sydney. On the way, Blake had provided intel reports on the man Moghadam had named operating out of Western Sydney. Haddad bin Halil was Max's first target and a name he was sure he would never forget. His orders were to provide support to Hulk and Kate to capture Haddad, if possible, or kill him, if necessary.

"Thank you, Minister," Hulk said ending the call and putting his phone in his pocket. "The Defence Minister has confirmed the order."

"Good," Kate said. "Let's go get this fucking piece of shit."

"Our boys are already close to the house," Hulk said. "They have set up near the Parramatta Train Station and are waiting for us before they move."

"We're about ten out."

"What's the plan, Hulk?" Max asked.

"The AIS tactical team will surround the safehouse and Alpha will lead a team in through the rear door of the property. I will lead a second team in through the front. You will sit in the car and observe."

"I'm not going in with you?"

"No, you will observe. The training wheels aren't off yet."

"Okay," Max said.

"See boss," Kate said. "I told you he was ready, he took the order without complaint, even though he looks a bit pissed and sad about it. You should let him come in."

"No, this is too big and he is still training," Hulk said to Kate before turning back to face Max. "You have potential kid, but I can't risk my guys with a recruit who is still wet behind the ears. We all have to learn how to crawl before we can walk. Got that?"

"Yes, sir," Max said trying to hide his disappointment.

"Good lad," Hulk said turning back to face the front. "But, be ready for anything, these fuckers can be tricky."

Hulk, Kate and Max met the team a block down from the Parramatta Station. Max watched and listened as Hulk gave the team their orders. Max noticed how calm and practiced he was, and he saw something he had not seen since Hulk had first approached him at university asking him to consider joining AIS – he saw a kindness in Hulk's eyes as he looked at each of his team members. He realised Hulk was concerned for his troops, as he would have been every time he led soldiers into battle, and Max was hit with a wave of admiration for the hard-arse old General and respect for his role and experience. He also realised why he was being asked to sit aside, Hulk wanted him to be ready not only for his team's safety, but also for Max's own safety.

The team synchronised their watches, they were to breach in exactly six minutes. The two teams climbed into their respective four-wheel drives and parted ways. Kate with two AIS agents and Hulk with Max and two other AIS agents. Hulk's team paused two doors down from the safe house to give Kate's team time to get to the safehouse's backyard via the rear neighbour's yard.

A minute out, Hulk accelerated, and the big car leapt forward before braking hard outside the safehouse. Hulk and the two agents jumped down from the car and ran towards the house, each leaping a small picket fence before running for the front door. Max sat in the car watching the team move when, all of a sudden, he heard an explosion and saw smoke billowing from the rear of the house. His heart raced, the adrenaline coursing through his system making him fumble as he tried to undo his seatbelt, so he could get out and provide support, but before he could he heard a screech of tyres and turned to see a van racing towards the side of his car. It t-boned Max's

Landcruiser, causing it to flip as the wheels hit the gutter. It was resting on its side as the van jumped the gutter and hit it again, knocking it onto its roof. Max was thrown about inside, hitting his head hard against the window. He hung semi-conscious from the seatbelt trying to regain his focus. His vision was blurred and his ears were ringing, but he thought he heard gunfire. He turned to face the house and saw the two agents beside Hulk laying awkwardly, the agent on Hulk's left was face down in the grass and the other was sprawled out on the small staircase leading up to the safehouse's front door. Max's heart skipped a beat as he saw Hulk throw his MP5 down onto the grass and raise his hands above his head.

Max undid his seatbelt and fell out of his seat onto the roof, his big frame falling awkwardly in the small space. He tried to open the door, but it jammed, so he spun around and started kicking it, inch by inch it opened with each kick until it came completely free. The terrorist who had been driving the van was walking across the lawn aiming his pistol at Hulk, he turned around when he heard Max kick open the door and fired a number of shots into the Landcruiser's door and window. Max recoiled back into the car as the window shattered, showering him with glass. He looked around trying to come up with a plan and saw the window opposite had been smashed in the collision. He crept quietly across the roof and out the window into the street, and he made his way around behind the overturned car. His head ached and he felt dizzy, so he reached out to steady himself against the car, as the terrorist unloaded several more shots into the Landcruiser. Max closed his eyes and shook his head trying to clear it. *Come on, I just need one shot,* he thought to himself. He opened his eyes and his vision focused on the tailgate of the Landcruiser. He took a couple of short breaths then quickly ducked his head and right arm out from behind the big car. He found his target just inside the picket fence and fired two shots, head and chest. The terrorist dropped to the grass and Max came out from behind the Landcruiser searching for Hulk. He sighted him standing at the top of the front steps and his hands behind his head. *Something is wrong,* Max thought as he raised his gun in Hulk's direction.

Max watched over the sight of his MP5 as Hulk walked forward, dropping down the first step, as a man came into view behind him, too close for a shot at that distance.

"Put your weapon down, Agent," the man yelled.

"Fuck you," Max yelled back. "You put yours down."

"This is not a negotiation, Agent, put your gun down or I will shoot your friend here in the back of the head."

"If you do that and I will shoot you between the eyes before he hits the ground," Max said.

Hulk smiled noting Max's defiance and his willingness to do what it takes.

"Okay, tough guy," the terrorist said taking aim at Max over Hulk's shoulder and opening fire.

Max dived for cover behind the picket fence, scrambling along its length to make himself an even harder target. As he moved, so did the terrorist who had taken out a knife and held it under Hulk's throat dragging him back towards a car in the driveway. Max tried to get to a position to fire, but was forced back by bullets which were splintering the little wooden palings. When the gunfire stopped, Max jumped up and ran with his gun up facing the car. Hulk was sitting in the passenger seat, his hands handcuffed to the handhold in the roof above the door, obstructing Max's line of sight to the driver as the car reversed out the driveway, scraping hard on the bitumen as it sped out onto the road and down the street in reverse. Max could see Hulk yelling something at him, but he couldn't make it out. He couldn't make the shot without hitting Hulk, so he just held his aim. Max looked around searching for a car to give chase, but there were none in sight. The Landcruiser was on its roof and the van which had hit it was leaking coolant from under its crippled bonnet. The terrorist spun his car and took off down a side street. He felt hopeless as he watched the car speed off with his new boss in the passenger seat.

Fuck, Kate, I hope she is okay, he thought as he ran for the backyard. He kicked open a tall gate at the side of the house and ran to the backyard with his gun at the ready. As he swept around the corner, he saw the whole rear section of the house was on fire and a large hole had been ripped open in the back wall where the backdoor and deck had once stood. The AIS agents were on opposite sides of the yard several metres from the flaming wall. They were both terribly burnt and not moving. Max scanned the yard and found Kate back near the fence laying in the garden next to a massive rottweiler. He ran over and dropped down beside her.

"Alpha," Max said grabbing her shoulders.

Max felt for a pulse taking a few seconds to find it then he lent down and listened to her breathing and watched her chest rising and falling. He checked for other injuries, but thankfully could not find any.

"Kate!" Max yelled shaking her by the shoulders.

Kate began to stir as a low growl sent a chill up Max's spine. He stole a quick glance over his shoulder at the big rottweiler which was on its feet gnawing and gnashing its teeth, and beginning to foam at the mouth. Max very slowly moved his hidden hand to reach for his gun without taking his eyes off the dog, but before he got the chance to fire, a small stick like object flew over his head and hit the dog on the nose. The dog stopped growling and searched the ground for the object, which it found seconds later and started chewing on it wildly.

"The way to every male's heart, I'm told," Kate said laughing.

"I guess so," Max said finally realising she had tossed the dog a treat. "You had that on you?"

"No," Kate laughed. "I found them on near the kennel over there."

"What happened?" Max asked.

"We jumped over and made our way towards the door, when this big slobbering arsehole started barking and ran for us. We scattered and I just happened to run towards the kennel and found the treats near the fence. As it was about to launch at one of our guys, I whistled and showed him the treat and he ran up the yard towards me. I signalled for the boys to go in, while I had it distracted. I remember seeing them reach the top step, but that's it, then a handsome prince woke me up. Did we get Haddad? Where is Hulk?"

"We were burnt. Hulk's been taken and the other four agents are dead. I took one of the terrorists out, but Haddad had Hulk in my line of sight and had me pinned down behind the fence."

"It's okay, Max," Kate said. "It sounds like you did everything you needed and could do. We need to call in."

Max helped Kate to her feet as she reached for her mobile and called Blake to relay what happened.

"Hermes, it's Alpha," Kate said as the phone connected. "I'm here with Prince, we've been burnt. Haddad's gone and he's got Hulk. Our team's dead."

"Acknowledged Alpha, please standby," Blake said.

Kate and Max stood staring down at the smart phone and listened to the chaos unfolding as Blake was yelling orders to the teams.

"Alpha, you there?" Blake asked.

"Here, mate," Kate said. "What are our orders?"

"With Hulk out of action, Shadow will take command. It will be up to him. I've started a track on Hulk's phone, he might not have it on him, but we might get lucky."

"Is Shadow there now?" Kate asked.

"No, he's en route. He's been in town briefing the Defence Minister and Prime Minister on Haddad and the Adelaide cell."

"Hermes, it's Prince," Max said. "How long until you know where Hulk's phone is?"

"Not long, I suggest you two get to the Bunker and await orders."

"Roger that," Kate said.

"Hermes?" Max said.

"Yes?"

"Can you please call us when you know where the phone is?"

"Yes, Prince," Blake said ending the call.

Max and Kate climbed over the back fence as sirens started to approach in the distance and neighbours were tentatively venturing out into the street to see what was happening. They hustled into Kate's Landcruiser and headed towards the AIS Bunker in Western Sydney. En route they got a call from Blake.

"The phone is still moving," Blake said. *"It's travelling along the Western Motorway towards Penrith."*

"We have to follow it," Max said. "We have to find Hulk."

"No, Prince," Blake said. *"Shadow wants you back here for a debrief."*

"That's bullshit, Blake," Max said. "We are close, we should follow and at least see if it's him."

"Codenames, Prince," Blake said. *"Shadow has given an order."*

"I don't know him, but I know Hulk and I know what he would do if it was one of us," Max said. "He'd come get us."

Blake sat in silence for a moment considering Max's point. On one hand he was right, Hulk would go to the ends of the earth to protect his agents, but on the other he had been given an order.

"You might be right, Prince, but we've got our orders," Blake said. *"I can't overturn them."*

"No one is asking you to mate," Max said. "Just let us know where he is and tell them we're coming in – as ordered. If they ask, I'll tell them you ordered us back and I ignored you. I'm just a stupid rookie."

"He's right, Hermes," Kate said. "We're best placed."

"I'm not sure about this," Blake said.

"We'll just find and follow them, then we'll report in," Kate said. "We won't make a move without backup."

"If you follow him you are to remain out of sight and you're not to engage," Blake said. *"Find him and then call it in. Got it?"*

"Roger, mate," Max said looking over to Kate. "Send us the map."

A few seconds later, the car's navigation system came on and a map with a little blue blinking dot appeared, before a route was highlighted. Kate slammed her foot down to chase the getaway car.

Chapter Twenty

In small suburban house in Western Sydney, Hulk sat duct taped to a chair. Blood dripped from his mouth and nose, and one of his eyes was closing over from the beating he had received, but he had yet to utter a single word to his captors.

"General Scott," Haddad said. "We know who you are and where you work. We also know you have captured our brother, Moghadam. Your team is dead and soon you will join them in the afterlife. Why not save yourself some pain and tell us where you are holding him, and I'll put a bullet in your head and be done with you."

Hulk said nothing, just sat staring Haddad in the eyes. He did not blink, just stared, trying to irritate him. It seemed to be working.

"Fine, we'll do it your way," Haddad said walking from the room.

Hulk took the chance to look around the room to see if there was anything he could use to escape. His knife and gun were on the other side of the room, but he could not get there taped to the chair, he could not get any momentum without alerting his captors. He strained against the tape trying to break it, but it was no use, they had layered it thick around his wrists and ankles.

Haddad came back into the room. He was a short man and had a wiry frame, especially compared to Hulk, although Hulk made even big men look relatively small in comparison. Haddad was wearing a loose-fitting pair of black linen pants and a white linen shirt which looked three sizes too big for him, but disturbingly, he was also now wearing a plastic apron and face shield which sat flapped open like a baseball cap visor. Ominously, he was also carrying a toolbox which he sat on the table next to Hulk's gun and knife.

"You know where this is going, General," Haddad said opening the toolbox without turning back to Hulk. "I am going to hurt you, a great deal, until you tell me what I want to know. Where is Moghadam and what does AIS know about our plans?"

Hulk sat in silence trying to mentally prepare for what was coming. Unlike Max, Hulk's determination was driven by hate, not love. He hated everything about men like Haddad and used it to shield him from breaking point, but he knew everyone broke, it was just a matter of time, and he was willing to drag this out until the bitter end.

"I hear some of your peers think you are God-like," Haddad said. "Well, one of my favourite Demigods was Achilles, let's see if you carry the same weakness."

Haddad rifled around in the toolbox and Hulk heard a couple of clicks, like a cartridge or magazine being loaded, then Haddad turned around wielding a nail-gun. Hulk began to breath in and out quickly and an anger burned in his eyes as if saying 'do your worst'. Haddad walked over and fired a nail through Hulk's left boot and left ankle, severing the Achilles tendon before piercing through the other side of the boot dripping with blood. Hulk thrust about in the chair and gritted his teeth, but he did not scream or speak. He kept his laser-like focus squarely on Haddad, the anger burning hotter in his eyes.

"You are a tough man," Haddad said walking back to the toolbox. "But, even the mighty Achilles fell, as you will. This is a heat-gun, General, seen one before?"

Haddad waved it around like a pistol.

"It generates a lot of heat to melt, blister and strip paint. That is one of the benefits of buying this little house, it needs renovations, so we invested in the best equipment. The combat gear you are wearing is no doubt tough and I am sure pretty resistant to some high temperatures, but I have been wondering, how long do you think it will last before it melts, exposing your skin? Let us find out."

He held the heat-gun above Hulk's abdominals and just below his right pectoral. The fabric of the combat shirt started to smoke within the first minute and Hulk could feel it starting to burn his skin. He clenched his teeth and stared with rage at

Haddad. After ninety seconds, the shirt started to melt, and Hulk felt the melting shirt and the intense heat from the gun burning and blistering his skin. Smoke poured into the air filling it with the smell of burning flesh and fabric. Hulk was squirming in his chair and trying with all his might to bust the tape holding his wrists. He was picturing choking the life from Haddad, but this time he did scream from the pain, which caused Haddad to smile and laugh, then he turned the gun off and watched the smoke swirling around Hulk's red face. He mockingly blew the smoke from the end of the gun, before resting its red-hot barrel on Hulk's right arm. It smoked as his flesh melted and Hulk again groaned in pain.

"Sir, it is him," one of Haddad's men said coming into the room and handing him a phone.

"Yes?" Haddad said and he listened intently for a minute. "Thank you."

Haddad handed the phone back to his man.

"Make the preparations," Haddad said. "Then come and takeover here, I need to leave."

"Yes, sir," the man said before leaving the room.

"General, I'm really sorry, but I have to go," Haddad said. "It seems your team has taken out our cell in Adelaide and I have been given orders to bring forward my own cell's plans here in Sydney. So, you might have won one little victory in Adelaide, but I can assure you, you will lose even bigger here in Sydney. What comes next is on you?"

"So, why don't you tell me what is coming?" Hulk asked. "Your friend is coming back in here to kill me anyway."

"The man finally speaks, it seems, General, that the best way to torture you is not through physical pain, but mental. So no, I will not tell you what is coming, but I will tell my men to try to keep you alive long enough to witness it. Although, they have been known to go a bit overboard with the torture. They killed the last agent of yours we captured far too soon. Hopefully, they will show you some restraint, but I would not count on it."

"Why don't you do it yourself you, big pussy?"

"Nice try, General," Haddad said walking from the room. "Do not die too quickly."

Chapter Twenty-One

After thirty minutes, the blue dot had stopped moving and Max gave Kate the address. She navigated through the side streets for an hour and parked two blocks down from the location pinged by Hulk's mobile phone.

"We need to see if he's there," Max said in the suddenly silent car.

"What do you want to do, go put your nose against the window, it would be suicide?" Kate said.

"Maybe," Max said. "Do you have any better ideas?"

"We should call it in and speak to Blake, he and Shadow will give us our orders."

"What's he like?"

"Who?"

"Shadow."

"He's a tough old son-of-a-bitch."

"So, I can't imagine he'll take this well?"

"No, he is going to be pissed we ignored his orders."

"So, why did you let me?"

"Because you were right."

"Yeah, it was the right thing to do, Hulk's in trouble."

"Yes. Let's just hope they all see it that way, otherwise we are going to be in the shit."

"Well, if that's the case, I vote we don't call it in just yet, let's wait for them to call us and if it goes to shit, I'll take the blame."

"No way, I'm in this too, Prince, but let's not do anything too stupid and when we need to, we will call it in."

"Agreed," Max said opening his door.

"Where are you going?"

"I'm going to take a sneak peek through the window."

"I said nothing stupid."

"It's only stupid if I get caught."

"Look, I fucking hate these guys more than you do kid and I've known Hulk for a lot longer, but that's just crazy."

"Yeah, probably," Max said as he stepped out, closed the door with a gentle click and headed for the house where he thought Hulk was being held, leaving Kate in the car.

Max got to the neighbouring house and decided to venture into that little yard. A small broken concrete walkway led down beside the house framing an overgrown weedy strip of grass with the wooden fence between the two properties. Max climbed into the long grass and peered through the cracks in the fence at the house holding his boss. The windows were covered by stale yellowing bedsheets which had been draped like curtains inside the house, obstructing his view, and he saw the paint was pealing among other issues that needed fixing on the house. He rustled quietly through the long grass, glancing through the fence when a hole or slit large enough appeared.

Still no signs of life.

In the backyard, he found a spot and crouched down to get a view of the neighbouring house through a hole created by a knot in the wood which had long since fallen free and he waited, watching and listening. There were some faint sounds, but nothing he could make out over the sound of the nearby roads, but then the hairs on his arm stood up as he felt something coming at him from the left. He spun instinctively and drew his silenced pistol, aiming for the source of the sound.

"Jesus Christ," Kate said before kneeling beside him. "It's just me."

"Sorry," Max said lowering his weapon. "The sheets are blocking the view. Nothing to report in as yet."

"Shadow just called and wants us back at the bunker. He sounded really pissed off."

"I don't understand why he wants us back there so badly, his boss and friend is being held and most likely tortured. Why not let us do some recon?"

"I don't know, Max, but," Kate said but was interrupted by the sound of a car leaving the house next door.

"Did you see who was in that?" Max asked.

"No, fuck, it sped off too quickly."

"Maybe we should call it in, Prince," Kate said.

Max was about to speak when a gunshot rang out from the house next door.

"Fuck this," Max said redrawing his pistol and in two quick moves hurled himself over the wooden fence.

"What the fuck, Prince?" Kate said through the wooden palings.

"I'm going in, with or without you."

"Oh fuck me," Kate said, before copying Max's acrobatics, launching herself over the fence before drawing her own pistol.

Max was already at the backdoor, trying the handle. It turned, so he quietly opened the door and crept into the empty kitchen. In the hallway running between the bedrooms and the lounge he found his first target. A man in his thirties, tanned skin with a short black beard, loose linen clothing and clutching a pistol in his right hand. Max held up a finger to his lips letting Kate know there was a target ahead. He holstered his gun and withdrew his hunting knife. The new blade glistened as it slid from its leather case. He briefly paused. This was his second kill, but the first up close and personal. He cleared his mind, before slapping his left head around covering the target's mouth and pulling his head back awkwardly. His righthand was already moving and it sliced deep and hard into the target's exposed throat. Blood dripped down over the knife as the target slumped and Max caught his weight and silently lowered him to the floor. The target had been standing in front of a doorway which lead to a set of stairs up to the second storey. Kate used hand signals to indicate she would sweep the ground floor. Max gave an acknowledged signal before indicating his intent to go upstairs. As he hit the second step another shot was fired from upstairs. They exchanged worried looks before breaking, Max took the stairs two at a time until he reached the small hallway leading to three rooms. He cleared the first, then the second and slowly, stealthily he moved to the third. He snuck a quick look around the doorframe and saw Hulk tied to an old wooden dining room chair near the window. A man dressed similarly to the guy downstairs was pacing back and forth in front of Hulk. Hulk looked in bad shape.

"You will tell me what AIS knows of our operations," the man said. "You will be used to barter for Moghadam's life and, if you are lucky, you will be traded for him. If not, I will kill you?"

Hulk had spent his time tied to the chair in silence since Haddad left, but on seeing Max's head around the doorframe he decided he had had enough of the silent treatment.

"Well, you got me," Hulk said. "Haddad couldn't do it, but you have, you broke me. I'm impressed. Although there is something you should know."

"Oh and what's that?"

"I might be injured and bleeding out, but I'll be the one staring down at your corpse before today is through and laughing knowing there's one less terrorist piece of shit in the world."

"Is that right, well," the man began but was silenced as a bullet slammed into the back of his head and exploded from the front of his face.

For a few seconds, Hulk watched his lifeless body standing in place, before it crumpled to its knees then fell to the carpet. Max was standing with his gun drawn the barrel pointing at him.

"No need for the second one son, you got him," Hulk said.

"Jesus," Max asked taking in Hulk's wounds.

He was bleeding from the ankle and what looked like a nail through his boot. He had a bullet wound in the left thigh, a burn on his right arm and a sickening burn, the black and red melted skin was showing through the hole in his shirt, on his stomach. Then Max noticed his left shoulder, blood was pouring from a small hole. At first, he thought it was another bullet wound, but then he saw the bloodied drill laying on the floor next to Hulk.

"Oh fuck," Max said running over and pulling down the stained curtain behind Hulk.

He ripped a strip from it and stuffed it into the shoulder, trying to keep pressure on it, causing Hulk to grimace.

"Are you okay?" Max said.

"I've been shot and tortured, but otherwise I'm just fantastic, Prince. How are you?"

"I'm a little shaken, but in comparison, I guess I can't complain."

"Well, you should have shot that arsehole through the car window like I was yelling for you to do in the yard, then maybe I wouldn't be fucking sitting here bleeding out," Hulk said. "But for what it's worth, thank you for coming after me."

"Shadow ordered us back, so I think I'm going to be in his bad books."

"Well, what you did wasn't exactly by the books, but sometimes it's not about that, it's about the result. Sometimes we have to break the rules. Wait, you said us, who is with you, where is the rest of our team?"

Kate walked through the door and at first, smiled at her boss before seeing his wounds.

"Good to see you're still with us, boss," Kate said looking down then laying a boot into Haddad's man. "Unlike this lifeless fuck."

"And, you too, Kate," Hulk said. "How's our team?"

"They're all dead, sir. I'm sorry."

"Shit. They knew we were coming. Haddad got a phone call warning him to get out. There's a rat somewhere in the ranks. Get me out of this fucking chair."

Kate ripped a long piece from the curtain and wrapped his thigh.

"We have to get you to the hospital," Kate said. "Where's the second bullet hole?"

"It was a warning shot," Hulk said nodding at the wall beside him. "He put the first shot into the wall to try to frighten me."

"Well, it might have been a warning for you, but it was like a starter's pistol for Prince. He leapt the neighbour's fence and was in here fast, Hulk. We did good with this one. Two confirmed kills on day one."

"Yeah, thank you both."

"Honestly boss, if it was me, I would have followed orders and headed for the bunker. Max encouraged me to ignore Shadow. He's going to be pissed."

"That's okay, you let me handle Shadow."

"Okay," Kate said cutting the tape on Hulk's wrists and ankles, when she saw the nail for the first time. "Oh fucking hell, we have to get you to the hospital."

"No, take me to the AIS bunker. The med-team there can deal with all this."

"They aren't equipped for this level of damage."

"Just do," Hulk said slumping unconscious in the chair.

"Get the car," Max said as he tried to wake Hulk.

Kate ran down the stairs as Max lifted Hulk up over his shoulder. He descended the stairs and ran into the front yard, down the small broken concrete path and kicked open the little gate. Kate skidded the Landcruiser's tyres, stopping it beside Max. He opened the door and as gently as possible rested Hulk in the backseat before climbing in the other side next to him. As the door closed, Kate accelerated, heading for the hospital.

"Hermes," Max said as his phone connected. "We've got him. We're en route to the hospital, he's in bad shape."

"Acknowledged, Prince," Blake said. *"What's your status?"*

"Alpha and I are fine. There are two dead terrorists at the address where the trace led us. Haddad escaped. Hulk thinks we might have an inside man. This is now the second time they've got the drop on us."

"Jesus."

"You're the only one I trust, Blake, can you think of anyone acting strangely?"

"No, but we've been out of here for weeks, at the Wool Shed. I'll keep an eye out."

"Thanks mate."

"Is that them," Lloyd said.

"Yes, sir," Blake said.

"Prince, this is Shadow," Lloyd said. *"We have not had the pleasure of meeting yet, but let me tell you, you have firmly placed yourself on my shit list and it's not a list you want to be on."*

"Let me cut you off there, sir," Max said. "We've got Hulk. He was being tortured and he's in a bad way. He's been shot, burned, bashed, he has a nail shot through one of his ankles and he had a hole drilled into his shoulder. So, with all due respect, you can save your lectures for someone who cares. We got him out. He'd be dead if we followed your orders. If you want to hold that against me, feel free, but I'll sleep soundly."

Max ended the call.

"Oh fuck, Max," Kate said. "Did you just hang up on him?"

"Yep, fuck that guy."

"He is the second-in-command of AIS and you're a new recruit. No one speaks to him like that."

"I just told it like it was, if he's pissed it should be at himself, not me. I'd do it all again in a heartbeat and if that gets me thrown out, well, so be it. As I said, I'll sleep easy knowing we got Hulk out of there. He should be thankful we saved his friend. Arsehole."

"That's all true, Max, and I'd do it again too. Hulk means a lot to me. I was just shocked that's all. Over a decade in the military following orders, you know?"

"Yeah, I get it. I'd be a terrible solider."

"Yeah, but I think you're going to be a great spy."

"Thanks, Kate."

Kate pulled up in the emergency department at the Parramatta Hospital and ran inside to get a wheel chair as Max climbed out and started to pull Hulk from the rear of the car. Max sat Hulk in the chair and they ran into the hospital calling for help. Doctors and nurses came running, as worried onlookers recoiled at the sight of Hulk slumped in the chair with his various wounds. The nurses wheeled in a bed and helped Max lift him onto it, before they rushed off towards an operating room as Max told them of the known injuries and how long he had been unconscious, he also explained they were federal agents. Max left the room as the doctors and nurses started preparing Hulk for surgery, attaching numerous wires, oxygen mask and cut free his clothing.

Chapter Twenty-Two

"It's me," Haddad said into his mobile phone. "I am on my way to the facility. Has Uri delivered the vials?"

"Yes, he has left them with your man on the ground," Wright said. *"He seemed upset about something. Do you know what it might have been?"*

"Do not worry about it."

"I'm not sure where you get off telling me what to worry about or not."

"It is all under control, relax."

"You relax. How are we progressing with Moghadam?"

"Everything is on schedule."

"Even so, do we know who has him?"

"AIS."

"The Australian Intelligence Service has him?"

"Yes."

"God have mercy."

"Hold your nerve, Archbishop."

"What if they find us?"

"They will not. You need to calm down."

"How can you be so sure?"

"I have General Patrick Scott the Head of AIS in my custody. They don't know anything."

"In your custody, what the hell are you talking about?"

"Nothing. Do not worry about it, relax."

"I am worried about it and stop telling me to relax. I think it is time for me to take over. I am worried you are going to make mistakes, like capturing the Head of AIS."

"You should know, Benjamin, the reason Uri was nervous."

"What?"

"I am the reason Uri was nervous."

"Why?"

"I have his family and the family of his aide, Abbas, in my custody. I told them I would kill the families if they did not go through with the plan."

"Jesus."

"Isn't that blasphemy in your religion?"

"Shut your mouth, Haddad. I am taking over. Release the families."

"What would you like me to do with the General?"

"He is your problem, you fix it. Daniel will be at the facility in an hour to pick up the devices, including those for Uri."

"Anything else, Your Grace, wishes?"

"Don't be a smartarse. We need to move forward our plans."

"When did you have in mind?"

"Hours, not days or weeks."

"Fine by me. We are ready."

"Good. Let's just get this done."

"Yes, sir," Haddad said as the line went dead. "Fucking idiot."

Chapter Twenty-Three

Max and Kate were sitting in the waiting area while Hulk was being operated on. They had been there for a couple of hours. Nervous patients and visitors had looked them up and down when they walked into the room dressed in their tactical gear. Max looked up and was surprised to see Flash and Blake walk into the waiting room, similarly dressed.

"What are you two doing here?" Max asked shaking their hands.

"We've got a couple of leads to chase down," Blake said. "Thought you two would want in."

"Fucking oath we do," Kate said making a couple of people hesitantly look at the team. "He's going to be under for a little while yet and I'd love to get my hands on these fuckers."

"Let's go, we'll fill you in en route," Blake said leading them out to the cars. "How's Hulk?"

"Doctor says he's pretty beaten up but nothing they can't handle," Max said. "As Kate said, he'll be out for a few hours, plenty of time to go find Haddad, that son of a bitch."

"We used the satellite to track his vehicle," Blake said as they climbed into Kate's car. "It drove around for over an hour, constantly changing direction and circling back, obviously looking for anyone who might be following him."

"But, we've got a location?"

"Yes," Blake said taking off his ring and placing it into a recess behind the volume knob in the car's entertainment system.

Access key recognised. Welcome, Hermes, scrolled onto the little screen. Max and Flash looked at each other, surprised by the new technology. Blake pressed a button to bring up a saved location on the satellite navigation system and started the guidance. A map appeared and Kate started following the blue line to Haddad's location.

"Where is that?" Max asked. "Darling harbour?"

"Just a couple of blocks back," Blake said. "Looks like some sort of warehouse."

"We're going in after him?" Flash asked.

"Yes, Shadow, although extremely pissed at Max, authorised the mission," Blake said. "Oh and you're going to need these."

Blake turned around and handed Max and Flash a silver ring each, like the one he had put into the car's dashboard.

"Welcome to the AIS," Blake said. "These rings are individualised security access keys. They will allow you access to AIS facilities and vehicles, and they are coded to secretly store data transferred via AIS mobile or tablets. They also activate AIS weapons. Our guns will not fire unless they detect the ring. It is a built-in safety feature, in case the weapon is lost or taken in a struggle. These are normally given to agents on graduation from the program at a little ceremony we have at our head office in Canberra. Hulk authorised both of yours to be created and Shadow told me to hand them over. I'm sure Hulk wishes he could have presented them to you personally and to officially welcome you to the team, but for now let me say on his behalf, well done on completing the Wool Shed. You are now among a very small number of people in the world, who share a very specialised set of skills and training, and an even smaller number of Australians who are tasked with defending our nation, allies and interests at home and abroad from threats. Welcome to the Australian Intelligence Service. Good luck and Godspeed."

"Hear, fucking, hear!" Kate said. "Well done, boys."

"Thanks," Max said taking the ring and placing it on his right ring finger.

"Thanks," Flash said putting his ring on the middle finger on his left hand.

Max and Flash smiled and congratulated each other and shook hands.

"There will be time after all of this to celebrate properly, but for now let's focus on finding Haddad and stopping whatever it is he is up to," Blake said turning back to make a call.

The car wove its way through traffic and down towards Sydney Harbour. Blake had confirmed the car had not left the warehouse and they were authorised to go in. A few blocks out Kate stopped the car and the four agents went to the back to gear up. Blake opened the rear door then removed a small panel on the wall inside the storage space of the Landcruiser. Inside was an electronic keypad and he entered a four-digit combination unlocking the weapons' hold. The floor lifted up on little hydraulic arms revealing a collection of gear. Blake and Flash filled their tactical vests, while Kate and Max refilled theirs. Blake handed Max a new pistol and MP5, and took two weapons for himself. Kate and Flash took their own guns from the moulded foam inlay within the Landcruiser's boot. They each pushed a comms unit into their ears, pulled on balaclavas and headed for the warehouse.

"Testing," Blake said.

"Copy," they each said one after the other.

"Prince, Alpha," Blake said. "You two flank right through the door. Flash, you and I will head left."

They each acknowledged the direction and shouldered their weapons in sight of the warehouse. They entered the grounds of the warehouse. Finding no targets, they proceeded to the main door, which Blake was about to open, when bullets slammed into the inside of the door and shattered its small window, showering glass down on Blake. Kate looked around and saw a security camera on the corner of the warehouse aimed straight at them. She fired a single shot and it exploded sending sparks, plastic, glass and electronics into the air and cascading to the ground. Blake gave a signal to Max and Kate to head around the warehouse to the right. He and Flash were going to go through the main door in sixty seconds. Max and Kate broke to the right and followed the path leading down beside the warehouse. Max was leading with his MP5 pressed tightly against his right shoulder, when up ahead a door opened and three men ran out. Two were carrying Uzis while the third had a pistol in one hand and a small silver metal briefcase in the other hand. One of the Uzi welding men turned to face Max and opened fire. The rapid fire drew a line along the dirt several metres in front of Max before tearing a line of bullet holes in the thin metal wall of the warehouse as Max nailed him between the eyes and in the chest and he fell to the ground. The second Uzi carrying man had turned to back to face Max, shielding the guy with the briefcase who took off running down the yard. He was sacrificing himself to put distance between Max and the briefcase. Max and Kate dived in separate directions as the bullets smashed into the stone path which they had been walking on. Max and Kate fired as they both hit the ground and two bullets simultaneously hit the blocker in the head, throwing it back with violent force and taking him off his feet. Max saw the man with the briefcase reach the back fence of the compound and start to climb over it.

"Go get that fucking arsehole, Prince," Kate said. "I'll help these two."

"You got it," Max said running at full pace towards the back fence.

He fired two shots that hit the fence and one that hit a tree just past the guy with the briefcase who had dropped to the other side of the fence and looked back towards Max and smiled. It was Haddad. He ran off through the big manufacturing plant yard next door as Max hit the fence. Max slung his MP5 over his back, put one foot out on the middle of the fence and used his momentum to leap to the top of the metal frame and haul himself up. He rolled over the top and as his feet hit the ground, he drew his pistol and gave chase, covering the ground with incredible speed, dodging a forklift as he ran. The driver slammed on the brakes and swore as he watched Max in his full tactical gear and balaclava run past and into the plant through the same door Haddad had used.

Inside the noise was deafening as conveyor belts rushed in every direction carrying bottles. One row running level with his head was rushing past, empty bottles heading down the length of the factory. A row at his waist was rushing back in the opposite direction completely full. Max noticed the shape of the bottles and labels and realised he was in a beer bottling facility, a local brew he had enjoyed a few times. Two empty bottles exploded next to his head throwing glass over him, he ducked for cover behind the waist high conveyor, stealing a glance through the bottles to see Haddad running for a side door. Max returned fire but missed Haddad as he stepped around a crate of beer cartons. Max ran after Haddad, but watched helplessly as he gunned down two workers in white coats who had crossed his path. Screams rang out over the machinery as other workers saw their colleagues get hit. Some came to help as Haddad kept running, until they saw Max. Two big guys blocked his path, readying to confront him, brave, but stupid.

"Federal Agent!" Max yelled. "Get out of the way!"

They did not move so he fire a shot into the ground at their feet and they stepped aside. He ran between them and told them to call an ambulance. Max tried to line up Haddad in the distance, but he kept pulling civilians into Max's line of fire, so he waited and ran harder, yelling at people to clear the way. He saw Haddad run through a door at the far end of the plant. Just before he got to it, Max paused, and used the door frame for cover. He ducked his head out to look for Haddad and two rounds struck the metal frame next to his face. He pulled back behind the wall and took the moment to get his breath back. He checked again, but Haddad as gone. He ran through the door and several workers from the factory stopped in their tracks on seeing Max.

"Federal Agent!" Max yelled over the sound of the machinery. "Where did he go?"

"That way," one of the men said pointing down the street.

"Thank you," Max said running out into the street.

He saw Haddad running behind a row of cars on the opposite side of the street using them for cover. The road ran down a hill ending beside the exhibition centre. There were large concrete barricades at the end to stop cars from getting access, but there was pedestrian access onto the boardwalk lining Darling Harbour. Max felt a cold chill thinking about the thousands of people who would be down at the harbour.

"I've got Haddad," Max said into his comms unit. "He's heading for Darling Harbour with some sort of briefcase."

"Copy, Prince," Blake said through his earpiece. *"Flash is en route to provide support. Alpha and I need to stay on site, we've got two in custody and bunch of information to sort through. I've called it in and two teams are on their way, one to you and one to me. Try not to let him out of your sight."*

"Ack," Max said ducking behind a car as a bullet smashed into the window.

"Prince, do you copy? Are you okay?" Blake asked hearing the gunshot.

"Yeah, this arsehole is firing at me again."

"Be careful."

"I'll try my best. I'll get back to you soon."

"Good luck and Godspeed, Prince."

"And, to you. Out."

Max ran down the footpath chasing Haddad who turned back occasionally to check where Max was and to fire, if he had a shot. Max did not fire because the distance was too great and he did not want to risk hitting someone walking out of a yard or business between them. Max watched as Haddad raised his gun into the air and opened fired wildly as he ran out onto the boardwalk. Max saw people running for their lives and then his blood turned cold as Haddad started opening fire into the crowd. He ran harder, but tried in vein to stop in his tracks, as a delivery truck reversed out from under the exhibition centre into his path. He ran into it, jumping at the last second and turning his shoulder in to take the impact, causing a bang and it stopped, blocking his way. He was stuck between the exhibition centre wall, the truck and a parked car. He jumped up on the bonnet of the car and leapt off running as fast as his legs would carry him, when his boots hit the street. He had lost Haddad, but ran the remaining metres down onto the boardwalk. People were crying and screaming, but when they saw Max they had one of two reactions, they either ran or froze in horror on the spot, fearing a repeat of what they had just witnessed.

"Where did he go?" Max asked one of the old men frozen in his place. "I'm a Federal Agent. That man is a terrorist, I need to stop him."

The old man could not speak, but looked to his right. Max followed his gaze and saw a trail of bodies and blood laying on the path. Some kind and brave people had stopped to provide first-aid to those injured. Max could hear the pain in their voices and cries. Max took off in the direction Haddad had obviously gone causing more people to panic and flee as they saw him. Sun was shimmying on the beautiful harbour and Max saw people on the far side stopping and staring trying to figure out what was happening. He ran past a couple giving CPR to a victim only a metre away from the water's edge. He felt angry and sad, but it was serving only to make him more determined. He was going to stop Haddad.

The trail of bodies and misery seemed to stop leading up to a mall on Max's left, so he headed in. Inside screams echoed on the glass and tiles, furniture had been overturned and a café sat empty as Max saw one of the waiters laying still in the centre of the dining area. His eyes open staring, devoid of life. Max felt guilty for not getting there sooner, maybe he could have saved this innocent young guy who was probably only a year or two younger than him. Max got to the other end of the mall and had not seen Haddad. He ran out into the sunshine looking for him, but all he found was a team of five police officers training their guns on him.

"Put down your weapons!" the oldest of the police officers yelled. "And get down on the ground!"

"I'm a Federal Agent!" Max yelled. "I'm pursuing a terrorist who shot all of those people."

"You heard me, put your gun down or we will open fire!"

"He's going to get away!"

"You have one last chance, throw down your gun and get on the ground or we will take you down!"

"Okay," Max said throwing his gun down and lying on the landing above the concrete steps of the mall. "But, at least send some of your guys in to check the mall."

"You just came from in there, a good Federal Agent would have seen the gunman, unless he's a liar and it was him who did it," the policeman said as two of his men came over and handcuffed Max.

"You are making a massive mistake," Max said as one of the two cops dropped a knee into his back taking the wind out of him as the other flexi-cuffed him.

"Or I'm making the arrest of my career."

"If anything happens, it'll be on you," Max coughed as the officers started removing his vest. "You will regret this."

Max was still lying face down on the concrete as he watched the crowd gather to applaud the police officers for arresting a suspect, then he saw Haddad smiling broadly at him through the crowd.

"Stop that man!" Max yelled towards Haddad. "You've got the wrong man, that's him there!"

"Sure it is," the policeman said not even bothering to look.

Haddad laughed, turned and walked off. Max tried to watch where he went, but the crowd was in the way. He was gone. *Fuck it,* Max thought to himself.

A few minutes later, there was a commotion to Max's right and he turned his head to see what it was. The crowd was murmuring and parting as five figures dressed like Max moved down the boardwalk towards Max. As the last of the crowd parted, Max saw the tactical gear and weapons, and Flash, leading the way. He had removed his balaclava, but the rest of his team were wearing them.

"Who is in charge here?" Flash asked as the policeman turned to face him.

"I am," he said. "Who's asking?"

"AIS," Flash said noticing Max on the ground. "Get him up."

Two of the guys with Flash ran over to Max and started cutting the cuffs.

"What the hell do you think you are doing?" the cop asked.

"I am a Federal Agent, I work for the Australian Intelligence Service, known as AIS. This man is one of our agents. He was in pursuit of a suspect. Where is the other man?"

"He took off, Flash, about two minutes ago," Max said. "Disappeared into the crowd, heading north, I couldn't see where he went because Captain Fuckwit here had me tied down and the crowd got in the way."

"You two head up and see if you can find a trail," Flash said to the other two of his guys before turning back to the policeman who was starting to sweat. "You are in a great deal of trouble."

Max got to his feet and gave the officer who had kneed him in the back a filthy look. Flash explained the situation to the cop as Max put his gear back in his vest, holstered his weapons and pressed the comms unit back into his ear. He heard the two team members looking for Haddad calling in their search.

"Prince, Flash, do you copy?" one of the team members said.

"Copy," Max said.

"We've got a couple of witnesses saying he went into the casino. Do you want us to follow?"

"Yes," Max said. "We'll meet you at the security office."

"Ack. Yes, sir."

"Hermes, did you hear that?" Max asked.

"Roger, Prince," Blake said. *"Watch your back."*

"Will do. Found anything at the warehouse?"

"Alpha is working on one of the guys and our backup team arrived and they're sweeping the place. I'll keep you updated. You do the same."

"Will do, out," Max said turning to Flash. "Let's move, Flash."

"Alright," Flash said. "Let's go and you lot better come too."

Max and Flash started jogging for the casino with the two AIS agents and the police team following.

Chapter Twenty-Four

"It's me," Haddad said into his mobile phone. "AIS found me at the warehouse and I had to flee. I got to the harbour and shot some infidels to cause a distraction. I am at the casino. I am going to have to move to Plan B, in case they catch me."

"I saw what you did," Wright said. *"You idiot, they will all be on high alert now. They are already closing in on you. How do you plan to escape and carry out your attacks now?"*

"I will find a way. Allah will provide a solution."

"He better, because I just found out you failed to kill the General and have been tracked twice. I am starting to doubt your talents, maybe I should find someone else to do this. I don't think you have the faith to see this through."

"Do not question my faith in my cause, I am doing this for my God, and how dare you question my ability to faithfully serve Him."

"We have different causes, Haddad. I am willing to fund your attacks to serve both our needs, but rest assured if you fail again, not only will I sever our relationship, I will kill you myself. Have I made myself clear?"

"Perfectly clear, although I would say it is nice to hear you have finally grown some balls, back to the Catholic ideals of the good old days, back to when you were ruthless and bloodthirsty, back to when you really had faith. It is about time."

"Watch yourself, Haddad. You are but a very small cog in a very big machine."

"What does that mean?"

"It means just do your job and do not fuck up again."

"Yes, sir," Haddad said ending the call. "Infidel."

Haddad walked out of the small storeroom and onto the main floor of the gaming room. The neon lights and bells and alarms of the poker machines flashed and rang out echoing in the large space. Men and women cheered at various blackjack and craps tables lining the room. It was dark and the smell of beer and wine filled the air assaulting Haddad's sensibilities. He was getting angrier with every passing step on the sticky flamboyant and hyper-coloured carpet. He hated western culture, hated the greed and over-indulgence. He felt like he was surrounded by animals, but a smile crept across his face as clenched the briefcase in his hand and thought of what was to come.

Chapter Twenty-Five

Max, Flash and their team bounded up the narrow escalator which led up towards the front of the casino then across the white tiles of the small mall encircling the casino and up the short staircase to the front door. The security guards put their hands on the guns and stepped forward to block the team's path.

"Australian Intelligence Service," Max said removing his balaclava. "Who is in charge here?"

"I am," the guard at the back said moving forward to meet Max.

"We believe a man entered the casino in the last few minutes carrying a metal briefcase. News may not have reached you yet, but this man has just shot a number of people on the boardwalk down by the harbour."

"Evacuate the casino," the guard said over his shoulder.

"No, wait," Max said stopping the guards. "We're not sure what his plans are. We don't want to startle him, he could hurt your guests."

"Okay, so what should we do?"

"Get this picture to all of the guards in the casino and on the doors," Max said handing the guard a photo of Haddad. "They should not approach him, they need to call it in and my team will take him down. What comms channel are you on?"

"Eighteen."

"We'll patch in. Get the photo to your security room so they can start sweeping with the cameras. Lockdown to the casino. No one new in. People can leave, but your door staff need to be watching for Haddad. Clear?"

"Yes, sir," the guard said walking back and radioing the security room.

"Right," Max said turning back to his team. "You two, go with Flash, head left and sweep towards the centre. You two, come with me, we will head right and sweep in towards Flash's team."

"Ack," Flash said as the team all nodded.

Max led the team through the casino doors and headed right with two of the AIS team. Flash went left with his small team, hugging the wall. Over flashing lights and ringing bells, and the general noise of the casino, Max scanned the crowd. A few people saw Max and hesitated, he gave them a thumbs up and waved calming them down, but they kept watching as he continued along the wall. As he approached the corner, he asked one of his men to stay and keep scanning the room. He and the remaining AIS agent followed the right-hand wall towards the back of the casino, constantly scanning the crowds as they went. Max watched as a man threw dice on the green felt table to his left, he screamed and jumped up and down hugging the woman next to him. They both smiled and cheered as customers nearby had a mixed look on their faces, some looked happy for the couple for their win, while others frowned in jealousy. Halfway down the room, Max asked the second guard to wait and keep watching for Haddad. Max walked to the back corner and scanned the faces in the room.

"Flash, got anything?" Max asked into his comms unit, knowing his team had mirrored his own on the far side of the casino.

"No, Prince," Flash said.

"Report in."

"Clear," Flash's first team member said.

"Clear," said his second before the other two gave the same response.

"Okay, head towards the centre of the room," Max said. "Stay alert."

Max headed on a slight angle toward the centre of the room, weaving through tables of rowdy customers and rows of poker machines. A couple of punters sighted him and gave him a wide birth as he walked past. Up ahead, Max saw a door in the back wall of the room open and Haddad walked out scanning the room, then they locked eyes.

"Freeze, Haddad!" Max yelled and drew his pistol as he ran towards Haddad.

Haddad drew his pistol and fired. Max ducked behind a poker machine as the light board above the gaming machine shattered. As the gunshot rang out, people screamed and started running. They tripped on tables and chairs, as they pushed and scrambled for the exits. Haddad fired again as Max ran between two of the machines trying to edge closer, the bullet smashing into a beer glass, shattering it and throwing glass and beer over one of the nearby gaming machines. Max fired twice from behind his cover and Haddad dived behind a blackjack table. Max fired another two shots as he ran out from cover, the bullets tearing into the blackjack table Haddad was using as cover. His gun shot up from behind the table and fired towards Max which forced him to run and jump over a small table. As he went over, he knocked over five or six glasses spraying alcohol over himself and the floor, and he dragged the table over to shield himself from incoming bullets. One round thundered in the base of the table as he hit the dirty carpet. Max heard gunshots all round him, but they were not aiming for him. He ducked his head up to see Haddad running back through the door he had entered through moments ago as Flash and the team arrived and started firing. Bullets hammered into the door and walls next to Haddad, and Max could not sure, but he thought he saw at least one hit Haddad.

"Prince, you okay?" Flash yelled.

"Yep," Max said getting to his feet. "Let's go, two of you stay here and watch the door. Shoot that arsehole if he comes out first."

"Yes, sir," the agents said.

The other two agents were already at the door and they went through. The first guy was hit with a volley of bullets sending him stumbling back out towards the casino floor. As he fell, the door stayed open resting against his side. Max saw Haddad run down a small corridor and into a room on the right.

"Get him an ambulance," Max said to the other agent by the door. "Flash, let's get this arsehole."

Max jumped over his fallen colleague and went through the door and down the hallway, closely followed by Flash. When they got to the door, Max quickly ran across the gap and took cover on the far side of the door, a bullet flew through and hit the wall opposite fractions of a second later.

"I nearly got you, Agent," Haddad yelled through the door. "Stick your head back out and let me finish this."

"Give up, Haddad," Max said. "We've got you surrounded, there is nowhere to run."

"That maybe so, but it will not matter."

"Why?"

"Because with Moghadam out of the way, I am in charge and I have instructed my brothers and sisters to rise up and execute our plans."

"And, what would those plans be?"

"Death, so much death. We will forever change your nation and the western world. You and your allies will feel what is coming for generations, until you finally give up, completely overwhelmed by our strength, and join your fellow infidels in hell for eternity, where you belong."

"How do you intend to do that?"

"Why don't you come in and have a look?"

Max and Flash exchanged worried and questioning looks, then Flash pulled out his mobile phone, opened the camera and stuck it around the door frame. He pulled it back just as a bullet hit the doorframe. He looked down at the phone and Max watched as his friend's expression turned to horror. He threw Max the phone and flung his body around and through the open door into a massive industrial kitchen and opened fire. Max did not have time to look at the phone, instead he dropped it and followed Flash into the kitchen. Haddad was halfway down a long stainless-steel bench which ran the length of the kitchen. It must have been more than twenty metres long. It was lined with half prepared food, some plated and some starting to boil over or smoke on the hotplates and grills. The kitchen was long vacated following the shots in the casino.

Max saw Haddad hiding behind a solid steel fridge door which was being peppered with bullets by Flash who was firing wildly. He had crossed over to the left-hand side of the room and was running towards Haddad in the open. Max was not sure what had made Flash react, but knew it must not have been good, given his friend had left himself so exposed. Max ran down the right-hand side of the kitchen bench, semi-shielded by it, training his gun on the open fridge door which was being pummelled by Flash's bullets. Max heard Flash's gun run empty and fired several shots into the door to keep Haddad pinned down, then Flash stopped and started looking at something on the bench, but Max could not see what it was. He continued firing his pistol at the door, but he knew he was getting close to empty, so started to drag around his MP5 from his back to his left hand, then click, the pistol ran out of bullets. Before he could get a shot off with the MP5. Haddad sprung out and fired towards Max, forcing him to duck behind the kitchen bench. Plates and food containers exploded showering him with China, plastic, glass and food and oil, as he took cover, then he heard two shots, not aimed at him or the bench and his blood ran cold. He went to stand, but again Haddad fired into the bench top keeping him pinned down. He knew Haddad was getting further away. He got to his feet, but stayed bent at the waist and knees trying to stay under the level of the benchtop, and he ran trying to get to the far end of the bench, keeping low.

Max got to the end and checked around the corner of the bench, he saw Haddad running for a rear exit with his briefcase, he was limping and trailing blood from his right leg. Max fired and hit Haddad in the right shoulder and he fell through the exit swiping blood down the door. Max walked out from behind the bench keeping the gun trained on the door, but stole a look to his left, Flash was lying motionless on the kitchen tiles. He had a choice, chase Haddad or help his friend. He took one step towards the exit, but stopped, turned left and ran to Flash's side, he dropped to his knees into a pool of Flash's blood.

"Get me an ambulance now!" Max yelled into his comms unit.

"They are already en route, sir," one of the agents said.

"Flash is down, Haddad's gone out the exit at the rear of the kitchen, get some agents around there now. He's shot in the leg and shoulder."

"Prince, it's Hermes. You need to stop Haddad."

"I can't, Hermes, Flash is in bad shape," Max said checking Flash's wounds.

"Shadow has given the direct order, our team will find Flash and help him, you must capture Haddad, he is your primary mission."

"If I leave, Flash will bleed out."

"I know and I'm sorry, Prince, I really am, but we cannot let Haddad escape."

"Then you better get some agents out the back because I'm not leaving Flash here like this."

Max listened as Blake yelled orders for the men to head to the rear of the casino to pursue Haddad. Blood was pumping from a wound in Flash's neck, Max reached up onto the bench and found a tea towel which he folded and placed over the wound, putting pressure on it.

"Prince, I'm sorry, you have to leave him," Blake said. *"Go after Haddad."*

"No, Blake. I'd do the same if it was you or Kate lying here too. The other agents will get Haddad. Oh my God."

"What is it, Prince?"

"Flash saw something when he charged into the room," Max said looking at the item in Flash's hands. "I found it. I'm going to need hazmat in here immediately."

"What have you got?"

"It's a small metal box with a test-tube in it, it looks like it's behind a glass shield. It's got some sort of liquid in it. It has a small biological symbol on it. Wait, there's something on the other side. Oh fuck."

"What Prince?"

"It's a timer, three minutes. How far out are hazmat?"

"A lot longer than that. Shit."

"I need to find a container of some sort."

"It'll need to be completely airtight, Prince."

"I think it'll need to be fairly solid, in case there is an explosive in it too. What about a cool-room, would that work?"

"Maybe."

"Fuck it," Max said as one of the AIS agents ran into the room. "Come over here, put pressure on his neck."

"Yes, sir," the agent said putting his hands on the bloodied tea towel on Flash's neck.

Max gently lifted the small metal box and its glass vial from Flash's hands, his fingers curling in slightly after letting go as Max freed it from his grip. Max walked quickly to the cool-room, opened the door and walked in, sitting the box in the back corner against the walls. He ran back out and looked around the kitchen until he found what he was looking for, and ran over and grabbed a pile of wooden chopping boards. He ran back into the cool-room and placed them on top of the little box then he tipped over the shelves in the cool-room to put more weight down on the boards and box, hoping to absorb any explosion. He ran out and closed the door, then tried to drag a double door fridge in front of the door in case any explosion forced it open. He pulled and tugged hard at the fridge, but it was fully stocked and would not budge. Max stepped back then ran and jumped at the fridge putting a foot into the side to spring up and pulling himself onto the top of it. He sat with his feet against the walls and hands wrapped over the lip at the top of the fridge. He pushed hard against the walls, the veins in his arms throbbing as he clung to the fridge trying to push it over. Slowly it started to tip, then it fell. Max threw himself back over the edge and onto the back of the fridge. It dropped hard wedging itself between the walls and resting against the door of the cool-room. Max slid down the back of the fridge coming to rest next to the wall, just as he heard the explosion. It thundered inside the cool-room. Max heard the boards and shelves get flung around inside, but the door did not budge. Whatever was in the vial should be circulating inside and Max hoped it was fully sealed. He looked down at his blood-stained hands and hurried back to Flash, just as the paramedics arrived. They set about working on Flash and after a few minutes, Max and the agent helped lift him onto the trolley. The paramedics hoisted it up and its wheels dropped into place, they pushed the trolley and Max ran with them heading for the waiting ambulance, leaving the AIS agent behind to guard the cool-room.

"Hermes, you there?" Max asked.

"Yes, Prince, go ahead," Blake said.

"The vial exploded in the cool-room, but I am pretty sure it is contained. The paramedics and I have Flash on a trolley heading for the ambulance and the hospital."

"Okay, Prince, thank you. Hazmat should be there soon, they will sort out the cool-room and let us know what we are dealing with."

"Did they pick up Haddad?"

"No, he got away."

"What? How is that possible, he was shot in the leg and arm?"

"I'm not sure, Prince, but we could use you on the ground there looking."

"I want to go with Flash."

"You can't help him, Prince. He's in good hands. I need your help."

The paramedics flung open the doors and wheeled Flash into the back of the ambulance. Max climbed in next to him, but turned to the paramedics when they were about to close the door.

"Wait," he said.

"Sir, we need to go," the paramedic said.

"I know," Max said turning back to Flash and resting his hand on his chest. "Get better brother, I'll be thinking about you. Stay strong. I'll be out to see you when I can. I'm going to get that son of a bitch."

Max patted Flash on the arm then jumped back out of the ambulance. The paramedics closed the doors and Max watched as it raced off.

"Okay, Hermes, I'm here. Where do you want me?"

"Thank you, Prince. Alpha and I are still at the warehouse. Come meet us up here and we will come up with a new plan."

"Ack, see you in a couple of minutes," Max said running up the street towards the warehouse.

Chapter Twenty-Six

"Uri, are you there?" Wright asked his phone.

"Yes, I am here," Uri said. *"What can I do for you?"*

"How is the second project going?"

"It is almost complete?"

"It works?"

"We have had several successful trials. Two-hour turnaround time."

"Two hours? That seems a long time."

"No, Your Grace, it's actually amazingly responsive."

"Okay, good to know. How long until we have enough for us?"

"For us?"

"Yes."

"A day."

"And for mass production?"

"More than a week."

"I have had to move up the plans. We need it sooner."

"That was not what we discussed, these things should not be rushed."

"Haddad was tracked and he set off one of the devices."

"When? It's not on the news. These bloody Arabs, I knew we could not trust them."

"It has only just happened."

"How do you know that?"

"I have many connections, in many places."

"So, it would seem."

"We need project two up and running. It is a vital part of the plan."

"I can talk to Hogan and see what we can do."

"Thank you, Uri."

"I will contact him now."

"Thank you. Oh and Uri, I heard about your family, I am sorry. I have told him to release them."

"Told him? He works for you now?"

"He knows the money is from me and I have told him I am taking over the operation."

"The money is from you?"

"I am funding the Arabs so they can purchase equipment and the virus. I will keep the money following to them, as long as they can deliver."

"Fair enough. Can you trust them, the Arabs?"

"At this point we don't have much choice, but I will try to manage them."

"An impossible task, Your Grace, but I wish you well. I will let you know when I hear back from Hogan. Oh and Benjamin, thank you for helping my family."

"Thanks, Uri."

Chapter Twenty-Seven

Max stood washing Flash's dried blood off his hands. It swirled and splashed in the dirty off-white basin, and Max watched it drain away slowly. When the water ran clear, he splashed some water on his face then stood dripping, staring at himself in the mirror. *What have I gotten myself into?* His mind was whirling, like the water in sink. He turned off the tap and headed out to see Kate and Blake.

"Sorry about Flash, Max," Kate said. "He's a tough fuck, he'll be right mate."

"Thanks, Kate," Max said. "He lost a lot of blood, it's going to be touch and go I'd say."

"What are you a doctor now too?"

"No, but my boyfriend is and we study together. Sometimes we read things to each other from our coursework, to discuss them out loud, it helps the ideas sink in. I've got a general idea about how things work and well, I'm worried."

"He'll be okay, Max," Blake said walking in and placing his hand on Max's shoulder. "Kate's right, he's tough and he's in good hands."

"Yeah I guess you're both right," Max said. "I guess, he'd want us to get on with the job. So, where are we at?"

"We've got five arseholes in custody," Kate said. "Our boys are doing a sweep of the warehouse, they haven't found a fucking thing yet and this bloody place."

"Blake said earlier you were working on one of the guys?"

"Yeah, he's taking a nap at the moment."

"He's not talking?"

"No, I had to get a bit rough with him. He'll talk though."

"Oh, okay."

"Max, you're going to have to get used to enhanced interrogation techniques at some point. It's the only thing these arseholes understand."

"I saw what they did to Hulk, it's barbaric."

"Yes, it is," Blake said. "We know that, Max, there is no joy on our part or desire to do it, but it is what works. Everyone has a breaking point."

"Hulk didn't break."

"He has years of training and he's a tough son of a bitch, he delayed the breaking point, he didn't stop it coming. He would have eventually broken. Your psychology courses must have touched on human breaking points."

"Yes, but I'm not sure this was how the lecturers intended for me to use it."

"It's how we intended for you to use it. Limited physical pain and discomfort, to confirmed terrorists and their sympathisers, with the addition of cutting phrases and emotional manipulation to draw out information which saves lives. That is why we do what we do."

"Okay, well, as long as it is to save lives. I'm not comfortable with it though."

"None of us are, Max. That's what makes us human."

"It's what makes us the fucking good guys, Prince Charming," Kate said. "They're fucking psychopaths and we need to get into their heads to stop them from doing shit like they did today."

"I get it, Kate."

"Do you? They tortured our boss, they shot people in the street, innocent people just living their lives, they set off a chemical or biological weapon of some sort and may have more, ready to go, and they shot your friend. They're the bad guys, Max. We need to stop them."

"Where is he?"

"That's my boy," Kate said pointing to a small room to her right. "Follow me."

Max followed Kate into the untidy office leaving Blake in the main section of the warehouse. Inside, a man in his mid-forties was hanging from outstretched arms which were tied at the wrists to a hanging neon light which was suspended from chains bolted to the roof. The old light was failing and it gave the room a brown glow rather than the vibrant white it would have in its original condition. His head was slumped to the left on his chest and his feet where barely touching the floor. He was a clean and well-dressed man in casual attire, washed-out blue jeans and a long-sleeved V-neck black cotton shirt. He had a neat trimmed beard which blended into his short dark hair. One of his eyes was closed over and his nose looked broken.

"He looks like a normal guy," Max said.

"That's their strength, Prince," Kate said. "Blending in. It's the new way of the world, they hide in plain sight, attack and disappear into the crowd. Fucking cowards."

"How do we know he's involved?"

"He was shooting at me when we came through the door."

"That'll do it."

"Yeah."

"Let's have a chat with him then."

Kate walked up and slapped the man hard across the face. He shook his head and groggily started to regain consciousness. Kate grabbed him around his bottom jaw and raised his head, she got only an inch or two from his face and starred him in the eyes.

"Wakey, wakey, you piece of shit," Kate said. "Time to talk, Omar."

"I will not be addressed in such a way by you, you filthy infidel whore," Omar said. "Get your whore hands off me."

"That's not the type of talk I meant," Kate said then she punched him crunching his broken nose and spraying blood down his face and over her hand which had been holding his jaw.

"You filthy bitch, I am going to kill you and everyone you have ever loved."

"Okay, that's enough," Max said stepping out from behind Kate.

Omar had not seen him standing there and took a moment to look him up and down with his one opened eye.

"Who are you?" Omar asked.

"I'm here to ask you a couple of questions, Omar, was it? I need to know who you are working with, what you have planned and where Haddad bin Halil is hiding."

"Get her away from me and I will think about answering you."

Kate let go and walked to the small office desk, she brushed a pile of paperwork onto the ground and sat on the desk. Omar starred at her with hate and contempt. Max walked forward and starred at Omar waiting for him to turn to face him.

"So, where is Haddad and what do you have planned?" Max asked as Omar finally turned back to look at him.

"Brother Haddad is hopefully getting ready to send many of your countrymen to judgement because their feet have slipped," Omar said.

"Their feet have slipped, what does that mean?"

"It means everyone is a sinner, some worse than others and it is time for them to meet Almighty Allah and be judged for their crimes against him."

"And, what pray tell are these crimes?"

"Take your pick. How about blasphemy, sodomy, adultery. How about invading our lands and raping our women and children? How about sitting idly by as your governments wage war which ravages our countrymen and nations to feed your greedy appetite for wealth, power and oil? How about claiming to be for freedom and liberty, but only as long it is how you describe it?"

"How can you justify hurting innocent people? If your problem is with the government, vote for someone else. If your problem is with how people live their lives and who they love, then get a life of your own. Who cares what they do?"

"Allah cares and so do I. I am justified in my actions because He has commanded my hands to work in His name."

"You see, Omar, before I came in here my colleagues and I were debating the use of torture to get information out of people like you. I was sceptical, but with an answer like the one you just gave, it is clear you cannot be reasoned with and I'm starting to warm to the idea."

"I can tell you have not got what it takes. Inflicting pain on people takes a certain character and it is not in you. I can see it in your eyes."

"Your people are responsible for the torture of my boss, the death of federal agents, the murder of many innocent Australians and tourists, an attempted weapons attack and your so-called brother, Haddad, shot a friend of mine and I'm not sure if he is going to make it. So, I'm giving you one last chance to do it the easy way, the pain-free way or my colleague here is going to hurt you really bad."

"I knew you could not do it, leaving it to this filthy beast of a woman. Pathetic."

Max walked over to the table where Kate was sitting and put his hands down on the table. He starred at the desktop for a few seconds. *Can I do this?* He asked himself. His mind was racing.

"What's it going to be Prince Charming?" Kate asked.

"He is going to get a woman to do his job for him, because he is weak," Omar said.

Max looked up at Kate, she noticed his eyes were glassy and reflective, he seemed to be pulsing with energy. She could tell his mind was working in overdrive, but then something changed. With every passing word from Omar, resolution was building, like he was reaching a decision.

"It is sad to see the great Australian Intelligence Service reduced to hiring such fragile little flowers, it is good for us though," Omar laughed.

Kate saw it in Max eyes, then he was gone. He moved so quickly, spinning and stepping towards Omar, then Kate heard a scream. Max had hold of an object which looked to be lodged in Omar's shoulder.

"You see Omar," Max said twisting the letter opener. "There is a clump of nerve-endings right here in the shoulder, even just pressing hard on it can cause discomfort, so I imagine this, hurts like shit. Tell me what I need to know and I will take out the letter opener. Continue to delay or hide information from me and we will see if a pen can cause just as much trouble on the other shoulder."

"I am going to enjoy listening to news of my brothers' success and the death of many infidel filth," Omar said through gritted teeth.

"How do they plan to do it? What is in the dispersal devices?"

"Oh, you have seen one then, ingenious right? One of my own designs, I am very proud of it."

"Tell me about it."

"Its timer counts down then sets off a small piece of plastic explosive which shatters the glass and clouds the surrounding area with whatever is in the vial. Chemical weapons are good and can be devastating if the device goes off in the right place, but biological weapons are the best. The thick blanket of biological disease will spread and infect anyone within fifty metres, but the true joy comes as each of those afflicted go about their lives helping spread it to others, within hours hundreds will be exposed and within weeks the nation and the world will become victims. It is all part of Allah's plan."

"How could He be part of a plan to wipe out the whole world's population?"

"Oh, don't you worry about us, there is a plan for the worthy, it is eternal life in paradise."

Omar winced in pain, but Max left the letter opener in his shoulder and walked over and lent against the desk next to Kate.

"He seems pretty proud of his work," Max said.

"Yes, he does," Kate said looking at Omar. "Fucking terrorist piece of shit. Where is Haddad?"

"Fuck you, bitch," Omar said.

"Wrong answer," Kate said jumping down from the table.

She walked over to Omar and ripped the letter opener out of his shoulder before stabbing it into his other shoulder, around the same spot as Max had put it. Omar screamed again but his hatred burned in his eyes. It was not only because of the pain, but no doubt, because Kate was a woman. Max had his doubts about torture, had his doubts about his new career and had his doubts about whether he could do it, but then he pictured those men and woman lying dead near the harbour, and he thought about Flash bleeding out in the casino's kitchen. His thoughts were mixed with a new fear he had never experienced before, Omar's threat of biological warfare. *I have to stop him, I can't let that happen,* Max thought to himself. Max pushed forward off the desk and moved Kate to the side with his left hand, she stepped clear and Max swung his right hand through the air with incredible force slapping a computer keyboard across Omar face. It shattered scattering letters and electronic components across the room.

"We don't have time for your bullshit, Omar," Max said. "Tell me where to find Haddad."

Omar started to complain, but Max heard a faint buzzing sound between his protests.

"Shut up," Max said backhanding Omar. "Do you hear that?"

"No, what?" Kate asked.

"Where's his phone?"

"It was on the desk, hang on," Kate said going through the items she had swept onto the floor.

She found it and handed it to Max.

"It's him isn't it," Max asked as he showed Omar the screen displaying the incoming caller's number.

Omar looked at the number and Max saw the recognition in his eyes. He swung around behind Omar and grabbed hold of the letter opener, pulling it harder and deeper into his shoulder, every millimetre tearing and opening the wound further.

"I want you to find out where he is," Max said lowering Omar into a chair then leaning in to speak right in his ear. "One wrong word and I will push the opener right through your shoulder. Got it?"

Omar just grunted, so Max let the pressure off the opener, slid the green arrow and pressed speaker.

"Omar, it's me," Max recognised Haddad's voice through the little tinny speakers. *"Omar, are you there?"*

Max tapped the letter opener, warning Omar.

"Yes," Omar said. "I am here."

"You got away from AIS?"

"Yes."

"Good, we need to regroup. Where are you?"

"I am still in the city."

"Can you get to the safehouse?"

"I think so."

"That is good news. I was shot in the leg, but it is just a small wound, Faisal bandaged it. The agent also grazed my arm too, but it is fine. Are you okay?"

"Yes."

"Good. I spoke to our friend. He is unhappy to say the least and he made some threats. I am getting tired of him. I do not care about his needs or his pathetic cause, his religion is done, his people have fled, too easily swayed by the weakness of the New Testament. That is why he will fail and we will prevail."

"Inshallah."

"Get to the safehouse, take one of the dispersal units and release it in our friend's building. It will send a warning and it will distract AIS, while we prepare for the next attacks."

"What will you do?"

"I am going to find out where Moghadam is and free him, we need him to come back and run the final operations in... "

"AIS have me, get out now, Haddad!" Omar screamed into the phone and the line went dead.

"Get it to Hermes," Max said throwing the phone to Kate. "Tell him to trace that last call. Let's hope Haddad keeps it on him."

"You got it," Kate said. "You right here?"

"We're going to have a little talk."

"Good luck," Kate said walking from the room.

"You may have just sentenced millions to death," Max said walking back out from behind Omar. "I was conflicted before, but let me assure you, I'm not now."

Max kicked Omar in the chest and knocked over the chair, Omar hit his head hard on the polished wooden floor and the sound echoed around the room. Max walked over and stomped down hard with his combat boots on the letter opener, feeling it move clean through the shoulder and pin into the floorboards.

"That's it," Omar said. "Come down to my level, feel what it is like to inflict pain. It feels good, does it not?"

"No," Max said. "But, in your case, I am willing to make an exception."

Max stomped down hard again on the letter opener breaking it and sending two twisting splinters of the blade through tendons and muscles surrounding his shoulder, blood started pouring out of the wounds.

"Tell me what I need to know!" Max yelled keeping the pressure down on the heal of his boot.

Omar's eyes started to roll wildly, he was beginning to blackout.

"Where is he, Omar? Who were you going to take out?" Max asked. "You are going to bleed to death here on the floor without medical attention. Tell me what I need to know."

"Benjamin," Omar said faintly.

"Benjamin who?" Max asked but Omar passed out. "Fuck."

"How's it going in here?" Kate asked. "Jesus, Max, what did you do?"

"He's unconscious," Max said feeling Omar's pulse. "But, we need to get him to the hospital. He was about to tell me his target. Benjamin is all he got out."

"Well that's no fucking help, there's probably several thousand Ben's in this city alone."

"Yeah, I know," Max said dragging Omar up over his shoulder.

"What are you doing?"

"Taking him to the hospital. When he wakes up, I'll be waiting."

"Okay, I'll come with you."

"Let's go."

Chapter Twenty-Eight

Max was standing looking through the glass into the operating room. A doctor was steadily working with fine, very slow, very precise movements. There were several nurses providing assistance, holding various implements, checking multiple machines and rushing equipment and tools in and out of the room. Flash was perfectly still, covered in a blue sheet with just his shoulders, neck and head visible. His pale face was turned towards the glass and the doctor was working on his neck where the bullet had struck. Max could see the blood on his neck and looked down as if remembering the sight of Flash's blood on his hands.

"Hey," Kate said. "Hulk has just woken up. He's asking to see you."

"Okay, thanks," Max said. "How is he?"

"Doctor says he'll make a full recovery."

"That's good to hear. I'll go see him now."

Max walked out of the observation room and headed down the corridor. It was stark white and had an overpowering smell of cleaning products. Doctors, nurses, patients and visitors were all filing in and out of the hallways. He found the ward he was looking for and went into Hulk's room.

"How are you feeling?" Max asked.

"I feel a bit useless in this fucking bed," Hulk said. "But I'm working on that. I hear you've had a big day?"

"You could say that."

"Kate tells me you put a suspect in the hospital?"

"She helped."

"I'm almost proud of you. I would be if you got the name first, but otherwise it sounds like you handled it okay. They'll wake him up in a few minutes and you need to go in and get the name."

"Will do."

"How are you holding up otherwise? I know it is a lot to take in."

"Honestly, I'm a bit shaken up, but I get it now."

"The job?"

"Yeah. He was on the phone to Haddad. I knew they were ruthless, but this is something else."

"They are driven by religion and it is buried deep within their psyche. It drives and motivates them beyond what most can comprehend. They've been brainwashed and these dark messages have been driven into them from the moment they learnt basic words and phrases. It's chilling at first, but."

"But what?"

"But we have similar traits. That's the ugly truth. You, me, Kate, Blake, Flash, our whole team. We are driven just as strongly to stop them winning, as they are to win. We have to meet them on their level. We have to play their game and by a different set of rules to match and then beat them. You see now why we have to do what we do right?"

"Yes, I get it, Hulk. I'm in, one hundred per cent."

"Good. I need you to be. You need to continue to work with Blake and Kate to find these arseholes and stop them."

"You got it, boss."

"Good lad. Why don't you go and wake that son of a bitch up and see what he knows?"

"Ack. I'll keep you updated."

"Make sure you do. Good luck and Godspeed, kid."

"Thanks, Hulk," Max said as he walked out of the room.

Max walked along the corridor thinking about his line of questioning and considering who might be involved and what may be coming next, when alarms began to sound. Max started to run as he heard the announcement calling for a doctor to go to Omar's room. Max ran into the room and saw nurses checking Omar's wounds. Max pushed forward to see for himself. He felt sick wondering if he had tortured Omar to death, but then he saw it, there was a scalpel handle hanging only an inch out of Omar's chest. He was dead.

"Did you see anyone leave this room?" Max asked the medical staff.

"No," one of the nurses said before turning back to Omar.

Max ran out of the room, grabbing the doorframe as he ran into the hallway, helping him make the turn and he ran as fast as he could back towards Hulk's room.

"What the hell is going on?" Hulk asked as Max ran into the room.

"Someone took out Omar," Max said. "He had a scalpel stabbed down into his chest, only the tip of the handle was visible, certainly not an accident."

"Fuck! I need to get out of this bed."

"No, you need to stay in it, but we need to get you out of this room."

"Just give me a gun."

"Yeah, okay, here you go," Max said handing Hulk his pistol. "I'm getting you out of here."

Max walked behind Hulk's bed and started wheeling him for the door.

"Alpha, are you on comm?" Max asked.

"Yes, Prince," Kate said. *"I'm here with Hermes in the observation room watching them work on Flash."*

"I'm en route with Hulk. Clear the room for a bed. Omar's been taken out."

"What?"

"Someone killed him. If they knew he was here, they know Hulk and Flash are here too."

"Got it. We'll clear a path."

"One minute out."

"Roger that."

Max turned the bed towards the observation room and ran for the door.

"Hey, slow the fuck down will you?" Hulk said grabbing at the bed.

"Hang on tight," Max said but before they hit the door it opened and Blake stepped clear.

"Thanks," Max said slowing the bed to a stop.

"Jesus Christ," Hulk said. "You're a lunatic."

"One of you need to stay here with Hulk and Flash," Max said. "The other needs to come with me and sweep the hospital."

"I'm with you, Max," Blake said. "Lead on."

"Lock the door behind us, Kate," Max said.

"Yes, sir," Kate said giving Hulk an impressed look and smile as Max and Blake left the room.

"Jesus, day one and he's already taking charge," Hulk said. "I have to admit I'm impressed."

"He's had a big fucking day too, boss," Kate said. "The only hesitation so far has been about torture, but he put Omar in here, so I guess he's getting over it."

"I guess so."

"You picked a good one boss. If he makes it through everything today, he'll be unstoppable."

"Well, let's just hope we can figure this all out and stop Moghadam and Haddad."

"Fuckin' ay! We'll get 'em."

Outside the room, Max and Blake were sweeping the hallways. Blake had ordered the hospital into lockdown and security guards had blocked all the exits. Patients, nurses and doctors were, wherever possible, locked in rooms or offices throughout the hospital. They nervously watched through the glass as Max and Blake moved past their doors in slightly crouched walks with their MP5s pressed firmly against their shoulders. Max heard squeaking on the tiles towards the end of the hall. Blake must have heard it too, because he stopped briefly to look at Max. They both nodded at each other and started for the T-intersection at the end of the corridor. Two men ran around the corner and stopped in their tracks on seeing Max and Blake.

"Freeze, Haddad!" Max yelled.

The two men spun and ran back to the T-intersection, Haddad went right limping slightly, while his comrade went left as two bullets hit the tiles behind them from Max and Blakes' guns.

"I've got Haddad," Max said.

"Got it," Blake said as they parted ways and went after their respective targets.

Max ran the length of the hallway following Haddad, the gap closing but not enough, because even with the limp Haddad was pulling obstacles into Max's path. Max didn't shoot. He needed Haddad alive, but he mostly didn't want to risk a stray doctor or hospital visitor getting in between them, given the lockdown had only just started. Up ahead Haddad took a right and Max sprinted to the end of the hallway, where he stopped and leaned against the wall, quickly sneaking a look around the corner, but there was no sign of Haddad. Max stepped around into the new corridor and raised his weapon. He moved slowly checking each room as he made his way down the hallway. He checked the third door on his right, it was locked. He was about to move to the next door when he saw movement in the room through the small glass window. Haddad was using a doctor as a human shield, his left arm was choking her around the neck, her arms were clutching at his trying to break free and Haddad had his Uzi pointing at her head. He was dragging her backwards towards an adjacent room and her shoes flailing around on the tiles trying to get traction, but Haddad was too strong. Max slammed the butt of his MP5 into the window shattering it. Haddad fired a burst of shots into the door and Max ducked behind the doorframe.

"Stay out of here!" Haddad yelled. "Or I will kill this infidel bitch!"

"Let her go, Haddad," Max said. "She's innocent."

"That's where you are wrong," Haddad said dragging the doctor into the other room. "No one is innocent."

Max checked through the window, reached in and unlocked the door, before quickly entering the room and following Haddad. As he checked around the doorframe of the adjacent room, Haddad fired a shot into the doctor's leg and smiled broadly as he saw Max's expression change. The doctor screamed and fell to the floor.

"You've made your point," Max said. "Let her go."

"You may wish to come in and swap places with her, Agent?" Haddad asked. "What did you say your name was? Agent what?"

"My name is Prince."

"Well, Agent Prince, why don't you come in?"

"Let her go and I'll come in."

"I am not sure if you noticed, but she is a crying mess and cannot walk."

"The doctor's safety is all that matters," Max said entering the doorway and pointing his gun at Haddad. "So, why don't you put down the gun. You are surrounded and you have lost."

"Okay, Agent Prince, you got me," Haddad said looking down at his gun before dropping it to the floor.

"Are you okay?" Max asked the doctor.

"No!" the doctor said.

"What's your name?"

"Victoria."

"Okay, Victoria, everything is under control, try to scoot towards me and through the door," Max said moving to the side as Victoria tried to painfully drag herself towards the door, before he turned to face Haddad. "And you, hands behind your head and get on your knees."

"How am I going to give you a round of applause with my hands behind my head?"

"What?"

"You just took down a terrorist, I suspect you want a round of applause for your efforts?"

"No, just shut your mouth and get on the floor."

"Okay, okay."

Haddad started to kneel, keeping his eyes locked on Max. As he got to one knee, Max looked down at Victoria who was almost at his feet. Haddad used the moment to spring forward knocking the MP5 from Max's hands and tackled him back into the doorframe tripping on Victoria who screamed as they fell on top of her. They wrestled. Haddad punched Max three, four, five times as Max rolled using his forearms to block the incoming blows. Max threw his right elbow forward smacking Haddad in the jaw and knocking him off onto the floor. Max scrambled on top of Haddad and mirrored his previous moves, unleashing several punches. Three connected and dazed Haddad, but he was not giving up. He pushed Max in the chest between blows then began thrashing about creating some space between the two. He lifted one knee and rammed it forward into Max's groin. Max recoiled and fell slightly. Haddad dragged his leg through Max's and kicked him hard in the chest sending him backwards onto Victoria who screamed again. Haddad slid on his back across the white tiles scuttling backwards trying to put distance between the two. Max rolled off Victoria and leapt forward onto Haddad's legs, trying to drag him in. Max punched his wounded leg, but he kicked and jostled out from under him, then they both got to their feet. Max jumped off his left foot, drew back his right fist and slammed it into Haddad's face, then threw a left jab into his solar plexus buckling him over. Max sprung forward throwing a knee up into Haddad's face sending him falling backwards into a small table sitting beside a patient's now empty bed before he fell to the ground. Max looked for movement, but Haddad looked out cold.

"Are you okay?" Max asked turning back to Victoria.

"No, I'm really not," Victoria said. "What kind of macho-bullshit is this? Why didn't you just shoot him."

"I need him alive. He's got some answers I need."

"What sort of answers?"

"He's responsible for what happened at the casino, at the harbour and to my two colleagues in your operating room."

"Oh my God."

"Yeah, I'll call for someone to come and help you, but first I have to secure this guy."

"Okay."

Max turned around, walked over to Haddad and bent down to turn Haddad over onto his back. Haddad swung around using Max's momentum to assist his swing and thumbed a steel bedpan hard into the side of Max's head, Max fell to the ground beside Haddad and laid still. Victoria screamed, calling for help as Haddad got to his feet. Blood was pouring from his nose, he spat a mouthful onto the ground and wiped his mouth, looking at Victoria in disgust. He continued to stare at her as he walked across the room, passed her and into the adjacent room. He picked up his gun and started for the door, but paused when he got to Victoria. Without looking down he fired a burst of bullets into her face and she fell to the floor.

"Do not fear, Agent Prince," Haddad said walking over to Max who was starting to come to. "I am not going to kill you, I want you to see the price of your failure. Everyone who dies today is blood on your hands."

Haddad flipped Max over and removed a set of handcuffs from his vest, and cuffed him to the steel bedframe.

"See you soon," Haddad said, striking Max on the temple with the butt of his gun.

Max slumped towards the floor, his arm holding his weight from his handcuffed wrist, as Haddad walked out of the room.

Haddad made his way quickly through the maze of corridors, checking the room numbers as he went and keeping a look out for AIS agents and security guards, then he found it, three-nine-eight. He flung himself around the corner and levelled his gun at where the bed should have been, but General Patrick "Hulk" Scott, the Head of Operations for the Australian Intelligence Service, was not there. Haddad stormed out of the room and started checking the nearby rooms for nurses. At the second, he opened fire into the door, shattering the glass. Screams rang out as he reached in and opened it. Four nurses, one male and three female, were huddled together in the far left-hand corner, they were hugging each other, whimpering and shaking as Haddad approached.

"Where is the patient from room three-nine-eight?" Haddad asked.

They didn't respond, just hugged in closer together, nervously shaking and crying. Haddad walked over and grabbed one of the girls by the hair dragging her to her feet. She kicked and reached out grabbing for her friends and colleagues, but their grip slipped and Haddad reefed her back.

"Turn around," Haddad said. "All of you!"

They slowly turned, their eyes red and cheeks wet with tears. Panic rested on their faces as they looked to their friend who was in fear for her life. Haddad had her neck clenched in his left hand and the Uzi pointed at her face.

"Tell me where he is," Haddad said.

"They took him," the young male nurse said.

"Where did they take him?"

"Operating theatre."

"I thought he was stable?"

"He was."

"So why did they take him back to the operating room?"

"They didn't take him to be operated on."

"When did they take him?"

"Not long after the man down the hall was killed."

"Who took him?"

"I don't know, a young guy. He had a vest on and black clothes, like a policeman, from a movie, like SWAT or something."

"Prince," Haddad said with disgust.

"Yeah, he was like a prince. Very handsome."

Haddad turned with hatred burning in his eyes.

"Handsome? You like men, do you?"

"What does that have to do with anything?"

"Everything," Haddad said shooting the man in the face before turning the gun, spraying bullets and killing the other nurses.

He fired the gun empty into the male nurse and squeezed the trigger again twice, the empty clicks ringing in the tiled space. He stood and starred at the dead man for a long moment letting the odd mix of hatred and satisfaction wash over him. He walked out of the room and headed for the operating rooms, reloading his gun as he walked. On his way, he found the security room and checked the security monitors which were scrolling through live feeds coming from various rooms around the building. He saw Max still unconscious and handcuffed to the bed. Several screens later he watched for a few seconds as Blake and his comrade, Faisal, exchanged fire through a small doorway. Faisal looked like he was pinned down, Haddad doubted he would make it out. Another solider soon to be met with open arms by Allah. The operating room flashed on the screen and Haddad saw Hulk, Kate and Flash, as well as various doctors and nurses. Hulk and Kate had weapons in the outer room, while Flash was still being operated on. He tapped the screen and headed for the operating room. He strolled down the corridors checking left and right as he went. A few rooms from the operating room he walked passed a drinks machine and stopped beside it. He checked the distance. Satisfied, he moved to the right of the machine and started rocking it back and forth, before tipping it over. It crashed to the ground and Haddad heard the drinks fall and roll around inside. He took up position behind the drinks machine, putting it between himself and the operating room door, then he opened fire ripping lines of bullet holes into the door.

Inside the room, Kate returned fire through the door as Hulk rolled off the bed for cover, groaning as he hit the floor and as stitches and bandages pulled on his wounds. The nurses in the adjacent room with Flash had stopped working and were ducking behind the bed and walls. The doctor though had thrown herself over Flash's body shielding him bravely.

"Are you okay?" Kate asked.

"Yes, just keep firing," Hulk said getting to his knees and steadying his gun with an outstretched arm on the bed.

“Prince, Hermes, you read me?” Kate asked into her comms unit.

“I’m here,” Blake said. *“I’ve got one guy pinned down, he must be almost out of ammo though, so hopefully won’t be long. What’s up?”*

“Some arsehole is shooting up our room, he’s got us locked down, but the door won’t hold up for long,” Kate said. “Where’s Prince?”

“We got separated, he went after Haddad.”

“Prince, you there?” Kate asked. “Prince?”

“I’ll find him, as soon as I take down this arsehole, then we’ll come for you.”

“Got it. Thanks, Hermes. As soon as you can mate.”

“Ack.”

Chapter Twenty-Nine

"Where are you?" Wright asked.

"I am at the hospital," Haddad said over the sound of gunshots.

"What is that noise?"

"Gunfire."

"Who is shooting?"

"I am and some other people too."

"Who are you shooting at?"

"A few people from AIS."

"Why?"

"One of my men was captured, I had to take him out and I thought I would take out a few more while I was here, including the General."

"How many?"

"I don't know."

"Are you going to get out?"

"Yes, I think so."

"You think so."

"I will be fine."

"Did Daniel retrieve the devices?"

"Yes, two for you and two for the Jews."

"And the casino?"

"What about it?"

"What were you thinking? You wasted a device and you have set them on our trail."

"I was trying to get away from them."

"You failed, Haddad."

"No, I am about to prevail."

"In case you are wrong, where is your remaining device?"

"It is safe."

"Where?"

"Do not worry about it."

"What if they capture you too?"

"They will not."

"Damn it, Haddad! Where is the device?"

"I have to go, I am a little bit busy," Haddad said ending the call.

"Oh Lord, give me the strength I need to get through this," Wright said dialling a new number. "Daniel, it's me. I need you to launch the first attack now and place the second device on the timer."

"Yes, sir," Curran said.

"Then I want you to find Haddad's safehouse and retrieve his second device."

"He won't be happy about that."

"He's in a gunfight at the hospital. He might not get out. You leave him to me."

"Where would you like his second device?"

"Bring it to the church for now, I need you on the road."

"Where am I going?"

"You are going to meet the Jews and help them execute their attacks. When they are successful, we will figure out a final location."

"Yes, sir. Understood."

"Good. Get it done. The Lord is with us."

"Their feet have slipped," Curran said ending the call.

"Indeed they have," Wright said putting the phone back in his pocket.

Chapter Thirty

Max woke and winced in pain, his head was aching. He tried to put his hand on the spot to check if it was bleeding, but the handcuffs pulled on his wrist. He opened his eyes slowly to inspect the cuffs. *Fuck,* he thought to himself. He looked around and saw Victoria on the tiles, lying in a pool of her own blood. *Oh Jesus, I didn't save her.* Max felt around in his vest for the keys to his cuffs and when he found them, he undid the cuffs and replaced them in his vest. He walked over to check Victoria, but there was nothing he could do, she had a line of bullets across her chest and face. Max felt sick and anxious, but overwhelmingly, he felt failure. His thoughts were interrupted by the distant sound of gunfire. He grabbed his gun and headed towards the sound.

"Hermes, it's Prince," Max said. "Do you copy?"

"I'm here, Prince," Blake said. *"Are you okay?"*

"Haddad got away from me. Is that gunfire coming from you?"

"There's two lots mate. I've got Haddad's friend pinned down near ICU, but Alpha, Flash and Hulk are under fire, I presume from Haddad. Get to them as fast as you can."

"On my way!" Max said running towards the operating rooms, clearing the hallways as he ran.

Max paused occasionally to get his focus, he was still hazy from being knocked out by the bed pan. He ran into the corridor leading to the operating rooms. Halfway along a drinks machine was on its side and there were bullet holes in the walls either side of it and chipped out of the plaster along the walls. He saw the door to the operating room was smashed to pieces. Max's heart raced, he felt lightheaded and steadied himself on the drinks machine. He shook his head to focus then jumped the drinks machine, before smashing through what was left of the door into the observation room. Hulk's bed was empty and there was blood on the tiles, then Max looked through the glass and his blood ran cold. Haddad was standing over Flash with a knife daggling over his neck, he was pointing his gun at Kate and a number of medical staff. Max recognised the doctor who had been operating on Flash. Hulk was propped in a chair nearby, blood was pouring between his fingers from the reopened wound in his leg. Haddad summoned Max into the room with the tip of his knife.

"Hermes, you there?" Max asked into the comms unit.

"Yes, Prince, did you get to them?" Blake asked.

"Yeah, but we've got a problem, he's in the operating room with a knife above Flash, Hulk is bleeding bad and he's also got Kate and the medical team in there. He's waving for me to come in."

"Fuck."

"My thought too. Have you got your guy?"

"Yes, I've got him in custody."

"Think he knows anything?"

"Not sure, but sometimes they share a fair bit of information in case one of them fails. Why?"

"I'm just flipping a coin."

"What?"

Max did not answer, he flung open the door to the operating room and walked in with his gun pressed against his shoulder, sighting Haddad through the short scope.

"Put your gun down," Haddad said.

Max's vision blurred and he blinked quickly to focus. Then he fired twice. The nurses and doctor screamed, as Max ran across the room, around the table and pointed the gun at Haddad's face. Haddad was on the floor. He was alive and spitting blood, laughing in pain. Max had driven bullets into both his shoulders, forcing him to drop the knife and the gun. The gun had scattered across the floor and Max stepped back to look for the knife. It had dropped onto the table next to Flash and pierced the mattress, close, but just far enough away from his friend. Max breathed a sigh of relief.

"Doctor, are you finished with Flash?" Max asked.

"Yes, we just need to clean up a little, but the nurses can do that," the doctor said.

"Good, can you please come over and check out this piece of shit on the floor?"

"Yeah, yeah sure," she said walking over with one of the nurses.

Most of the other nurses went about finishing off Flash's post-operation clean up as Max walked over to Hulk and Kate who was working with the remaining nurses to bandage Hulk's leg.

"That was some stupid shit," Hulk said. "But, ballsy."

"Fuckin' 'ey," Kate said. "You got some big stones on you kid and you can shoot, two shots to disable and not kill, risky but good work."

"I checked with Hermes first," Max said ignoring the fact he was still suffering from the blow to the head. "To make sure he got his guy, in case I missed."

Hulk looked at Kate and she smiled and looked away.

"What?" Max asked.

"It's just, well, it's been a day from hell, Max," Hulk said. "Most of our long-term guys would struggle and I have to say you've handled yourself above and beyond what I could have imagined. How are you holding up?"

"I've done some things today that I would never have thought possible until a few months ago and well, it's been tough, but I'm coping just fine."

"That might be true, but I want you to see Doctor Carter as soon as you can."

"Yes, boss."

"I mean it, Max. That's an order."

"Okay, Hulk."

Blake walked in with Haddad's partner in crime, who had his hands cuffed behind his back.

"Everyone okay?" Blake asked looking around the room, taking a moment to look at Max, before turning to Hulk.

"We're fine," Hulk said. "Haddad's in some pain, thanks to Prince, but we're fine. You okay?"

"I'm fine thank you, General. This is Malik Faisal."

"Well, I think we should get out of here, so we can have a conversation with Faisal and Haddad."

"Call Shadow, tell him to prep the rooms."

"Yes sir, you got him, Max?" Blake said pushing Faisal.

"Sure," Max said grabbing Faisal by the front of the shirt. "He's not going anywhere."

Chapter Thirty-One

Kate turned the Landcruiser into the driveway of a storage compound in Western Sydney. She waved her access ring in front of the sensor and the gates slowly swung open. Max was in the backseat looking through the window. He thought it just looked like a normal storage facility. Three rows of massive sheds, high razor wire fences and a lot of cameras. Kate followed the concrete road between the middle and last sheds, until a big door rolled to the side in the large steel storage shed at the rear of the facility. Kate drove through, closely followed by an ambulance and chase car with four AIS agents on board. Max, Kate and Blake climbed down from the four-wheel drive when it pulled up at the far end of hanger-sized open space. It was lined with small rooms, but the space in the centre was just a large high-roofed open area. There were a number of cars parked inside.

"What is this place?" Max asked.

"The AIS Bunker," Blake said.

"Yes, sorry, I know that, but how's it work, it just looks like a big empty shed?"

"Well, up here we have a bunch of holding cells and interrogation rooms, plus there is a medical centre over there which is where Flash will be until he gets better, now the surgery is complete the AIS doctor and nurses will look after him. Downstairs there is a secure communications facility and weapons vault. It's being expanded to add staff sleeping quarters and kitchen facilities, and some conference rooms. It will be up and running fully in the next year or so."

"Right. Sounds impressive."

"It will be, it's not at the moment, it's really small and cramped. Doesn't matter anyway, we'll be staying up here today."

"Okay, cool."

"Oh shit," Blake said as an older man walked out of the room ahead.

"What? Who's that?"

"Shadow."

"Oh shit."

"Hermes," Lloyd said. "Get in there and sort out those cameras will you, the monitors are not working properly?"

"Yes, sir," Blake said hurrying off for the holding cells.

"Alpha, I have to say I am very disappointed in you. You disobeyed orders."

"Yes, sir," Kate said. "But, we got Hulk out and I think that has to count for something?"

"It does, but this is not the organisation for questioning orders and certainly not a good example to set for new rookies."

"It was all me," Max said. "Kate wanted to follow your orders and come back straight away, but I forced her to follow the lead and we were right to do so."

"Max, you don't have to," Kate said before she was interrupted.

"Mr Shaw, my name is Greg Lloyd, but people call me Shadow. I have heard a lot about you and your performance today. Do not for one-minute think that it excuses insubordination. I do not care what you think is right or wrong, got it?"

"Yes, sir," Max said. "But."

"No, Mr Shaw, no buts, you will listen and follow orders. No questions."

"I have a question," Hulk said being wheeled over in a wheelchair by one of the AIS agents who had followed the ambulance. "Why don't you let it go?"

"Your tone would suggest it's not really a question, Patrick."

"Well, what do you know, decades in intelligence has finally paid off, you can read me well old friend. No, it wasn't a question, let it go. These two are the reason I'm here and they have performed beyond the call, Greg, so let it go."

"Yes, okay."

"Yes, what?"

"Yes, General," Lloyd said embarrassed. "Did they tell you he also ignored me, letting Haddad get away from the casino?"

"We have Haddad now."

"We would have had him hours ago, if Mr Shaw could follow orders."

"And, Flash would be dead," Max said. "Your order was bullshit, I wasn't going to let him die."

"It wasn't your choice to make."

"Well, you weren't there, much easier to pass on a shit order from your comfy chair in the bunker than to be there watching your friend bleed to death."

"You have no idea what I have seen or done throughout my career you insolent little shit, how dare you question me."

"Fair enough, you're right. I'm sorry, but there was no way I was letting either Flash or Hulk die. That's just not who I am."

"Well, you better get used to the idea. In this game, your friends can die in an instant."

"Not if I have anything to do with it."

"You can't save everyone."

"No, but at least I will try."

"You arrogant," Lloyd said before being interrupted.

"Enough," Hulk said. "We are, where we are, and for what it is worth, I can't fault Prince's performance. Let's move on."

"Fine. The rooms are set up and ready."

"Good, thank you, Greg," Hulk said pointing to the observation room. "Take me in there please, Agent."

Max and Kate followed Hulk, who was being pushed in a wheelchair by an AIS agent, and Lloyd into the observation room. It had rows of monitors with live vision coming in from the nearby interrogation rooms. Max watched the monitors, Blake was in one of the rooms adjusting the camera. Another agent dragged Haddad into the empty room and taped him to a steel chair, as two other agents wrestled Faisal into a similar steel chair and taped him down in the room where Blake was finishing up.

"Well, here we are kid," Hulk said. "What do you think? Want to give it a shot?"

"Interrogation?" Max asked.

"Yeah, it worked with Moghadam, and was working on Omar. You've been in Haddad's face today, why not give it another go?"

"Are you sure?"

"Get in there before I change my mind, but don't put him in the hospital without getting information first this time."

"Yes, sir."

Max walked into the interrogation room with Haddad and waited by the door until he looked up.

"You," Haddad said spitting blood which had stained his teeth. "They must be desperate sending you in here. How old are you?"

"Why?"

"I thought most western children got a paper run while they were at school, not jobs in intelligence."

"Why did you kill the doctor?"

"Who?"

"The doctor at the hospital, Victoria. She didn't do anything to you, she was innocent. You didn't need to kill her."

"It upsets you, doesn't it?"

"I just want to know why."

"Why? I will tell you, why, because there is no one in this country or any of your allied friends' countries that is innocent. She might not have pulled the trigger herself, but she was complicit in the deaths of many of my people."

"How do you figure?"

"Your country and your allies sent troops into the Middle East and killed thousands of truly innocent people. Women and children by the hundreds piled up in the streets. I saw it with my own eyes. Government after government elected in this nation all follow the Americans and the British blindly into war. Now the war is coming to you, time for you to feel the pain we feel."

"So, what sort of pain do you intend to inflict?"

"The kind which will forever change the face of your country."

"When?"

"Any minute now."

"You're telling me that an attack is going to occur in the next few minutes."

"Yes."

"Why did you tell me that?"

"Because it is too late for you to stop it."

"Where?"

"Downtown."

"Here is Sydney?"

"Yes."

"What is the target?"

"It's a place which will show you the power we now possess."

"What sort of power? What is in the vials?"

"It is a new weapon, very powerful, very potent, very lethal."

"What do you hope to get out of this?"

"We want the troops out of the Middle East and we want retribution."

"Do you seriously think that if there is a successful attack, they'll negotiate a troop withdrawal?"

"No, but when they find out this attack is just an example and when they find out exactly how many more attacks we have planned, they will want to negotiate."

"How many more?"

"A lot."

"What are the targets?"

"Nice try."

"Okay, well, what do you want me to know?"

"What time is it?"

"It's nine pm."

"The first attack should have just happened. They're going to want you back next door."

"Are you in pain?"

"Yes, but the look on your face is helping me through it."

"I can assure you that you haven't felt anything yet," Max said as he walked out of the room.

"Lockdown the building and the harbour, shutdown the bridge, the trains and the airport," Hulk said into the phone. "We need a hard perimeter surrounding the area. No one, repeat, no one, in or out until we are sure. Given the timing, it has to be the same substance as the casino and if so, we have a Code Red. Yes, thank you. Get it done and call me back."

"What happened?" Lloyd asked.

"A device was detonated at the Sydney Opera House," Hulk said. "It was small, but we think it was like the one at the casino, a dispersal device. I've ordered a lockdown, but it's in the ventilation system already and circulating. It'll be at one hundred percent saturation within the building in minutes. We can't let anyone out, we can't risk it spreading."

"Was there a show on?"

"Yes, a musical. The theatre was full."

"Oh God."

"Yeah, it's going to be bad."

"Do they need us in the city?" Max asked.

"No, the local police and the feds will shut it down, and we have some guys en route. They will handle it. Our job is to stop it happening again."

"What would you like us to do?"

"You've got him talking, you need to go back in and find out everything you can. Blake you head in and start working on Faisal, we need times and locations, and names. I want to take these fucking people down and I want to put a stop to them. Am I clear?"

"Yes, sir," Max and Blake both said before heading into their respective interrogation rooms.

Haddad was smiling and started to laugh as Max walked into the room.

"What's so funny?" Max asked.

"I can see in your eyes, your pain," Haddad said. "It went off. Tell me, how many killed in the initial explosion? No, don't worry, it will not matter once the contents spread, they will all die."

"What is in the cylinders?"

"Oh, it is a special little concoction. It is not important. What is important is that within twenty-four hours of infection more than eighty percent of those who come into contact with the substance or an infected person will die. And, let me tell you, it is not a pleasant death, it will be violent and nauseating."

Haddad smiled broadly and laughed as Max stood and contemplated what he had just heard. His mind was reeling. He thought about Carter's conversation about breaking points and torture. *Can I really do this?* Max asked himself. *If I don't, will more people die? How many has he already killed? Can I stop further bloodshed?* Then he pictured a biological attack in the Opera House. Pictured men, women and children with blood pouring from their eyes and mouths, and convulsing on the floor. Max walked over to a small table which was resting against a wall in the interrogation room. It was covered in tools and equipment, as well as first-aid kits and bandages. He grabbed a two-litre jug shaped plastic bottle and turned back to Haddad.

"Do you know what this is?" Max asked.

"You would not dare, you do not have the balls, you fucking child," Haddad said.

"You see, Haddad, I've been struggling with the idea of torturing people and killing people since I started here with AIS. It just seems wrong on some level."

"I knew it. Why don't you put the bottle down and let a real man come in here."

"Oh, I hadn't finished. You've helped me see past the issues I had because I can see the evil in your eyes and the pure pleasure you are getting from knowing innocent men, women and children are dying as we speak thanks to you and your organisation. And, well, I think you've helped me on my road to becoming a good agent."

"How did I do that?" Haddad asked.

Max took off the lid and poured a quarter of the jug into the bullet hole in Haddad's right shoulder. Haddad screamed in pain as the acid bubbled and burned its way into the wound. He shook and thrashed about in chair as Max stepped back and watched. *Fuck, I can't believe I did that,* Max thought, but tried to push it out of his mind and not let it show on his face.

"So, what's it going to be, Haddad?" Max asked. "Are you going to tell me what I need to know?"

"Fuck you," Haddad spat still fidgeting in his chair with pain evident on his face.

"Wrong answer," Max said walking over and pouring more of the clear acid into Haddad's wounded shoulder.

Haddad screamed in pain then passed out. Max's heart and mind raced. He wondered if he had killed him.

"Max, come in here," Hulk said over the intercom.

"You're doing good kid," Hulk said as Max walked into the observation room. "I must admit I didn't think you had it in you, but I'm impressed."

"I think I killed him," Max said.

"No, he's just passed out from the pain. Give him a minute then get back in there. There is a small pouch inside the first-aid kit which was ammonia sticks inside. Snap one under his nose and he'll wake up."

"Got it."

"Do what you need to do to get the information."

"Yes, sir. Can I ask what's happening at the Opera House?"

"It's in lockdown as are the four blocks in a radius around the building. There is a police boat border on the harbour and all transport, including the ferries are shutdown."

"Are there paramedics inside yet?"

"The Department of Health, Fire Brigade and HAZMAT, and the Federal Police are prepping up to go in."

"You heard what Haddad said about the infection rates and timings, and the violent deaths?"

"Yes, Max. I've passed it on the teams on the ground. Are you okay?"

"Yes, I think so."

"It's not easy to hear, kid. I understand, especially on your first day in the field, but this is a real-life example of why what we do is so important, the good, bad and the ugly of what we do."

"Yes, sir. I'm starting to get the idea."

"Good. Now get back in there."

"Okay," Max said walking from the room.

He found the bag and snatched up an ammonia stick from the kit, walked over to Haddad and snapped it under his nose. Haddad shook his head and pulled away from the smell as Max threw the stick across onto the table. Haddad was still groggy and his eyes were closed, so Max slapped him hard across the face and a stinging sound echoed around the little room.

"Wake up you son-of-a-bitch," Max said.

"You hit like a woman," Haddad said.

Max punch Haddad straight in the nose, breaking it, sending his head flying back and spraying blood down his face.

"Is that better?" Max asked causing Haddad to laugh.

"Your anger is amusing," Haddad said.

"It might be now, but let me assure you, Haddad, by the time we finish here it won't be."

"You won't break me."

"Yes, Haddad, I will and I'm going to enjoy it," Max said punching Haddad in the eye then twice in the mouth sending a tooth out onto the floor.

"You broke one of my teeth."

"Well, let's even that up," Max said punching him again twice in the face.

Haddad spat out blood and another tooth onto the floor.

"There we go," Max said all balanced.

"You filthy infidel," Haddad said. "You have no right to touch me."

"You are a terrorist," Max said grabbing Haddad by the throat and slowly pressing his thumb into his windpipe. "You are responsible for the deaths of hundreds in the Opera House and you tell me there's more to come. How can you possibly think your God would approve?"

"Spare me. You would never understand."

"So, why don't you tell me?" Max said releasing his grip.

"I already told you. It is retribution, for Iraq, Syria and Afghanistan. For the thousands of innocent children and women your country killed by dropping bombs on their houses. For starting wars for oil and corporate greed. And yes, for your worship of false idols and your flagrant disregard for the one true God's laws."

"Our disregard for His laws? Well, tell me this, what about murder? How's He feel about that?"

"It can be justified."

"That's bullshit. Who gets to choose which rules get followed and which ones to disregard? Is it you? Who put you in charge?"

"Allah spoke to me."

"And told you to release a biological weapon on women and children? Some sort of an eye-for-an-eye thing? Seriously? Don't you find it hypocritical that you can come in here and bitch about the loss of your innocents while doing exactly the same thing?"

"The difference is Allah is on my side."

"You claim to know what He wants, tell me this, does He give you any other information?"

"What?"

"Does He give you any other information or does He just tell you to kill people from a far like a fucking coward?"

"I am not a coward. I served in the military for twenty-four years, and yes, Allah speaks to me often."

"Well, tell me this," Max said walking over to the table. "Did He tell you what happens next?"

"Yes, many more of your countrymen are going to die."

"No, I meant about what's going to happen to you next?" Max turned around and clicked a pair of plyers in his hand.

"You think you can scare me?"

"No, I'm just asking if He warned you?"

"Warned me?"

"Yeah, did He warn you that I was going to take out your teeth one-by-one until you talk?"

"No, you won't."

Max strode across the room, grabbed Haddad by the throat, again choking him.

"Open your mouth," Max said.

Haddad clenched his jaw and tried to turn away, but Max was far too strong. Max drove his thumb into a pressure point under Haddad's ear, next to his jaw. He pressed so hard his thumb was starting to ache.

"You see, Haddad, you're right I am young, in fact, I'm still at university. But, I am a quick study and I love to help people I know with their studies. Someone very close to me is training to be a doctor and he just so happened to recently have an exam on nerves and pressure points. As I was quizzing him, the information stuck in my mind and I know there is one just there. Can you feel it?"

Haddad tried to pull away in pain, but Max kept hold.

"Look at me, you son-of-a-bitch," Max said driving his thumb in deeper. "The pain stops when you tell me who is involved and where I can find them."

Haddad did not speak, so Max pushed the plyers between Haddad's lips, opened them and slid one side into an opening created by one of the teeth Max had previously knocked out. Max closed the plyers around the closest tooth.

"It's up to you," Max said. "Just tell me what I need to know. Give me a name."

Haddad just starred at Max, so Max moved the tooth slightly and watched Haddad shift comfortably in the chair.

"You don't want this," Max said. "Tell me what the plan is."

Haddad stayed silent. Max gripped the plyers tightly then ripped the tooth out. Blood spilled out of Haddad's mouth onto his shirt and he swore at Max, screaming in pain.

"Honestly, I've only just started learning Arabic," Max said. "Did you just call me a bad word? Oh, my poor sensitive ears. Here, can you look after this for me?"

Max opened the plyers and dropped Haddad's tooth onto his leg.

"One down, should we bet on how many before you talk?" Max asked wiping the blood from the plyers onto Haddad's shirt before putting them back in Haddad's mouth. "Well, you're missing two from the top and one from the bottom, I guess we should even that up, maybe I'll get one from the back?"

Haddad mumbled and Max recognised a few words, like infidel and pig. He pointed the plyers at a wisdom tooth, closed them around the tooth and tried to pull it out. It was stubborn, so Max started moving it back and forward slowly, Haddad was starting to violently pull away and grunt wildly. Max grabbed him by the throat and pressed his thumb hard shutting the airway.

"The sooner you realise I am serious and I will not stop, the better it will be for you," Max said twisting the plyers.

Haddad's eyes went wide, but he did not speak. Max was starting to feel a rising anger. He felt slightly confused by Haddad's willpower in the face of obvious overwhelming strength. He was beaten, so why keep fighting it. Max took hold of the plyers tightly until his knuckles went white, then he levered the tooth out, smashing the molar next to it. Haddad passed out as more blood gushed from his mouth. Max dropped the plyers and jogged out of the room, he quickly looked around the vast hanger and found the door he was looking for and sprinted for it. He ran into the bathroom and kicked a stall door open, then vomited in the toilet. After a minute, he steadied his breathing and walked over to the basin, splashing water on his face and rinsing his mouth. He stood watching the water drain, thinking about what he had just done. He knew Haddad was a terrorist and he knew Haddad had more information to give, but he was starting to doubt whether he could do it. He composed himself, turned off the tap, it let out a squeal on the final turn, then walked back out into the large shed, his face still dripping with water.

"Are you okay?" Blake asked.

"Yeah, I just needed a minute," Max said.

"It's a lot to handle, Max, it's okay to talk about it. You made it through the course mate and now you're in, we will look after you. It's not a test, not a trick. If you need help, we will give you everything you need. The reality of what we have to do is scary and traumatising. Trust me, it gets better, but what you are feeling right now shows just how good a person you are. It shows you are human. You're supposed to feel like this. If you didn't, I would be worried."

"Thanks, Blake."

"It's been a trying couple of days on top of what you've been through over the last couple of months."

"Yeah, it sure has."

"But, that's why you made it through the course, you're made of some superhuman qualities which drive you to perform. Even when you're exhausted and full of doubt, you will continue, because you know it's what you need to do."

"I can't stop thinking about those innocent people I saw him shoot near the harbour and the pain and suffering of those poor people in the Opera House who are finding out that most of them will die within hours. I want to hurt him, Blake, on some level, I want to see him in pain. I want him to pay for what he has done."

"I get that."

"But, I'm struggling with actually doing it."

"Well, that's normal, Max. Thinking about things is a lot easier than actually doing them."

"Yeah, but I think the worst feeling is guilt or maybe it's worry."

"You have nothing to be guilty of or worry about, Max," Blake said reaching over and taking Max's hand. "You didn't do these things and if more attacks happen and we fail to stop them, it won't be your fault. Haddad and his mates did this, not you. The guilt is on him and his team, and them alone. Got it?"

"Yes, thank you, Blake," Max said looking him in the eyes and feeling the warmth of his hand, that same warmth he felt in the Wool Shed that night and seeing nothing but love and friendship in his eyes.

"I'm here for you, Max, don't forget that," Blake said.

"I won't, thank you, Blake," Max said.

"Alright, you okay? We should head back over and see what we can find out."

"Yes, I'm okay now, thanks. I just needed a moment. Let's go see what he's got to say."

Max and Blake walked over to the observation room, where Hulk had been watching their exchange through the door in the shadows.

"You alright, kid?" Hulk asked.

"Yes, sir," Max said. "I'll be fine, sir."

"You will be or you are?"

"I am."

"Good. For what it's worth, you're doing well. Even I would be struggling to get this piece of shit to talk. He's trained to resist, that's why it's taking this long. Keep it up, okay?"

"Yes, sir."

"Here take this," Hulk said passing Max a small black pouch. "He's being hooked up to a drip and his wounds are being bandaged, it will make him feel like he has won, because we're the good guys, patching him up. Not willing to let him die. But, this shit, well, it will make him wish we had killed him."

"Okay."

"Head in when you are ready."

"Thanks," Max said taking a small bottle of water from the observation room.

Max lent against the doorframe watching as the AIS nurse finished setting up the drip. Haddad was still slumped in the chair, but his shoulders and mouth were stuffed with gauze and taped in place where it was possible. The nurse packed up his supplies and walked out of the room, nodding to Max as he went. Max walked over to the little table and sat down the black pouch Hulk had given him. He got out another ammonia stick and snapped it under Haddad's nose. Haddad woke and started to frown as his body came back online. The pain starting to flood his system again. Max dropped the small broken stick onto the table and grabbed his water and took a drink.

"How are you going, Haddad?" Max said. "Still with me?"

"Sadly, Allah has not yet called me to his side, but I rejoice knowing it is coming soon," Haddad said spitting out the gauze.

"No, Haddad. No, it's not. Why don't you open your eyes and see for yourself?"

Haddad opened his eyes wincing from the light. He blinked a few times before he sighted the drip and the empty bandage packets laying on the floor beside him. He turned and looked down at his shoulders, one after the other.

"It is amazing," Haddad said. "You know what I have done, but you still can't take that final action. Can't let me die."

"Don't speak too soon, Haddad. It wasn't compassion that bandaged those wounds. You've still got a story to tell me. Do that, then you can go be with your God."

"He is waiting for me in paradise. I will be rewarded for my service in His name."

"And, don't forget the virgins. Seventy-two, right?"

"That is correct. A worthy reward for my labours."

"Well, aren't they lucky girls? I presume they will be girls?"

"Of course, they will be, what kind of disgusting insinuation are you making?"

"Well, you never know these days. I thought I should keep an open-mind that you could wish for seventy-two men or many thirty-six of each. Did He tell you what you would get when He spoke to you?"

"You disgust me. Your blasphemy and insolence will see you punished when you arrive for judgement."

"Maybe, but I've got a few more sins to do first."

"What?"

"I have a few more sins I need to make before I leave here, like causing you more pain than you have ever felt."

"You cannot hurt me and I will not talk."

"Oh, I can and you will," Max said walking over to the table to retrieve the little black pouch.

Max unzipped the pouch slowly to create an anxious tension in the room. He pulled out a syringe and small glass vile with a clear water-like substance inside.

"I had lesson a few weeks ago on how this chemical works," Max said sitting the pouch on the floor before slowly drawing back the syringe filling it from the little glass vile right in front of Haddad's eyes. "I'm told it burns, wait is that what they said? No, no, it was that it feels worse than that, worse than burning. What was it he said? Oh that's right, he said it's like your veins are on fire and you are burning from the core out, over every inch of your body, like your blood is acid and like it is trying to rip its way through your organs and skin. Let's give it a go, shall we? You can tell me after if his description was right. If you make it through, of course, sometimes it has been known to cause heart failure or stroke. Doesn't matter, we'll find out in a minute."

Max lent over and very slowly inserted the needle into a small opening in the cord running the drip into Haddad's arm.

"Or I guess you could just tell me what I need to know?" Max said holding the needle still.

"Fuck you, infidel scum," Haddad said bouncing in his chair trying to brace for what was coming.

"No, Haddad, fuck you," Max whispered in his ear then depressed the needle very slightly.

Less than two millilitres of the fluid entered the line then Max pulled the syringe out and stepped back. Haddad started to scream and shake and cry. He instantly started to sweat, his face turning red, almost purple, and his veins all pumped tightly, Max could see them bulging in places as Haddad gripped the chair with all his might. It went for a full minute before Haddad calmed and slumped in the seat. Conscious and breathing heavily, he was exhausted and he looked like he had just run a marathon with the sweat drenching his clothes and skin. Max walked over and stood leaning in with his face only an inch from Haddad's face, he grabbed him by the hair and threw his head back.

"Was he right?" Max asked. "Like lava pushing from your core out? It certainly looked painful."

Haddad did not respond. Max was not sure if it was deviance or exhaustion.

"That was only two millilitres," Max said waving the syringe in front of Haddad's eyes. "There is another ten in here. If I give you all of it in one go, you'll die, you can go and see, Allah. Your pain gone, paradise awaits. Just tell me what I need to know and I'll give you the rest."

Haddad did not speak, but he was starring at the needle, his eyes showing him deep in thought. Max waited, creating silence and tension, making it seem like Haddad was in control.

"Okay," Haddad said finally. "I will tell you. As long as you kill me after."

"Deal, what are the other targets?" Max said letting go of Haddad's hair.

"A football game at the Olympic Park here in Sydney and a gathering tomorrow morning in Canberra."

"What gathering?"

"A ceremony to honour your war dead."

"The dawn service?"

"Yes."

Max's mind raced. Lachlan was in Canberra for a job interview and to do practical training with the private hospital which Hulk had organised for him. Max was to go down in the morning and they were going to look for houses over the weekend. Lachlan was going to the dawn service, they had spoken about it last night. Max felt sick as he looked at his watch. It was already after midnight.

"Are there any other attacks planned?" Max asked.

"No," Haddad said.

"Who is going to lead the attacks?"

"The one in Sydney is a man named Benjamin Wright."

"How do I find him?"

"He'll be the first name on a search of the internet."

"He also goes by Reverend Wright."

Max took out his phone and searched the name.

"The Archbishop of Sydney?" Max asked.

"Yes," Haddad said.

"The Archbishop is going to release a biological weapon at the football?"

"Yes."

"Why?"

"You'll have to ask him."

"Okay and in Canberra?"

"Katzenberg. David Katzenberg."

"Who is he?"

"He is a Rabbi in the national synagogue in Canberra."

"Is this a joke?"

"What do you mean?"

"A Muslim, a Rabbi and a Catholic."

"Yes."

"All planned to release biological weapons across the country?"

"Why is that so hard to believe?"

"What is their goal?"

"As you have demonstrated so aptly today, the world is turning away from religion. At times of stress and terror, people return to their faith."

"So, you conspired to bring about a nationwide revelation, a mass return to faith through spreading fear?"

"Yes. I have told you everything, now do what you promised. Kill me. Allow me to see, Allah and feel His embrace."

"Not yet, I have to see if your information checks out first."

"It will. Do what you said you would."

"I will," Max said. "Just not right now."

"You promised! Where are you going? Get back here!" Haddad screamed as Max left the room.

"Do you think he is lying?" Hulk asked as Max walked into the observation room.

"No, I don't actually," Max said. "It felt like the truth."

"I agree, but I tell you, if it is true, we are getting into something bigger than we thought. Blake go run those names passed Faisal."

Max took a seat next to Hulk as Blake left the room.

"Good job today, kid," Hulk said.

“Thanks, Hulk.”

“I mean it, you’ve been through the ringer, and you haven’t missed a beat. I was sceptical at points during your training, but you’ve gone above and beyond what I expected.”

“I was wondering, I think I know the answer, but I’m struggling with it, but can I ask you a question?”

“Yes.”

“Lachlan is in Canberra.”

“And you want to call him?”

“Yes.”

“I’m sorry, but you can’t. We can’t create panic.”

“What about the service?”

“What about it?”

“Can we shut it down?”

“We are trying. Shadow is on the phone to the Prime Minister and Home Affairs Minister as we speak.”

“What happens next?”

“We try to verify the names and any meetings the three of them had, then we track them down and ask them some questions.”

“I meant about the service.”

“If the Government shuts it down, the terrorists will know we are onto them and it could spook them into releasing it early or somewhere else.”

“And, if they don’t shut it down?”

“We are going to Canberra.”

“Okay,” Max said turning back to the window to watch Blake with Faisal and checking his watch.

Blake was pacing back and forth, asking Faisal questions. One after the other. Max continued to check his watch and with each passing second his fear and worry for Lachlan was growing.

“That’s it,” Max said standing up. “I can’t take it anymore.”

“You can’t take what?” Hulk asked.

"This arsehole is lying, Hulk, and he's enjoying it. Look at his face. He knows Blake is getting nowhere."

"So, what do you think we should do?"

"Bad cop time," Max said walking from the room as Hulk smiled to himself.

Max stormed into the interrogation room and Blake stopped talking when he spotted Max and moved aside. Max drew his pistol and shot Faisal in the knee cap, shattering it and spilling blood onto the floor.

"Jesus," Blake said. "What are you doing?"

"Get out, Hermes," Max said.

"But."

"No, get out."

Blake left the room and Max walked over to Faisal.

"Were the names he gave you correct?" Max asked.

"Fuck you," Faisal said through gritted teeth.

"Wrong answer," Max said stepping back and firing again.

A bullet smashed into Faisal's other knee and he screamed.

"You are crazy!" Faisal yelled. "Okay, I will talk, I will talk, but not to you, let the other man back in."

"Fair enough," Max said walking out, pausing in the doorway. "But, you lie to him or fuck around, I'll be back in here and the pain will continue."

"Get out of here!"

Max walked passed a slightly shocked Blake.

"Sorry, I needed to speed things up," Max said.

"Looks like it worked," Blake said. "Good job."

"Let's see what he's got to say," Max said walking back into the observation room as Blake headed into the interrogation room.

Max took his seat and watched through the glass. Faisal was protesting and flapping about, asking for morphine and complaining about Max, but Blake calmed him down and he started talking.

"Well, what do you know?" Hulk said. "He's singing. Well done, kid. We'll make an agent out of you yet."

Blake walked back into the room.

"He confirmed the names and locations," Blake said. "Want me to get a plan together?"

"Yes, head down and see where Shadow got to with the politicians," Hulk said. "Then gear up. You, Alpha and Max are going to Canberra. That good with you, Max?"

"Yes, sir," Max said.

"Blake, go get Kate and your kit."

"Yes, sir," Blake said heading for the bunker.

"What about the Sydney site?" Max asked.

"I'll lead a team out to pick up the Archbishop," Hulk said.

"You can hardly walk."

"I'll figure that out. I wanted to speak to you about what happens next."

"Okay."

"When you get to Canberra, I want you to go pick up the Rabbi, find out who he is working with and bring them in. You can take them to AIS Headquarters for questioning. Until we have proof, you'll need to hold off on the physical stuff. Got it?"

"Yes, of course, sir."

"Good. It's just."

"We could be being played."

"Exactly."

"Then what happens?"

"Shadow will stay here and keep working on these two just in case."

"Okay."

"Once you've got your target and the information you need, you should keep your plans with Lachlan. Maybe surprise him and spend a few hours with him. We need you to keep up appearances."

"I wish I could just tell him. I'm sure he'll understand."

"Not yet, Max."

"Okay, Hulk. I understand, but what if I need to come in to help?"

"I'll get the hospital to call him in too."

"Just how wide is your reach?"

"That's for me to know," Hulk said smiling at the question. "Seriously, kid. You're doing great. I know the stuff with Lachlan is painful, but it'll get better."

"Okay, got it."

"Well, holy fuck, Batman," Kate said walking into the room. "Seems Robin's got his big boy pants on today."

"Are you ready to go?" Hulk asked ignoring her.

"Yes, sir," Blake said from behind Kate.

"Good. Get to the plane."

"Yes, sir," the three of them said heading for the car.

"Fucking proud of you, Prince," Kate said patting Max on the back. "Like a duck to fucking water. Now, let's go get this son of a bitch."

Chapter Thirty-Two

"Hello?" Curran asked into his mobile phone.

"Daniel, it's me," Wright said. "They have Haddad."

"AIS found him?"

"The stupid man stormed the hospital trying to kill the General, but he was easily beaten, given the number of agents on site."

"Well, that was pretty stupid."

"Yes, well done with the Opera House."

"Thank you, sir."

"Did you find the other devices?"

"Yes, I'm planting our second one now, then I'm headed to meet Uri and Katzenberg."

"Good. You need to hurry, we cannot be sure what Haddad will say to AIS."

"You think he would give us up?"

"I think he is weaker than he lets on. Who knows what they will do to him?"

"Torture?"

"They will torture him, without doubt."

"How do you know that?"

"I know a few people who work there."

"Are you telling me everything I need to know?"

"Don't get captured."

"Archbishop, do you know what they are doing to him?"

"Yes."

"Tell me."

"You don't want to know."

"I do."

"Well, he has bullets in both shoulders, he is missing several teeth and he's just about to be pumped full of what I am told is a chemical which makes your veins feel like they are on fire."

"Jesus."

"Given the circumstances, I will let that slide."

"Forgive me, Father. You can take the man out of the military."

"But, not the military out of the man."

"Yes, sir. Sorry, sir."

"It is okay, Daniel."

"How do you know what they are doing?"

"I told you, I have some contacts in AIS."

"They must be pretty close to the action to know what is happening in a room like that."

"Yes."

"I hope you don't mind me asking, Father, but is he – I presume it's he – is he connected to us in anyway?"

"There is a bigger game at play, Daniel. Our role is important and our cause is righteous, but there are others involved and their cause is their own."

"You mean, apart from the Jews and the Arabs?"

"Yes."

"Who?"

"I cannot tell you that."

"I think given the circumstances and the risks I am taking, I deserve to know."

"You might be right. You are with me, aren't you?"

"Of course, sir. I am with you until the end. Their feet have slipped."

"Bless you, Daniel. Okay, I'll tell you. His name is the Pilot. He is funding our cause."

"Why? What's he getting out of this?"

"Chaos."

"Why would he want that, if he works for AIS?"

"As I said, we are just one part of a much bigger scheme."

"I would argue, Archbishop, that there is no bigger, nor higher calling than getting people back to the church and showing them the path to our Lord."

"You are right, Daniel. I am using him, as much as he is using us. We needed money. There is no higher calling than the work you are doing in our Lord's name and in His service. Thank you for what you are doing."

"Thank you, but not everything is about money, Your Grace."

"It is when you have to buy weapons and fund the campaigns we will need following the attacks. We need money for those things."

"Of course, I'm sorry, now I understand, Father."

"Good. Thank you, Daniel. Now, you need to get going."

"Yes, Your Grace," Curran said as the phone line cut out.

Wright's car stopped and he climbed out in his full regalia. The purple sash flapped in the breeze as he walked towards the barricade.

"Father," a young policeman said. "I'm sorry, but it is off limits for the public, I can't let you through."

"I have clearance," Wright said. "Archbishop Benjamin Wright, please check and hurry, people are suffering, they need to reach out to God."

"Just a minute, sir," the officer said before taking his radio up. "Command, come in, I have an Archbishop Wright at clearance twelve. He says he has authorisation to proceed?"

"Copy, twelve," the radio squawked. *"The Archbishop of Sydney has been cleared by AIS to enter. Please let him through."*

"Roger that," the officer said. "Sir, please come through."

"Thank you," Wright said walking through the barricade carrying a silver briefcase. "May God be with you."

"And you, Your Grace."

Wright wove his way quickly through the crowd of police and emergency services personnel rushing around the barricaded Sydney Opera House. He ducked down a small set of steps and found a lone man dressed in paramilitary fatigues.

"Archbishop Wright?" the paramilitary man asked.

"Yes."

"I work for AIS, the Pilot asked me to let you in."

"Yes, thank you."

"You know what's in there right?"

"Yes, son. God watches over me. Please open the door and follow me in."

"Follow you, I wasn't told about that."

"Yes, you'll be fine. Trust me."

"Trust you, I just met you."

"Do you want me to call the Pilot and ask him what you should do?"

"No, sir. Please. I'll follow."

"Good, let's go."

The paramilitary man waved his access key on the sensor and the small Opera House security door opened allowing the two men inside.

"Here take this," Wright said handing the paramilitary man a tall gold goblet as he spun his open silver briefcase on the desk inside the door.

Inside the case, another dispersal device sat unarmed and strapped into a foam inlay on one side. On the other, an inlay for the goblet now sat empty but it was completely framed by four long cylinders which ran the length of their sides of the case. They were full of a deep red liquid. Wright took out one of the cylinders, unscrewed the small white cap and poured some of the liquid into the goblet the paramilitary man was holding. He screwed the cap back on then passed the container to the man with the goblet. He took out another long cylinder, then locked his briefcase and placed it against the wall under the table.

"Please, take a sip," Wright said. "It will protect you."

"From the virus?" the paramilitary man asked.

"Yes."

He took a sip and offered the goblet to Wright who just took it back and sat it on the table.

"You aren't going to drink it?" the paramilitary man asked.

"I have already taken a dose of the antidote, when this batch was delivered to me earlier," Wright said. "I need you to bring the spare bottles and I need you to take my phone and record me with the people. Can you do that?"

"Yes, Your Grace."

"Good," Wright said picking up the goblet and handing him the phone. "Let's go upstairs."

The two men walked upstairs into the Opera House. Federal agents in biological suits stopped on seeing the two men. The agents had been moving people between rooms behind heavy plastic sheeting.

"Sir, when they said you were coming in, I presumed they meant you would wear a HAZMAT suit," an agent said. "You will be infected now."

"No, agent," Wright said. "God has spoken to me and I am here to help heal these people."

"Sir?"

"Move aside, agent," the paramilitary man said. "He has clearance from AIS."

"Yeah, fine. Okay."

The agent stepped aside and Wright and the paramilitary man walked over to the first room. He pulled back the plastic sheet and entered. He waited until his follower came in and started filming. People were already showing symptoms and they looked up at the priest from their growing misery.

"My brothers and sisters," Wright said addressing the room and in front of his recording camera. "What has happened here today is a tragedy. The devil's work has been unleashed on us and it is truly horrific. What will happen to each of us next I'm told is unspeakable. Pain and suffering like we have never felt, but I know God protects me and he will take away my pain in this world or the next. But, what about you? Are you free of sin and ready to take your place by His side, in His glory, in His eternal paradise or have your feet slipped?"

"Let me tell you, each of us in our lives have moments where our thoughts and actions have thrown us into sins against our Father. Our feet have slipped! Indeed, we are born into sin and we need to live lives reflecting and embracing His will to be taken into His light. Have you lived such a life or have your feet slipped? Have you accepted God into your life and your very soul, or have you ignored and denied Him, turned your backs on Him? For those of you who fall into the latter category when you arrive for judgement in the hours to come, you will be cast aside, thrown from the heavens into the fiery pits of hell to burn in your eternal punishment for your feet have slipped!"

"But, for those of you who, even know, truly open your hearts and minds to our Lord, rest assured, He will hear your prayers. He will reach down and stop this awful virus, if indeed, you make amends and confess your sins in time. But know, even if the worst should happen, if at that time you are free from your sins, He will be waiting for you with open arms to welcome you to His kingdom, His home with many rooms for each of us to live in eternal happiness by His side. Father, please hear my prayer, bless my brothers and sisters gathered here today who sip the blood of Christ from this cup and confess to you their sins. Protect them from this virus and plague, but if we are too late and they should fall, embrace them in Your love and allow them to walk with you in the heavenly kingdom. Amen. Now, who would like to confess and drink their share of the blood of Christ, our Lord and Saviour?"

Chapter Thirty-Three

Max was sitting in the backseat of the black Landcruiser. Kate had told him he was barred from driving unless it was an emergency after witnessing his performance behind the wheel at the Wool Shed. Blake was sitting in the front passenger seat as the car raced down the slipway past the Canberra airport. Max looked through the window watching the crew set about refuelling the AIS Gulfstream. Its white paint was shining, almost sparkling, under the lights of the Royal Australian Air Force base lights. Kate took a hard-right turn and hit the accelerator heading towards the city.

"He's a senior religious figure, Kate," Blake said. "We can't just go in and drag him out by the hair."

"Why the fuck not?" Kate asked. "If he's guilty, fuck him!"

"We don't know if he is guilty."

"A known terrorist named him."

"Yeah, I know that, but what if he was lying?"

"Who?"

"Haddad."

"What do you think, Prince? Think he was lying."

"No, I don't," Max said. "But, I haven't been doing this for long."

"Oh fuck that, Prince. You can read people, that's one of the reasons you got the fucking job. Tell me, if you had to say, yes or no, no grey area, is he involved?"

"Yes."

"See, Hermes. Let's just go break the door down and drag him out. We can strap him to a chair and put Prince in a room with him, that should scare him. It'd scare the shit out of me, given what he's done today."

Max felt the hair on his arms stand up and a shiver ran down his spine as he relived the torture in his mind. *It was worth it,*

Max thought. *I needed to protect people, I needed to protect Lachlan.*

"No, Kate," Blake said. "We are going to bring him in quietly and ask him some questions, we will leave a team at his house to search it and the cyber guys are already working on hacking his computer and phone."

"Fine."

"It's approaching two, the service starts at five thirty," Max said. "How are we going to get the information we need in that time?"

"I don't know," Blake said.

"We need to shutdown the event."

"The Prime Minister and Minister for Home Affairs have said no. They told us to secure the site."

"What the fuck's wrong with them?" Kate asked.

"They said 'then they win'."

"My boyfriend is going to be there."

"Lachlan is going to the dawn service?" Blake asked.

"Yes."

"Okay, well, we can't have that."

"Hulk told me I couldn't warn him."

"You can't, but I can get him out of there."

"How?"

"He's got a job at the hospital, right?"

"Yes."

"I'm going to get them to call him into work."

"You can do that?"

"Yes, I will call the director now."

"Thank you, Blake."

"You won't be able to concentrate if he is at risk, I need your head in the game," Blake said unlocking his phone and dialling a prestored number. "Director Hayes, it is Lieutenant Commander Blake Smyth, I work for General Patrick Scott and the Australian Intelligence Service. Yes, sir, I did know you were on deployment together. Well, sir, I need you to do us a favour. I understand the General asked you to hire Mr Lachlan Farrell. He's doing some practical training with you now. Yes, sir, I'm sure he is very capable and I'm glad to hear that. I need you to bring him in to work today, in fact, I need you to bring him in now. Yes, sir, I know it's a weird request, but I would be very grateful. Excellent, thank you, sir. One more thing, can you please have your bio team on standby? No, sir, nothing to worry about, at this stage, it's just a precaution. Okay, great. Thank you again, sir."

Blake pressed the end button and put the phone back on the charging plate under the dashboard.

"He's calling Lachlan in to work," Blake said. "He won't be at the service."

"Thank you, Blake," Max said leaning forward and touching him on the shoulder.

"That's okay, Max. Right, let's focus on how we are going to do this."

"I still think we should shoot the fucker and drag his arse back to AIS," Kate said. "Do you seriously think he's going to come quietly if he's involved?"

"You might be right, about the coming quietly bit, not the shooting bit," Blake said.

"So, what do we do?"

"How about a little role-play?" Max asked.

"Kinky, I like this idea already," Kate said.

"What'd you have in mind, Max?" Blake asked ignoring Kate.

"Why don't we break in, blindfold him and take him somewhere to question him pretending we work for Haddad?" Max said.

"Snatch and grab," Kate said. "That could work. What do you think boss-man?"

"Let's do it," Blake said. "We're two minutes out. Max, check the weapons."

"You got it."

Kate pulled the car up a few doors down from Katzenberg's house. Max and Blake got out and went around to the rear. They holstered their weapons and grabbed some cable ties and a black hood from the weapons hold. They left the door opened and headed for the house, completely dressed from head to toe in black tactical gear. At the property next door, they rolled down their balaclavas and drew their silenced pistols. Max circled around the back of Katzenberg's house while Blake waited at the front door. On the count of twenty, Max picked the lock and entered the rear of the house. He swept silently room by room from the backdoor through to a set of stairs leading up to the first floor. He waited for a few seconds before being joined by Blake. Max led the way with Blake only a step behind the whole way up. On the landing at the top of the stairs, they both froze in place hearing a sound to their right. Blake used hand signals to tell Max to check it out, while he scanned the rest of the rooms upstairs. As Max approached the door of what he assumed was a bedroom and readied himself for entry, the doorbell rang downstairs. Max looked around at Blake, who put a finger over his lips. Max stepped quickly through the corridor and into the bathroom, just as the bedroom door opened and a tall, thin man walked out wearing just a pair of black dress pants which he was doing up. He headed down to the door and opened it. Max heard a brief exchange before the man and his new companion walked up the stairs and into the bedroom. The second man was shorter and younger, and he was carrying a lot more weight around the midsection. Max and Blake tiptoed quietly to the edges of the door and listened.

"Are we ready to go, Uri?" Katzenberg, the taller man, said.

"Yes, everything is in place, David," Uri said. "I was able to get a batch of project two to Wright. He was happy enough with that to start him off. We will produce more over the coming days to help cleanse our followers."

"Good and our first device?"

"It's with Abbas."

"And, he is ready?"

"Yes, but are you, David?"

"What do you mean?"

"Are you sure we want to go ahead with this, getting involved with the Arabs? Are we really going to achieve what we set out to? They seem to be getting ahead of themselves in Sydney."

"Yes, which is good for us. They will take all the blame. We are just using them to get the job done. AIS is probably already blaming them."

"And if they don't? What happens if the people find out? Won't it have the opposite effect?"

"They won't find out. Haddad and Moghadam will take the fall for all of the attacks and the people will come running back to us."

Max and Blake nodded to each other, then Max flew around the doorframe and into the room.

"Get on the floor!" Max yelled levelling the gun at Katzenberg.

"You heard the man," Blake said mimicking the moves aiming his gun at Uri's face. "Get on the floor!"

"What is this?" Katzenberg asked. "Who are you?"

"If you answer any of my questions with lies or I think you are trying to hide something from me, I will be your worst fucking nightmare," Max said pistol whipping the Rabbi. "So, get on the fucking floor!"

Uri dropped to his knees straight away and Blake pushed him down onto his stomach with his combat boot kicking him between the shoulder blades. Katzenberg got down slowly and Max copied Blake, kicking him onto his stomach. They both cable-tied their suspects' hands before Max dragged a black hood over Katzenberg's face. Blake looked around the room and found a business shirt hanging on a nearby chair, he tied it around Uri's face as a makeshift blindfold. The two agents led their captives down the stairs and out in the front yard. As Max walked down the little staircase to the front lawn, he heard Kate on the comms unit warning him of something, but he did not catch it. He looked up and saw a man frozen at the front gate.

He was a young man, maybe just slightly older than Max, and like Katzenberg and Uri, he too was wearing a black suit and tie, with a white shirt. He wore a small round rimmed pair of reading glasses and he had a small backpack hung over his right shoulder.

"Stay right there," Max said locking eyes with him. "Don't you move."

The young man hesitated, then turned and ran.

"I've got him, Max," Blake said. "Go get that arsehole. Get on your knees!"

Katzenberg and Uri both got down to their knees, as Max ran across the yard and down the street after the young man.

"He ran into a yard three doors down, Prince, sorry I didn't see him coming to the gate sooner, he must have come out of the shadows next door," Kate said over the comms unit. *"Where do you want me?"*

"Get to Hermes," Max said.

"Roger that."

Max ran down the foot path and into the yard Kate had pointed out. He sprinted along the driveway and into the backyard just as the young man was climbing over the back fence. Max ran hard then jumped up and pulled himself over the fence. The young man was already halfway across the yard as Max landed and gave chase. The two men ran out into the street one after the other. Max looked around and realised it was not just any street, it was ANZAC Parade which led up from Lake Burley Griffin to the Australian War Memorial where the special dawn service was to take place. There was already a large crowd starting to arrive. Several people watched in fear as the two men ran towards the memorial, Max still wearing his balaclava and combat gear which must have been a frightening sight. A few people stopped or ran in the opposite direction as they saw him. Max started to gain on the young man as they got within fifty metres of a police barricade. The young man had moved his backpack around to the front and was fiddling with the zipper. He was going for the device. Max drew his pistol.

"Stop!" Max yelled. "Federal agent!"

The young man kept running, but checked over his shoulder to gauge the distance between him and his pursuer. A line of police officers started to take notice of Max and the young man, and reached for their pistols.

"Freeze!" one of the officers said as he and his team took cover behind their vehicles taking aim at Max and the young man.

The young man stopped and Max slowed, taking several steps to the left to move the police out of his line of fire, but keeping the gun aimed at his target. The young man was still trying to open his backpack.

"Put the bag on the ground and put your hands up," Max said.

"Both of you put your weapons and bags down, and put your hands up," the police officer yelled.

"I'm a Federal Agent. This man is a suspected terrorist. I will not put down my weapon. I will fire at him if he does not put down his bag."

Max watched as the bag hit the ground and the young man raised his hands, but in one he held a small metal device.

"You don't want to do this," Max yelled at him.

"Put down your guns," Abbas said. "Or I will detonate the device."

"This is not your fight, Abbas. Yes, I know your name. I heard Katzenberg speaking about you earlier. You won't be able to blame anyone else for this, it will be drawn straight back to you and your religion. It will not have the effect you were hoping for. In fact, you will destroy your religion and maybe all religion. But, this hasn't gone too far, only you and I know what is going on here. Put down the device and I promise I will try to keep it that way."

"Rabbi Katzenberg said no one would find out. He said the Arabs would take the blame, he said people would flood back into the synagogue and renew their faith in Judaism. He said we would restore religion across the country."

"I'm sorry, Abbas, but that's not going to happen now. Please don't destroy your faith. This isn't what you believe in, harming helpless men, women and children. Look up there at the crowd gathering, they don't deserve to die."

"What have I done?"

"You haven't done anything yet, just put the device down, very slowly and we can all walk away from this with a clear conscious."

Abbas started to lower his hands. He was shaking and started to cry.

"I'm sorry," Abbas said stopping and holding the device in front of his face, starring at it.

"It's okay, Abbas, just sit it on the ground and we can talk about it," Max said.

"I can't go to gaol. I can't live with what I have done."

"Please Abbas, just put the device down, you haven't done anything wrong yet, we can talk about it."

Abbas turned and faced Max.

"Don't do it, Abbas," Max said. "Just put it down."

"I'm sorry," Abbas said moving his thumb above the detonation button.

Max fired twice hitting Abbas in the forehead and the neck. Abbas did not fall straight away, his lifeless body just stood motionless for several seconds. Max leapt forward, spiriting harder than he thought possible and jumped forward as Abbas's legs buckled and his body started to fall to the ground. He dropped his pistol and reached out with both hands catching the device less than a foot from the bitumen. He laid still on the ground trying to get this breath back, winded from the fall, then he dragged his arms in and inspected the device. The cylinder was intact.

"Sit it down," the police officer said as his team circled Max.

"I'm a Federal Agent," Max said. "This is a biological weapon, I need to secure it."

"You need to put it down. Until we can verify your identity, you are under arrest."

"You're kidding right?"

"No, put the weapon down and put your hands behind your back."

"This is the second time this has happened and I'm starting to get annoyed by it. We're on the same team."

"That might be the case, but you are carrying a weapon, covering your face and you killed a man in the street. What would you have me do?"

"Okay fine, but you need to call the HAZMAT team, secure this area and do not under any circumstances move this device once I sit it down."

"Just sit it down."

"Okay," Max said gently sitting the device on the ground.

"Now, shuffle back and away from the weapon."

Max slid backwards about a metre from the device then one of the cops dropped a knee into his back before cuffing him and pulling the balaclava off.

"Oh, for fuck's sake, again with the knee," Max said. "That all they teach you boys?"

Max heard sirens approaching, the sound was echoing across the lake and up the parade. An officer stood him up and walked him to a nearby police car, and shoved him into the backseat. He watched out the window as a couple of the police looked at the device. One of them looked over at him and he shook his head. The officer smiled then looked away as Kate's Landcruiser pulled up a few metres away. Max watched as Blake walked up the parade, took off his balaclava and produced a small plastic card which he showed the lead officer. Max could not hear what was being said however he did notice the officer's body language change, he seemed suddenly more rigid, then he looked down at his feet. Blake handed him a mobile phone and the officer listened intently for a minute then handed it back to Blake and started walking and pointing at the device and at Max. Blake walked over to the device and pointed in Max's direction. The officer ran over to the car and let Max out.

"Agent Shaw," the officer said. "I'm sorry for all this, we needed to be sure of who you were before could let you go."

"And the officer who dropped a knee into my back?" Max asked. "Was that necessary given the fact I could have been an agent?"

"I will reprimand him."

"Don't worry about it, I probably would have done the same. We've got a job to do."

"Yes, thank you, sir."

"Let's get to it," Max said as he walked over to join Blake.

"You okay?" Blake asked.

"Yeah, what's the plan?"

"An AIS team is one minute out, they are going to take the device back to AIS Headquarters for analysis."

"Where are Katzenberg and Uri?"

"They're tied up in the back of the Landcruiser. We will take them back to AIS HQ as soon as the team arrives and secures the weapon."

"Got it. I think it's intact. I had to shoot him, Hermes."

"I know. I heard you on the comms unit. You did well."

"You heard me?"

"Yes, your unit was on active while in pursuit of the suspect, so we could track you down and listen in. You did the right thing, Prince. You talked him down, I thought you had him too."

"I did, but then something got to him. I don't know why, but he went for the button."

"Sometimes they are too far gone, Max. You did everything you could and you saved lives. It must have been a hell of a jump from where you were standing to catch it."

"Too far gone?"

"Yeah, brainwashed beyond the point of return."

"I don't think that's what it was."

"What do you mean?"

"He was upset, certainly conflicted, but it was doubt. He said, 'what have I done?' He hadn't done anything yet."

"Maybe he knew he was going to get arrested as soon as he put it down and realised he'd thrown away his life?"

"Yeah, maybe," Max said as the AIS HAZMAT Unit pulled up.

"Over here fellas," Blake said pointing to the device.

The HAZMAT team unloaded a clear plastic and rubber sealed container from the rear of the large combat truck. They were wearing full bio-suits with self-contained air supplies. As they were loading the device into the container, Blake and Max walked back to their car.

Chapter Thirty-Four

Curran sat in his van watching as Katzenberg and Uri were dragged out of the house by AIS agents. He was almost in disbelief. When he agreed to help, the archbishop had been adamant, so clear, they would never be found. They had discussed at length how the Arabs would take the blame and how the Catholic Church would swing open their doors to welcome in new and returned believers. The church would rise again to its former greatness and the people would be saved. He would help save their souls for God. That is what the archbishop had promised. It was the least he could do.

The archbishop had found him in a military hospital in Sydney, rushed home from Afghanistan for emergency surgery after suffering horrific injuries in a bomb blast. His commanders, those lying bastards, manipulators, abusers, had forced him and his team into the building, even though intelligence said it was rigged with explosives. He lost his whole team in the blast.

In the Sydney hospital, his wounds refused to heal and doctors were not sure he would ever recover, but then the archbishop came to visit and it was as if God Himself had reached down and connected the two men. Curran's wounds began to heal in the days that followed the visit and his strength started to return. When he left the hospital, he found Wright and became a devoted follower and believer. He had helped Wright to show people the power of God, to help people find His way and His light – the same light that had saved him. His feet had slipped, like so many others, but now he was doing God's work. He was spreading the word of the Lord.

All the evil he was part of was necessary, but would not hurt the church. Islam would be blamed he was told, but now it was all coming undone. He had just heard on the radio that the archbishop was inside the Opera House taking confession and blessing the victims, some were already claiming to be feeling better and the conservative radio host was extolling the virtues of the Catholic Church and of the archbishop who had rushed in putting himself at risk. This is what they had been working for to show people the power of the Lord, but now Katzenberg had been captured and the Arabs had failed, he was starting to doubt the archbishop. He wondered if he had been lied to again.

"More lies," Curran said to himself. "They are all the same. Manipulators. Users. Abusers!"

He fidgeted with his phone considering whether to call the archbishop, but then he saw Abbas walk to the front gate of Katzenberg's residence. He watched as Abbas initially froze in place at the gate, then he took off followed by an AIS agent who ran like an Olympic sprinter after him.

"Oh Lord, give me strength!" Curran said again to his empty van.

The AIS agents pushed Katzenberg and Uri into the back of their SUV, and sped off down the road after Abbas and their other agent. Curran slammed his hands down on the steering wheel then grabbed the wheel and violently thrust back and forth like he was trying to rip the wheel from the car.

"Argh!" Curran yelled before getting out his mobile. "Answer you lying son of a bitch!"

"Hello," Wright said.

"They got Katzenberg and Uri, and they are chasing Abbas down the road."

"Calm down, Daniel."

"You fucking calm down! You lied to me!"

"I did not lie to you."

"You said the Arabs would take the blame, but AIS keep getting closer and closer to us!"

"They don't know about our involvement."

"How can you be sure? Did your friend from AIS tell you that?"

"Yes."

"Well, he has to be lying to you. How else would they have found the Jews?"

"Calm down, Daniel."

"Stop telling me to calm down! You are just as bad as them! Those arseholes who killed my brothers! They were fucking liars like you are! You get into our heads and your words spread like a virus, and we just do as we are told."

"I am not like your old army commanders, Daniel. I speak only in the service of God."

"How can I be sure of that? How can I be sure this isn't just another lie?"

"You felt it, didn't you? In the hospital, when I first met you. The power of God. He was there as He is here now, with us. He saw your pain, He saw your suffering, He saw how your wounds refused to heal and saw your anguish. Do you remember?"

"Yes."

"Do you remember His warmth washing over your skin, remember His love healing your wounds, remember Him taking away your pain?"

"Yes."

"That is how you can be sure, Daniel. The Lord has blessed you and He is with you, with us."

"Yes, Your Grace."

"I'm not the commander who ordered you into that building, Daniel, I didn't plant that explosive and I didn't pull the trigger, but I did show you the way."

"Yes, Your Grace."

"Do you have the devices?"

"All but one. I already gave Abbas the one for the service."

"But you have the others?"

"Yes."

"Where is Abbas?"

"They are chasing him down the street. Katzenberg and Uri are in the back of an AIS car."

"AIS have them?"

"Yes, don't you listen to me? That's why I am calling. They are getting closer to us!"

"Okay, okay, right. Yes, I hear you. What are you planning to do?"

"Now the Jews have been stopped, I will need some help to plant the devices. I think it is safe to assume the dawn service is now off limits."

"I agree. You'll head for the other targets?"

"Yes, but first I'm going to get some help and cause a distraction."

"Yes, okay. So, Plan B."

"Yes, I got the explosives from Abbas. I don't have any other choice. I will get help and our work will weaken their response."

"I guess not. Make the arrangements and get it done."

"Of course. What will you do, Your Grace?"

"I have spoken to Hogan, project two is rolling. The antidote seems to have started to work at the Opera House, so I'll stay here for a little bit longer and hopefully do some interviews, then I'll head back to the church. When you have finished get back here and you can help me distribute the antidote amongst our followers, then set about welcoming those seeking the light. You will be a saviour of our people and a true man of God."

"Understood. Thank you, Archbishop."

"Thank you, Daniel. God is with us. What we do is for Him."

"Their feet have slipped."

"Their feet have slipped," the archbishop said as the call ended.

Chapter Thirty-Five

Max was pacing in the corridor of the AIS Headquarters building in Canberra. He had met a number of the analysts and agents who were on site in the old concrete establishment, but he couldn't remember most of their names. He was tired and worn out from everything he had been through. Blake had told him the old building was built in the nineteen sixties, like the majority of the government buildings, when the Government had decided to create a national capital. It apparently was an old Defence Department building and from the look of it, it had not had a good clean since the day it was built. There was dirt caked thick on the outside of the windows. The walls were stained yellow from decades of cigarette smoking, when you were still allowed to smoke inside, and the once blue carpet was worn back to the underlay in some sections and to concrete in others. Every corridor was streaked black up the centre from foot traffic. Old solid metal safes and filing cabinets lined the worn grey cubicles which each had a series of outdated built-in desks and office chairs which looked ready to collapse at any minute. The computers though were all brand-new, state-of-the-art, with the latest in-house and off-the-shelf software. They stood out in their relatively ancient looking surroundings.

Max noted the varying ages, races and genders of his new colleagues. He had thought a majority might be like Hulk, old white men, former defence force personnel, but he was happily wrong. There were a few of them scattered around, but there was no one defining type of person, that gave Max some comfort because it meant he was not the only different one. He was drinking one of the strongest coffees he had ever tasted, but he needed it. One of Hulk's personal assistants had gone to the mess and got coffee and bacon and egg rolls for the team, while they tied Katzenberg and Uri up in the basement, leaving them there to sweat, having told them they knew who they were and that they had killed Abbas.

"How are you feeling?" Carter asked joining him in the corridor.

"Hi, Doc," Max said. "I didn't realise you were here."

"Yeah, I escorted Moghadam back from the Wool Shed. I hear you've had quite a hard start to the world of espionage."

"I don't really know what I was expecting, but this is well beyond that."

"Are you handling it okay?"

"I don't really think I've had time to process it."

"Well, from what I hear, you are to be congratulated."

"Is that right?"

"Yes. You saved the General, twice, and Flash, you apprehended several suspects and stopped two biological weapons from killing thousands of people. I would say congratulations are in order."

"I couldn't save the people at the harbour or in the Opera House or Victoria, the doctor out in Western Sydney."

"You can't save everyone, Max."

"I'm certainly going to try and I'm going to hold these people to account for what they have done."

"That's part of why we are here," Carter said opening the door to a nearby conference room. "Why don't you come in and take a seat?"

"Yeah, okay," Max said walking in and taking a seat across from Carter.

Carter sat in silence for over a minute. Max knew what he was doing, so he sat in silence too. After two minutes, Carter broke the silence.

"Normally, that works," Carter said.

"The silence?" Max asked.

"Yeah."

"Most people like to remove the awkward by filling the silence?"

"Yes. This is what happens when we recruit a top-of-the-class psychology honours student."

"I guess."

"How are you feeling about Haddad?"

"I think he's a piece of shit."

"I meant, how are you feeling about what you did to him?"

"I know. My answer stands."

"Interesting."

"Why is that interesting?"

"Because last time we discussed torture, you had very mixed feelings about it."

"I still do. It wasn't a pleasant experience, I threw up halfway through."

"That's a good sign, means you're human."

"Glad to hear it."

"Anything else about the experience you want to talk about?"

"It worked."

"I'm sorry?"

"He was tough and well, the things I had to do, God, but he talked. He broke and told me about his co-conspirators, that's what led us here. The torture worked."

"And, you saved thousands, Max. All those people at the service, let alone the people they would have infected had they left the area, which they would have. You, Max, you are the reason they are alive."

"Something is bothering me though."

"You don't like praise?"

"No, not about that, about the guy from this morning, Abbas."

"The guy you shot on ANZAC Parade?"

"Yes."

"You're worried about taking his life?"

"No. Well, yes, but that's not what I was talking about."

"What were you talking about?"

"He said he was sorry for what he had done."

"What he had done? You stopped him."

"Yes, that's my point."

"Maybe he meant sorry, in general, not for a specific action, plus he knew he'd been caught."

"That's what Blake said."

"And, you don't agree with him?"

"I'm not sure."

"That's not an answer. Tell me what you are thinking."

"I think he did something else."

"Like what?"

"I don't know."

"Prince, are you on comm?" Blake asked over the comms unit Max had forgotten was in his ear.

"Yes, Hermes," Max said. "Were you listening to all that?"

"All what?"

"I'm just talking to Doctor Carter."

"Oh no, Prince. No, I've been with the analysts, I went off comm."

"Okay, doesn't matter anyway. What's up?"

"Can you get Carter to show you to the operations room?"

"Yes, we're on our way."

"Good. See you in a minute."

"Can you please take me to the operations room? Blake needs me."

"Yep," Carter said standing and heading for the door. "Let's go."

They walked through a maze of corridors then headed up to the seventh floor. The elevator doors opened and they walked into a dark room, spanning the entire seventh floor of the building, the only light was coming from two large projector screens running down the left hand wall and a bank of computers. A couple of flood lights lit up the entry ways, but there was no natural light, all the windows were completely blocked out. Max couldn't tell if they were just covered in thick curtains or if the windows had been taken out and replaced with concrete. It was too dark to tell. Blake was sitting at one of the computers in the middle of the room with several analysts.

"Max, Ian," Blake said. "We've been looking into Katzenberg, Uri and Abbas. Katzenberg's computer and phone have high security, we are still trying to hack into it. Uri Rothstein is a businessman, he runs a company called Rothstein and Hutchinson. This is where is gets interesting. It's a chemical company based here in Canberra."

"How is that interesting?" Carter asked.

"Emails."

"Emails?"

"Yes, we hacked into his company email system and found numerous emails from the CEO of a company called, Hogan, Stevens and Hill Pharmaceuticals. Uri's company manufactures some of the chemicals the pharmaceuticals company uses."

"I'm still not following," Carter said.

"Several of the emails mention, a rapid, exponential increase in demand for a particular new drug they've been working on. They call it project two."

"How do we know they are linked?" Max asked.

"Because we also have the photo and video files of the testing."

"This is graphic so get ready," Blake said. "Roll it on the screen."

One of the analysts pressed a series of commands into their computer and one of the screens on the far wall changed to the black screen with white writing. It said 'Project One' then a video started rolling. It was a time-lapse of a man in a white laboratory. He started out normal enough, then he started to go pale and yellow, before breaking out in purple and red blotches. After eight hours in the room, he was violently ill. After twelve, he was convulsing on the floor and foaming from the mouth. Sixteen hours after exposure he was dead.

"Jesus Christ," Max said.

"Play the next clip," Blake said as the analyst hit play.

The screen changed, 'Project Two' was displayed on a black screen before footage began to roll. It was the same room, but instead a young woman was sitting quietly in a steel chair. She went through the same symptoms. After ten hours, she was violently ill, but someone dressed in a bio-suit entered the room and injected her with a needle. She stopped vomiting and laid still on the floor for around an hour, before she stood up, got back in the chair. An hour later, she was looking around, cognisant and she spoke to a new person in a bio-suit who entered the room to check her vitals and hook her up to a drip. Not long after that, a doctor walked in without the bio-suit on and they left the room together.

"And, it's the same virus and the antidote?" Max asked.

"Yes. Here is the live footage from the Opera House," Blake said as the analyst changed the screen.

CCTV footage from inside the Opera House panned through several different rooms. The HAZMAT staff were inside putting people into different rooms according to their symptoms. Some were starting to become violently ill, while others were experiencing earlier symptoms like blotchy skin. Around a quarter were still yet to show any symptoms.

"Who is that?" Carter asked tapping the screen above the moving image of Wright.

"That is the Archbishop of Sydney, Benjamin Wright."

"He went in there?"

"Yes, he's been taking confession and offering people wine from the gold goblet in his hand. Interestingly enough, some of the people who had symptoms hours ago, who drank out of his cup, are starting to stabilise."

"You think he has project two, the antidote, in the cup?"

"Yes."

"Fascinating," Carter said rubbing his chin in thought. "You think he's trying to convince people God is healing them?"

"Yes."

"A miracle of his own making. Fascinating."

"Okay," Max said. "So, we know where that arsehole is, I presume Hulk is going to get him. What are our rules of engagement with the others? We need to find these other devices."

"The link has been established for Uri and the weapons, we do what we need to do," Blake said. "Do you want to take the lead?"

"You're the boss, Blake, I'll do whatever you need me to."

"Okay, well, how about you take Uri and I'll take Katzenberg?"

"Done, where are they? Let's go."

"Excuse me, sir," an analyst said as Blake and Max made to leave. "You need to see this."

"What is it?" Blake asked.

"I'll put it up on the screen."

Max and Blake turned to face the screen, it was mirroring a phone which was open on the messages screen, it looked like an exchange between someone and Uri.

"Whose phone is this?" Blake asked.

"Abbas's," the analyst said.

"And, the conversation is with Uri?"

"Yes, sir."

Max read the messages from top to bottom, it was clear they were both involved with the planned attack on the memorial service, but one message got his attention.

"Stop scrolling," Max said. "Go back up, please. There, stop. 'I've delivered the other package and van to the Arab. He gave me our first device, but he has the others.' He handed over a package to someone with the other devices."

"You were right," Carter said. "He was saying sorry for something else."

"Yeah, the question though is, who?"

"And, where is he, how many devices does he have and what was the package?"

"Let's go find out," Blake said heading for the elevator.

As the doors opened, an explosion rang out shaking the building and throwing Max and his colleagues around the room. The building shook and filled almost instantly with smoke. Fires broke out everywhere and the sprinkler system kicked in to try to douse the flames. Debris, bodies, office equipment and tables and chairs were all violently thrown around the seventh floor becoming lethal projectiles.

Max had been slammed against the far wall and was knocked out by the force of the impact. He came to under an overturned desk. He tried to move but felt the weight of the heavy old desk holding him down. He was on his back and the desk was pinning his legs and crushing his chest. He felt suffocated, not only from the weight of the table, but from the smoke. He tried to lever his arms out to the side to get hold of the table, but his left arm was under his back and he could not move it, so he started to rock from side-to-side. At first it was very slow, moving it a little bit, but then it started to rock. He felt it digging into his ribs and shins, and thought he would be lucky to get out without one or both breaking. Finally, the table shifted to the left and he rolled his body, pushing with all his might. The table fell to the side and Max pushed it over freeing himself. He felt his ribs as he tried to get his breathing under control, they were sore, but he did not think they were broken. His shins were the same. He stood up and took in the room. The wall where the screens had been hanging was completely blown out. The wind was whipping in and whirling around the room. There were spot fires, and paper, office supplies and furniture, as well as the brand-new computers had been strewn around the room. Blake was laying against the wall next to the elevator, his neck at an awkward angle. Max ran over and checked his neck, Blake coughed and groaned, and rolled over.

"Are you okay?" Max asked.

"Yeah, I think so," Blake said. "What the fuck happened?"

"I don't know, an explosion. The whole side of the building is out."

"My team. Where's my team?"

"I don't know, Blake, I was knocked out under that table. I saw you and came straight over."

"Can you please help me up?"

Max helped Blake to his feet and the two of them began combing the room for the analysts and Doctor Carter. They found two of the analysts that had been helping them with the computer files. They were laying several metres from their computers, completely still. Blake checked their pulses, but it was no use they were both dead, cut down in a hail of shrapnel. The third analyst had been over near the projector screens and had fallen from the building to her death. Blake was shattered, he was kneeling over the two analysts on the floor, a look of pure anguish on his face. Max put his hand on his back.

"I'm sorry, Blake," Max said. "Come on, we need to find Carter and get out of here."

"They were just doing their jobs," Blake said. "They didn't deserve this."

"I know, mate, there will be time to remember them, but I need to get you out of here."

Max helped Blake back to his feet and as he stood, he saw Carter for the first time. He was sitting against the back wall watching the two agents.

"Come on, Doc," Max said. "We have to get out of here."

Carter just starred at them.

"Doc?" Max said. "Let's go."

He did not move, so they ran over and saw why Carter was not moving. He was pinned to the wall beside a filing cabinet by the metal leg of an old desk that had blown apart. The leg had pierced his stomach and punch right through him and into the wall.

"Oh fuck!" Max said.

"It's," Carter said couching up blood. "It's okay boys, after all the times I put you and our colleagues into the field, I'm well overdue, I guess, I had this coming."

"No, don't say that," Blake said. "You've done an amazing job here and thanks to you, our country is a safer place and a better place. You've served our nation with merit and distinction, Ian. We couldn't have done it without you. We couldn't do our jobs without you."

"Thank you for saying that, Blake."

"We need to get you out of here," Max said.

"I'm not going anywhere, Max."

"That's bullshit, we're going to get you to a doctor, they'll fix you up. You'll have a nice scar, but you're going to be fine."

"No, Max. I'm not. Thank you though, for caring. Never let your loving human side die. This job will throw everything at you and you'll want to give up or you may want to shut down your feelings and emotions. Don't. Your human nature is what matters, it is why you're going to be one of the best agents I've seen – you already are. Find your motivation and make sure you hold tight to the people that are special in your life and embrace love. Let it wash away all the shit that comes your way. You have a gift, Max, and your country needs you."

"We need you, Doc."

"Thank you, both. Blake, please tell my wife and children I love them, and that they are all that mattered to me in the world. Tell them, I did what I did, so they could live in peace and happiness."

"Of course, I will," Blake said taking Carter's hand.

"Hug Lachlan extra tight when you see him, Max."

"I will."

"You both need to go, the building is unstable. Look after each other, care for each other and go and get these arseholes, will you?"

"We will," Blake and Max said together.

"I know you will," Carter said smiling as he closed his eyes.

Chapter Thirty-Six

Max knelt over Carter's body, just staring at him. The man who had helped him through training at the Wool Shed. The man who had explored his deepest thoughts and emotions. The man who knew more about him than even Lachlan. He had failed, again.

"Max," Blake said putting his hand on Max's back. "Max, I'm sorry, but we need to go."

"Why did this happen?" Max asked.

"I'm not sure, Max. I'm sorry all of this is happening around you, it's not fair. Ian Carter was a very close friend and colleague of mine, I understand how you feel."

"I'm sorry, Blake, I know you were close. It's just, I'm struggling, mate. I am scared of failing, scared of more deaths piling up. I'm scared of losing more friends."

"I understand, Max. We work in a difficult environment, but it's not always like this. This is easily the worst day I've experienced since joining AIS."

"I'm not sure whether that's comforting or not."

"It's okay to be scared, Max. We all are. I am too."

"The thing is, Blake," Max said turning back to face Blake. "I'm also scared of something else."

"What?"

"I'm scared of the anger building up inside me, scared of the hate I'm starting to feel for these people and I'm scared of what I will do to them once I find them."

"I understand, Max," Blake said helping Max to his feet and keeping hold of his hand. "You care, Max. It's a strength, not a weakness. Like Ian said, your integrity and honour, and your love, are what will keep you grounded. Use the anger and hate to drive results, and trust that you will know where the line is and you will stop when you need to."

"You're placing a lot of faith in me, Blake."

"Yes, but I know you can do it."

"Well, let's go see if you're right," Max said squeezing Blake's hand before letting go, drawing his pistol and heading for the fire exit.

Max and Blake swept down the fire stairs each taking a corner, pausing and letting the other go down to the next, providing cover. On the fourth floor, the stairs were cracked and on the third, a few stairs were missing. Max and Blake jumped the gap, but on the second floor the gap was too large, so they entered the door on the second floor. It was completely devastated, fires were burning around the room, and desks, chairs and cabinets had been thrown from their places. They saw bodies of their AIS colleagues lying around the room, some were dismembered, others were on fire. The sprinklers that were still attached to the roof were trying in vain to overcome the fires, but they were failing. Max and Blake dodged through the wreckage and debris, and headed for the fire stairs on the opposite side of the room.

"Hermes, Prince, are you on comm?" Kate asked over their earpieces.

"Yes, we're here, Alpha, are you okay?" Blake asked.

"Fucking Moghadam has escaped. The explosion guttered the ground floor, collapsing the roof of the basement. We were pinned down, while some arsehole was shooting at us, covering Moghadam so he could get out. He climbed the concrete and ran out through the space where our fucking front door used to be."

"Where are you now?"

"I'm out the front with everyone who has gotten out so far. I'm trying to log into our surveillance system to get an ID on the car they left in, but the fucking servers were in the basement, they are probably on fire."

"Contact the Bunker in Sydney, they will have back-ups."

"Yeah, they are checking now."

"Good, we are on our way out now."

Max and Blake fled down the fire stairs, leaping gaps in the concrete, and finally ran for the foyer of the AIS building. The door was missing and beyond the gap they saw the disaster zone that was the foyer. Tiles had been uplifted and thrown into the walls, some had literally pierced into the concrete like large porcelain ninja stars. The wood panelling was in splinters on the floor and chunks of concrete had even been ripped from the wall. The glass panel that held the government crest had shattered and turned to dust, there was only a small shard left sitting on the floor, and all of the doors and windows were smashed in and were speared around the room and scattered over the floor. One of the security guards had a large chunk of glass hanging from a wound in his chest. Max and Blake walked out into the carpark to meet Kate.

"Is this everyone that made it out?" Max asked looking around at the small group of AIS agents assembled.

"So far, yes, but we have rescue teams coming in to sweep the building," Kate said.

"Have you spoken to Hulk?"

"No, not yet. I spoke to Shadow. He's running the Sydney operations and now running the search for our getaway vehicle."

"Did they pick up the archbishop and the device?"

"Hulk is with the team at the football stadium, no word on the archbishop as yet."

Max's phone rang.

"Hello," Max said answering the phone.

"It's Hulk, are you okay?" Hulk asked.

"Yes. I'm here with Alpha and Hermes."

"They are with you?"

"Yes."

"Good, put Hermes on the phone," Hulk said and Max passed Blake the phone.

"Hulk, it's Hermes," Blake said holding the phone out. "You're on speaker phone."

"Where is your phone? I tried you once already. Are you all okay?"

"It was on my desk inside. The three of us are fine, but General, I'm sorry to tell you Carter is dead, as are an untold number of our colleagues. The building is devastated, Hulk. The whole front wall is missing. Glass and concrete everywhere."

"Do you have a number?"

"No, but it's not going to be good, sir. There are maybe fifty people standing out here with us."

"Only fifty?"

"Yes, sir."

"Jesus."

"I'm sorry, sir."

"Me too," Hulk said pausing momentarily. *"There will be time after all of this to mourn our friends and colleagues, but we need to finish this first."*

"Sir, there is one more thing. Moghadam got away and Katzenberg is dead."

"What about Uri?"

"He is tied up in the back of my car, boss," Kate said.

"Good. You might need to have a word with him. There is more to all of this, I just can't put my finger on it."

"You're right, Hulk," Blake said. "Before the explosion Prince, Carter and I saw videos. They were videos of the trials for the biological weapon which was released in the Opera House. They were horrific."

"How does that link to Uri?"

"They were on his email."

"Prince, are you listening?"

"Yes, Hulk," Max said.

"When we hang up, I need you to have a word to Uri."

"Yes, sir."

"Anything else, Hermes?"

"Yes, there was a second video. There's an antidote."

"An antidote?"

"The email chain spoke about an exponential increase in demand for the product and a need for rushed mass production. The Archbishop is at the Opera House and we think he has it with him. Some of the people he heard confession from and gave a drink from his goblet are starting to stabilise."

"Son-of-a-bitch. Fake fucking miracles."

"Looks like it, sir."

"Okay, we'll pick him up. Who were the emails exchanged with?"

"Phillip   Hogan   of   Hill,   Stevens   and   Hogan Pharmaceuticals."

"What do we know about him?"

"We had started the search, but then the explosion hit."

"Alright, Hermes, get in touch with Shadow and let him know what is going on. Tell him what you told me. Get him to arrest Hogan. I'll call the Prime Minister and get him to nationalise the company, so we can control the production of the antidote. Prince, go talk to Uri, and Alpha, track that vehicle then the three of you go get those arseholes."

"Yes, sir," they all said.

"Good luck everyone. Keep me posted."

The line went dead.

"Can I borrow this?" Blake asked.

"Of course," Max said pressing his thumb to the sensor unlocking the phone.

"Thanks," Blake said as Max started for the car. "Max?"

"Yeah?"

"There's, I'm sorry, I didn't mean to look, but there's a message from Lachlan. Do you want to check it?"

"Yeah, it's okay, thanks for telling me. He will be letting me know about the hospital I'm sure."

Max took the phone and checked the messages.

Hey Maximus, I'm sorry to be a pain, but I've been called into the hospital. I'm not sure how long I'll be here, but I guess

I'll just have to play it by ear. I will call when I can. Sorry I'll miss the open houses. I've let the hotel know you are flying in, they have a key waiting for you. I can't wait to see you. I miss you so much. Love you, Lachie xx

Max quickly wrote a message back.

Hey Lachie, that's okay. My flight is delayed anyway, so I might not get to see all the houses either. But, I'm definitely looking forward to seeing you tonight. I miss you and love you too, so much! Good luck today. Love you, Max xx

"Thanks, Blake," Max said.

"No worries. Sorry."

"You're not the one lying to your boyfriend, you don't have anything to be sorry about."

"Neither do you, Max. It's for the greater good."

"Yeah. I better go talk to Uri."

"Sure," Blake said turning away slightly embarrassed.

Max walked over to the rear of Kate's car. Kate was pacing nearby, swearing at someone on the phone, but stopped to hit the unlock button when she saw Max. She walked towards him, as he opened the back door of the Landcruiser.

"Well keep fucking looking," Kate said ending the call.

"Haven't found them yet?" Max asked as sirens in the distance started to get closer.

"Not yet, but they will. What's the plan here?"

"We are going to have a little chat with Uri here," Max said looking into the rear of the car.

Uri was crying in fear and looked like he had wet himself.

"Hi Uri," Max said. "My name is Prince and I work for the AIS."

Max grabbed Uri by the hair and dragged him half out the door.

"Look at what you have done," Max said yanking Uri's head around, so he could see the damage to the AIS building.

It was completely devastated. Floors up to level seven had been totally gutted. The whole side of the building was blown out, smoke, fire and water were streaming out into the air or cascading down to the ground.

"You and your friends are responsible for this," Max said. "They are federal agents who are dead in there. If this was any other country you would get the death penalty. Here, you will definitely get back to back life sentences for every person you have killed today."

"I didn't. This wasn't me."

Max pushed Uri back into the rear of the car, pulled out his pistol and shoved into Uri's mouth. Uri shook and his eyes went wide.

"I don't care about your life and I certainly don't give a shit if you rot in gaol," Max said. "But I had friends in that building and I have people I care very deeply for in this city. Tell me what I need to know or I will bring in the death penalty just for you."

Uri tried to speak, but the gun was getting in his way.

"Before you speak," Max said clicking the safety off on his pistol. "You should know I read your emails and watched your little videos. It is taking all of my self-control not to just pull this trigger and be done with you. Do not lie to me. Do you understand?"

"Yes," Uri said as Max pulled out the pistol.

"Start talking."

"I'm innocent, I got roped into this by Katzenberg and Wright. They said we would just be scaring people. They said we wouldn't hurt anyone."

Max dragged Uri by the hair back out until his head was hanging from the back of the car, looking down at the concrete of the carpark. He put the pistol against the back of Uri's head. Uri started to cry as Max chambered a round.

"They wanted people to flood back into the churches and synagogues," Uri said.

"And what did you want?"

"I wanted that too."

Max fired a round past Uri's right ear. The bullet slammed into the concrete. Uri had stopped breathing, then started to sob.

"My company will make millions, possibly billions, with antidote sales if this thing spreads internationally."

"So, you were using them?"

"And, they were using me. Please, please, just don't kill me."

"What about Hogan?"

"He's a die-hard Catholic. The money was just a bonus to him, he's a true believer."

"One of Wright's flock?"

"Yes."

"And, Wright is in on all this too?"

"He's in charge now Moghadam is missing."

"How many devices are there?"

"Six."

"One in the Opera House, one in the casino, one at the football stadium, one with your dead friend, Abbas. So, two left, where are they?"

"Abbas is dead?"

"Yes."

"How?"

"I shot him in the head. Same thing I'm going to do to you, if you don't tell me where the other two devices are."

"Curran."

"Who?"

"Daniel Curran."

"Who is he?"

"He works for the archbishop."

"And, he has the devices?"

"Yes."

"Was he the man Abbas text you about earlier?"

"Yes."

"What was the package that Abbas gave him?"

"Please," Uri said crying.

"It was the explosive used here wasn't it?"

Uri said nothing so Max whipped the pistol into the side of his head.

"Yes," Uri said.

"So that's why Abbas said he was sorry. Where can I find Curran?"

"I don't know."

"What the remaining targets?"

"The memorial service."

"We stopped that one, what were the others?"

"I don't know, we planned everything separately, so no one knew what the others' plans were, in case."

"In case, what?"

"In case any of us were captured."

"Convenient excuse."

"It's the truth, I swear, he didn't tell me."

"How many attacks were supposed to be carried out here in Canberra?"

"Two."

Max fired into the ground beside Uri's head again as Blake walked over.

"Was Abbas going to carry out both those attacks?"

"Yes."

"Well, what was his second target?"

"Defence."

Max sat the hot end of his pistol barrel on Uri's neck burning the skin and making Uri squirm and cry out in pain.

"Why are you doing this?" Uri asked.

"Because you lied to me," Max said. "You told me you didn't know the other locations."

"I meant, I meant, I didn't know the Arabs' and Curran's locations."

"So, Defence, you mean Russell Headquarters?"

"Yes."

"Okay, Hermes, call and tell Defence to be on the lookout."

"After what happened here, they will be on high-alert," Blake said.

"Which buildings were they targeting Uri?" Max asked.

"The Secretary and military Chief's building," Uri said.

"Let's go, Alpha," Max said as he pushed Uri into the back of the car and slammed the door down.

Max, Blake and Kate jumped into the Landcruiser and sped off for the Defence Headquarters building, as fire and ambulance services arrived at the devastated AIS building.

"If the weapon is activated, I am going to throw you inside and lock the door," Max said to Uri. "You will suffer the same fate as your victims. You've seen the movie, it's not pretty, so start thinking about how I can stop this happening. Where can I find Curran and Moghadam?"

"No, please don't put me in there," Uri said. "I don't know how to find them."

"Well, start thinking."

"Prince, Defence says they raised their security and will be watching for the two men. I'm getting the Bunker to send through their photos."

"Good. It's still pretty early, there shouldn't be many people there, right? I mean, they should stand out?"

"It's always a bit busy up there, but it should be easier than it would be later in the day."

"How's he going to get in?" Kate asked. "I mean it's bloody insane, you've been there a thousand times, Hermes. Plus, they're on high alert, there'll be troops everywhere."

"I don't know, but we need to find him," Blake said. "With AIS down, more pressure will be put on defence to step up to fill the gap, but they are also running two wars and various peacekeeping missions as we speak. We can't let them fail."

Chapter Thirty-Seven

Kate stopped the car in the defence headquarters main carpark across the road from the compound's buildings. Troops had already secured the driveways under the buildings and were standing guard on all the doors. A number of camouflage wearing military personnel were starting to search the hundreds of cars parked nearby. They carried mirrors to look under the vehicles and torches to look through the windows.

"Alpha, stay with Uri," Blake said climbing out of the four-wheel drive. "Prince, come with me."

"Yes, sir," Kate said. "Good luck and Godspeed."

"Let's do it," Max said getting out and following Blake. "What's the plan?"

"We are going to head in and check the security plans, then we'll figure out what to do next."

"Okay," Max said suddenly conscious of the fact he was in full combat gear walking towards armed soldiers on the main doors of the defence headquarters building, one of the most secure facilities in the country.

"At ease, boys. I am Lieutenant Commander Blake 'Hermes' Smyth and this is Agent Max 'Prince' Shaw from the Australian Intelligence Service. Who is your commanding officer?"

"I am," a young man said walking forward with his hand out to shake hands. "Corporal Jarrod Pollock".

"Corporal, you heard what happened at AIS?"

"Yes, sir. Sorry for your losses."

"Thank you, I appreciate that. What have they told you about the threat?"

"They have given us these two photos, sir. One Abu Moghadam and the second is a man named, Daniel Curran."

Blake studied the photos then showed Max. Max took a moment to memorise Curran's face and nodded to Blake.

"Well, keep an eye open, boys," Blake said. "We aren't sure how they will try to get in, but it is vital they are stopped. I need you to take special notice of any devices they may also have in their possession. They are extremely dangerous. The vials need to remain intact."

"Understood, sir," Pollock said.

"Thank you, all," Blake said as he and Max headed for the door behind the security team.

Inside the big marble foyer more guards were manning security check points and sign in desks. Max followed Blake to the security desk. A large wooden Department of Defence crest was mounted on the wall behind the guards.

"This building is in lock-down, gentleman," the old guard said as several soldiers turned with the weapons on the ready. "State your business."

"Lieutenant Commander Smyth and Agent Shaw of AIS," Blake said. "We are here on the direction of General Patrick 'Hulk' Scott the Head of the Australian Intelligence Service to monitor operations and help secure the facility."

"I think we have it under control, thanks boys."

"It isn't a request. I am taking over."

"Well, Commander, I'm not sure you have the clearance, rank or experience needed for such a task and even if you did, as I said, we've got it covered."

"What's your name?"

"Allan Miller. Former Colonel, Australian Army."

"Well, sir, firstly thank you for your service. Secondly, who and where is your commanding officer?"

"He's gone out for," Miller was interrupted.

"Blake," an older woman dressed in army fatigues said coming through the security screens. "Nice to see you, kid."

"Great to see you too, ma'am," Blake said shaking her hand. "Major General Susan Whitlam, may I introduce you to Agent Max Shaw. Max, this is General Whitlam the Head of Defence Intelligence."

"Nice to meet you, Agent Shaw," Whitlam said shaking Max's hand. "I hear you have had a hell of a first day?"

"Yes, ma'am," Max said looking inquisitively to Blake. "Nice to meet you too."

"General Whitlam receives hourly briefs from AIS on our operations, that's how she knows who you are."

"Oh okay," Max said. "Makes sense."

"So, they won't let you in hey?" Whitlam said. "You'd think they would have a bit more respect considering everything you have both done today."

"The former colonel and I were just discussing how AIS was taking over the facility and operation. He seemed ready and willing to help."

"Yeah right," Whitlam said looking at Miller who had not flinched since the General had entered the room. "Is this true, Allan?"

"Yes, ma'am," Miller said. "Just sorting out security passes for the two agents."

"Thank you, but they don't need them," Whitlam said walking towards the glass security screens. "Come on, boys, let me show you where we have set up."

Whitlam buzzed her security tag on the little panel and the eight foot high glass doors slid open and closed behind her as she walked through. Blake pointed to Max's ring then waved his own in front of the sensor. The doors opened for him and he walked through. Max tapped his ring on the large grey box, the doors opened to a little positive sounding buzz and small green light. Blake and Whitlam were waiting next to a large group of men and women dressed in camouflage combat gear, including green, black and brown face paint. The group was checking their weapons and more than one eyeballed Max up and down as he entered.

"I've set up a temp office and command centre here," Whitlam said opening the door of a nearby conference room. "Come in. Everyone listen up. This is Hermes and Prince from AIS. If they tell you to do something, do it."

"Yes, ma'am," the group of soldiers and aides said as they went back to setting up computers and surveillance gear.

"The screen is showing our external cameras, the internals are still being connected to this system, it shouldn't take much longer."

"Do you have views on all the roads surrounding and leading up to the compound?" Max asked.

"Yes," Whitlam said pressing the remote control on the desk in front of her changing the video feed. "This is the front leading up to the main square. This is the road leading into the back of the building and the loading dock. These feeds are various side roads and roads within the compound."

"He's not coming in here," Max said mostly to himself.

"What's that?" Blake asked.

"Nothing. I'm just thinking aloud."

"Tell us, son," Whitlam said.

"He's not coming in through the front door. This is now one of the most secure facilities in the country. They would be crazy to try to get in."

"So, what are you thinking, Max?" Blake asked.

"Three possibilities. First, Uri could have lied."

"You spoke to him. Do you think he was lying?"

"No, I don't think so, he was petrified, but he broke quickly which leaves me with some doubt considering what it took to get information out of the others."

"Trust your instincts, Max. What's your gut saying?"

"He didn't lie, this is at least one of the targets."

"So, what's the second possibility?" Whitlam asked.

"He could detonate the device on the front lawn and expose everyone in the square."

"But, most of the chemical would escape, limiting the impact."

"Which leaves us with option three."

"Which is?"

"He's not coming in the front door."

"He's coming in somewhere else?" Blake asked.

"Exactly."

"There isn't anywhere else he can get in," Whitlam said. "We have all the entry and exit points covered."

Outside the conference room door there was some commotion. The phones started ringing on the table and aides looked at their mobiles. Whitlam looked at her mobile, but she did not need to see the message.

"They are coming in the front door," Whitlam said pressing the remote.

The screen on the wall changed and everyone in the room turned. The security cameras showed twenty men running for the front doors or hiding behind their vehicles for cover, firing at the defence personnel guarding the building.

"Go, go, go!" Whitlam yelled into her comms unit.

The troops near the lobby started yelling and running for the door with their weapons raised. Blake and Whitlam had walked out into the lobby as the troops fled out, down the stairs and joined Corporal Pollock's team in defending the building. The military teams were pushing back hard and fast. Three of the insurgents were already down. Blake had his pistol out, as did Whitlam who was still shouting orders at the troops. The doors were locked and barricades were being placed behind the glass doors. Blake walked back into the command centre where he found Max standing up next to the screen. Max was staring intently at the screen, his face was only inches away.

"What are you doing?" Blake asked.

"He's not there," Max said.

"Curran?"

"Curran and Moghadam, neither of them are out there."

"What?"

"They aren't out there and none of the guys in the square are carrying devices or packs."

"What are you thinking, Max?"

"Coming through the front door is suicide."

"They are trying, right now."

"No, Blake, their men are trying or trying to distract us at least Moghadam and Curran aren't. Pull up the internal cameras and start cycling through them," Max said to one of the aides who started rapidly clicking through internal security camera feeds.

"How could they have gotten in, Max?"

"I don't know, but maybe they snuck in before the place was completely sealed?"

"They would have needed security passes, synced to our system, and, or."

"Or, what?"

"Or DFA's system."

"DFA?"

"Department of Foreign Affairs."

"What about them?"

"Tunnels."

"Slow down, Blake. What are you saying?"

"There are tunnels, linking a number of buildings in Canberra. They were built during World War II, so people could move freely between the buildings unseen, but more importantly, safe underground. Do we have cameras in the tunnels?"

"No, sir," the aide said. "The DFA tunnel is no longer in use and the others are collapse in permanently closing them."

"Where is the DFA entrance?"

"Basement, level three."

"Thanks. Max, let's go."

Blake and Max headed for the elevator. The doors opened on level three and they fanned out with their pistols drawn. Max pointed to a painted on signpost which indicated the various directions for tunnels and carparks. Max and Blake split up, left and right, to wrap around the large stale concrete basement. Max headed along the right wall, observing the cars and checking the various tunnel gates as he walked. Locked.

He could see the rubble in some blocking the way. Max got to the tunnel leading to the foreign affairs department. It was wide open and the padlock was sitting in two halves on the polished concrete floor.

"He's in the building," Max said as Blake arrived.

"I've got to call this in," Blake said taking out Max's mobile and dialling the number. "Ma'am, it's Hermes, they're in the building. The DFA tunnel is wide open and the padlock is cut. Get the surveillance team to sweep the footage and shutdown the ventilation systems. Yes, ma'am."

"Where is the air-conditioning system located?" Max asked.

"It's an isolated system in case of attack."

"So, it can't spread the chemical?"

"No, not if it is released outside the building."

"And, if it is released inside?"

"If it is released in the ventilation room, it can definitely spread throughout this building and the adjoining buildings."

"They are all connected?"

"Yes."

"That doesn't seem real smart."

"No, not today it doesn't."

"Hermes, Prince, are you on comm?" Kate asked.

"Yes, Alpha," Blake said. "Go ahead."

"Well, it's a complete fucking shit show out here."

"Yeah, are you okay?"

"We're fine, that's not why I contacted you. Uri looked out the window when the gunfight started. He saw a familiar car in the lot."

"Whose?"

"His."

"What?"

"His car was in the parking lot."

"How did it get there?"

"Two of his guys were part of the attack."

"Were?"

"They were two of the first to fall."

"So, he was more involved than he let on."

"Yep."

"Alright. Many more still on their feet?"

"Yeah a few, but our boys have nearly got them."

"Good."

"I checked the car. When it was all clear."

"Did you find something?"

"Yes, that's why I'm fucking talking to you."

"Right."

"We found plans to the defence headquarters."

"Any hints on where they were headed?"

"No, there's no markings on it, but I found a second blueprint."

"Of what?"

"DFA."

"Foreign affairs?"

"Yes."

"We're at the tunnel between defence and DFA. The gate is open and lock is cut."

"Think they might hit both?"

"They have two devices," Max said.

"Defence and DFA, on top of AIS, would cripple our intelligence, war and peacekeeping missions around the world."

"Fucking oath."

"No time to talk about it now," Max said. "Alpha, can you get to DFA?"

"Yes."

"Go, now."

"On my way."

"You should go too, Hermes."

"Why?"

"Defence have got this place locked down. I'll help Whitlam flush out whoever is here. DFA security and Alpha will need help."

"He's right, Hermes. One of you should come."

"Got it, on my way."

"Good. See you there."

"Ventilation room?" Max asked.

"Two floors down, turn right. Can't miss it."

"Got it. Good luck."

"Likewise," Blake said turning and running through the tunnel towards DFA.

Max took off back across the carpark towards the elevator. As the doors opened on level five of the basement, Max ducked his head around the corner and saw three bodies lying in the hall, in pools of their own blood, their camouflage fatigues staining red. Max walked quietly down the hallway, willing his combat boots to stay silent on the polished concrete floor. He stepped lightly past the bodies, keeping his pistol trained on the door to the ventilation room. When he got to the door, he slowly and softly turned the handle, and it opened with a small click. He paused for a second, waiting to make sure no one heard him, then inched open the door.

Inside he saw massive old furnace units. They stood more than two metres high, the same wide, and around four metres long. They were arranged in long lines, Max was not sure how big the room was, but it looked like several football fields. A third of the way down the room, the furnaces stopped and a large glass room ran along the righthand side of the massive space. Max noticed the glass was blue almost black as he got closer. As he walked along the corridor framing the glass box, he realised it was the server room. The large black servers' lights blinked and flashed inside. There was no rhythm or pattern to them. They seemed completely random. Max kept moving, hugging the concrete wall, aiming his pistol towards the end of the hall. Beyond the sever room, Max saw the air-conditioning units which filled the rest of the massive underground basement. They were not quite as big as the furnaces, but they were large and again, they were in two long lines. Between the first two, Max found another body face down, her camouflage uniform covered in blood. Max looked up as a door to his left opened and Curran walked out into the hall.

"Freeze!" Max yelled.

Curran spun and fired two shots at Max, before ducking behind an air-conditioning unit.

"You're too late," Curran yelled as Max dove for cover. "The timer is set."

"You don't have to do this, these people don't deserve this, they are innocent."

"They are not fucking innocent! They lied to me! You won't see active duty, you'll see the world, we'll pay you to study, it'll be an adventure. Fucking arseholes!"

"You were in the army?"

"Yes. Eight years. Eight fucking years of their lies and bullshit! Eight years of watching my friends get shot and blown up. Eight years of them ordering us to do horrific things to truly innocent people just trying to live their lives. Eight years of war over oil, not freedom or democracy. They deserved to be punished for everything they have done."

"And, what about the innocent men, women and children who will be affected if this spreads outside the building? What about the innocent victims you have sentenced to death in the Opera House? Why are you doing this?"

"They are not innocent. Their feet have slipped!"

"What do you mean, their feet have slipped?"

"Deuteronomy thirty-two, thirty-five. 'Vengeance is Mine, and retribution, in due time their foot will slip; For the day of their calamity is near, And the impending things are hastening upon them.'"

"Is that what this is about for you, bringing on the day of calamity?"

"'And I saw the dead, the great and the small, standing before the throne, and books were opened; and another book was opened, which is the book of life; and the dead were judged from the things which were written in the books, according to their deeds,' Revelation twenty, twelve through thirteen."

"You want to send people to their judgement day? Why? What did those women or children in the Opera House do to deserve this?"

"They sat in silence as the government marched troops into false wars. They turned their backs on the Lord and let sodomy, homosexuality, blasphemy, greed, adultery, false gods and false idols become acceptable. The commandments have been abandoned and the seven deadly sins rule the world."

"What about thou shall not murder?"

"'You must show no pity: life for life, eye for eye, tooth for tooth, hand for hand, and foot for foot' and 'whoever sheds man's blood, By man his blood shall be shed' and 'Then all the men of his city shall stone him to death; so you shall remove the evil from your midst,' Deuteronomy nineteen, twenty-one, Genesis nine, five through six, and Deuteronomy twenty-one, twenty-one."

"So, you think manipulating a few phrases from the Bible gives you some justification for what you have done? You are a murderer! You will be the one who faces judgement and I don't think a righteous God will forgive you."

"You are just a tool of the system. They are using you. You need to see the light. You need to turn your back on them. Your feet have slipped!"

"I have seen the light," Max said jumping up from behind the air-conditioning unit and firing three shots into the lights above Curran.

Glass and plastic rained down on Curran and he leapt to his feet and ran for the nearby unit, firing at Max as he ran. Max fired at Curran and moved forward several units before needing to duck back behind cover. Bullets hit the metal air-conditioner as Curran fired towards Max. The harsh sound rang out through the large space. Max returned fire, until his gun clicked empty. As he reloaded, he heard footsteps thundering towards him. He chambered the clip and a round, but Curran was only a metre away. Curran dived and tackled Max sending the pair backwards into a metal air-conditioning unit before falling to the floor. Max tried to free his arms, but Curran had him in a bearhug pressing Max's elbows into his ribs. It was suffocating and excruciating. Curran's years of service and countless hours of training gave him the edge over Max. Max struggled to try to free himself, but it was no use, Curran was too strong. Max's mind was racing as his vision started to blur because his breathing was restricted. Max thought about his training and thought about Hulk kicking his arse. *What would Hulk do?* Max thought to himself. *Whatever it takes.*

Max could hardly move his left arm, but with the little movement he had he reached for his knife. Using his fingertips, he eased the knife out of its leather holster then grabbed the handle and stabbed it into Curran's leg. His range was small and the knife did not go in far, but it achieved the result. Curran let his grip slip and Max violently threw his head forward breaking Curran's nose. Blood sprayed from Curran's nose and he let go of Max. Max rolled to the side and scrambled across the floor towards his pistol. Curran grabbed Max's leg and dragged him back, away from the gun. Max kicked and kneed Curran as he pulled himself on top of Max. When his face got closer, Max threw his elbow hard into Curran's temple. Curran was dazed, but undeterred. He dragged himself onto his knees and punched at Max. Max shielded his face as Curran threw punch after punch into his forearms, chest and ribs.

Max waited and waited, punch after punch, for his opportunity, then it came. Curran's rate slowed. Max threw a short, hard punch straight up and into Curran's throat. Curran grabbed his neck, and his mouth opened and closed like a fish trying to drag in breaths. His eyes went wide. He pushed Curran in the chest with both hands, sending him flying onto his back.

As he rolled on the floor, clutching his neck, Max stood up and walked over to his pistol. He picked it up, checked to ensure a round was in the chamber and turned back towards Curran, but he was gone. Max looked around trying to find him. He ducked his head around the unit to watch as Curran ran through the door he had originally used as Max had entered the room.

Max sprinted after him. He kicked the door open and ran through. There was a maze of metal ventilation ducts running through the room. They were connected to a series of large metal boxes, which looked like the air-conditioners in the other room. Max checked the first one as he walked past, it was stamped with a company logo. It was some sort of air-filtration system. Max walked between the ducts searching for Curran, the lights shimmered on the silver surface following the bumps and grooves of the ducts with each step he took.

Max leapt forward tackling Curran into the vents. The two wrestled, punching and kicking each other, then they separated and squared off, bouncing around like boxers in the ring. Curran limped forward and threw a couple of punches in Max's direction which he blocked. Max kicked Curran's wounded leg and he shuffled back. Max leapt off his left foot into the air and smashed his right fist into Curran's face with a vicious jab, before winding him with a left hook to the stomach. Curran buckled over and Max sprung forward driving his knee up towards Curran's face, but he dodged the blow and used Max's momentum against him, sending him into a pile of spare ventilation tubing. Max fell into the soft metal cylinders and disappeared under them. Curran took off as Max tried to crawl out. They crunched and creaked under his weight, until he finally pulled himself clear, scrambled out and gave chase. He rounded a bend in the ducts and saw Curran ahead taking the vent off one of the filtration units.

"Stop, Daniel!" Max yelled levelling his pistol at Curran. "You don't have to do this. It's not too late."

"It is too late," Curran said ripping the cover off the system.

Curran threw the grate to the side and reached into the filtration unit. Max ran towards him, but paused as Curran pulled out the live biological dispersal device.

"Put it down, Daniel," Max said.

"I just need to push a couple of buttons and this goes off, spreading the virus into the air vents and wiping out this country's top brass," Daniel said.

"Please, Daniel. No God would want this."

"What if I want it?"

"You don't. You signed up for service. They didn't force you to it. You had a job to do to protect Australians, to protect innocent people. Yes, some of the things you had to do and the things you saw were horrific, trust me, after the day I've had, I get it. But, you were doing it for the right reasons. You aren't here now, doing this, for the right reasons."

"Archbishop Wright, he showed me the way. When my wife left and took my daughter, when I got back and couldn't sleep at night without waking up in a cold sweat from reliving every shot I took and every friend's death, night after night. When the wounds torn into my skin by an explosion in a building, these arseholes sent me into in Afghanistan, would not heal. He took me in, helped the Lord find and heal me. He helped me find the light."

"No, he distorted the words of the Bible and manipulated you for his own purpose. He used your anger and anguish, and turned you into a weapon, fuelled by false words."

"No, no, he wouldn't do that!"

"He did, Daniel. I'm sorry, but he did."

Curran stated to lower the device. He was staring at it and slowly moving it towards the concrete.

"'I will destine you for the sword,'" Curran said softly to himself. "'And all of you will bow down to the slaughter.'"

"That's it, Daniel," Max said. "Just sit it down gently."

"'Because I called, but you did not answer, I spoke, but you did not hear. And you did evil in My sight And chose that in which I did not delight.'"

"No, Daniel. Please, just sit it down."

"Their feet have slipped," Daniel said looking up at Max.

"Don't."

"Their feet have slipped," Daniel said looking down at the device and quickly moving his hand towards the buttons.

Max fired three shots, one into Curran's head and the other two into his chest. Curran fell backwards, still clutching the device. It sat perfectly in his hands and rested on his chest. Max walked over and checked the device. The timer was still counting down.

"Hermes, can you hear me?" Max asked.

"Yes, Prince," Blake said.

"I found Curran and the device."

"Where is he?"

"He's dead and I have the device."

"That's great, Prince. Well done."

"It's been activated."

"How long?"

"Four minutes."

"Okay, that's plenty of time. You need to get it to Whitlam. She has a containment unit. Go to the elevator, meet her on the ground floor. I will call her now."

"Got it," Max said. "Moving now."

Max gently picked up the device and started walking rapidly for the elevator. He kicked open the door to the basement and started making his way past the air-conditioning units, then the server room. He kept watching the clock ticking down. There was two minutes left, as he hit the button for the elevator. He watched it, each click felt like time was speeding up, while the elevator was taking an eternity. The elevator arrived and Max stepped in and pressed the button for the ground floor. Tick, tick, the numbers kept flicking over as the elevator rose. The doors opened on the ground floor and Whitlam was waiting with her team.

"Here, Agent Shaw," Whitlam said pointing to a clear Perspex container.

Max walked out of the elevator and gently placed the device inside the container after one of the military guys lifted the lid. He pulled his hands out and the officer closed the lid, she checked the seals then clicked eight locks into place and pushed a small button on the computerised panel attached to the side of the box setting off a small beep. A row of small red lights flashed twice then held a solid green. It beeped twice.

"All clear, ma'am," the officer said.

"Good get it in the vault," Whitlam said as two officers picked up the container and ran for small metal box not much bigger than a refrigerator. "We have a camera set up in the vault."

Whitlam and Max walked over to the conference room and watched as the officers loaded the Perspex container in the metal vault and shut the doors. The screen went black until Whitlam turned on the light inside the vault using her laptop.

"Ten seconds," Max said as the device came into focus.

The explosion was ferocious flames erupted from the device and the green chemical cloud rushed and coated the Perspex. The box bounced, but did not fracture. The colours were mesmerising as they swirled around the box.

"Ma'am," the officer said. "The box held up, the chemical is contained."

"Good news," Whitlam said. "Thank you."

"Hermes," Max said into his comms unit. "You there, mate?"

"Yeah, Prince, but I'm a bit tied up at the moment," Blake said.

"I just wanted you to know, we stopped the device. It was safely detonated in the containment unit."

"That's good."

"What's happening on your end? Any leads?"

"You could say that."

"What's going on, Blake?"

"We found Moghadam, but he's captured Alpha. He has barricaded himself and Alpha in the DFA bunker."

"The bunker?"

"Yeah, it's a secure facility under the building. It's there to talk to world leaders on encrypted channels."

"Does he have the device with him?"

"I don't know."

"I'm on my way."

"Good, I could use the back up. Hulk, called by the way, he is en route. The device at the football field was a fake and Wright somehow snuck out of the Opera House and we can't find him, but Shadow's managing the search."

"Shit, another device is out there and this radical lunatic has it. When will Hulk be here?"

"Soon."

"Good. I'll be there in a couple of minutes," Max said heading for the elevator.

Chapter Thirty-Eight

"You failed, Your Grace," the Pilot said. *"I'm not really sure how you managed it, but you did."*

"I did everything we discussed," Wright said. "Didn't you see the interviews and footage from the Opera House, I've delivered miracles."

"No one in The Network gives a shit about your miracles, you selfish fuck, and no, you did not do everything we discussed. If you had, you would have succeeded and all of this would have been blamed on the Arabs, but now AIS know you are involved."

"AIS is wounded, the explosion in Canberra took care of that."

"AIS has numerous facilities, all of which backup and sync to each other for this exact reason. Yes, you have crippled them, personnel-wise, but they will recover quickly and the data will still be intact. You were supposed to create chaos and fear, and while you may have achieved that to a small level, it is not enough. AIS is closing in on the last of the devices now."

"There were too many moving parts."

"That was your call."

"The Arabs wanted an assurance we were in this with them, so they wanted us to carry out some of the attacks too, and Katzenberg and Uri, he despised them. He wanted their hands covered in blood as well. Some sort of sick symbolism."

"They were smarter than you gave them credit for, now you are going to wear the blame."

"And, the church?"

"I will do what I can to limit the damage to the church, but you need to get out of the country, at least until we can spin this and try to erase your involvement. We will go into overdrive with the footage of your so-called miracles, maybe that will work."

"Right, yes. Okay. You can do that?"

"We can, our reach is far and our hands never idle."

"Just how big is this group you are part of?"

"If you get through the next few months and we can control the message, I will bring you in closer and you can see The Network for yourself."

"How am I going to leave the country? Won't AIS be looking for me?"

"Yes, they are. You are going to leave on a private jet which is waiting for you at the airport. It has been cleared to leave when you are on board."

"Where am I going?"

"Rome. Well, the Vatican to be precise. You are going to do some training. It seems you are on your way to becoming a Cardinal."

"Cardinal?"

"Yes, congratulations. I'm sure they'll love that apparent miracle shit you pulled at the Opera House."

"Thank you."

"You need to go now, AIS are on their way."

"Oh, umm, right. Yes, of course. I will pack now."

"You have ten minutes, a car will be waiting downstairs. Silver BMW."

"Thank you, Pilot. You have done me a great service. I will not forget it and I will keep you in my prayers."

"You need to go."

"Yes, just one more thing, what about Curran?"

"If Mr Curran survives that alone should prove the existence of your God. AIS are onto him and as much as it pains me to say, they have this new agent. Prince, they call him. He is the best I've seen. He has been all over these attacks and bested you all, more times than you have won, that's for sure. Curran's good, well trained, but the little Prince, he just has a tenacity and strength I've not seen in a recruit or many full

agents as a matter of fact. If he finds Curran, I'm not sure Curran wins."

"I pray you are wrong and that he completes his mission."

"Pray hard, Your Grace."

"If my prayers are answered, will you send him to Rome?"

"Yes, he will join you. If he makes it."

"Thank you."

"You need to go now, Your Grace. I will be in touch when it is safe to do so."

The line disconnected and Wright stared at his phone. The words Rome and Cardinal were on repeat in his mind, before his thoughts turned to Curran. He hoped he was safe.

"Lord, please forgive your son, Daniel, for the things done in your name," Wright said kneeling before the alter. "He went forth into the world to spread your message and to bring the people back to your church. If he fails, may you raise him up to Your glory and embrace him in Your light. Merciful God, please also forgive me for the sins I have committed to advance our cause. I did what I had to do, what the Good Book instructed, but I'm not without sin and I ask for your forgiveness, oh righteous and forgiving God. Please watch over me, as I take the next step in my training to become a Cardinal and move higher in the ranks of Your church and help spread Your message to the masses. Amen."

Wright stood and walked quickly to his residence beside the cathedral. He packed just the essentials and headed out into the alley behind the grand old buildings. As promised the BMW was waiting and he climbed into the backseat. It made its way gently out of the alley onto the main road and sped off towards the airport, as sirens sounded and red and blue lights flashed on four police cars that rushed past in the opposite direction. He turned back and watched as they were joined by four on the other side of his cathedral. A swarm of police officers in riot gear stormed the church. He turned back breathing a sigh of relief.

Chapter Thirty-Nine

Max ran at full sprint through the tunnel connecting defence and DFA. Whitlam's troops had killed or apprehended all the attacking forces in the square. On Max's request, she was preparing a small unit and second detonation container to aid the AIS team at DFA. He had decided not to wait. Blake and Kate needed his help.

"Prince, are you almost here?" Blake shouted over the comms unit.

"Yes, I'm in the tunnel," Max said. "What's that sound?"

"Gunfire. A second attack squad has just hit DFA. I'm pinned down behind the security desk on the ground floor. The guards are falling fast here."

"Hold on, Hermes. I'm nearly there."

Max ran harder and faster, down little slopes and up gentle rises in the long dark concrete tunnel, until he ran flat-out into a similar underground basement carpark to the one he entered at defence. He searched for the elevator, but instead found the stairs. He leapt up them three at a time. As he ran, he dragged his MP5 around and pressed the butt of the gun into his shoulder.

He heard gunfire and glass smashing on the other side of the ground floor door. He opened it, but stayed behind the cover of the concrete wall. Three men were about to enter the foyer through the smashed windows. Four DFA guards outside were dead on the grass and a long row of attackers were firing at the building. Two guards in the lobby were firing wildly with their pistols at the men coming through the glass, but they were cut down where they stood. Blake was behind the security desk firing. He took down the man on the far side of the lobby, but the other two started firing in his direction, forcing him to take cover. Max ran into the lobby firing at the closest man. He shot him in the neck and through the arm. The man turned as he was falling and fired at Max. Max dropped to a knee and fired four more shots into him. He was dead before he hit the floor. The second man had spun around too and was bringing his gun around to fire at Max, but before he could, Max fired three shots and Blake bounced up from behind the desk and fired two shots. All five hit him and he dropped to the floor.

"Prince, this way," Blake said running for a door across the foyer.

Max ran, firing through the glass at the attackers outside who were starting to move closer to the building. He ran through the door as the first of the invading force stepped into the foyer. Bullets hit the doorframe either side of him. Blake slammed the door shut and the two agents ran fast for a rear corridor.

"Where is Kate?" Max asked.

"Downstairs," Blake said. "Moghadam has her locked in their communications room."

"What's his plan?"

"I think he called these guys in to help him escape."

"Right, so it's you and me against all of them?"

"Yep."

"Fuck. How long do you think we can hold them off?"

"Not long."

"Long enough for Whitlam's crew to get here?"

"Maybe, if we position ourselves well."

"Call her, tell her to speed it up. You've been down there. Roughly tell her where we will be positioned."

Blake called Whitlam as they ran down the stairs. Max looked around the antechamber outside the communications room. As Blake had described to Whitlam, there were four old wooden workstations in the centre of the room and a bookcase on the right. There was also a bathroom door on the left. The entrance to the communications room was at the back of the room.

Max dragged the closest workstation in next to the door of the bathroom, as Blake aimed at the door. He swept the computer and other equipment and supplies off the desk onto the floor, before doing the same to a nearby workstation, then he pulled it over and stood it on its side in front of the first desk. Finally, he and Blake dragged the book case over and stood it in front of the workstations. Blake gave it a final shove as a bullet slammed into the bookcase next to his hand. He bounced around behind the shelves and workstations, their makeshift cover, and knelt next to Max. Max used hand signals to tell Blake to go left, while he climbed up on the first workstation. Max gave Blake the three count then they both started firing. Blake shot several rounds around the left-hand side of the bookcase, hitting the first guy between the eyes and dropping him to the floor. Max shot over the top of the bookcase taking out the second and third men trying to get through the door. The other men retreated to regroup.

Max fired two warning shots into the wall outside the door, but the attackers were not holding back. A metal can bounced into the room, it was about the size of a spray can. Before Max had the chance to take in what was happening, Blake had sprung left and toe punted the can back out through the door. The flashbang grenade detonated in the hallway outside the antechamber. The sound was deafening and the flash was harsh in the doorway. It must have been awful in the hallway, the concrete walls amplifying its effects. Blake and Max both took the opportunity to run at the doorway and opened fire into three of the men they could see staggering around and when they fell, fired blindly passed them. Another flashbang bounced towards them, this time, Max slammed the door shut and they ran back behind their cover. The door shook as the grenade went off, but it held. They waited, watching the door, but not for long.

The door fractured and sent wooden shards into the room. Blake and Max unloaded round after round into the space where the door had hung only moments prior. Max emptied his clip and started to reload as Blake's run dry. As Max clicked a fresh magazine into his MP5, two men stormed through the door. He took the first guy down with one shot, but the second man took two shots, he made it almost to the bookcase before the fatal shot hit. His lifeless body dropped to the floor next to Blake as the third wave of attackers split into the room. Blake and Max showered them with bullets cutting them down in the doorway.

"What are they doing?" Max asked. "They aren't getting in here."

"They are sacrificing themselves to run us out of bullets," Blake said.

"That's committed."

"They think seventy-two virgins await, they are doing Allah's work, so He will reward them for being martyrs."

"Religion is a powerful motivator. Curran was under the same influence. He sprouted a bunch of Old Testament references at me. Stuff about judgement day and God's vengeance."

"This is what we have been trying to tell you, Max, throughout your training. We have to match their passion and sometimes do terrible things to stop them, but look at them, lining up to die. They are fuelled by their faith and it is more important to them than anything in the world. They are literally willing to die for what they believe in."

"Aren't we too?"

"What's that?"

"Aren't we willing to die for what we believe in too? I mean look at where we are standing."

"Yes, but," Blake said firing at two more men in the doorway.

"But, we are on the good side?"

"Yes, we defend those who can't defend themselves and protect those who need protection."

"Curran was on our side once too."

"Military?"

"Yes. It messed him up pretty bad. He spoke about the things he had seen and been forced to do for his commanders."

"Yeah, I understand. Working in the Navy and now with AIS."

"Things like watching friends die?"

"Yes, sadly."

"I don't know if I can handle that. I mean Flash and Hulk."

"You saved them, Max."

"What about Kate, locked in there with some psychopath? What about Carter? What about you?"

"We'll be okay, Max, and we are going to get Kate out of there. We will be fine."

"I like your confidence. How do you get through it?"

"I know why I am here, I know why we are all here and I know why we do what we do, and why it is important. And, when I can, I talk it out with friends, like you."

"Well, when we get out of here, we can definitely have a drink and debrief."

"Sounds good to me," Blake said as the two of them fired over and around the bookcase.

The men at the door stopped firing and stopped their advance. Max and Blake looked at each other, trying to figure what was coming, then they heard the door behind them open. They both turned and levelled their weapons at the door.

"Put down your guns, AIS agents," Moghadam said through the door. "I have your foul-mouth friend here. I will kill her and all of us with this device if you don't let me leave."

"Why don't you leave the device in there and come out with your hands up?" Max said.

"Is that you? The agent from that shed in the outback?"

"Come out here, Moghadam."

"We are coming out," Moghadam said. "Don't shoot."

Moghadam walked out clutching Kate around the neck. She was bigger and stronger than him, but in his other hand he had the device.

"It is you," Moghadam said. "It is a small world after all."

"Let her go," Max said. "And put the device down."

“No, I don’t think so. You both need to put your guns down and we are leaving. My men are waiting for me.”

“Not sure there are many of them left out there.”

“They did what was necessary. Allah, will thank them.”

“I doubt it. They tried to kill us.”

“But, you killed them. Maybe it is you who Allah will not thank.”

“I’m sure if He is indeed up there watching, that’ll be the least of His issues with me.”

“Indeed Agent, you like everyone in this country and in the West, have slipped.”

“Our feet have slipped?”

“Yes.”

“And, yours? They’re on solid ground, are they?”

“I am but a vessel and an agent for my God, I do what He commands.”

“If that’s true, He’s an arsehole.”

“How dare you!”

“No, he’s not the arsehole, you are! I don’t think He asked you to do anything, I think you twist His words to manipulate people and justify your own twisted bullshit, and I think He’s going to tell you that when you meet Him.”

“No, He will greet me in paradise and thank me for what I have done!”

“You have failed, Moghadam. I stopped Curran. We stopped Abbas. Soon we will mass produce the antidote and get it to the remaining people in the Opera House. Katzenberg is dead and Uri’s in custody. Most of your men are dead. Put down the device, it’s over.”

“Most of that is true, but I hate to tell you there is no antidote.”

“Yes, there is, maybe they just didn’t tell you about it.”

“I knew they could not be trusted. It was the Jews wasn’t it?”

"I think they all knew, but they must have been happy for you to miss out. I guess your cause wasn't worth saving in their eyes."

"Nor is theirs' in mine. I will make sure to pay the others' a visit when I leave here. Put down your guns."

"Don't either of you fucking dare!" Kate said. "Shoot this motherfucker!"

"Quiet bitch," Moghadam said tightening his grip on Kate's throat. "Or I will detonate this right next to your head."

"Just do it, you big pussy!" Kate said. "If the roles were reversed, I'd have already killed you."

"Shut up!"

"Oh fuck this!" Kate said throwing her head back violently against Moghadam's nose and breaking it.

Moghadam released his grip and Kate fell forward. Max fired six shots into Moghadam as Blake dived off the table and caught the device only a few inches off the concrete floor.

"Hoo-fucking-rah boys!" Kate said. "About bloody time, I have been listening to him drone on and on for what seems like a fucking eternity."

Outside the door one of Moghadam's men yelled something in Arabic.

"Alpha, behind the cover!" Blake said as three men rushed the door.

Kate jumped behind the workstation as bullets slammed into the bookcase and the walls in the antechamber. Max and Blake returned fire until their MP5s ran dry.

"I'm out," Blake said.

"Me too," Max said drawing his pistol.

He and Kate fired whenever one of the men tried to enter the room. Kate took down one guy with a bullet to the neck. Max shot one of the men in the arm and he pulled back behind the concrete wall. They kept firing until both weapons clicked empty.

"I need another clip," Kate said.

"I don't have another one," Blake said.

"I'm out too," Max said.

"Well, fuck, least we shot that son-of-a-bitch," Kate said pointing to Moghadam. "Maybe we should set this off, so his friends outside the door can't use it on anyone else. This building will be empty now. Just us and them."

"We can't," Blake said. "It could spread."

"Just an idea. It's been a pleasure, boys. Max, I know we have only known each other for a short period of time, but you my friend were fucking born for this job. I've never seen anything like the shit you pulled off over the last couple of days. Made me proud. And, you Blake, well, you know I love ya and I'd fucking straighten you out any day if you wanted me too."

"Thanks, Kate," Blake said smiling. "You'd be the first person I'd call if I changed my ways."

"Yeah, thanks Kate," Max said smiling at Blake's comments. "It's been a crazy time, but I would do it all again, knowing we made a difference."

"You sure did," Blake said.

"Fucking oath you did," Kate said.

There was a noise by the door. Two of Moghadam's men started slowly making their way across the room, then outside there was a commotion. Gunfire rang out. It echoed down the corridor and into the antechamber. The two men in the room stopped and turned back. Kate and Max jumped off the table, both ran for the two distracted men.

Kate grabbed her guy's gun wielding hand and he fired his gun dry into the wall. She headbutted him in the back of the head then bit a chunk of flesh from his neck. He screamed and turned towards her clutching his neck with one hand. Blood was spilling through his fingers. She spat the bloody flesh into his face as he lashed out violently with one arm trying to punch her. Kate danced back and squared up, slapping his hand down and countering with her own punches. Slap, left. Slap, right. He started to get weaker as the blood loss kicked in. He tried one last haymaker, but she grabbed his arm and punch the elbow folding it back on itself in an unnatural way breaking it. He screamed in pain, then fell to his knees. Kate punched him as hard as she could right on the nose and he went out cold.

Max punched his guy in the back and swatted the gun out of his hands. It scattered across the floor. He ran after it, but Max grabbed him and spun him around then punched him in the face. The man staggered back, Max jumped off his left foot and threw a ferocious right jab into his face. As he landed, he pivoted and slammed a left hook into his liver. He hunched over and Max threw a violent right uppercut into his head forcing it back at tremendous speed. He fell to the ground next to his comrade, out cold. Max checked his pulse.

"Fuck me, Max," Kate said. "Has he got a pulse? That last shot looked like it snapped his neck."

"He'll live," Max said.

"This is Echo Team Two," a voice said from the corridor. "Identify yourself. You have ten seconds to comply before we come in."

"Stand down, ETT," Kate said. "AIS Agents, Matthews, Smyth and Shaw."

"Anyone else in there?"

"A pile of dead ones and two who will need a doctor, then a gaol cell."

"Roger that, coming in."

"Thanks for the backup, Captain," Kate said shaking the officer's hand.

"Anytime, Agent. All clear in here. Do you have the device?"

"Yes, it's on the table behind the bookcase."

"Roger that. Bring in the containment unit."

Two officers in military fatigues came into the room holding a clear Perspex case like the one Whitlam and Max had used at defence. They placed the device inside, sealed it, then took it from the room, closely followed by the army captain.

"So, I guess I didn't have to get all fucking sentimental," Kate said. "Geez, I show the smallest bit of girliness and then we don't die. Fuck."

"It was a nice moment, Kate," Max said. "I appreciated it. Oh and don't worry about the girlie stuff, you more than countered that by biting a chunk out of that fucking guy's neck."

"Yeah, fuck, Kate," Blake said. "That was brutal, but on the other thing, well, I couldn't think of two people I'd rather be in a jam with."

"Aright, Jesus," Kate said. "Let's get the fuck out of here."

The three agents headed up to the DFA lobby. The military had shut it down. Men and women in uniform were milling about. Whitlam walked across the foyer, pushing Hulk in a wheelchair.

"Well, it seems congratulations are in order," Hulk said.

"The two devices have been secured or detonated safely," Blake said. "And, the crews are all dead or in custody."

"What about the third device?"

"It's not here."

"Where is it?"

"I'm not sure, we'll need to question the two guys downstairs and go through Moghadam and Curran's phones to find a lead, but maybe it's with Wright wherever he is."

"Yeah maybe."

"Any leads?"

"Not yet, but Shadow is on it. He'll find him."

"Good."

"Can you go and secure the phones and start that process?"

"Yes, sir," Blake said heading off to get the phones.

"You two can question the men downstairs, we need to find Wright and the device."

"Yes, sir," Kate said heading for the stairs.

"Max, just a minute," Hulk said.

"Yes, sir," Max said.

"How are you holding up?"

"I'm fine, Hulk. It's been a wild ride."

"Yes, it has and you've done an incredible job. I'm proud of you, kid. You've handled more than I though possible of any of my team, let alone someone in their first week on the job. Well done."

"Thanks, Hulk. It's been tough, but I didn't do it alone. You've put together an incredible team, I know they've had my back the whole way."

"They always will."

"And, I'll always have theirs. This is a tough job, but I understand now why we are here."

"That's good to know, kid. You'll always have a place in my team."

"Thank you, sir. Can I ask, how is Flash?"

"He's out of the woods. He will make a full recovery."

"Oh that's great news. I look forward to getting back to Sydney to see him."

"I'm sure he'd be happy to see you."

"How did you go with the pharmaceuticals guy?"

"Mr Hogan is now working with us to roll out the antidote at the Opera House. His company is now part of the Federal Government, we federalised it for this operation."

"Okay, I better go down and help Kate, I guess."

"Thanks, Max. When you're done, you should go and see Lachlan."

"I'd like that, thank you."

"Head down and help Kate. Let me know what you find out."

"Will do," Max said heading for the antechamber where he left the two unconscious terrorists.

Chapter Forty

Max took a long hot shower, letting the blood, sweat and dirt of the last two days wash away. The two men in the antechamber and a search on Curran's phone confirmed Archbishop Wright had the final device, but he had fled the country. Hulk and Shadow were running a search for the plane and his destination. Hulk had assured Max that they would track him down and find the device.

The warm water ran down over his naked body refreshing and reviving him, he was starting to feel human again. He thought about everything he had seen and done over the last few days, from torture and death to the lies and complex discussions with psychopaths on religion. He thought about his training and his career. It was going to be a tough job, but he meant what he had said to Hulk, it is a necessary role to ensure people are protected from those who seek to do harm. He wanted to do his part to ensure innocent people, like Lachlan, were safe from terror. No one should live in terror and he wanted to do his bit to stop its spread.

He thought about Lachlan and how much he loved him. He could not wait to see him, he missed him so much. It had only been a couple of days, but they were some of the toughest days of his life and he wanted to hold his partner and feel his love. He still felt guilty about having to conceal his real job from Lachlan, but given the horrors faced over those few days and the real likelihood of attacks and panic, he knew Hulk was right, he could not tell him just yet. And, even when he did, he was not sure he would tell him the whole story. Lachlan would understand his desire to help and he would come around to the idea of him being a spy, but he was not sure he would accept how much Max's own safety was on the line and how often.

Max climbed out of the shower and dried off, his skin was red from the heat of the water. He looked himself up and down in the mirror, his eyes looked tired and he had a few marks from the fights he had been in, but all considered, he looked fine. He got dressed into a clean pair of jeans and a tight black t-shirt. He put on his boots and a jacket rolling up the sleeves, put on his watch, then grabbed his phone from the charger, checked it quickly, no news from Hulk, so he put it in his pocket. Finally, he picked up his new ring, his AIS access key. He studied the small silver band, then placed it on his finger and headed out of the hotel.

He made one stop, before heading to the Kingston Foreshore restaurant where he now sat looking at the sunset shimmering on the water. It was reflecting off his mirror-lensed Oakleys as he sat drinking a cold beer. He had the *Times*, Canberra's local newspaper spread over the table in front of him, opened on the real estate section. He had circled a few places with a yellow highlighter. He also had a manila file sitting on the table. Inside was a photo, biography and a number of speeches from the Member of Parliament he was going to work for as a cover job. He had spent an hour reading the file, before turning to the real estate section.

Lachlan walked along the boardwalk which circled Lake Burley Griffin. Max watched as he searched each of the bars and restaurants, looking for him, then they locked eyes and smiled broadly. Lachlan bounced up the stairs, two then three at a time, Max stood and walked to him and they hugged for the longest moment, then kissed passionately in the fading afternoon sunlight. They walked back to the table and sat discussing their days. Lachlan spoke with enthusiasm about his new job and new colleagues, and the challenge his career was going to be, but he sounded happy and excited. Max was so proud and so happy for him. Lachlan asked Max about his day and Max told him all he had learnt from the manila folder about the Honourable James Johnston MP, then they sat looking at the houses Max had circled in the newspaper and planned their future together.

"What's this?" Lachlan asked pointing to Max's new ring.

"I wondered how long it would take you to see it," Max said. "Just a little something I picked up this afternoon."

"It's nice," Lachlan said. "Although, I'm not sure we should be wasting money on stuff like this before we move house. It's going to be expensive for the first few months until we are set up."

"Yeah, it is, but we'll be fine. I just wanted something to symbolise a new beginning."

"Symbolic, nice idea," Lachlan said looking down at the table.

"And, there isn't anybody else in the world I would rather be doing it with, starting a life together," Max said placing a small box on the table in front of Lachlan.

"What's this?"

"Open it."

Lachlan opened the box and saw a silver ring, almost identical to Max's AIS ring. He had picked it up on the way to the restaurant.

"Someday, this will be replaced by an engagement ring, but for now, I want you to know how much I love you and I want you to know you are my world and I am going to spend the rest of my life with you," Max said.

"You are so sweet," Lachlan said with a tear in his eyes. "I love you too, Maximus, more than anything in the world. Oh and the answer will be yes, when you ask."

They both smiled, hugged and kissed each other passionately.

Epilogue

He sat sipping on short black espresso from the small white square shaped cup, watching the traffic, both on foot and in the various vehicles rushing past. His mirror-lensed glasses reflected the sun and hid his eyes. He watched the men at a nearby table and tried to listen to their conversation, but the parade of tourists and locals was making it difficult to hear. The three men he was watching finished their drinks, stood and two of the men sat down their briefcases on the table while they paid their cheque. When they left, the two men swapped briefcases.

He sat for a few seconds, then stood himself and put some cash on the table for his coffee, then followed two of the men who had set off down the ancient cobble stone street, as the man with the second briefcase headed in the opposite direction.

"I'm following the target," Max said. "They handed off the briefcase, it's heading south."

"We're on it," Blake said. *"You're authorised to proceed."*

"Acknowledged."

"We just say Ack."

"Ack. Got it."

Max followed the two men over an ornate bridge with marble statues of demons and angels, past the Castel Sant'Angelo and up the steady incline to Saint Peter's Square. He followed the target into the grandiose Basilica. Max had never seen anything so magnificent. Michelangelo's masterpiece complete with its own towering concrete cupola. It was a vast space filled with thousands of tourists, but Max kept his eye on the target as the two men headed for the rear exit which was off limits to the public. Max watched as they headed through the door, there was security everywhere, he needed a distraction. He walked over to a group of tourists who were listening to their guide on their headsets. Max bumped into one of the men at the rear of the group who stumbled forward and fell over a red rope which was fencing off a priceless painting. A number of guards came running and other tourists stopped to help the man up. Max disappeared in the crowd, snuck past the guards and out the door following his target.

As he walked along the streets of the Vatican, Max wondered what secrets the winding cobble stones would have seen and heard over the years.

"Prince, it's Hermes," Blake said over the comms unit. *"Are you there?"*

"Yes, Hermes," Max said. "I'm still on their trail. Did you pick up the briefcase?"

"Yes, we have the vial and the device. It's secure."

"Good to hear. He's about two minutes out from the residence."

"Ack."

The two men separated and Max kept following his target. He walked along the streets and down side lanes, until finally he walked up the stairs of an ancient residential block. He made his way to the third floor then strolled along the balcony to his room. He walked inside and closed the door. Max walked along the balcony, like he had all the time in the world, he checked the windows of the apartments next to his target's. Empty. He knocked on the target's door. When it opened, Max shoved the target hard back into the room and he fell to the floor. Max locked the door and shut the curtains.

"Who are you?" Wright asked sprawled out on the floor. "Don't you know who I am and where you are?"

"The only name you need to know is Prince," Max said. "I work for the Australian Intelligence Service. Your name is Benjamin Wright and you are the Archbishop of Sydney, soon to be Cardinal Wright. And, yes, I know exactly where we are, we're in Vatican City."

"Well, how dare you come in here like this and treat me with such disrespect."

"Save it for your mate."

"My mate?"

"Yeah, the bloke upstairs."

"Blasphemy!"

"It's nothing compared to what you have done."

"What are you talking about, what are you doing here, Agent?"

"You know exactly what I am doing here. You are responsible for the murder of two hundred people and the attempted murder of millions."

"I do not know what you are talking about."

Max threw a handful of photos down on the floor next to Wright and he watched as he looked through them and grimaced, then he got to the photo of Curran and paused on it.

"Daniel Curran," Max said. "Friend of yours?"

"I've never seen him before," Wright said.

"For a religious leader, you sure lie a lot. You brainwashed Mr Curran into doing your dirty work, trying to release a biological weapon at the defence headquarters and foreign affairs department, and at the war memorial ceremony, and you were responsible for actually releasing the substance at the Sydney Opera House and at the casino. Oh and a few minutes ago, you sold the last vial of the biological weapon to a known terrorist, he's in custody, by the way, and the device is in our possession."

"Even if all that was true, you are in Vatican City. As you said yourself, I'm about to be made a Cardinal. You can't touch me."

"Yes, I can," Max said dropping a knee into Wright's chest.

"You can't kill me."

"Oh yes, I can do that too. Tell me, Your Grace, should I leave these photos here, when I do?"

"They prove nothing."

"No, but this does," Max said holding up a thumb drive. "Conversations, text messages, emails, witness statements, even a couple of your speeches are in here – powerful stuff.

Tell me, how would you like to be remembered? An old man who had faithfully served the church for decades or as the man who unravelled religion as we know it?"

"You can't do this, I was trying to save the church."

"If it was up to me, we would plaster your name and your brainwashing speeches all over the internet and television, until everyone in the world knew what you had done, bringing down this corrupt institution once and for all. Like Einstein said, 'The word God is for me nothing but the expression and product of human weaknesses, the Bible a collection of venerable but still rather primitive legends. No interpretation, no matter how subtle, can change anything about this.' Your actions have confirmed to me that indeed there is no God, Your Grace, for if there was, He would never have let you get this far. But."

"But, it's not up to you?" Wright smiled. "Thankfully. Now, please leave me in peace."

"What happens to the church is not up to me," Max said as he stabbed a needle into Wright's neck and injected him with a small amount of clear liquid. "What happens to you though, well that's in my hands."

"What was that?" Wright asked. "What did you inject me with?"

"I wanted to inject you with a small amount of your own biological weapon, give you a bit of your own medicine, eye for an eye, so to speak."

Wright panicked and his eyes went wide.

"There's the recognition I was looking for," Max said grabbing Wright by the neck. "You saw the videos, didn't you? Saw what the substance did?"

"Please, no," Wright said. "The antidote, I need more of the antidote, I don't want to die like that."

"You won't, sadly, that's not what I injected you with. And don't worry, you won't be the man who destroys the church either," Max said letting go of Wright and picking up the photos and USB drive, putting them in his pocket. "It's more than you deserve though, Your Grace, because your feet have slipped."

Max stood up and Wright clutched his chest. He started squirming and rolling on the floor, he was sweating and convulsing, and his face was screwed up in pain and his jaws were clenched. After a few seconds, he stopped moving and Max checked his pulse. Nothing.

Max opened the door and walked out into the morning sunlight, he headed down the stairs and found a side gate, slipped out into the Italian street and disappeared into the crowd.

The End.

Max Shaw will return in *Shaw Confrontation*.

www.jwpublishing.com.au